Readers have fallen in love with
The Child on Platform One

'Such a gorgeous book. I loved and believed in all the characters, and thoroughly enjoyed their stories. The ending moved me to tears *****'

'OMG what an incredible read. It was so emotional. I was engrossed from start to finish and would highly recommend this book *****'

'This book was incredible... The story is realistic and believable. Once you start reading you will not want to stop *****'

'An emotional, haunting book filled with secrets throughout. Excellent *****'

'I loved the book and the way it was written. I will be reading more novels by Gill Thompson as her interweaving of events with fictional characters is remarkable *****'

'This was a great book! There are secrets in this book you will not see coming . . . Heartwarming *****'

'It's not your normal evacuee story as it's intertwined with other stories which I really enjoyed. It had me gripped. I will be looking out for more books by this author *****'

'This is a very good book. I recommend you read *****'

Praise for *The Oceans Between Us*

'A warm-hearted tale of love, loss and indefatigable human spirit'   Kathryn Hughes

'A heartrending story'   Jane Corry

'A mother's loss and a son's courage . . . A heartrending story that spans the world'   Diney Costeloe

'Gill Thompson has brought us a beautiful tale of a mother's love whilst also tackling a very dark and awful period in British and Australian history. The emotion that comes from the pages of this book is palpable. And that ending, oh my goodness. I will be thinking about Jack and Molly for a long time to come. This is a wonderful book'   *Emma's Bookish Corner*

'It has opened my eyes to the injustice done to so many . . . A thought-provoking and interesting read'   *Shaz's Book Blog*

'*The Oceans Between Us* truly pulls at your heartstrings. With themes of salvation, longing, self-preservation, inequality, betrayal, forbidden love, friendship, loyalty, the search for justice and a place to call home, along with human endurance, this novel will touch your soul'   *Mrs B's Book Reviews*

The
Child on
Platform
One

GILL THOMPSON

REVIEW

First published in Great Britain in 2019
by HEADLINE REVIEW
An imprint of HEADLINE PUBLISHING GROUP

First published in the UK in paperback in 2020
by HEADLINE PUBLISHING GROUP

1

Cataloguing in Publication Data is available from the British Library

ISBN 978 1 4722 5801 4

Typeset in Garamond MT by Palimpsest Book Production Ltd,
Falkirk, Stirlingshire

Printed and bound in Great Britain by Clays Ltd, Elcograf S.p.A.

HEADLINE PUBLISHING GROUP
An Hachette UK Company
Carmelite House
50 Victoria Embankment
London EC4Y 0DZ

www.headline.co.uk
www.hachette.co.uk

To Leonie and Corinne
With love from your adoring Grandma

If understanding is impossible, knowing is imperative, because what happened could happen again.

Primo Levi

Prologue

Prague, 1930

Eva had already scraped back the piano stool and was about to slide the music books into her bag when Professor Novotny lifted a hand to delay her.

'Just one more minute, my dear.' His thin finger pointed skywards, in imitation of the number. 'I have a piece I would like you to take home.'

While the professor rifled through the tottering pile of manuscripts on top of the piano, Eva cast a glance at the wooden clock on the wall. Four thirty. She hoped this wouldn't take long. Already the conservatoire rehearsal room was gloomier than when the lesson had started, shadows stretching across the floor. *Come on. Come on.* She placed her fingertips on the yellow keys, allowing the cool ivory to calm her.

'Ah, here it is.' Professor Novotny was wheezing from the effort of finding the score. 'Hector Berlioz. It's a villanelle from *Les Nuits d'Été*. One of his lesser-known pieces.' He switched on the overhead light and the room brightened.

'A villan . . . ella?' Despite her anxiety about the time, Eva was intrigued. She stood up as her teacher gestured for her to relinquish her place at the keyboard and positioned herself to the side of the piano, ready to watch Professor Novotny play.

'Yes. A secular Italian song.' The professor sat down on the padded piano stool with a thump. 'This one is a celebration of spring and new love. Perfect piece for a young girl.' He reached for the round black glasses on a cord round his neck, put them on as though preparing to play, then removed them again. The glasses swung loose on their moorings. 'There's to be a concert at the Rudolfinum next year, a tribute to Berlioz's work. I thought you could perform the villanelle as your first public solo.'

Eva drew an indignant breath, but the professor flapped his hand at her.

'Those children's competitions don't count.'

Those *children's competitions*! She straightened her back. Hadn't she won every one? Even the prestigious Dvořák Prize for Young Talent. A memory of lifting the heavy metal cup and hearing a crescendo of applause flashed into her mind.

The professor propped the folded pages of music against the metal prongs of the rest. 'I'll play you a bit. Please turn the page for me.' The glasses were perched in position.

Eva took up her place behind her teacher, trying to remain still; it would be rude to appear impatient. But inside her head she was begging Professor Novotny to play only a few bars. She knew he worked her so hard because he was proud of her, and she was keen to be the best she could, but the ornate hands of the clock showed twenty to five now. Today of all days she couldn't afford to be late.

'Listen. You'll hear the lovers wandering through the woods to gather wild strawberries.'

Eva flushed at the word 'lovers'. Sometimes Professor Novotny spoke to her as though she was older than sixteen. But as he started to play, she did indeed hear the light, tripping sound of footsteps, and felt the freshness of the spring breeze on her face.

She peered over the professor's shoulder. Beneath his tapered fingers, the printed notes skittering across the manuscript became an airy melody. Teasing, joyful. Eva had always seen notes as people. The rows of joined quavers – the short notes – were gangly lines of boys sporting over-large football boots at the end of their thin legs; or a straight band of dancers performing the Lúčnica, in black shoes, with their arms linked. The single crotchets – twice as long as quavers – were teachers, ramrod straight in front of a class. And the long minims were powerful generals, commanding their army's attention by their stillness. But if Eva were a note, she'd be a really long one: a breve, strong and alone, surrounded by space and silence.

The professor finished playing with a flourish, then handed her the score. 'Homework. Start tonight.' The notes hovered in the air before the spring promise of the tune was smothered by the advancing autumn dusk. The sun must be even lower now. Eva's stomach clenched. An allegro beat started up in her head.

She thrust the manuscript into her bag, then put on her coat. 'Thank you, Professor Novotny, I'll be sure to practise.'

'Make sure you do. I want to hear you play it perfectly at your next lesson.'

'Of course.' Eva's hand was on the doorknob, its polished surface greasy under her fingers. She darted another look at the clock. Nearly five. This villanelle had claimed even more time than she'd realised. She'd have to run like a' wolf dog.

'Goodbye, my dear.'

'Goodbye, Professor Novotny. And thank you for the lesson.'

The professor bowed, the overhead light he'd snapped on earlier illuminating his bald head. Eva made her escape.

She ran through the darkening streets with the music bag clamped under her arm, her chest burning, her breath ragged. Yet in spite of her urgency, Berlioz's melody still skipped through her head, and she tuned her footsteps to the chords pressed out by Professor Novotny's liver-spotted hands. She was running through the woods with her lover, away from the stifling confines of the city, her senses alive to the sound of the birds and the sweet-sharp perfume of the strawberries. She could feel the boy's breath on her cheek, his mouth on her lips, perhaps – if her face hadn't already been red, she'd have blushed – his body pressed against hers. Only the pungent smell of coffee seeping out from under the door of the Kotva reminded her where she was. As she darted past the café, shadowy shapes lifted cups to their lips, gesticulated in conversation, or blew plumes of smoke from Stuyvesants whose tips glowed red in the gloom. How lovely to linger at the table with friends rather than having to rush home for the curfew.

Eva glanced up at the sinking sun. Mutti would have finished the chores by now, the challah already baked and resting on the lacy cloth, its plumply plaited crust shining with egg wash and oozing a fresh bread smell. She would have put on her grey dress, wrapped the gauzy scarf around her hair and

4

gone downstairs to light the candles, whose silver holders gleamed from the polish that she'd given them earlier.

Abba, in his shiny black suit and prayer shawl, would have filled the Kiddush cup with sweet wine, his lips rehearsing the blessing for daughters that he'd speak later with his warm hands resting on Eva's head:

May you be like Sarah, Rebecca, Rachel and Leah.
May God bless you and guard you.
May God show you favour and be gracious to you.
May God show you kindness and grant you peace.

If Abba had fathered sons, he'd have asked God to make them like Ephraim and Menashe, two brothers who lived in harmony. But there'd been no sons. Only Eva. A beloved only child.

A mist was rising from the surface of the Vltava, and Eva inhaled the wet air as she sped along the pavement. She couldn't risk stopping to cough properly, so she tried to clear her throat in shallow breaths whilst running. She wasn't used to going so fast. Most days her lesson ended on time, so she walked to the Josefov via well-lit streets. But with sunset approaching, the quickest route home was through the cemetery.

An animated mosso beat pulsed through her. Should she risk it? Perhaps the gates closed at curfew. Mutti had told her again and again to stick to the main roads. They'd be full of people on their way home from work. Longer but safe. Yet Eva paused on the pavement to peer at the winding path through the tombs. The ancient stones were crammed together as if the graves had been hastily dug, not placed in ordered rows like a modern cemetery. Wind threaded through the trees, causing the branches to shiver. To stifle the jump of her heart, she imagined she was performing at the Rudolfinum on a gleaming black Steinway, to a shadowy audience awed to silence by her playing.

She placed her palm against one of the dark metal gates and it yielded slowly. Perhaps it was a sign she should go through the cemetery. She could make up for some lost time this way.

Trying to rekindle Berlioz's melody, to renew the thrills of spring and blot out the fears of autumn, she crept through the gate. The dew had already fallen and the leaves were damp underfoot. Creepers clung to her stockings and she had to kick her feet out to dislodge them. It would be foolish to run; the gravestones were too crowded, the path too meandering. But she hastened her steps, her senses alert for danger.

Inside the cemetery, tall horse chestnuts and sycamores diffused the low sun's rays. Gravestones loomed either side of the path, inscribed with old symbols and ancient lettering. Abba had told her once that some of the graves held as many as ten bodies, all piled on top of each other to conserve space. In spite of her serge coat, Eva shivered.

She was halfway through when she heard the thud of boots, a harsh laugh, a sharp cough.

She froze. 'Who's there?'

No reply, but beyond the shadowy stones she caught a glimpse of biscuit-coloured cloth. Blood pounded affrettando in her ears.

'Who's there?' she asked again. Her voice sounded hoarse.

A uniformed figure stepped out from behind a tree. A youth, maybe late teens, with a sweep of blond hair across his forehead.

'What have we here: a young lady?' His tone was leering, mocking.

Eva pulled her coat tighter, trying to ignore the gallop of her heart.

Another youth stepped forward. Then another. She wheeled round. Two more came up behind her. She was surrounded by five young soldiers, all wearing red armbands.

Was this what Mutti had feared when she'd warned her not to go into the cemetery? Eva had nodded solemnly at the time, but in her head she'd dismissed her mother's advice. All parents said things like that, didn't they? Of course she was careful. Although recently, even Eva had felt uncomfortable at the sight of German boys standing on street corners muttering to each other and pointing at passers-by. Those Hitler Youth seemed to be everywhere these days.

Surrounded by a ring of menacing young men in their distinctive uniforms, she wished desperately that she'd heeded Mutti's words and ignored her lateness. Saliva pooled in her mouth, her throat too dry to swallow.

The first youth advanced towards her. 'Don't be frightened, pretty girl.'

Eva stood her ground, trying not to show her fear. But when she opened her mouth to shout for help, the boy reached forward and slapped his palm against her lips.

Eva darted terrified glances at the other boys.

The pressure of the youth's fingers slackened, but he kept his hand close to her mouth, in case she tried to cry out again.

She clenched her fists.

'Such beautiful clothes,' he murmured, dropping his hand to stroke her coat. Eva couldn't stop herself flinching. Or inhaling his sour breath.

Slowly he undid her grey buttons.

The other boys were watching, waiting.

'Hold her arms.'

Eva struggled as the youth tried to take off her coat. But the boy behind her grabbed her wrists, until the garment was yanked off her and tossed onto the ground.

The youth reached forward again. He touched Eva's cheek softly, then ran his finger under her chin, around her neck and down to the dent of her throat. He carefully edged up a section of the gold chain she always wore. She found herself mesmerised, in spite of her fear.

'What a nice necklace.' It was almost a whisper.

Did he want to steal it? Eva reached down and hooked her own finger under the thin metal links, pulling the whole chain out from under her collar so he could see the gold star on the end, the star that usually lay hidden under her blouse.

The boy gently removed it from her grasp, prising her fingers open one by one, and held the star up to the fading light.

The chain tightened against the back of Eva's neck. She muted a protest at the pain.

'How interesting.' The boy's eyes were on her face, but his words were addressed to his companions, who jeered and laughed.

The spell was broken. The boy let the pendant go abruptly. 'She's not for me.' His expression hardened and he shoved

Eva away. 'All yours, Otto.' He turned round and gestured to the smallest of the youths to come forward.

Eva let out a long-held breath as silently as she could. Dare she flee? The first boy had his back to her now; perhaps this was her chance. She lowered her head to charge through the gap.

But as the smaller boy was shoved forward by his mocking companions, their circle tightened to prevent his escape, blocking Eva's too.

The lad approached her. He was slight, with hair so blond it was almost white and eyelashes so fair they were nearly invisible.

If he had been on his own, Eva could have defended herself. She was no coward. She'd have kicked and punched and spat until the boy released her. But surrounded by a leering wall of soldiers, she had no chance. She reached behind her, fingers scrabbling against the top of a gravestone, searching for a weapon. But if there'd been any stones placed along the rim, they'd long since vanished.

'Come on, Otto, not scared, are you?' The first youth, who'd retreated to become part of the wall, goaded the lad who was now standing in front of Eva.

'Yes, come on, Otto, our balls are freezing.'

The boy laughed, the strangely eerie cackle betraying his nervousness.

Although the youths spoke German, Eva understood them perfectly. All the families in the Josefov spoke German at home. Her stomach tightened and her breath rasped in the cold air.

'Please don't hurt me, my parents are waiting.' Her voice

came out thin, reedy. Why couldn't she make herself sound threatening? Perhaps she could appeal to the boy's sense of honour. He seemed hesitant; maybe she could persuade him. If he realised how important it was for her to get home, he might leave her alone.

But as the other youths catcalled and whooped, making strange gestures with their hands, the boy responded to their raucous taunts. His eyes narrowed and his mouth pressed into a threatening line. He hawked up a gob of phlegm and spat on her. She let the slime trickle down her cheek, too terrified to wipe it off.

He yanked at her pendant and it broke immediately, the chain abandoned to the autumn leaves. A whoop went up from the group.

A different youth tore off her blouse in one violent movement. Another cheer.

Then they were all mauling her, ripping her skirt and stockings in a frenzy, their straining, sweating faces contorting in the moonlight, the air thick with their beery stench. And at the same time they were singing some ugly drinking song that had them bellowing out loud, flat notes in a terrible cacophony.

Eva wrapped her arms tight across her chest, desperately protecting her cream camisole. But someone wrenched her hands away and stripped it off her, the delicate fabric that Mutti had hand-sewn tearing under his fingers.

She was thrust backwards and pushed down onto her own coat, her head thumping against the soft lining.

Then the boys came at her again.

*

Afterwards, it was an owl that first penetrated her conscious-ness, hooting mournfully through the cold air. Her fingers dug into the wet earth; she inhaled the musty odour of leaves. But the animal reek of her own blood was still there. She curled her bruised body into a ball, trying to shut out the black miasma and the memory of the boy's nervous laugh.

The time for the Shabbat blessing had long since passed. Eva's anxious parents would be presiding over an empty table, asking themselves again and again where their devoted daughter could have got to, when she knew that all good Jews must be indoors by nightfall, on this most sacred of evenings.

Part One

1933–1939

1

Hampstead, London

Even from under Will's bed, Pamela could hear Hugh hollering. She stretched out her hand another inch, wincing at the resulting pain in her armpit, until her scrabbling fingers reached the sock. Then she pushed herself backwards so that she and the sock were free of the bed's bulging underbelly.

'Coming!' She shook the sock. So much dust had accumulated. Her son had only been home four weeks, and goodness knows how the sock had got there. But at least he had a complete pair now. She lifted the lid of his trunk, located the other sock – he'd never bother to find it himself – rolled the two neatly into a ball, then pushed them down the side. 'The trunk's packed now, Hugh,' she called, pressing the lid shut.

There was a rapid tattoo of footsteps on the stairs and Hugh burst into the room. 'Will's in the car already,' he said as he hoisted up the trunk. 'Gosh, Pamela. What on earth have you put in this?'

Pamela grasped the other handle and followed her husband onto the landing. 'The school wanted me to pack his cricket bat and pads for the new season, remember. So the boys can get some practice in.' They'd had to take Will to Harrods to

15

buy cricket whites. Pamela smiled at the memory of her son emerging from the changing room pretending to bowl to Hugh, who'd mimed a batting action in return. What a mercy Will had inherited Hugh's strong, lean body and was good at sport. Pamela had worried herself sick that he'd be bullied when he first left for Cheam. But luckily his aptitude for team games had gained him respect among the other boys and teachers, and he'd settled in well.

It was tricky hauling the trunk down the stairs, and more than once it bumped against her knees. She hoped her stockings wouldn't ladder. Hugh would get even more cross if she had to run upstairs for a new pair, but thankfully she couldn't feel the telltale give of silk. Her dress came down to her calves anyway, so nothing would show as long as she was standing up. Besides, they wouldn't hang around at the school – a quick embrace, strictly no tears, then Will would be off with his friends and she and Hugh would return to the car for the sad, silent journey home.

'What's Kitty doing anyway?' said Hugh as he took the trunk's weight from her to manhandle it through the front door.

'Cooking. We've the Pallisers coming for supper tonight, remember.' Hugh often invited guests over for the evening after they took Will back. Pamela had long since guessed he wanted to take her mind off missing him.

'She should still come and help.'

'It's all right.' Pamela took the handle again as they carried the trunk down the drive. 'We're nearly there now.' She always felt awkward getting Kitty to do things. She knew she ought to treat Kitty as a servant rather than a friend, but it just didn't feel right to order another woman around. When she was growing up, they'd all helped Mum. There certainly wasn't enough money for servants. And even if they'd been able to afford them, people would just have said they were hoity-toity.

She slid into the back seat next to Will as Hugh slammed the boot shut. She put her arm round her son and he leant in for a cuddle. Pamela swallowed. She dreaded the time when Will stopped hugging her, or allowing his thick dark hair to be smoothed. Even now, when he was very tired, he would snuggle up to her on the sofa, his warm body pressed into hers. Once, when he thought she wasn't looking, she caught him sucking his thumb. Hugh would have chastised him for that – 'Boy of your age behaving like a baby, disgraceful' – but Pamela imagined he'd have to suppress all self-comfort at school; it wouldn't hurt to regress a bit once he was home.

At eleven, he was on the cusp of puberty. Perhaps by the time he came back for Easter he'd be taller, broader. She must make the most of his affection now. The journey to Cheam took less than two hours. He wouldn't be hers for much longer.

Will turned his head to look out of the window, releasing himself slightly from her embrace, although he didn't push her away.

'Are you all right?' she asked.

He looked back and nodded.

'Looking forward to the new term?'

'Rather. I can't wait to meet up with Merrow-Jones and Carter – find out what they got for Christmas.'

It must be hard for Will hearing about his friends' presents, when his own family didn't celebrate Christmas. Another problem with not sending him to a Quaker school. Pamela

17

squeezed his shoulder. 'That's good. And I expect you'll want to show them your new cricket whites.'

Will put his hand over hers. 'Everyone has cricket whites, Mother. But I'm looking forward to going down to the nets to practise.'

Pamela forced a smile. 'Indeed.'

'You'll have to show us your new skills when you're next home,' called Hugh over his shoulder.

'Can't wait,' Will replied.

'Nor me,' added Pamela. 'Only four weeks until the next exeat.'

'I can't believe you've counted!'

Pamela looked at her son's laughing face, the flushed cheeks, the bright eyes. Of course she counted: the weeks, the days, the hours. She never stopped.

As soon as they returned to Hampstead and Hugh had parked the car, Pamela rushed up the stairs to Will's room. A fug of stale air met her when she pushed open the door. Already it smelled closed in, desolate, almost as if Will hadn't slept there for four blissful weeks of the school holidays. Pamela went over to the bed to gather up her son's old striped flannel pyjamas and fold them carefully. They were too small now. They'd had to buy new ones for school, along with the cricket whites.

Kitty would be wanting to wash them then tear them up to make dusters. But Pamela wouldn't give them to her just yet.

It was an effort to powder her face, concealing the slide of tears, and go downstairs to check on Kitty. They'd planned the menu together days ago: mock turtle soup, creamed chicken, spinach and new potatoes, and pears à la condé. Pamela had deliberately chosen a plain menu. Something deep inside her still rebelled at extravagant food, and besides, the Pallisers were going through a tough time financially. They'd had to let their cook go: Josephine had to prepare their meals herself now. Pamela felt quite embarrassed that Hugh's career was on the up while their friends were struggling. She wanted to treat them to a nice meal without making them feel uncomfortable.

Kitty was stirring the soup on the hob. Behind her, on the huge kitchen table, bowls, plates and tureens were laid out with military precision. A half-stripped chicken carcass lay beside them, next to the bowl of pears. Pamela looked round anxiously to check Felix was nowhere in sight.

'All right, Kitty?'

'Yes, ma'am. All under control.'

Pamela glanced at the chicken again. 'Perhaps you could boil the carcass up for broth tomorrow. That'll be fine for my lunch.' They'd always done that at home. Mum could make a chicken last three days sometimes. Even with the six of them. Mind you, by the last day you'd be lucky to find a thin strip of it among the watery mass of pearl barley and vegetables.

'Very well, ma'am.' Kitty twisted a knob on the stove and the bubble of soup slowed a little.

'Is there anything I can do?'

Kitty glanced round the immaculate kitchen. 'Perhaps the place cards . . .' she murmured.

'Of course, I'll write them straight away.'

'Very good, ma'am.'

19

Pamela departed to fetch her fountain pen from the drawing room bureau. Above the noise of the soup, she thought she heard a sigh of relief.

Later, as she stood in front of Hugh to fasten his black tie, she found herself marvelling once again how the shy Quaker boy she'd met at the meeting house had turned into this successful, confident man. The more Hugh progressed in the Foreign Office, the more he seemed to shed his frugal upbringing, embracing the fancy lifestyle, the expensive clothes, the rich food with alarming ease. He even seemed to enjoy the concerts and operas they were obliged to go to. And sometimes Pamela felt a little ashamed that she did too.

She smoothed down her blue silk dress in the mirror. The colour was muted, the cut simple. She never wore jewels. But despite that, the figure reflected back at her still looked more like a society hostess than a girl with a modest, puritan upbringing. She firmed her lips as she dabbed Chanel perfume on her throat. Had she and Hugh been so easily changed by money? Her relief work, collecting clothes and food for German children, reminded her almost daily that many were less fortunate than they were. She really hoped that the more influential Hugh became, the more good they could do to help those poor persecuted families.

At dinner, the talk was all financial. Wall Street . . . the gold standard . . . budget reforms. Pamela found it difficult to concentrate. She was too busy checking the soup wasn't too salty or the potatoes overcooked. Making sure Kitty had refilled her guests' wine glasses, and that Hugh wasn't drinking too much. When they had first started to entertain, they had had long discussions about the morality of serving alcohol. It went against all their Quaker teaching, but Hugh felt they shouldn't impose their own beliefs on their guests, and Pamela had reluctantly agreed. These days Hugh joined them without a qualm.

It was a relief when Kitty brought out the port for the men, and she could lead Josephine into the sitting room for coffee.

Josephine had been quiet during the meal and Pamela wanted to draw her out. She poured the steaming coffee from the jug and handed Josephine a cupful. 'Things no better?' she murmured. By now it was second nature to emulate her friends' educated tones; she'd long since abandoned the accent she'd grown up with. Another compromise on authenticity. But Hugh had persuaded her how important it was for her to fit in.

Josephine shook her head. 'If Philip doesn't find more work soon, I reckon we'll need some of those provisions you're collecting for foreign children.' Her mouth twisted.

Pamela set the jug down sharply and some of the coffee spilled onto the table. She dabbed at it with her handkerchief. 'You know we'll help in any way we can.'

Josephine sighed. 'Yes, I know. It just seems strange that you're doing so much for the Germans when there are English children starving.'

Pamela half turned to pour a cup for herself. 'Quakers don't see different nationalities. People are all the same. If there's a need, we'll try to meet it.'

'Very commendable,' murmured Josephine, sipping her coffee.

Pamela smiled thinly. She knew the Pallisers resented her helping the German children, but she wasn't going to give up her charity work. Not for anyone.

Thankfully the conversation soon turned to their own children. Josephine and Philip also had a son, James, in the year above Will at Cheam. Luckily he was on a scholarship so they hadn't had to withdraw him. Sometimes they shared lifts, although they always went separately after the Michaelmas holidays. There was no room for both boys with all the luggage for the new term.

The Pallisers' girls were still at Sarum Hall, despite the increasing struggle to find the fees. Pamela envied Josephine, who could walk her daughters to school in the morning and collect them in the afternoon. How lovely to have your children dine with you each night, to be able to peep into their bedrooms when they were asleep, see their tousled hair on the pillows, hear the rise and fall of their breath, to comfort them when they had bad dreams. Pamela tried not to think of Will shivering under a grey blanket, struggling to sleep on the lumpy mattress in the chilly dormitory. It seemed the more you paid for your child's education, the more spartan their accommodation. But at least it had been their choice to send Will away to school – well, Hugh's anyway. How terrible for those poor German parents who'd sent their children to England hoping to protect them from their increasingly hostile country and wondering whether they'd ever see them again.

Thankfully their guests were gone by midnight. Pamela was dying to struggle out of her corset and put on her flannel nightdress. She sat at her dressing table smearing on cold cream as Hugh sat up in bed rustling a rather creased copy of the *Times*.

'Josephine all right?' he asked. His voice floated out from behind the paper.

'I think so.' Pamela started to brush her hair. She no longer gave it a hundred strokes as she used to when she was a child and it had hung over her back. Now it was shorter, the waves framing her face. She'd had a Gallia perm only last week and she didn't want to weaken it. She laid the brush down and fluffed up her hair with her fingers. 'I think there's been rather a lot of belt tightening, though.'

'Philip said as much. Can't be easy for the poor chap.'

'Indeed.' Pamela climbed into bed and burrowed under Hugh's paper. 'Although I feel envious of Josephine having her girls at home with her.'

Hugh folded up the paper and dropped it onto the floor. He put an arm round Pamela and leant his head against hers. 'I know you miss Will terribly, darling, but it's good for him to be at Cheam. He's mixing with the right sort.'

Pamela pulled away a fraction. 'The right sort? Other Quakers are the best sort, Hugh. He must go to Leighton Park after Cheam. It's important he attends a Quaker school.'

Hugh turned round to plump up his pillow and dislodged her. 'The Pallisers are hoping to send James to Marlborough – if he can get another scholarship. I think we should at least consider it.'

Pamela turned onto her back. 'I thought we'd agreed. You were happy at Leighton, weren't you?'

'Yes, of course, but my father wasn't in the FO.'

Pamela caught a waft of port as Hugh exhaled. 'Don't you ever worry that we're losing sight of our beliefs?'

Hugh closed his eyes. He was so still that Pamela wondered if he'd fallen asleep. 'I'm still a Quaker at heart,' he murmured eventually. 'There are plenty of us in government. We can do more good from the inside.'

Pamela turned back towards him. But Hugh was already snoring lightly. The conversation would have to wait.

2

Eva hated flock wallpaper. She loathed the mock-velvet patterns, brushed matt by years of grimy fingers, the tawdry sheen of the paper, the ridiculous artifice that aspired to grandeur but achieved only prissiness.

Today the gold patches, almost green in the half-light of dawn, were the colour of bile. She closed her eyes, more to block out the queasy sight of the bedroom walls than to attempt sleep. It was too late for that; she'd had the nightmare again, still horribly vivid after three long years, and her ears rang with the sound of hideous laughter. She wouldn't drop off again now, although Josef still snored beside her, vibrato grunts emanating from his large nose. Maybe the catarrh was already bubbling through his nasal passages. He'd thought last night he was getting a cold. Or a 'viral infectious disease of the upper respiratory tract', as he'd told her in his precise scientist's voice. Josef didn't catch common colds.

Sometimes Eva couldn't believe how much her life had altered since that night in the cemetery. She was so far from the naïve young girl who'd run home from her piano lesson just three years before. Now she was mired in marriage and responsibility; an obedient wife to a much older husband. Hardly the future she'd imagined for herself. That terrible night had changed everything.

She turned quietly onto her side, triggering a corresponding lurch in her stomach. Her intestines felt liquid, formless. Had she eaten last night? Oh yes. The memory of the thick beef stew she'd spent half a day preparing and stirring caused her mouth to flood with gall. Josef had enjoyed it, smacking his lips and telling her what a good cook she was, how red meat was thought to boost iron levels. But Eva had only taken tiny bites, enough to erase, at least temporarily, the metallic taste she'd had for the past few days.

She swallowed down the nausea the memory provoked, and tried to ease herself up the bed. Perhaps that would make her feel better. But even the effort of moving made her dizzy, and she let her head loll against the wooden bed frame. She closed her eyes again. Never one to lose his appetite when ill, Josef would be demanding his breakfast soon. She needed to tiptoe to the bathroom, tug her long linen nightdress over her head, coax the ancient taps into providing more than a trickle of water and have a quick stand-up wash before hurrying back to the bedroom to choose another dull outfit from the nondescript blouses and skirts that populated her wardrobe. She had a sudden sensation of emerald silk caressing her skin and the finest of stockings smoothing her legs, but she shut it out. She'd promised herself she wouldn't think of what might have been. The more disturbing memories she suppressed entirely.

As she continued to lie propped up against the headboard, trying to garner some strength and free her ears of haunting sounds, she was conscious of Josef coming-to beside her. After clearing his throat in a series of staccato coughs, he dredged up some mucus and swallowed it back down with a martyred shudder. Then he started to make gloomy little noises, intended, no doubt, to alert her to the life-threatening nature of his condition. The waking-up routine was even longer than usual today.

'Good morning, Josef,' she said.

'Good morning,' he replied, but his voice was full of self-pity.

Clearly this was Eva's cue to ask after his health. 'How are you?' she dutifully enquired, trying to sound as solicitous as the occasion demanded.

Josef pushed up his greying fringe with thin fingers. 'Feel my forehead,' he begged plaintively. 'I think I have a temperature.'

Eva did so. Her palm slid across a thin film of sweat. 'Maybe, although it is stuffy in here.' Josef had insisted on the heavy gold drapes to match the sickly wallpaper when they'd first bought the apartment. Eva had been too weary and resigned to protest. She was still only nineteen and had been married to Josef for two years now, although it felt much longer than that.

'Fetch a thermometer, *Liebling*.'

Eva dreaded having to get up, but she needed to disguise her own ill health from her husband, otherwise he'd be adding gastric influenza to his list of other ailments. She lurched down the passageway to the bathroom, opened the cabinet, took out the thermometer, then returned to the invalid. As she shook down the mercury, Josef pulled a handkerchief from his pyjama pocket, filled it with a rush of green mucus, then inspected the contents. Eva's stomach heaved. She just managed to thrust the glass tube between Josef's pale lips before staggering back to the bathroom, thrusting up the toilet seat and depositing the scant remains of last night's supper into the pan.

She remained kneeling over the bowl for a few moments until she was sure her stomach was empty. Then she stood up on straw-like legs, rinsed her mouth and splashed her face with water before reaching into the cabinet again. There was a small jar of balsam there. If she told Josef to hold it under his nostrils to clear his nose, he wouldn't be able to smell any lingering traces of vomit on her.

When she returned to the bedroom, his head was on one side, his eyes glazed with imagined fever, the thermometer still protruding from his mouth. She pulled it out and held it up to the light, squinting at the mercury.

'What is it?' Josef asked hoarsely.

Eva turned and smiled. 'Just a little high. Nothing to worry about.'

'I knew it.' Josef's head banged against the bed frame. 'I had a feeling I was going to be ill. I do suffer so with these respiratory tract infections.'

Eva firmed her lips as she handed him the balsam.

'Can you get me a little hot lemon, *Liebling*? And then perhaps a newspaper? Reading might take my mind off my infirmity.' He held the jar under each nostril in turn with a shaking hand, then sniffed loudly. 'You'll need to contact the Institute too. See if Paní Kratz will let you use her telephone. Tell them I'm far too indisposed to come in to work. Dr Svoboda will understand.'

'Of course.' Eva forced a smile. 'I might be a while, though. I'll have to go down to the market.' She was pulling clothes out of the wardrobe as she spoke. Josef hadn't thought to ask why she wasn't yet dressed; luckily he was too caught up with his own indisposition to notice hers. She slipped on a brown skirt and a pale green blouse, drew a pair of stockings up her legs, then rammed her feet into stout lace-up shoes. She'd fetch her headscarf and the wicker basket from the hook in the hall on her way out. Josef didn't approve of her wearing rouge, so there was nothing she could do to relieve the pastiness of her face. She'd just have to hope a brisk walk would put colour in her cheeks.

'Goodbye, Josef,' she called as she unbolted the heavy wooden front door. 'I'll be as quick as I can.'

'Hurry home, *Liebling*,' the thin voice called back, followed by a series of theatrical coughs.

As she made her way down the road, having called Josef's co-researcher from their kind neighbour's house, Eva felt stronger than she'd expected. Perhaps the fresh air had revived her. It was strange how she could be so sick one minute, then almost right as rain the next. This wasn't like a normal bout of gastric trouble. From nowhere, a conversation with Mutti darted into her mind: 'I was sick as a dog with you, Eva. Funny thing was, I always felt better as soon as I'd emptied my stomach. By the end, I almost welcomed the vomiting.'

Eva stopped in her tracks, her mind running through the dates. It was Pesach the last time she'd had to buy pads; she remembered how the cramps had squeezed her pelvis as she'd sat with Josef at her parents' table waiting for Abba to say the Kiddush as he poured the wine. She counted on her fingers. Pesach was six weeks ago. She smoothed her coat over her belly. Could she be pregnant? She glanced at her watch. She hadn't even started the shopping yet, and she needed to get back to Josef, but later, maybe if he slept, she could write to Mutti.

The thought of her mother's loving concern, the spark of hope in her brown eyes, put a bubble of joy in Eva's own heart. She'd been so busy feeling miserable, convinced she was suffering from an illness. But a baby! That would be marvellous. A new life might blot out the memories.

As she wandered past the fruit stalls at the market, choosing the plumpest, most thin-skinned lemons for Josef's drink, and delving into her purse for koruna – ridiculous amounts things cost these days – she was composing a lullaby to a newborn child, cradling him in her arms as she sang, filled with hope for this new chance.

How funny that her lugubrious middle-aged husband, so objective when it came to science but so irrational about his own health, was to become a father. How had they made this baby? Had there been a time when the fires of mutual passion had overcome Josef's caution and Eva's malaise? Had he put aside his hypochondria and she her lethargy for a night of unbridled lust? It must have been that evening when they'd celebrated the official end of abstinence. She had a brief memory of wine, laughter . . . a fumbling of buttons and zips, tangled limbs, an unusual urgency . . .

Her marriage certainly wasn't the one she'd imagined for herself when she'd been a young piano student with dreams of romance, but Josef had always been kind, and taken care of her in his own way. She should be grateful for that. And what had happened to her hadn't been his fault.

She tried to imagine what their baby would look like, and stifled a laugh at the thought of a red-faced infant with Josef's embroidered black kippah sliding around on top of his little head. Would the child be good at facts like Josef, or a musician like herself? Perhaps having a baby would rid Josef of his hypochondria. On the other hand, it might make him worry twice as much. She debated whether she should tell him. If he knew she were pregnant he'd be analysing her every mouthful for nutritional content, forever calculating the baby's weight and size, perhaps even succumbing to a little nausea himself out of sympathy. She pressed a palm against her stomach. Maybe she'd keep this to herself for a while. Wait until Dr Aaronovich confirmed it. Although, really, the signs were too strong for doubt.

As she walked back up the road inhaling the warm May air, she wondered whether having this new life inside her would finally put the past to rest. She blinked back the memory of Professor Novotny's reproachful eyes when she told him she wouldn't be performing the villanelle at the Rudolfinum, or anywhere else for that matter. She swallowed down the visceral pain of not being able to practise, to enjoy the keys coming to life under her strong fingers, the melodies in her ears, the joy that rippled through her body when she played. But it was her parents' shock and sadness that had wounded her most.

They'd tried to be gentle with her. Mutti had spent hours making chicken soup and little cakes, tempting Eva with small mouthfuls whilst her throat closed and her stomach heaved. Abba kept wrapping her in bear-like hugs, but Eva saw the haunted look on her parents' faces. Their hopes had been shattered too.

She'd spent a year at the sanatorium in the Carpathian mountains, recovering her mind and body. The rumour went out in the Josefov that she'd had tuberculosis. Her parents did nothing to quash it. But the family moved out to Pilsen soon after. A new start. Although the sense of what might have been travelled with her.

All she had to remind her of that time was a beautiful melody she'd composed. A lullaby, really, to soothe her shattered spirits. She thought of it often, even now, to comfort herself.

She was married before she knew it. Not to the handsome young man of her dreams in a vibrant celebration of dancing and feasting, but in an almost funereal ceremony to middle-aged widower Josef Kolischer. 'Thank goodness Kolischer will take her on,' Eva had heard her father whisper to Mutti one evening when he thought Eva was in her room. 'He's done very well at the Institute; he'll be able to provide for her. And most importantly, he's been married before. It's sad that his wife died without giving him children, but Eva is young and fit and they can have a family together. And hopefully she'll grow to love him in due course.'

Love? Eva had never known that feeling. She felt numb most of the time, lifeless, despite Josef's kindness. But perhaps she'd feel love for the baby. She stroked her stomach again. By the time she'd bought the lemons, and a copy of *The Prague Press*, her heart was lighter.

'What kept you so long?' Josef was still propped up against the pillows. 'Did Paní Kratz let you telephone the Institute?'

'Yes, she was very kind.' Eva handed him a teacup full of

hot lemon and honey. 'Drink this, Josef. I bought you some aspirin too.' She handed over a couple of chalky tablets.

Josef thrust them into his mouth, then tipped back his head, wincing as he swallowed. 'Thank you, my dear. I've been suffering so much. I'm sure men feel pain more than women.'

Eva's stomach rumbled, and the nausea surged again. 'I'm sure you're right, dear,' she replied, before hurtling back to the bathroom.

She felt better once she'd eaten a little dried bread. She couldn't even face any of Mutti's home-made jam. By the time she returned to the bedroom to check on Josef, he was buried behind the newspaper, only his laboured breathing signalling his presence.

'How are you feeling now?' she asked him, delving behind the paper to feel his forehead again.

No reply.

'Josef?'

The paper rustled and lowered, revealing Josef's thoughtful expression. 'That Jew-hater Adolf Hitler has made another speech. He claims he . . .' The newspaper was raised again whilst Josef searched for the article. '. . . will never attempt to subjugate foreign peoples.' He looked at Eva, his illness temporarily forgotten. 'Perhaps he's just all bluster and no action. I don't like to be complacent, but this might be better news than we'd feared.' Since the Enabling Act back in March, they'd been concerned what the new German chancellor would do with his increasing power.

'Perhaps.' As Eva picked up Josef's empty cup, she suppressed the image of biscuit-coloured cloth and red armbands. A leering face and white-blond hair. She shivered. Nothing would ever make her trust Germans again.

Josef's expression turned anxious.

Eva certainly wasn't going to explain her reaction. Partly to drive away Josef's worries, but mainly because a flash of guilt reminded her it was his baby too, she lowered herself onto the bed beside her husband, gently removed the newspaper, took his cold hands in hers, and told him her own good news.

3

'You haven't forgotten the department ball on the fifth, have you, darling?' asked Hugh as he reached for another piece of toast one morning at breakfast.

'Of course not,' replied Pamela, her own toast suddenly turning to sawdust in her mouth.

'It's going to be quite a showy affair. You'll need to wear something that's up to the mark.'

Pamela swallowed painfully. 'Don't worry. I won't let you down.'

'Righto.' Hugh stood up and dropped a kiss on the top of her head. 'Must dash. See you this evening.' He left the room, still clutching his toast.

Pamela smiled absent-mindedly back. But as soon as she heard the slam of the front door, she wiped her mouth on her napkin and rushed upstairs. Bother. The fifth was only a week away. She'd intended to visit that nice little Jewish tailor in Golders Green ages ago, but had become absorbed in her refugee work and let it slip her mind. She dabbed a bit of powder on her face and sprayed on some perfume. That would have to do. Thankfully she'd already put on the skirt from her tweed suit that morning. If she popped the matching jacket over her blouse, she'd look perfectly smart. 'Just off to see my seamstress,' she shouted to Kitty.

A disembodied voice drifted back from the kitchen: 'Right you are, Mrs Denison.'

She grabbed her bag from the hall table and clattered out of the front door.

As she sat on the Tube, breathing heavily from exertion, she realised she'd failed to telephone ahead. She'd just have to hope Mrs Brevda wasn't too busy. Why on earth did she always leave things until the last minute? She bit her lip and gazed around the carriage. Two schoolgirls sat opposite her, whispering behind their hands. Next to them was a middle-aged woman wearing a hat like a fruit bowl. Every time she moved her head, a pair of cherries wobbled with her. Pamela pretended to suppress a yawn in order to hide a laugh, and realised that she'd come out without her own hat. The truth was, clothes bored her, and she still felt uneasy at unnecessary finery. She certainly didn't want to let Hugh down, but she hated having to dress up for functions. It would be much easier for him to go to these events on his own, whilst she stayed at home with her knitting or a book. She wasn't really cut out to be a political wife. But that was what she was and she had to play her part.

The train swayed along the track and shuddered to a halt. Luckily it was only one stop. Pamela got out and exited the Tube, making her way along Golders Green Road until she reached Mrs Brevda's. She pushed open the door, triggering a tinkling bell as she did so, and entered the dark interior, which smelled of new fabric and sewing machine oil. The seamstress was sitting at the back of the room as usual, her eyes fixed on a piece of dark green cloth that she was guiding under the needle with one hand, whilst turning the wheel furiously with the other.

She only stopped when Pamela coughed, and only then after making sure the needle was down, pinning the fabric in place.

'Mrs Denison. What a surprise!'

Pamela smiled. 'I'm so sorry, Mrs Brevda. I should have telephoned ahead. But I need an evening dress made urgently.'

The seamstress frowned. 'How urgently?'

Pamela cleared her throat. 'The end of next week?'

'That's hardly any notice at all, but I'll see what I can do. What did you have in mind?'

Pamela looked round the little shop, her mind blank, and eventually lighted on a roll of iridescent purple silk. 'That's nice,' she said, fingering the fabric admiringly. It was striking, but not showy. And it would look splendid under the chandeliers of the Whitehall ballroom.

Mrs Brevda stood up, dragged the roll from the shelf and dropped it on the table where she'd been sewing, releasing a slight puff of dust. She took one end and stretched out a yard or so. 'Good choice, my dear. If I cut it on the bias, it'll move beautifully. Mr Denison won't be able to keep his eyes off you.'

Pamela laughed. 'I doubt that, but I agree the fabric is perfect. Do you think you can make me something in time?'

'Hmm. Wide or narrow skirt?'

'Oh, narrow, I think.'

'Good. That will take less time. And sleeveless, I take it?'

Pamela nodded. 'But nothing immodest.'

'Of course not.' Mrs Brevda drew a piece of paper and a

pencil across the table and quickly made a couple of sketches. One had a sweetheart neckline and a nipped-in waist, but Pamela thought it looked a little young for her. The second had a mandarin collar, and a slightly flared hem.

She pointed to the second drawing. 'That one gets my vote.'

The seamstress put a tick by the chosen sketch and motioned Pamela behind a dark curtain at the side of the shop. 'Pop your suit off, please, and I'll come in and measure you.'

Pamela did as she was told, and Mrs Brevda entered the cubicle, unwinding the tape measure that was usually slung around her neck. 'I have your measurements from last time. Let's just check if they've changed at all.'

Pamela stood on a rickety stool in the makeshift changing room whilst Mrs Brevda stretched the tape measure this way and that, muttering to herself and jotting down figures. She wound it round Pamela's waist. 'Still no bump to conceal, then?'

Pamela blushed. 'Will is fourteen now. And Hugh only wanted one child.'

Mrs Brevda took the tape measure away and stood back. 'Shame. With a war coming, everyone with sons must be worried.' She put out a hand and helped Pamela down from the stool.

Pamela's legs felt suddenly weak. 'Do you think there'll be a war, Mrs Brevda?'

'Well, you're the one with a husband at the Foreign Office, but most folk around here think it's only a matter of time.'

'Surely not.' Pamela sat down abruptly on the stool. Mrs Brevda had confirmed what she'd feared deep down. Perhaps she'd been too content to accept Hugh's assurances that everything would be all right.

'Many of us have families back in Europe. That Hitler's a madman. He's just passed a whole lot of laws against Jews. My people no longer feel welcome anywhere. Prague's a beautiful city.' The seamstress sniffed. 'Much more elegant than London. But I'm glad I came across when I did. Jews are leaving Czechoslovakia and Germany just as quick as they can.'

Pamela forced a smile. 'And I hope we're making them welcome here.'

Mrs Brevda sniffed again. 'Some people are. But Hitler's getting greedy. He's like that Kaiser Wilhelm all over again. If he starts treating the rest of the world like he's been treating the Jews, then countries will have to respond.'

Pamela got shakily to her feet. 'I'm sorry you feel so vulnerable, Mrs Brevda.' She wished she could reassure the seamstress, but maybe Hugh was hiding his concerns from her. Thank goodness there were Quakers in government. They'd be sure to do the right thing.

Mrs Brevda nodded. 'I'll ring you in a week.'

Pamela left the shop thoughtfully.

As Hugh twirled her expertly round the dance floor, Pamela suppressed a surge of pleasure at the way the silk dress flowed. Mrs Brevda had done an excellent job. The ball gown fitted her perfectly – nothing too tight or revealing, and very comfortable to wear. She'd known it was perfect the minute she'd picked it up, modelling it in the changing room under the seamstress's critical eye.

We certainly don't feel like a country contemplating war, Pamela thought to herself as she watched Hugh's Foreign Office colleagues drinking, smoking and laughing. All around her were women in gorgeous frocks, opalescent under the lights, moving with grace and fluidity. The whole effect was of shifting shapes and colours, like looking through the kaleidoscope Will had had as a child.

They sat down for a breather, and Hugh grabbed a glass of champagne from a passing waiter, ignoring Pamela's look of reproach.

'I forgot to tell you earlier,' he said. 'I have to go to Czechoslovakia on FO business in a few weeks' time. Wondered if you'd like to come along for the ride? Might be fun.'

Pamela twisted her wedding ring round her finger in an absent-minded gesture. It had come from Asprey's and she was always terrified of losing it. She had no idea what Czechoslovakia would be like, but maybe it would be nice to spend some more time with Hugh instead of staying at home as usual. She could probably ask someone to take over her refugee work for a while. And it would be good to find out for herself a little more about what was happening in Europe. She was so insulated in her London life. Perhaps there was something she could do to help people whilst they were in Czechoslovakia.

'All right,' she said. 'That would be lovely.'

Hugh leant forward and she caught a whiff of alcohol. 'Did I tell you how beautiful you're looking tonight?'

It was Pamela's idea to go skiing. She was sitting under the dryer at the hair salon, leafing through a copy of *Harper's*

Bazaar that Madame Adrienne had handed her. Everyone knew that Madame Adrienne wasn't really French, but Pamela was content to go along with the charade. Pamela could never make her fine hair as thick and wavy as Adrienne could, and these days Hugh was more than happy to foot the bill. Sometimes she worried she was spending too much time and money on her appearance, but Hugh assured her it was her duty to keep herself attractive; all the other ministerial wives kept up with the latest styles.

As she flicked through the articles on fashion and beauty, searching for something more interesting, an advertisement caught her attention. It featured a woman in plus fours and a red Fair Isle jumper, posing against snow-covered mountains. There was a jaunty cap on her head; she was clutching a pair of ski poles and beaming. There was a caption under the picture: *This Winter to Czechoslovakia.* Pamela realised how weary she was of leaden English skies; the short, dark November days; the dull routine at home. Even her charity work had become monotonous. She only came alive when Will was back, and now that he was at Marlborough, he was often invited to friends' houses for days on end, reducing the time spent with his parents. How could they compete with the noise and laughter other boys' homes offered, full of lively siblings keen to play tennis or take Will to dances? Despite Pamela's best efforts, the winter break was always quiet with just the three of them. She hadn't really given Hugh's proposed trip to Czechoslovakia much thought. But what if they combined the Foreign Office business with a skiing holiday? She pictured Will hurtling down an icy slope, his face flushed with excitement, she and Hugh following more cautiously, smiling at their son's enthusiasm. That would give them all a trip to remember.

When she made her suggestion at dinner that evening, Hugh looked up from his soup bowl in surprise. 'But you can't even ski!' he almost shouted.

Pamela broke into her bread roll. 'I know, but I used to ice-skate as a child. It can't be that different.' She had a brief memory of a strange stiff-legged walk across a frozen pond, her breath coming out in a cloud, her arms flailing in all directions. It had taken her a whole morning to learn to bend her knees, to glide rather than lurch, to allow her fixed grin to soften, shifting her gaze to the frosted reeds on the far side of the pond rather than staring anxiously at the ground as her brothers laughed at her. But she'd mastered it. Her father said she was a natural.

'Skiing's not at all the same,' said Hugh, reaching for his own bread roll. 'You'll be traversing a mountain, for a start.'

'Yes, I know. But I can have lessons.' Pamela dipped her spoon into her soup, pushing it away from her towards the top edge of the bowl, like she'd seen Clementine Churchill do. 'Or I could just watch you and Will. You're both bound to be good. Think of all that rugby you used to play!'

Hugh sat up straight. His stomach, which had started to slump towards the table, straightened with him.

Pamela smiled. 'And I bet Will takes to it straight away. It'll be such fun.'

'Hmm.' Hugh wiped his mouth with his napkin. 'I'll think about it.'

*

Two days later, Hugh returned unexpectedly early from Whitehall and slapped a pile of travel brochures on top of Pamela's bureau, where she'd been writing to Will.

She turned round, smiling at his triumphant expression. 'The skiing holiday! We can go?' Her body tingled with excitement. Will would love it.

Hugh chuckled. 'It was so quiet in the office, I thought I'd take the afternoon off. Passed Inghams on my way to the station so popped in for a few of these.' He leant forward to spread out the pile of brochures. 'You choose!'

'That's terrific. Thank you, darling.' Pamela tidied the brochures into a neat stack. 'I'll just finish writing to Will, then I'll have a look.'

'Righto.' Hugh turned to go out of the room, miming a ski manoeuvre as he did so.

Pamela laughed and picked up a pen. *PS*, she wrote at the bottom of Will's letter. *Guess what?*

Two weeks later, they were in the Krkonoše mountains. The ski resort was basic but adequate. Hugh had completed his business in Prague in record time, whilst Pamela and Will visited the castle and the Charles Bridge, took a boat trip on the river and attended a couple of concerts at the Rudolfinum. Then they all caught the train to the resort.

Ever since she'd seen the picture in the magazine at the hair salon, Pamela had pictured herself standing on the snow against a piercing blue sky, a pair of ski poles in her hands and a healthy glow on her cheeks. For once, Will didn't mention any of the treats his friends were having that Christmas. A ski holiday clearly made *him* the object of envy. Pamela felt a pang of guilt that they could afford such extravagance. But she'd work extra hard for the refugees when they got back to make up for it.

The reality was even better than the picture. Each day brought a blue- and pink-washed sky with a hard white sun glittering through the trees. By lunchtime, there was even a little warmth in the air. Hugh had tried to persuade her to stay at the chalet drinking hot chocolate, or to take an afternoon stroll round the resort, but Pamela was determined not to miss out. To be honest, she didn't find skiing easy, but she wasn't going to admit it. It was hard work traversing a mountain and she always seemed to lag behind. Will and Hugh strode out in front, learning so quickly and making it look effortless. Their skis never seemed to cross and they never slipped sideways or had to pause for breath like Pamela did. The instructor and guide they'd hired was kind and waited for her each time, even when the other two didn't bother to check on her. 'You're getting better, Meesees Deneeson,' he said in his broken English, his eyes crinkling against the sun's glare. 'Keep going, not long now.'

In the afternoons, after long lunches on the restaurant terrace halfway up the mountain, with Will champing at the bit with impatience, they carried on skiing on their own. On the last day, Hugh proposed that they traverse higher up, then ski down the mountain.

'Are you sure you want to come with us?' he asked Pamela, winking at Will. 'We want to make the most of the last day. We'll be on the train by this time tomorrow. But it might be too much for you.'

Pamela swallowed. 'I'll be fine.'

44

'We'll look after you, Mother,' Will added, putting an arm round her. But Pamela thought he looked a bit embarrassed.

She set off between them, trying to slide the skis along as fast as she could.

As they climbed higher up the slope, the temperature cooled. A swirling wind buffeted their jackets and an icy blast numbed Pamela's ears and the tip of her nose. She rewound her scarf around her head, pulling the front of it over her face. Even so, the wind clawed at her, trying to gouge her throat and snatch her breath. She didn't dare open her mouth to speak, but nodded bleakly at Hugh as he signalled to her to keep going. She gripped her ski poles. She'd been stupid to agree to go up the mountain; she was a liability. Hugh and Will would have had much more fun on their own, without her holding them back. But she hated missing out.

She risked a glance down the sheer slope in front of her, almost blue where the sun didn't reach it. Her legs felt flimsy, and terror tightened her stomach.

'All right?' Hugh was smiling at her. How could he look so relaxed and excited when they were all facing certain death?

Pamela tried to stretch her lips in return; her mouth was too dry to speak.

Will was already standing at the top of the slope, turning his head from side to side as if rehearsing his route down.

Hugh nudged Pamela's back, and she slid her skis along the hard snow in front of her, at right angles to the slope, digging her poles in hard to stop herself slipping. Miraculously, she started to move forward.

'That's my girl,' said Hugh.

She didn't dare turn round to acknowledge him. She couldn't

45

look at the slope to her right either. Just fix your eyes straight ahead, she told herself, as she inched across. Eventually she reached Will. She had to force herself to resist grabbing his arm.

'Ready, Mother?' His face was glowing despite the cold. Like Hugh, he didn't show a scrap of fear.

'All right,' said Hugh, panting slightly. 'I think it's best if Will goes first, otherwise he'll get impatient.'

Will laughed.

'But you must stop every few hundred yards to see where we are. Pammie, you go in the middle and I'll bring up the rear.'

Pamela nodded. She'd be safe between her two men, wouldn't she? She closed her eyes for a second, imagining them all back at the chalet, toasting their tired feet in front of the log fire, sipping hot chocolate, laughing at the day's adventures. How she wished they were there now. That she didn't have to get through the next few hours. But it had been her idea to go skiing. She really mustn't hold them back. She wanted Hugh and Will to be proud of her, for Will to tell his school friends about his brave mother. She took a deep, shuddering breath.

Will had already launched himself down the slope and was zigzagging smoothly down the first section. She heard the faint whoosh of his skis and saw the puffs of snow spray out from under the blades. His dark hair was just visible under his cap, and she knew his cheeks would be red and his eyes shining. Despite her terror, she felt a brief surge of pride. Her glorious, intrepid son. What a future he had ahead of him. Although she'd resisted Marlborough for as long as she could, she had to admit that the school was making a fine young man of him: he was kind, hard-working, truthful. All good qualities for a Quaker boy.

'Come on, Pammie. You've got to go sometime.'

Pamela turned her head slowly to acknowledge Hugh's comment. Even that small gesture threatened to unbalance her body. She wobbled slightly.

'Plant your poles to the side, then turn,' shouted Hugh, sounding like the ski guide but without the accent.

Pamela swivelled her upper body, drove the ends of her sticks into the hard snow, hearing the crunch of ice as she did so, then edged her skis round until she was facing down the slope. The blades slid on the slippery surface; it took all her strength to straighten them. Her rigid arms shook with effort.

'Well done. You're right in position. Off you go!' exhorted Hugh.

She pushed herself slowly forward. Instantly the ground fell away from under her and she was hurtling down the slope.

'Turn!' Hugh's faint voice drifted down to her.

Turn? Oh yes, of course. She dug in her right blade, leant out as the instructor had drummed into her, and allowed her left ski to follow. At first nothing happened, then suddenly she'd turned and was rushing towards the side of the slope. She dug in her left blade and turned again. Despite the terrifying speed and the huge strain on her muscles, a little part of her was elated. She was skiing! Properly downhill skiing!

'Well done, Mother!'

She allowed herself a glance down, and there was Will in

front of her, stationary on the slope, banging his poles to loosen the impacted snow, his skis locked in position.

Pamela forced her legs into a shaky snowplough and juddered past Will, coming to an abrupt stop ten yards beyond him. She didn't dare turn round, but felt Hugh whoosh up behind her, then Will joining them.

'Good work, Pammie! That's the hardest bit done.'

Pamela nodded, still looking down the mountain. There'd been a few expert skiers at the top, who had easily outstripped them, but clusters of black shapes lower down the slope suggested they would soon have company.

'Ready?' Will wasn't even out of breath. But then he'd had a while to rest. Pamela wanted to dig herself into the snow, take off her skis and sleep for hours until her exhausted body recovered. But the sooner she set off again, the sooner she'd be back at the chalet, basking in the warmth of the fire and Hugh and Will's pride, telling herself she would never, ever put herself through that again.

'Yes, let's go,' she said.

Hugh chuckled. 'You're getting a taste for this.'

Pamela didn't reply. She just forced her legs into a parallel position and set off again.

Warmed by a watery sun, the snow was softer further down the mountain. There wasn't the gritty feel of ice under her blades and she could ski more smoothly now. She followed Will's line, tracing diagonal patterns down the slope. How marvellous to be guided down the mountain by her son. She watched Will's firm figure ahead of her. Already he seemed more manly. This ski holiday had done him the world of good; he was so protective of her, so delighted by her progress. How splendid that he'd always be there to look after her.

It was the noises that alerted her first. Warning shouts, a sharp scream of pain, then strangled cries of panic. Pamela looked down the slope. A child had fallen and was sobbing loudly, lying awkwardly on the snow, skis and poles strewn down the mountain. Will had already skied past and was trying to make his way back up the slope to help. Two other skiers, doubtless the child's parents, were following suit, their stiff postures revealing their anxiety. Pamela altered course to reach the child, but instead of slowing down as she'd intended, she found herself picking up speed. Suddenly she was careering down the slope, unable to stop. She shrieked for Will, but he was too far away. And Hugh was too far behind to help. At this rate she was going to hit the child.

She dug in her right blade and veered off course, mere yards before impact. But now she was rushing headlong towards the edge of the mountain. What should she do? She was rapidly advancing on the forest that lined the slope. The snow was icy here, the trees denying the sun its softening warmth. She hit a slippery patch and shot towards a tree; tried to sit back to slow her approach but only accelerated further. Her leg slammed into the trunk, and she fell back, winded, onto the snow.

Before the pain made all conscious thought impossible, her first response was relief that she'd avoided the child. Her second was how red her blood looked against the white snow.

4

The first Czech words Pamela learned were for painkillers. And she used them often, particularly *morfin*. Her leg had been pronounced broken at the scene. Two local men arrived after half an hour with a sledge, and Hugh and Will helped lift her gently onto it. Even then she'd screamed with pain.

The ambulance took her twenty miles to the nearest hospital, an agonising jolt along mountain roads, despite the fact that they'd given her *morfin* by then. After an interminable wait for an X-ray, a lugubrious doctor informed them in broken English that she'd snapped her shin bone. Luckily the break was clean, so after her leg was swathed in plaster of Paris, and raised on a hoist, there was nothing to do but wait until it mended. Six weeks, the doctor said.

'Six weeks?' repeated Pamela, tears misting her eyes. 'But my husband has to return to work and my son's school term starts soon. Can't I go back to England with them on the train?'

The doctor shrugged. 'You can,' he said, 'but the best way is to stay here.'

Hugh nodded. 'I'm sure he's right, Pammie. You don't want to make things worse. I hate leaving you here on your own; I'll miss you terribly. But I know you'll be safe and well looked after.'

'How will you manage on your own?' Pamela wailed. She'd waited for Hugh to say 'I told you so' when she first had the accident, but to his credit he'd remained silent. Nevertheless, the reproach still hovered between them.

He pressed her hand. 'You mustn't worry, darling. Kitty will look after me. And we can write. You'll be home before you know it.'

Pamela looked sadly at Will. All that fresh-air ruddiness had disappeared from his face and he looked paler than he had before the holiday. 'I'll miss your next exeat,' she said.

Will wiped his eyes with the back of his hand. 'I'll write too, Mother. Every day. I promise.'

'Not every day, darling. You'll be far too busy.'

'Every day,' said Will firmly.

Pamela gave him a shaky smile, then hugged both her men in turn, taking comfort from Hugh's strong shoulders and the tightness of Will's embrace. Hugh smiled brightly, but Pamela could still see the concern etched on his face. It was only after they left that she allowed herself to cry properly. And then she cried for a very long time.

It wasn't until her sobs subsided to shuddering gulps that she became aware of the woman in the next bed looking at her pityingly. She said something that sounded like 'tack leeto'.

Pamela shrugged apologetically. 'English.'

The woman nodded and pointed to herself. 'Ada,' she said.

That must be her name. 'Pamela,' she replied, mimicking the woman's gesture.

Ada smiled. She must have been around Pamela's age, but she had missing teeth like an old woman. Pamela wondered

51

if she'd lost them in an accident. Like Pamela, she had her leg in a cast.

Pamela couldn't think of anything else to say after that. She was aware of the woman still looking at her, so she turned her head to avoid her scrutiny, pretending to observe her surroundings, although they were already all too familiar. The ward was basic but clean: twelve metal beds in two neat rows, each with a pink blanket and starched white sheets. There was an elderly lady in the bed opposite Pamela's who moaned at intervals like a wounded animal. Two middle-aged women were further down the row, one knitting, the other staring blankly across the room. In the bed the other side of Pamela, a young girl with a pale face and lank hair huddled under the blanket, her eyes closed. Pamela wondered what was wrong with her. The other beds were empty.

After a while, a smiling young nurse appeared. She made her way down the ward, tidying, smoothing and checking, until she reached Pamela's bed. She picked up Pamela's hand, encircling her wrist whilst she consulted a silver watch pinned to her uniform, then nodded briskly before moving on to Ada.

Pamela lay back on the pillows. The initial onslaught of pain had eased, or been numbed by drugs. All she felt was a throbbing, a heaviness around her leg and an intense itching that had her eyes watering with frustration at her inability to ease it. Six weeks! However was she to pass the time? She had a copy of *Murder on the Orient Express*, which Hugh had given her recently, on the small table beside her bed, but she was trying to eke it out, a few pages a day, so that she didn't finish it too soon. She doubted if the hospital possessed any English books, and although Hugh had promised to send her some magazines, they probably wouldn't arrive until after she'd left.

She tried not to think about Will packing for school with no one to find his socks or fold his clothes. Kitty would do her best, but she'd be busier than ever in the house without Pamela to work out menus or write shopping lists. She just hoped Hugh wouldn't shout at the poor girl too much. Really, he had no idea how to handle her. And what about her refugee work? They'd have to do without her for weeks at Drayton House; she normally went there most days to help pack the clothes that people had sent in for the children. Sometimes she'd press a little jumper to her face, or hold up a pretty dress, and imagine a Polish or German child wearing it, taking comfort from the warm fabric. Then she'd fold it with care, hoping her concern would be caught in its fibres. She curled her fingers into a fist and thumped the blanket. It was too much. And all because she'd wanted to give Will a good holiday!

She felt Ada staring at her again. The woman was muttering something unintelligible. Pamela gave her a watery grin and Ada made a sad face in return. Then she hauled up a carpet bag from the floor, dragged it onto the bed and rummaged inside it for a while, before locating a small bar of chocolate. She eased off the purple wrapper, snapped the chocolate in two, then lobbed one section carefully across to Pamela. It landed right in front of her. Pamela laughed and made a thumbs-up sign. Ada responded similarly. They both bit into their chocolate at the same time and exchanged glances of enjoyment. It really was good.

'Choc-ol-larder,' said Ada.

Pamela repeated the word, trying to imitate the woman's

accent, then offered the English version, which Ada echoed. 'Good,' said Pamela.

After that, Ada pointed to her bed, her blanket, her sheets, her nightdress. Each time she gave the Czech word; each time Pamela repeated it then supplied the English equivalent.

Pamela was getting used to Czech voices now. The soft, guttural sounds, the strange way they pronounced the letter 'r' – half rolling, half a 'j' through clenched teeth. It certainly wasn't easy. But she wasn't going to be beaten either. She pointed to her leg and raised her eyebrows.

'No-ha,' said Ada.

'No-ha,' Pamela repeated. Then, 'Leg.'

They identified various body parts, then tested each other. By the time the lunchtime trolley rumbled down the ward, Pamela realised that two hours had passed. Two hours when she hadn't thought about Hugh, or Will, or the awful frustration of being stuck in a hospital bed. As she scooped up spoonfuls of potato soup (bram-bor-ova pol-ev-ka) and chewed on thick black bread (zhit-ney kleb), she told herself that she would manage somehow.

Ada didn't seem to want to continue their lesson after lunch. She was fussing with her nightdress, rubbing at her sallow cheeks and pulling her fingers through her hair. When the door to the ward burst open and two young children hurtled through it, followed by a small, weary-looking man in a checked suit, Pamela realised why.

Ada held out her arms, and her son and daughter jumped onto the bed to greet her. 'Oh-pat-rin-yeh!' she gasped. Her wince of pain made her meaning all too clear. The children froze, then gently snuggled into their mother's embrace.

Pamela swallowed. She turned her head away as Ada's husband leant forward to kiss her. Perhaps now was the time to indulge in Agatha Christie.

She picked up her book from the bedside cabinet, but after only a few pages, she was conscious of the rise and fall of a child's breath and the faint smell of milk. The little girl was standing beside her, staring at her open-mouthed. Pamela lowered her book and smiled. The child held up a grubby doll. It was made of calico, unadorned except for some coarse wool hair, with cross-stitched eyes and mouth. Pamela shook the doll's padded hand solemnly. The child giggled, then made the doll dive under Pamela's blanket. Pamela pretended to look for it whilst the little girl laughed even more. Eventually she produced the doll from under her bedclothes with a flourish. The child's dark eyes lit up.

Ada said something curt to her daughter, whose shoulders slumped.

'It's all right,' said Pamela, signalling to Ada that she was happy to play with the girl.

Ada nodded gratefully, and the game continued.

By the time her family had left, Ada's face was pale. She lay back on her pillows and closed her eyes.

Pamela picked up her book again. Clearly the language lessons would have to wait until tomorrow. But at least a few more hours had passed.

A procession of red ants was inching its way up Pamela's shin, the soft scrape of their hair's-breadth legs causing such a frenzy of itching that the urge to rip off her plaster and claw at her skin until she drew blood was overwhelming. She woke up suddenly, her forehead clammy, her heart thundering. The walls of the ward closed in on her. Soft blue light illuminated the sleeping forms in the other beds. The old woman's moaning had stopped, replaced only by wheezy sighs. The air was fugged with the smells of antiseptic and warm humanity.

From the end of the ward came a tap-tap sound like Morse code. Pamela raised her head. A large, frowning nurse was squashed behind a desk, knitting furiously, a fat ball of wool jerking across the medical records piled up in front of her. Pamela caught the glint of metal in the moonlight and imagined seizing one of the long needles and thrusting it down the side of her plaster, blissfully easing the incessant itch. She bit her lip. She couldn't even get out of bed to use the toilet; she had to perform in a bedpan behind a discreetly placed screen.

She closed her eyes and tried to picture herself knitting. When she'd been pregnant with Will, she'd spent hours making him little matinee jackets and bootees. Mum had taught her well. And as he grew up, there were scarves and bobble hats, until the need for school uniform and a new-found desire to choose his own clothes had made him reject his mother's home-made efforts.

An image of Ada's daughter's doll darted into Pamela's mind. She could probably work out how to knit a few little garments to cover its grubby nakedness. It would be worth it to see the shine in the child's eyes, her wide smile of pleasure. And it would be a way of thanking Ada for her kindness. She smoothed the bedclothes as far as she could reach. For once she was looking forward to another day.

Lots of careful miming to Ada, and Pamela's insistent donation of some of the holiday korunas left in her purse, resulted in Jan, Ada's husband, bringing in a bulging paper bag and depositing it on Pamela's bed the next time he visited. Pamela shook out the contents: three balls of wool – paintbox colours of red, blue and green – and three pairs of needles of varying thickness. Perfect. She beamed at Jan and reached over to take more money from her bag, but he shook his head. Pamela shrugged, keeping the smile in place.

The little girl, whom Pamela now knew as Agata, had brought in her doll again. Pamela pointed to it and the child carried it over. A further mimed dialogue indicated a request for a blue hat, a red jumper and a green skirt. Under Agata's careful scrutiny, Pamela took up a strand of blue wool and cast on. Fifty stitches should do it. She'd knit straight for a few rows and then taper. Perhaps she could even make a pom-pom for the top. She was so busy knitting that it took her a while to realise Agata was perched on the bed next to her, her head resting on Pamela's stomach. How long had it been since Will used to do that? Since he'd started at Marlborough, the hugs had become perfunctory, and he only kissed her when bidden. She inched her upper body nearer this small, trusting child, enjoying her warmth, and tried to knit as fluidly as possible so as not to disturb her.

She'd have been happy to cuddle the little boy too, but he remained by his mother. He had a toy plane in his hand and was making it duck and dive over Ada's bedspread. Pamela smiled across at him, but he avoided her eyes.

Pamela's Czech improved daily. She still had her lessons with Ada, and now Agata was trying to teach her too. She'd often sit with Pamela once she'd spoken to her mother, watching her knit and testing her on newly acquired vocabulary. Even the doctors and nurses joined in, explaining in halting English what they were doing, then changing to Czech and getting Pamela to repeat their words. She was a willing pupil and gradually became fluent in the basics.

Before long, there was a small pile of doll's clothes on Pamela's bedside table. After she'd snipped the last strand of green wool from the little skirt, she held it up for Ada to admire. Ada tried to smile, but failed. Pamela stared at her. She'd been so occupied the last few days, she hadn't noticed that her neighbour was more gaunt than ever, her eyes a dull brown. Her lunchtime tray, which she'd returned listlessly to the bedside cabinet, still held half a bowl of now congealing soup and a whole hunk of bread. Pamela wanted to speak to her new friend, to ask if she was all right, but she didn't have the words. She'd have liked to wipe her forehead or hold her hand, but she was impotent with her leg strung up like this. And by now Ada's eyes were shut, the faint rise and fall of her chest the only indication of life.

Pamela picked up a letter from Will. He'd kept his promise: flimsy blue envelopes with a British postmark arrived every few days, usually in batches after a gap, thanks to the vagaries of the postal system. She'd already read this one several times, but no matter. As she immersed herself in her son's lively descriptions of Latin lessons and rugby practice, the hospital sounds muted and it was her own beloved child who commanded her attention.

Pamela's first thought was how odd it was that Ada wanted a language lesson at two in the morning. Then, as consciousness surfaced, she realised that the Czech woman wasn't speaking to her; she was muttering unintelligibly in her sleep. She watched her neighbour thrash her head on the pillow, and winced as Ada's leg pulley creaked in protest. The disturbance brought the rapid tread of the duty nurse, who put a hand to Ada's forehead, then grabbed a screen from the side of the ward, hauled it across the room, and placed it beside Ada's bed, shielding her from Pamela's worried gaze. She was left to interpret the thuds and rustlings coming from behind it. At length the screen was moved away, more gently this time, and Ada's face looked calmer.

But she was still unconscious the next morning, and when Pamela saw the livid rash on her chest, she signalled to the nurse in alarm. Again the procedure with the screen, although this time the noises were more frantic. Eventually the nurse sped off, returning a few minutes later with a doctor. Pamela listened to the urgent exchange between them, but couldn't make out any of the words.

Several medical staff visited Ada during the day, carrying syringes, tablets and various medical implements, but still the screen remained in place. Pamela was too worried to knit or read her book, so she just stared into space, listening anxiously to her neighbour's staccato breaths when it was quiet, or the rapid conversations of the doctors as they attended her. Whatever could be the matter with Ada? It seemed very serious. Pamela's stomach clenched whenever a doctor arrived, and soon her heart seemed to be one continuous beat of fear for her kind fellow patient.

After lunch, Jan and the children visited. Jan blanched when he saw the screen by Ada's bed. A doctor approached and spoke to him in a low tone, which produced increasing signs of alarm on his face. Eventually he put his arms round his children and herded them towards Pamela. Pamela realised at once what he meant. 'I'll look after them,' she said, motioning for Jan to return to his wife.

She pulled Agata up onto her bed. The little girl had brought her doll with her and was content for Pamela to help her dress it with the clothes she'd knitted. The boy, Tomas, stood like a statue, his dark eyes fixed on the screen by his mother's bed, behind which his father had also vanished. He'd brought his toy plane with him but made no attempt to fly it.

The children stayed while the ward grew dark. An orderly brought Pamela's supper, a little smoked meat with some red cabbage and potato dumplings, which she shared with Agata, but Tomas refused to eat. By now, the nurses and doctors had stopped coming to Ada's bed. Only the occasional rasping breath escaped from behind the screen. And then not even that. When Jan's howl of grief tore through the air, Pamela hugged Agata to her. But she couldn't reach Tomas, and was powerless to put an arm around his shuddering shoulders. She was trembling too with the horror of it all.

Eventually Jan emerged. His eyes were red and his frame appeared slighter than usual. He shakily nodded his thanks to Pamela, drew the children behind the screen for one last goodbye to their mother, then led them slowly back down the ward.

Pamela was left to listen to the sounds of orderlies heaving Ada's body onto a stretcher and carrying it down the corridor, whilst her heart ached for the woman's poor husband and children, and for the new friend she had lost.

And despite her best attempts to conjure Will and Hugh's healthy, smiling faces as they'd waited for her at the bottom of the ski slope, all she could see as she tried to sleep were the haunted expressions of Ada's little family.

She doubted if she would ever forget them.

5

The early morning was their special time. Miriam woke at five as usual for her bottle, and Eva tiptoed out of bed, leaving Josef snoring, and made up the feed in the chilly kitchen before padding back to lift the little girl out of her cot and hold her close, keeping her warm while Miriam sucked eagerly, her brown eyes seeking Eva's own. With the curtains drawn the room was shadowy, the air thick with thumb-suck breath. At nearly three, Miriam was heavy now, but she still curled into Eva as though remembering when she'd been a part of her body. Her birth had been straightforward: the capable, stout midwife delivering her with ease whilst Mutti looked on and Josef and Abba sat talking and praying in hushed voices outside. In the last few months of pregnancy, Eva had tried to block out her fears, the memory of pain and terror, but she needn't have worried. Miriam came easily, and afterwards Eva was pierced by a joy so exquisite she wanted it to last for ever.

She looked down at the drowsy child. It was amazing how Miriam could even suck in her sleep, her little pink mouth pushed back against the teat, her starfish fingers pressed against Eva's chest. You're all mine, she thought. I'll never give you up. She felt a sharp dart of fear as she thought of the palpable tension in the Jewish quarter. After the Nuremberg laws of last autumn, Jews were no longer allowed to marry Aryans, and German Jews had been denied their citizenship. A few families in the Josefov had already fled for Britain, but Josef dismissed them as panic-mongers.

Yet Eva had still shivered when, back in the summer, she'd pushed Miriam in her pram past newsstands and seen pictures of Hitler smiling as he presided over the Berlin Olympics. There was something about him that made her uneasy. Maybe it was the uniform; ever since the night in the cemetery, the sight of German uniforms caused an instant lurch of panic. She held Miriam closer. She'd protect this child with every breath in her body.

*

Finally back in England after her long weeks in Prague, Pamela was urged by Hugh to take things slowly. She stayed indoors resting through a cold, wet spring, then, as it turned into summer, spent long days stretched out on a garden chair, reading, or closing her eyes against the glare of sunlight, often lulled into sleep by the drone of bees, letting the warmth of a benevolent sun seep through her skin and into her bones.

After she'd left the hospital, she could smell the stench of carbolic soap and disinfectant for weeks; it was only here in the garden that the peppery scent of geraniums and the opulent sweetness of roses finally replaced it. But the memory of Ada's white face was harder to blot out.

By September she longed to get back to her charity work again. At least that way she'd be useful. Hugh insisted on driving her to Drayton House when he could, or summoning a taxi when he couldn't. Pamela made sure she was home in time to comb her hair and pinch her cheeks before he returned. She didn't want him to see how exhausted she was, or how much her leg still hurt when she stood. More often than not, she had to sit down to sort out the clothes.

As the days wore on, she realised the dew was lying longer on the grass in the mornings and the tight green bramble berries at the end of the garden were beginning to redden and loosen in the languid sun. One bright October Sunday, after Hugh had left for his club, Pamela decided she was well enough to make the journey to Whitechapel for a long-overdue visit to her parents. She caught a crowded bus to the high street and headed south on foot until she got to Buckle Street. Although she'd put her flat shoes on, it was still hard not to limp. It would be a relief to hang up her coat in Mum's dark, narrow hall, and be shepherded inside to drink tea in the immaculate parlour.

But her normally calm mother greeted her anxiously, darting glances up and down the street before bolting the door behind them. That was strange. Her parents normally locked the door only at night. 'We can trust everyone around here,' her mother would say. 'No matter how poor, no one steals from a neighbour.' Sometimes she would return from shopping to realise she hadn't even closed the front door, that it was gaping open at the hinges, but nothing would ever have been touched.

Pamela followed her into the kitchen. It was brighter there than in the hall, and easier to see the sallowness of her mother's face, the new lines that fanned from her eyes, the droop of her mouth.

'What's the matter, Mum? You don't look well.'

Mum grabbed the kettle and filled it with a stream of cold water that beat a tattoo against the metal, then set it on the hob again.

'Mum?' Pamela persisted against the slow crescendo of the kettle's whistle.

Mum was clattering teacups and spoons on a tray that she'd covered with a starched tea towel. She reached into the cupboard and pulled down a Huntley & Palmers biscuit tin, decorated with a hunting scene. It was strange how Mum felt the need to treat Pamela like royalty since she'd got married. Bread and dripping had been good enough for her when she'd lived at home.

Finally the kettle boiled. Mum warmed the pot, spooned in tea leaves and lifted it onto the tray, where it infused a red knitted tea cosy with fragrant steam.

She carried the tray into the parlour, then finally sat down on the sofa next to Pamela and looked her in the eye. 'It's your pa. He's gone down to Cable Street.'

'Cable Street?' Pamela's hand went to her mouth. At once she realised the reason for her mother's concern. 'Nothing to do with that protest?'

Mum nodded mutely.

Hugh had told her that Mosley and his lot were marching into the East End today. If he'd known Pamela was planning a visit he'd have warned her off for sure. She knew there'd be a crowd – the excitement on the bus had been palpable – but she'd imagined she'd be safe so far north. Whatever had made her normally sensible father decide to join in?

'He's been muttering about the fascists for weeks,' said Mum. 'What that lot are saying about Jews is shocking. The

East End isn't standing for it. They've been barricading the streets to stop the Blackshirts getting in.'

Pamela reached for her mother's hand. When had the skin become so loose and liver-spotted? 'I'm sure the police will sort it out, Mum. And Pa's not one to fight.'

'No, love. But he's not one to accept injustice either.'

Pamela bit her lip. 'Is anyone with him?'

Mum nodded. 'A couple of the elders. Norman Townsgate and Ray Dunning.'

'Oh, that's good. They're both sensible men. I'm sure he'll be fine.'

Mum reached for her best jug and poured milk into their teacups. 'I hope you're right.'

Pamela stayed with her mother until dusk muted the dim light of the parlour still further and the air grew still. They'd exhausted their news long ago. For once, Mum was barely interested to hear what Will had been up to. She didn't even ask about Hugh. Pamela talked about the clothes she'd been knitting, and described at length the books she'd read, but eventually, weary of Mum's monosyllabic replies, lapsed into silence.

She'd lit a fire earlier, and was just about to draw the curtains, wincing at the jolt to her leg as she stood up, when Mum stopped her.

'I need to see your father coming home.'

Pamela slumped in her seat again. She stared at the wall as the minutes ticked slowly by. As a child she'd spent hours painstakingly stitching the sampler that now hung above the mantelpiece. *Blessed are the peacemakers*, it said. *Matthew 5:9*. She still found it hard to lower her eyes to where the telegram had sat all those years ago.

The boy had brought it round one midsummer morning, looking at her sympathetically as she'd taken it from him with trembling fingers. She'd propped it on the shelf above the fire, and Mum's eyes had gone to it straight away when she came in from the outside lavatory. But she hadn't opened it. That task had fallen to Pa when he returned from work. By then her eyes had already been red-rimmed, and she had given up trying to keep busy. The telegram had confirmed their worst fears for their son. Poor dead Tommy. Mocked and jeered at for refusing to fight, sticking to their family's Quaker beliefs, then killed carrying a stretcher. Her parents had never got over their grief.

When the clock chimed six, Mum insisted that Pamela go. 'You might have to wait a while for a bus as it is. I'll get Pa to pop to the telephone box on Camperdown Street when he's back and give you a ring. Go on, Hugh will be getting worried.'

Pamela went into the hall and reached for her coat. Hugh would indeed be worried when he got back from his club. Especially when he found out where she was. She gave her mother a hug, conscious of Mum's narrow shoulders and fragile frame. Surely she'd been taller when they'd last met?

'Look after yourself, Mum. And don't worry.'

Mum firmed her lips into a thin smile and ushered her out of the door.

'You did what?'

Pamela had never seen Hugh's face go from pink to red so quickly. She didn't dare look him in the eye. 'I didn't go anywhere near Cable Street.'

'But you knew about the march. You knew things were going to get violent. Whatever possessed you?'

Pamela raised her head. 'I thought it would be a peaceful demonstration. You keep telling me Mosley's losing his grip. Pa wouldn't have gone along if he'd known things were going to get ugly.'

Hugh almost threw a spoonful of sugar into his tea, the metal clanging against the delicate porcelain. It was a mercy the cup didn't break. 'I'm sorry, Pamela, but your father's a misguided idealist. I work with the government, remember.' He put down his teaspoon to adjust his tie. 'Pit a bunch of red-blooded fascists against a group of Jews and Labourites – and throw a few police into the mix – there's bound to be trouble.'

Pamela got clumsily to her feet and walked over to the small table beside Hugh. She brushed the stray sugar grains from its mahogany surface into her handkerchief and balled it into her pocket. 'The Blackshirts have behaved outrageously towards the Jews. You know Pa's a pacifist; he only wanted to go along to show his support.'

Hugh took a loud slurp of tea. 'And how would being beaten black and blue,' he looked at her over the top of his teacup, 'or worse, help anyone?'

She took a deep breath. 'Sometimes we have to stand up for the things we believe in.' She took her napkin and wiped a film of moisture from her forehead.

'Your father's an old man, Pamela. Easy target. Mosley's lot don't have scruples. He could have been smashed to a pulp, run over by one of those mounted policemen, clapped in gaol . . . then how would your mother cope?'

Pamela took several attempts to retrieve her handkerchief from her pocket. She finally located it, ignoring the snowfall of sugar, and rammed it against her mouth.

'Anyway.' Hugh's voice softened. 'Thankfully all is well this time. Your mother rang before you got home. Your father's safe, with no more than a small bruise. He had the sense to avoid the thick of it. Apparently he's badly shaken, but at least he survived.'

Pamela slumped into a chair. 'Thank God.'

Hugh came over to her and stroked her hair. 'There's too much unrest these days. Feelings running high at the slightest provocation.'

'People are struggling to make ends meet,' Pamela murmured.

'Difficult times.' Hugh returned to his chair. 'The Home Secretary's called a meeting first thing tomorrow to chew this over. All this furore in Europe isn't helping either.'

Pamela closed her eyes. She felt a bit faint suddenly. 'Do what you can, Hugh. Remember your faith.'

Hugh held out his cup. 'Of course I will. Now, is there any more tea?'

6

As Pamela put her hand to her mouth to stifle a yawn, a ball of blue wool fell off her lap. She glanced at the clock. Midnight already, and still no Hugh. He normally telephoned if he was going to be late, but there'd been no word. She rolled up the ball, stuck the needles through it and placed it on the small table beside her. Since her time on the Czech ward, she'd kept up her knitting. There was more and more demand for baby clothes for the refugees, and this was a much better way of occupying her time than reading *Murder in Mesopotamia* or taking tea with Josephine.

But she couldn't wait for Hugh any longer. To be fair, he had warned her that these latest cabinet discussions would go on well into the evening. Eden and Chamberlain were at loggerheads as usual. 'One of them will have to go,' Hugh had told her over breakfast that morning. 'It's only a matter of time.'

Pamela was half asleep by the time the sound of tyres on gravel and a brief flare of light in the bedroom stirred her. She heard the trudge of Hugh's weary footsteps on the stairs and watched him peel off his clothes and leave them in a pile on the floor. She bit back an admonition as he slid into bed beside her without even washing his face.

'Hugh?'

'Mmm?' His voice was already drowsy.

'What happened in the cabinet?'

'Stalemate,' he muttered, and fell instantly asleep.

At breakfast the next morning there was the shrill sound of the telephone. Kitty went to answer and announced that the call was for Hugh. Hugh put down his paper and marched into the hall. Pamela strained to listen over Kitty clattering in the kitchen, but Hugh's tone was too low.

Eventually he returned and sat down heavily. 'Eden's resigned,' he said.

'Oh.' Pamela glanced at the door, but the noises from the kitchen suggested Kitty wouldn't be in for a while. 'Is that a good thing?'

Hugh rubbed the space between his eyes. 'I think so, yes. Clears the way for Halifax. He'll go cap in hand to Grandi and that'll stop Hitler in his tracks.'

A picture flashed into Pamela's mind of the telegram on the mantelpiece, her father's shaking hands, the wail of grief from her mother, the months of silent pain. 'We must avoid another war at all costs,' she whispered.

Hugh nodded as he spooned in some porridge. 'Chamberlain's a good man. There are lots of us behind him. It won't come to that.'

'Thank God.' Pamela tried to eat her own porridge but her fingers couldn't seem to grip the spoon. She laid it down. Will was sixteen now. Already there was talk of Oxford. He was only four years younger than Tommy had been when the sniper had got him. What kind of coward could kill a man who was only trying to retrieve bodies from the battlefield to give them a Christian burial? She took a sip of tea to quell the heave of nausea.

Hugh looked across at her. 'There won't be a war,' he repeated. 'Will won't get called up. I'll fight for peace with every bone in my body.'

Pamela smiled shakily. 'Do,' she said.

But three weeks later, Pamela was listening to the news on the wireless when Hugh arrived home. He crouched down beside her and took her hand as Chamberlain condemned 'the use of coercion, backed by force, against an independent state in order to create a situation incompatible with its independence'.

'He failed,' she said.

Hugh gripped her fingers. 'He was completely ignored. France and Italy too. Hitler just marched straight into Austria.'

Pamela wiped her eyes with her other hand. 'So what now?'

'We do all we can to protect Czechoslovakia. That'll be next on Hitler's list.'

Pamela thought of little Agata's trusting face, Tomas's brave attempt to be a man when all he must have wanted was to sob like a boy, Jan's despair at having to be both mother and father to his children. She thought of the kindness of the hospital doctors and the patience of the nurses. They'd all taken a lost and frightened English woman to their hearts.

Hugh put his arms round her as she buried her face in his jacket. 'Neville Chamberlain's cousin died in the Great War. Machine-gunned down. He's determined to keep our boys safe at all costs.' He prised her head up gently. 'The man's so pro peace you'd think he was a Quaker!'

Pamela laughed weakly.

'That's my girl. Neville's talking of meeting Hitler face to face. One or two of us'll go with him. We'll make the wretched fellow see sense and that'll be that.'

Pamela grunted. 'That's what you said about Austria.'

'He caught us all napping. It won't happen again.'

She grabbed his hand. 'You have to protect Czechoslovakia.'

Hugh squeezed her fingers. 'We will.'

Pamela sighed as she turned off the wireless.

*

'And again, Miriam.' Eva stood behind her daughter's plump little figure, trying not to wince as the child plonked away at the piano keys. 'No, let me show you.' She leant forward over Miriam's shoulder and played the scale herself. Even after all this time, her fingers knew exactly what to do. The notes rippled. 'Now you.'

Miriam stretched out fingers that hadn't lost their baby chubbiness. 'I can't reach.' She turned round to Eva, pouting.

'Then you must try.' Eva gently returned her daughter's hand to the keyboard. 'Practice is the only way your muscles will learn. If you keep trying, you'll be able to do a little more each day. That's how I learnt.' She looked down at her own hands with their prominent veins and housework-reddened knuckles. Even at Miriam's age, they had been long and slim. The poor child had inherited her father's squat fingers, not her mother's slender musician's ones.

73

As Miriam bashed away again, Eva stared into the middle distance, musing on what might have been. Her parents had never had to make her practise; she drove herself. In fact, if anything they had to stop her. 'Go out and play, Eva,' her mother would beg. 'This is no life for a child, sitting hour after hour at the piano. The Meyer children are down the street – run and join them.' But Eva would shake her head and return to the keyboard, playing the same piece again and again until she got it right.

Would she have been a celebrated pianist by now, giving recitals all over the world? She'd barely played since the incident. For the first two years of their marriage, she and Josef hadn't even owned a piano. Then, when Miriam came along, Eva persuaded Josef to buy her a modest upright one, even though it cost several months' wages, in the misguided hope that she could rekindle her ambition through her daughter. She'd sung Miriam lullabies from the day she was born, and if she didn't sing herself, she found something appropriate on the wireless for Miriam to listen to, even during the early-morning feed. The child had grown up with music. What a shame she seemed to have no aptitude for the piano. Sometimes Eva wondered whether, if she had another child, it would show more promise.

When she'd composed her own lullaby, back in those terrifying months at the sanatorium, the discipline of writing the music, checking and changing the notes until they were perfect, had made her feel safer, more secure, when she'd otherwise felt so untethered. She often thought of the yellowing manuscript and wondered if other hands had found it, other fingers had played the notes she'd put together so lovingly. She'd probably never know now.

The fat little legs were swinging backwards and forwards as Miriam sat at the piano stool; she couldn't reach the pedals. She was playing middle C again and again, swapping fingers as she did so, until it sounded like some demented bell.

'Enough, Miriam!' In spite of her cross tone, Eva couldn't resist leaning forward to kiss the little girl's neck beneath her dark hair. It was still her favourite place; there was something about the back of a child's neck, as if all their tender innocence was concentrated there, warm and sweet. She kissed the top of Miriam's head too. 'Off you go and play. I think you've done enough for one day.'

Miriam wriggled off the seat. 'Thank you, Mummy.' She ran out of the room on sturdy little legs: off to her bedroom to find Lilli, no doubt, desperate to put her thumb in her mouth and give the doll a cuddle, before she started to plait her hair or rearrange her clothes. How strange that she could spend hours looking after her doll, when even five minutes at the piano seemed to be too long.

Eva took her daughter's place on the stool and absent-mindedly played the first few bars of the Berlioz villanelle. She never had got round to learning it as she'd promised Professor Novotny she would, although somehow the refrain had always stayed in her mind. She thought the melody would haunt her, associating it as she did with that terrible night, but strangely it proved more of a comfort. Over the years it had come to symbolise her girlish hopes for romance. The sweet boys of her dreams, who'd never been realised. Instead she'd met with a pack of predators who'd stolen her virginity and her youth. Josef was a good man, despite his hypochondria.

But he wasn't her Prince Charming. That man would only ever exist in her fantasies now.

She stood up. She'd promised Josef she'd make him some chicken soup, insurance against another of his impending maladies, and he'd be home soon. She traipsed into the kitchen, removed the chicken carcass from the larder, wedged it into the pan, then covered it with water before setting it on the stove. She'd chop the onions and carrots whilst she waited for it to come to the boil. Mutti's old recipe worked every time.

Her parents had been delighted when Miriam came along, almost as though she'd made up for the past. Such a shame they didn't live nearer. But they came out to Prague several times a month by train, always bringing a new gift for their granddaughter: a soft toy Minnie Mouse, a miniature tea set, a little rocking chair that Abba had carved himself. He'd spend hours playing hide and seek with Miriam too, or letting her climb onto his back before carrying her around on all fours.

'What a pity there are no other children,' Mutti had said as she handed over yet another hand-knitted jumper.

'Well, *I* was an only child,' replied Eva.

Mutti firmed her lips. 'That wasn't our intention.'

'Nor ours!' Eva blinked away an image of a little blonde girl who seemed to want to talk to her. She'd tried so hard to bury the memories.

Mutti put her arm round her. 'I know, dear. You've had a difficult time. We must thank Adonai for Miriam.'

And Eva had smiled at her daughter as she bounced up and down on her grandfather's back. 'Indeed we must,' she said.

When she returned to the larder to retrieve the vegetables, though, she found only carrots. Bother. She must've run out of onions. She'd have to walk down to the market to fetch some more.

She went to the bottom of the stairs. 'Miriam! We'll have to go into town. Please come downstairs quickly.'

She waited a few seconds, but there was no answering scuttle of footsteps. She sighed and started to trudge upstairs.

Miriam was in her bedroom, rocking Lilli, her eyes closed like an adoring mother. It was a familiar sight. But she was doing something else that stopped Eva in her tracks. As she cradled her doll, she was humming to her in a clear, sweet little voice. And the tune that came out of her mouth was the Berlioz villanelle. Pitch perfect.

Eva swallowed. Her daughter was no pianist, she'd known that deep down for a long time. But what she hadn't realised was that, maybe, she had the makings of a singer.

'Miriam,' she said gently, squatting down in front of her daughter, 'that's a lovely song, but we need to go to the market.'

Miriam stopped singing with a frown. 'Must we? I want to stay here.'

Eva nodded. 'I'm afraid we must.' She held out a hand. 'I can't leave you. But we can sing together on the way.'

Miriam scrambled up, her face full of resentment, and followed her mother out of the room.

Winter was finally melting into spring, but a raw wind still blew in their faces as they made their way down the road. Eva had wrapped a bright red and green scarf round Miriam's face, yet another one that her mother had knitted. Only Miriam's dark eyes were visible, watering with the cold. Her mittened hand was pushed into Eva's as she plodded solemnly along. It was too difficult to sing with their faces covered; maybe they'd do a little concert for Josef later. He'd like that.

But there'd be no hot soup to greet him if they didn't get the onions in time. Eva tugged on her daughter's hand. 'Hurry up, dear.'

Miriam's little footsteps quickened.

Despite the late hour, the market was still vibrant. Eva inhaled the sharp odour of vinegar wafting out of the pickle barrels as they drew near. The old peasant sat on the corner as usual, clutching squares of thick white paper. Beside him, his wife, in a vividly embroidered skirt, cradled rounds of yellow goat's cheese on her lap.

'Mummy?' Miriam looked at Eva questioningly.

'Very well.'

Miriam took off her mitten and fished out the largest pickle from the barrel. The man chuckled as he wrapped it in paper, and Eva gave him twenty heller. Then they walked on, Miriam munching happily.

An oompah band on the pavement blared out jaunty music as they hurried into the marketplace. The vinegar smell was replaced by the earthy odour of vegetables and the faint scent of flowers. Peasants sat on stools or squatted on their haunches in front of produce fanned out on blankets. As she and Miriam hastened along, pushing their way through the bustle of shoppers with net bags and wicker baskets haggling, gossiping and bartering with the sellers, Eva glanced at the bright fruit, the wooden crates of dirty vegetables straight from the fields, the waxy cheeses, the fragrant herbs hanging in bunches and the piles of fish with their clouded eyes. At the nearest vegetable stall, she seized a couple of large onions, their brown-paper skin coming loose in her hands, and thrust them at the farmer's wife, who twisted a sheet of newspaper into a cone and dropped them in. Eva handed over some coins and smiled her thanks. Then she grabbed Miriam's hand to hustle her home.

But as they walked up the road, strong gusts now buffeting their backs, she heard the roar of an engine. It drowned out the market sounds, the whip of the wind and the rasp of her own breath in the cold air. Everywhere people were looking up, shielding their eyes against the low sun's rays. Eva followed their gaze and saw a small unmarked plane dipping in and out of the clouds, sheets of paper falling from it like white leaves. She pushed Miriam to the ground and threw herself down beside her, clutching her daughter tightly, her heart pounding, her eyes squeezed shut.

Not until the plane's drone became a distant buzz did she dare to look up. An elderly woman in front of her was being helped to her feet by her equally elderly husband. Her shopping bag had split open and potatoes and apples had escaped and were rolling down the gutter. Eva tilted Miriam's small face towards her. 'Are you all right?'

Miriam nodded, although her skin was as white as the papers that had fallen from the sky.

Eva tugged her gently up and retrieved the bag of onions, still mercifully intact.

A young man in a dark suit came up behind them. 'Is your little girl hurt?'

'No, she's fine, thank you.' Eva smoothed Miriam's hair and

rearranged the scarf around her head. Her own fingers were numb, shaky. She was aware of a distant mocking laugh, and swallowed to shake down the memory.

'What happened?' she asked the man.

He was reaching up into a horse chestnut tree at the side of the road. One of the pieces of paper dropped by the plane was trapped in a low branch. He shook it loose. It was a leaflet, with a message printed on it in black ink: *Sagen Sie in Prag, Hitler last Sie grüssen.* Tell everyone in Prague that Hitler says hello.

The man spat on the paper, then hurled it into the hedge. 'Just because Austria's lying down for him, he thinks he can bully *us*.' He spat again. 'No chance.'

Eva took a deep breath to steady the accelerando beat in her chest, then tugged her tired daughter home as quickly as Miriam's small legs could manage.

It wasn't until Miriam was in bed, and Eva was ladling out a belated bowl of chicken soup, that she told Josef about the leaflet. Miriam had picked up on her mother's anxiety on the trip home, and Eva didn't want to frighten her further. It had taken several renditions of their villanelle duet and a long cuddle with Lilli to pacify Miriam enough for her to fall asleep. But the frightening message on the leaflet had clutched at Eva's heart all evening.

'What will we do, Josef?' she asked as he slurped the soup. Her own stomach was too unsettled to eat.

'Nothing. It's just scaremongering.'

'But it was a plane. It could have dropped a bomb!'

Josef wiped a splash of soup from his beard with his fingers.

'Perhaps you and Miriam should stay in the house for a while. Just until we know what's happening.'

Eva passed him her napkin. 'But how will we eat? And Miriam needs exercise.'

Josef blotted his beard, then folded the napkin into a square. 'We'll get Carmels to deliver the groceries. I know it's expensive, but needs must. And you'll just have to get Miriam to run around inside.'

Eve nodded. 'She can do some more piano practice. That will keep her busy.'

'Poor child. You push her too hard.'

Eva bristled as she collected Josef's bowl. 'But I did twice as much at her age.'

'I know, *Liebling*. You told me. But Miriam doesn't have your talent.'

'Or my determination.'

'Maybe not.' Josef sighed and leant back in his chair. 'Perhaps you should try something else. I thought she sang well this evening, in that little duet you performed.'

Eva smiled at the memory. 'She has a good voice. Maybe I can play for her.' She stood up to go into the kitchen.

'Are you going to get me some more soup?' Josef's plaintive enquiry followed her out. 'I think I have another respiratory infection coming.'

Eva went to stir the chicken broth that had been simmering on the stove. But as she did so, the afternoon's events flashed into her mind again. The streets had been busier than usual, filled with Jewish refugees who'd arrived in Prague from Germany. You were more likely to hear German than Czech or Yiddish in the Josefov these days. Thank Adonai she had got Miriam back safely. But for how much longer would their home be a sanctuary?

*

In Britain, things dragged on for the whole summer. A summer of speculation and anxiety. A summer of cloud and rain and sudden storms while the country held its breath. In July, everyone was issued with gas masks. Pamela shuddered as she stowed them in the under-stairs cupboard.

It was early autumn before Hugh went out to Germany with Chamberlain. 'Chap's never flown before,' he told Pamela. 'Sixty-nine and never been in an aeroplane. Hope I won't have to hold his hand.'

But he returned grim-faced. 'Chamberlain's convinced himself Hitler's an honourable man. Said he'd given him his word.'

'And is he?' asked Pamela, as she sorted out Hugh's dirty washing ready for Kitty.

Hugh tugged a clean jumper over his head and spoke from its depths. 'He's a determined man, that's for sure. I think we'll have to go back.'

He was right. Two weeks later, he accompanied the Prime Minister to Munich. Pamela went to the Everyman to see *Carefree* the following afternoon and caught Hugh's grinning face on the newsreel as he stood behind a determined-looking Chamberlain, waving his agreement with Hitler.

'Well done,' she said as she stood in the hallway to welcome him home.

'Chamberlain's confident,' Hugh replied, wiping his feet energetically on the mat. 'He's calling it "peace for our time".'

'Peace. Thank God.' Pamela offered her cheek for a kiss.

'Thank God,' echoed Hugh.

The next day Hitler's troops crossed the border between Germany and Czechoslovakia and marched into the Sudetenland.

7

'Mrs Denison. Yoo hoo!'

Pamela snapped to attention as a large woman in a voluminous tea dress swept down the narrow walkway, between tables overflowing with second-hand clothes.

'I've another bundle for you,' Margery Weston wheezed. She slapped an assortment of garments in front of Pamela. 'Someone's just dropped them off at the front desk. I've no idea who, but they look in good condition.' She drew a man's dress shirt out of the pile. It was pale blue and appeared hardly worn. 'It requires some cufflinks. I'm sure we can find some somewhere.' Margery's shiny moon-face beamed.

'Thank you, Mrs Weston,' said Pamela. 'I'll start on them directly.'

Margery nodded and bustled back down the aisle.

Pamela looked down at the child's knitted jumper she was clutching. It reminded her of one she'd made for Will years ago in dark green wool with a speckling of lighter green. It had stretched on her needles and was much too big by the time she'd finished. But he'd grown into it in the end.

She pictured Will on his last exeat. Although he'd regaled them with the usual school tales, and moaned about the increased amount of homework, he'd been quieter overall. Preoccupied. Hugh had taken to offering him a small glass of port after dinner, now that he was sixteen, and lingering with him at the table. Pamela usually took her coffee into the drawing room and tried to concentrate on her book until they joined her. Once she'd asked Hugh what he and Will spoke about. 'Men's business,' he had replied, winking, and Pamela had turned away, a little hurt. She hadn't asked again.

She pressed the jumper to her face. Like most of the clothes, it smelled slightly musty, but was perfectly serviceable. She added it to the pile of children's winter garments, then drew Margery Weston's bundle towards her. This time she really must concentrate.

By lunchtime, there were four neat stacks of clothes on the table in front of her: jumpers, hats, shirts and trousers.

'Luncheon, ladies,' Mrs Weston called, clapping her hands.

Pamela smoothed down her skirt and went to join the other women in the canteen.

Normally they had a chat over their soup and sandwiches. Pamela had got to know her co-workers well, and there was always family gossip to be exchanged. Today, however, was different. They'd all heard the news on the wireless that morning, and Margery Weston had an announcement.

'Following the escalation of violence against Jews in Germany,' she boomed, 'we are going to step up our aid efforts.'

Pamela looked round the room. Eileen Jackson sat next to Margery, her plain, honest face full of indignation as she nodded furiously. Little Beth Seddon had her hands to her face. Pamela glanced at her sympathetically. Hugh had sketched in the details when he'd returned late from the House last night. Synagogues had been torched, Jewish homes, schools and businesses vandalised. It was thought around one hundred Jews had been killed. And it wasn't over yet.

'I intend to fly out to Berlin in the next few days,' continued Margery. 'I want to speak to the Jewish women's organisations. Find out what's going on from the ground as it were. If necessary, we'll try to get the children out.'

Agata and Tomas sidled into Pamela's mind. She'd been concerned for them as soon as she heard about German troops invading the Sudetenland. Now Agata's bright little eyes pierced her memory again, and she pictured Tomas's expression of stoical resignation. Thank goodness they weren't Jewish. They might stand more chance than others.

'I'll help,' she said, raising her hand.

Margery turned. 'Thank you, Mrs Denison,' she said. 'Let's wait until I'm back from Germany and I'll be able to supply more details.'

Pamela nodded. She was tired of knitting, and planning Hugh's dinner. He'd managed without her before, all those weeks she was in the Prague hospital. She wanted to do something active. Her body tingled with suppressed energy.

By the next committee meeting, Margery was back. She stood up to give her report, her voice ringing out boldly. Pamela wished she had her confidence.

'I had a very successful time in Berlin,' she intoned, pausing to beam at her audience. 'Our little delegation met with Wilfrid Israel and concluded that unaccompanied children should be granted entry into Britain. I will be presenting my findings to the prime minister forthwith.'

There was a murmur of approval in the tightly packed room.

'Let us redouble our efforts to support these children.' She marched off the platform and into the sorting room, a line of volunteers following her eagerly.

But Chamberlain refused.

'You must be able to do something,' said Pamela. She tilted her spoon a little too much and a few drops of soup splattered her blouse. She grabbed her napkin and dabbed at them.

Hugh picked up his own spoon with exaggerated care and drew it slowly across his bowl. 'I'll contact the Jewish and Quaker consortia in the morning. See if we can get a delegation up to approach Hoare. Bypass Neville.'

Pamela nodded. 'Thanks, darling. Something has to be done. Those poor children.'

Hugh reached for his bread roll. 'Poor parents, too. Ghastly. Wouldn't want to be a Yid right now.'

'Nor me.' Pamela pressed her napkin to her lips. 'Do what you can, Hugh. Remember this is why you're in government. To make a difference.'

Hugh tore off some bread and placed it in his mouth. He chewed it thoughtfully.

*

Eva was late getting to the Wilson station, and by the time she arrived, the train was already on the platform in a billow of steam and a blast of whistles. She pushed through the crowd of passengers, scanning their heads to see if she could glimpse Abba's distinctive shtreimel, its brown fur bobbing above the headscarves, fedoras and woollen caps. But it was only when the platform was almost empty that she made out the two familiar figures trudging towards her. They look old, she thought. Abba was weighed down with bulging carpet bags, one in each hand and a third slung across his back. And Mutti, waddling along as fat as a babushka doll, seemed to be wearing a whole wardrobe of clothes.

'Welcome!' Eva hugged her parents. 'What a lot of luggage! I thought you were only staying for a week.' Was it her imagination, or did Abba and Mutti exchange a glance?

Mutti laughed, a little nervously, Eva thought. 'Well, I never know what to wear for Purim. So I thought I'd bring plenty of clothes to choose from.'

'I see.' Eva smiled, to ease the creases out of Mutti's anxious face. 'And Abba, did you decide to bring your whole wardrobe too?'

Abba shrugged. 'There've been thieves in Pilsen. They find out when people are away, then ransack their houses. Jews especially. You can't be too careful these days. It's been chaos ever since Hitler took over the Sudetenland.'

The guard blew his whistle and the train chugged away. Eva took one of Abba's bags, wincing at the weight. 'How terrible,' she said.

She led her parents along the platform and across the concourse, skirting a large group of children in the centre. It was odd to see so many youngsters without their parents. And standing so still and silent. Eva wondered where they were going. Each child carried a bag or case; brown labels hung round their necks as though they were parcels. She thought of Miriam safe at home with Josef, awaiting her grandparents' arrival, and felt a surge of relief that they'd all be together.

'Miriam is looking forward to seeing you again,' she said over her shoulder. Her parents were struggling to keep up.

'Who's she going to be at the festival?' asked Mutti.

'Queen Esther,' Eva replied. 'I ran up her costume from an old bed sheet.'

'I'm sure she'll look beautiful.' Mutti stopped to catch her breath.

'Let's get home as quick as we can.' Eva grabbed another bag from a protesting Abba, took her mother's arm, and the three of them made their way out onto the street.

'*Now*, Miriam,' Eva whispered. Miriam picked up the cymbals that lay in her lap and clashed them together loudly. Their neighbours, who were stamping their feet or rattling graggers, smiled at the little girl, dressed in her long white gown and gold belt, with a gold crown tilting precariously on her head. Once the noise had subsided, the rabbi resumed his reading. Eva looked round the synagogue. Conical lamps hung from the ceiling, their glow picking out the shiny headdresses of the children and the glint of the menorah. A faint odour of ketoret spices competed with the smell of polish. The familiar words of the Megillah washed over her:

'Then Haman said to King Xerxes, "There is a certain people dispersed among the peoples in all the provinces of your kingdom who keep themselves separate. Their customs are different from those of all other people, and they do not obey the king's laws; it is not in the king's best interest to tolerate them. If it pleases the king, let a decree be issued to destroy them."'

There were the usual boos and hisses every time Haman's

name was mentioned, although this time Eva thought she heard a few people whisper 'Hitler!' instead. Despite the festive atmosphere in the synagogue, she couldn't suppress a shiver. Haman had wanted to destroy the Jews. Would history keep repeating itself?

Mutti, sitting beside her, took a sharp breath.

Abba and Josef were seated towards the front, in the men's section. Abba looked small beside Josef. He seemed to have shrunk over the years, and since this business in the Sudetenland, there were more worry lines on his face. Josef had been as pleased as Eva was that they were all under one roof for the duration of the festival.

But neither Eva nor Josef had expected the announcement. Eva had just served up the hamantaschen and Miriam was reaching for one of the fruit-filled pastries when Abba cleared his throat and asked if they could stay for longer than the planned week.

'Of course, Abba,' Eva replied, glancing at Josef for re-assurance.

Josef nodded his agreement, but his face showed concern. 'What's the matter, Father-in-law?' he asked.

Abba sighed and reached for Mutti's hand. 'The truth is we no longer feel safe in Pilsen. Half the town seems to have decamped to Prague. The Rosenbergs and the Zeleznys have been arrested. The cemetery's been desecrated; the rumour is the synagogues will be next.' He released Mutti's hand to take a sip of wine, then grasped it again. 'Some days we have no water, no electricity. Food is scarce . . .'

Eva saw her father's eyes glaze with tears and rushed across to comfort him. 'I had no idea things had already got so bad,' she said. 'There's been very little news reaching Prague lately. Why didn't you tell us sooner?'

Mutti fiddled with her fork. 'We kept hoping things would get better. General Kloud has managed to hold the Germans off for months. The weather's been on our side too. So much mud!' She shuddered. 'But recently things have got worse. Now that we've managed to get out for Purim, we think our best option is to stay until things die down.'

'Of course.' Eva went to hug her mother. 'Stay with us as long as you want. You'll be safe here.'

She caught an exchange of glances between her father and her husband. 'Kolischer?' Abba murmured.

Josef reached for a pastry. 'My work at the Institute gives us immunity,' he said. 'You'll be safe under our protection. Eva's right. Please stay as long as is necessary.'

Beside Eva, Mutti let out a low sigh. 'President Hácha won't stand up for the Jews like Esther's uncle did,' she said, 'but we are certainly less vulnerable here.' She picked up her own hamantasch and turned to her granddaughter. 'Now, Miriam. Tell Granny all about Queen Esther.'

A few days later, Eva woke early from the usual nightmare. She shook her head to release the sound of nervous laughter. There was a strange light in the bedroom; even the flock wallpaper glowed white-gold instead of its usual sickly yellow. She raised herself from the pillow. Josef was snoring, as usual, beside her, but he'd be bound to wake if she got out of bed to investigate. Besides, it was so warm under the thick winter quilt. She let her head drop again and pulled the covers up over her ears. Maybe ten more minutes.

But then she heard the crunch of boots on ice. Of course, it must have snowed during the night; that was the cause of the strange light now flooding the room. Snow was familiar, but the noises from outside weren't. She sat up abruptly. Guttural shouts penetrated the curtains: the shout and rasp of commands, then the rat-tat-tat of drums. There was a bang as Paní Kratz next door slammed her bedroom shutters closed, and Eva wondered if she should do likewise. She tiptoed over to the window, ignoring Josef's sleepy groan, and drew the curtain back a fraction. Through the narrow strip of window, she glimpsed a blur of red, black and yellow. She eased the curtain back further. It was a German flag, fluttering from the window of the flat opposite.

'Eva? What's the matter?' Josef was sitting up now, feeling for his glasses on the bedside table.

Eva's stomach lurched. She swallowed drily. 'Germans,' she whispered. 'Everywhere.'

Josef shot out of bed.

They all clustered round the wireless as Josef twiddled the knobs, trying to coax some human sound out of the static. Then President Hácha's trembling voice filled the room, informing them that Prague would be occupied by the German military at six thirty a.m. There was to be no resistance.

Eva looked at her father's face, almost translucent in the early-morning light. She saw the tracery of veins, the deep set of his brown eyes. He's an old man, she thought. And a frightened one. Mutti's fingers fluttered at her throat; Josef was sweeping his hand down Miriam's hair again and again, smoothing the springy curls as if his life depended on it. Miriam knew better than to protest.

Eva stood up. She couldn't bear to listen to the radio a minute longer. 'I'll make breakfast,' she said. Anything to keep herself busy, to fill her family with food – bread and preserves that would keep the gnaw of fear from their stomachs. There was still some ground coffee in the tin. She'd make it strong and black: good for the nerves. Perhaps breakfast could make everything better. She escaped to the kitchen.

By the time she returned with a laden tray, Mutti, Josef and Miriam were kneeling by Abba, who was speaking the prayer for protection over them. Eva deposited the tray quickly on the table and joined them. She put her arm round Miriam and felt the warmth of the child's body. Despite his fragile appearance, Abba's voice was calm and strong.

'May our daytime be cloaked in your peace. Protect us . . . Keep far from us all evil; may our paths be free from all obstacles from when we go out until we return home.'

Their joint 'amen' sounded through the chilly room.

Later, Josef ventured out to get food. He returned empty-handed. He told them that the vegetable stands were still tightly wrapped with tarpaulin; the few stallholders who'd shown up had stood silently in the empty marketplace watching as German soldiers toppled the statue of President Masaryk. He described the loudspeakers that had been mounted on lamp posts and trees, the German flags strung from windows and lining the street. 'Just one Czech flag,' he said, 'hanging limply from a lightning rod.' The snow in the street had been trampled into ice, and Josef had slipped and slid several times as he puffed his way up the road.

Eva handed him a cup of hot coffee. He wrapped his white fingers around it.

'Thank you, *Liebling*. I touched the mezuzah a few times on my way in, I can tell you.'

Eva swallowed. 'Are we still going to be all right?'

Josef put his cup down. 'I think so. Dr Svoboda and I have been working on the new antisera for months now. We're on the verge of a breakthrough. The Nazis are supportive of our work. They'll protect us.'

'But what about the way the Jews are being treated in Germany? They're in fear of their lives. You don't think we should move out? Take my parents with us?' Eva had a sudden vision of her mother piling all her clothes on again, Abba loaded up with even more cases.

Josef took another sip of coffee. 'I can't leave my work at the Institute. Let's ride this out and see what happens. There is always panic at times like this. Things will settle down, I'm sure.'

Eva closed her eyes. She knew Josef worked hard, that he was proud of what he'd achieved. This current research was huge: creating a drug to kill infection could save millions of people from a needless death. But her mind couldn't blot out the vibrato drone of motorbikes, the cacophony of frightened voices, the thud of snowballs on metal as a few brave young men vented their anger on the approaching tanks, the thud-thud of goose-stepping soldiers. And behind those recent sights were the deeper memories: of biscuit-coloured uniforms, red armbands, mocking laughter . . .

Abba came into the room. 'Adonai protected the Israelites from the angel of death. He's been protecting our people for hundreds of years. He'll keep us safe now, I promise you.'

Eva hugged him. 'I hope you're right, Abba,' she said.

Eva hadn't been sure whether it would be safe for Miriam to return to school, but when nothing had happened after a few days, Josef insisted. 'We haven't been told not to. The Nuremberg schooling laws don't apply here. As long as you accompany her there and back, I'm sure it will be fine. The Germans aren't going to attack children. Besides, it's better she keeps busy.'

So Eva walked her daughter along the slippery pavement, trying to ignore the groups of German soldiers and the swastikas swinging from the lamp posts. A fine, powdery snow was falling, and both of them had to lower their heads to prevent the swirling flakes from stinging their faces. It was a relief to enter the warmth of the school cloakroom, to unwind Miriam's thick scarf from her neck, remove her wet coat and hang it, dripping, on her peg. But she couldn't help noticing that many of the other pegs were empty.

She reached out to fluff up Miriam's hair, flattened by the damp, and wipe the moisture from her reddened nose. 'There we are, *Liebling*.' She took Miriam's hand and led her into the classroom, where the smiling teacher was waiting to greet her.

'Good morning, Miriam.'

'Good morning, Fräulein Munk.' Miriam went to sit at her desk.

'Not many children today,' remarked Eva, looking round

the room. She caught sight of some neat sums written on the blackboard, the first task of the day, no doubt. As usual, the odour of chalk and old books hung in the air. But no cooking smells. The children didn't have lunch at school. Instead there were separate morning and afternoon sessions. In some poor families, who could barely afford footwear, those who had been schooled in the morning came home to give their shoes to their siblings so they could wear them in the afternoon.

'No.' The teacher firmed her lips. 'Some families are still frightened to send them. And . . .' she leant forward and lowered her voice, 'there's a rumour that the Liebnitz twins have gone to England.'

'On their own?'

Fräulein Munk nodded.

'But aren't their parents worried about the family being split up?'

The teacher shrugged. 'Of course, but at least they'll be safe.'

An image of Josef's confident expression came into Eva's mind. 'Do you think the danger is that high, Fräulein?'

'We'll do our best here to keep the children happy. The department has told us to carry on as usual. But if it was my child . . .' She broke off to watch Miriam lift the lid of her desk and remove a pile of little exercise books. 'I'm not sure what I'd do.'

Eva watched Miriam too. A prickling sensation began at the base of her neck. 'I'll be back at one,' she said to the teacher. Her tongue felt too heavy to get the words out. 'Please keep her safe until I return.'

Fräulein Munk stepped back as two boys hurtled into the

room. 'Slow down, please,' she said, holding up a hand. The boys came to a halt in a staccato fashion and proceeded more slowly to their desks. The teacher turned back to Eva. 'Of course,' she said.

Eva left the room.

As she hurried back home, she remembered the scene at the Wilson station. All those children with cases and brown labels. Was that what they were doing? Going to England? Blood pounded allegro in her ears. Perhaps she should tell Josef.

But at dinner that evening, Josef was adamant. 'She stays with us, *Liebling*. It's unhealthy in England. All that rain and fog. No place for a young girl.'

'But surely occupied Prague isn't any safer? The place is full of Germans!' Eva shuddered at the memory of sweating, heaving bodies, the terrifying stabs of pain, the filth, the cold despair. Her pelvis ached with remembered soreness.

'I keep telling you. I'm a scientist. I deal with reason and fact. No one has threatened us. Or our child.'

'But it's no secret that Hitler hates Jews,' said Mutti, emerging from the kitchen with a bowl of boiled potatoes. 'Look at what he's done already to those in Germany.' They'd all read the reports in the newspapers of Jewish shops, synagogues and houses being smashed up. Recently Jews had been evicted from their homes without notice, their radios shattered, and they were now all under a curfew.

Josef picked up his knife and fork. 'Some Jews, yes. But I don't pose a threat. I'm useful to the Nazis. They're pleased with my work. We're all safe as long as I'm at the Institute.'

Abba said nothing, just reached for the potatoes with an anxious frown.

The next day, Eva lingered at the school gates after she'd dropped Miriam off. There was usually a group of mothers there, enjoying a few minutes' gossip before they went home to start the day's chores. Normally Eva avoided them – gossip bored her and she didn't feel she had much to contribute – but today she hovered at the fringes. As soon as there was a lull in the conversation, she asked the question she'd spent half the night framing. 'I've heard the Liebnitz twins have gone to England. Does anyone know how they got there?'

One of the mothers, a stout woman with a green headscarf and a grizzling toddler clamped to her leg, turned round. 'I think Frau Liebnitz has English relatives. She got in touch and they invited the boys over. It can't have been an easy decision.'

The rest of the women, like a chorus from a Smetana opera, shook their heads and made sympathetic noises.

'So it's impossible to get our children to safety unless we have relatives abroad?' said Eva.

The woman shrugged. Inside the group, the conversation had moved on and she was eager to contribute.

But as Eva made her way back home, she heard the rapid beat of footsteps. She turned round to find the mother of one of Miriam's friends hurrying after her. Frau Golder. A tall woman with a permanently anxious expression.

'Good morning,' said Eva.

The woman returned her greeting, then glanced around. The street was deserted. Just an emaciated-looking pigeon pecking in the gutter for food. Nevertheless, she drew closer to Eva and lowered her voice. 'I heard you asking about sending children away.'

'Yes,' Eva replied. 'I don't trust the Germans.'

'I agree,' said Frau Golder. She delved into her handbag. 'There's a British man you can go to. His office is in Vorsilska Street.' She handed Eva a small, tightly folded piece of paper. 'You can ask if he'll take Miriam.'

Even the words made Eva's heart freeze. It took several attempts to open up the paper with her suddenly numb fingers. There was an address on it, written in black ink. 'Thank you.' She touched the woman's arm. 'Will you go to see him too?'

'I'm a Gentile, even though my husband's Jewish,' Frau Golder replied. 'We don't believe Eli is in danger. Although we did consider it for a while when someone gave me the address.'

Eva nodded. A person's Jewishness was determined through the maternal line. She tucked the paper into her pocket. 'I'll let you know how I get on.'

The woman turned back towards the school.

8

The following day, after Eva dropped Miriam off at school, she hurried to Vorsilska Street. There'd been a frost during the night and the roofs had crystallised: tiny flakes, like grains of sugar, nestling in the crevices. There was no need to ask directions to the Englishman's office: the queue snaked all the way down the road. She joined the end of it, behind a woman carrying a small baby swaddled in a bright shawl and holding the hand of a dark-haired older child. The woman smiled a greeting.

'Your children are very young,' Eva said.

The woman nodded. Wisps of black hair escaped from her headscarf and her brown eyes were bleak. 'The baby is only just weaned. Inka . . .' she gestured to the toddler, 'is three.'

'Aren't you worried about sending them away when they're so tiny?'

'Of course.' The woman bit her lip.

Eva was cross with herself. What a stupid question.

'My husband and I have discussed it endlessly,' said the woman. 'It'll break my heart to see them go. I can't imagine my life without them.' Her chest rose and fell rapidly. 'But at least it gives them a chance. And we'll get them back in a year or so, when the Germans leave.'

Eva thought of the determined procession of tanks rolling

into Prague, the terrifying rows of goose-stepping soldiers, the huge banners of Adolf Hitler. Would the Germans ever leave? 'It must have been a hard decision,' she said.

'Terrible.' The woman's eyes glazed. 'But the right one.'

A sharp gust whipped across the street, ruffling the woman's scarf and lifting tufts of the toddler's hair. The little girl cried out and her mother absent-mindedly smoothed her tangled curls, drawing the child closer into her coat as she did so.

Eva pictured Miriam's sweet face, her plump limbs, the still-baby smell of her, and her heart heaved. She turned away to hide her own tears. How could she bear to lose her daughter? But how could she bear the worry and fear of keeping her here either? It was indeed a terrible decision. But at least the woman's husband had made it with her. Eva was planning this in secret. It was wrong to deceive Josef; it went against all Jewish teaching. But the memory of that night in the graveyard wouldn't go away. She thought about trying to talk to Josef again, persuading him of the danger. But she could never tell him her own terrible experience of German cruelty. Her parents had been unable to save her then; she had to protect her own daughter at all costs. This was the only way.

It was twelve o'clock by the time she reached the head of the queue. The Englishman had kind eyes behind horn-rimmed glasses. He sat at a huge desk scattered with files and pieces of paper.

Eva sat down in response to his gesture. She gave Miriam's name and address.

'Photo?' The man looked up from his writing.

Eva's hand went to her chest. 'I haven't one,' she said. 'I didn't know.'

The man sighed softly. 'We must have a photo,' he said. He put down his pen. 'We send the pictures to people in England, you see. They choose which child they will take.'

'Yes, of course.' She'd have to take Miriam to the photographers in the Staré Město tomorrow after school. And hope her daughter's brown curls and bright eyes would appeal to an English family.

'Come back as soon as you can,' said the man. 'You'll need to bring a little money too.'

'Money?' Eva felt stupid. Why hadn't she thought of this? But Frau Golder hadn't mentioned it.

'To help provide for the child.' The man looked apologetic. 'I'm sorry, but our own funds are limited.'

'Of course.' Eva stood up. 'I'll come back as soon as possible.'

'Thank you, my dear. In the meantime, Miriam is on my list. As soon as I have the money and photo, I'll put them on file. Then I can let you know when a family has come forward for her.' He took a rubber stamp, rocked it on an inkpad a few times, then pressed it firmly on the piece of paper in front of him.

Eva swallowed, shook the man's outstretched hand, then left the room on shaky legs.

When she and Miriam returned home later that afternoon, Mutti was looking out of the window as usual. Since the Germans had arrived, Mutti seemed to have shrunk into herself. She no longer bothered to have her hair permed and set; she just pinned it back with hair grips, or covered it with a scarf, even indoors. Her eyes were dull and her skin pasty.

102

Eva had tried to keep her mother busy; there was certainly more cooking with the five of them, and sometimes queuing for food took all day, but there were still idle moments when Mutti's spirits sagged and that listless expression came over her face. It was there now.

'Mutti.' Eva drew her mother away from the window and made her sit down at the kitchen table, where Miriam was drinking noisily from a glass of milk. 'I've been thinking of making some more clothes for Miriam. She grows so quickly, and it's impossible to find stuff in the shops now.' She threw a stern glance at Miriam, who obediently started to sip more quietly. 'I wonder if you'd like to help. You're so much better at sewing than I am.'

Mutti smiled. 'You always preferred piano practice to needlework.'

'I know. Perhaps I should have listened to you.' If she hadn't been so obsessed with music, she'd never have been at the conservatoire in the first place. Her stomach clenched at the thought, and she took a steadying breath. Germans were savage, merciless. Miriam should be protected at all costs. She took her mother's hand. 'Can I make the most of you whilst you are here? I thought we could plan ahead, make Miriam clothes for the next year. Then she will have enough if the shops run out of material.'

Mutti's dull eyes brightened a little. 'What a good idea. I have garments I no longer need. Silly of me to bring so many, really. I'll cut up some of them to adapt for Miriam. That'll be much cheaper.'

Eva had been hoping her mother would say that. In truth, the shops' supplies were already dwindling. And she didn't have the money to buy fabric anyway. Especially as she had to find the welfare payment for Miriam.

While her mother dashed off to her room to look through her clothes, Eva prowled round the apartment. How could she raise some money? She had no jewellery apart from her wedding ring. And she couldn't sell that. Josef would be appalled. But what else of value was there? She wandered over to the piano, sat on the stool and fingered the keys. It was obvious Miriam had no aptitude or inclination to play. And Eva certainly wasn't about to resume her long-abandoned career. The piano had cost hundreds of thousands of koruna. She would contact Thomann's tomorrow and ask if they would buy it back.

Josef would be impressed by her thrift: she could tell him they needed the money for Miriam. That wouldn't be a lie. Although he would think it was for clothes and toys, not provision for a passage to England. She'd agonised about telling Josef she was planning to send Miriam away. He was so blinkered by his job at the Institute, so adamant she'd be safe in Prague. If he knew of her brutal experience of Germans, he might be persuaded, but that would be to give up her secret. And she couldn't do that.

'This old shawl would make a pretty dress,' said Mutti, emerging from the bedroom a few days later with a large square of red and orange cloth draped over her arm.

Eva took the material and stretched it out across the old wooden table in the kitchen. 'I'm not sure it's big enough for a dress,' she said. 'Miriam is growing so quickly. Maybe a skirt.'

'A skirt. Yes.' Mutti reached for the scissors. 'And perhaps a scarf with the leftovers.'

'Shall I ask Pani Kratz if we can borrow her sewing machine?' asked Eva. 'All this hand stitching must be hard on your eyes.'

Mutti looked across at the window. The sun was hazy through the lace curtains, but it was definitely brighter than it had been a few weeks ago. Spring was on its way at last. 'I can see perfectly well if I sit over there,' she said. 'I like hand-sewing. And it keeps me busy.'

Eva picked up the scraps of material as her mother snipped. One piece was long and narrow. She wrapped it round her fingers. It was fraying at the edges, but maybe, if she hand-stitched it too, it would make a ribbon for Miriam's hair. The little girl's brown curls now reached down to her shoulders and had to be tied back for school. But in the evenings, when she tugged her hair loose, she let Eva brush it as she sat by the fire, stroke after stroke, until it was smooth.

Eva felt a familiar lurch of dread. Was there a woman in England who would tie Miriam's hair in ribbons, or brush it free of tangles? Would she let her wear the little home-made dresses and skirts, the carefully embroidered blouses, or would she try to impose English clothes on her?

'What's the matter?' asked Mutti.

Eva realised she'd been winding the ribbon round her hands for several minutes. 'I'm fine,' she said. 'Would you like some coffee? There are still a few grains left, I think.'

Her mother shook her head. 'Save it for Abba. He'll be cold when he gets back.'

Abba had taken to wandering round the streets during the

day, after Josef went to work and Miriam to school. Eva had no idea what he did. Sometimes he'd come home with talk from the Kotva. More whispered news about the poor Jews in Germany now being taken away in trucks, losing their jobs, their businesses, perhaps their lives. But Josef would always reassure him. 'This is Prague, not Berlin. Remember your son-in-law is conducting important research at the Institute. My work will keep us all safe.' And Abba would nod and reply, 'And Adonai will keep us safe too. We trust in Him.'

But poor Abba didn't have anything to keep him busy like Mutti. Eva's parents had been with them for over a month now and showed no signs of returning home. Things had quietened down since that terrifying March morning, but there was no doubt Prague was in Nazi hands. The other day, someone had even planted a swastika on St Wenceslas's statue. Tread patterns from German tanks were bitten into the cobbles. Every so often the street would echo with the sound of fists hammering on doors. The ruddy-cheeked farmers from the market now had faces white as snow.

'There.' Mutti's deft fingers had already cut four pieces of fabric from her old shawl. She stood up stiffly and went over to the window to thread the needle, her eyes squinting against the light. 'Why don't you hem that ribbon, Eva?' she asked. 'There's another needle in my pincushion. And plenty of thread in the basket.'

Eva reached for the squat shape on the table, pierced with bright-headed pins and an upright needle. She drew the needle out and took a red cotton reel from Mutti's sewing basket. 'All right. I have an hour before I need to leave to pick up Miriam.' She pulled a length of thread and bit it with her teeth, ignoring Mutti's frown, then held it up to the light to push it through the narrow slit. She fashioned a knot at the other end and started to stitch.

'So,' said Mutti, keeping her eyes on her own sewing. 'Is this just to keep me busy, all this needlework?'

'Of course. And to provide Miriam with clothes for the next year.'

Mutti's deft fingers pushed the needle in and out of the cloth much quicker than Eva's could. As a child, her hands had been too busy playing the piano to sew. Although it was housework that exercised them most these days.

'And there is nothing you're not telling me?'

Eva stabbed her finger with the needle. A plump bead of blood appeared. 'Of course not, Mutti.'

Mutti kept sewing. She still hadn't looked at Eva. 'Because, you know, if you were planning to send Miriam away, without consulting Josef, that would be a terrible defiance of your husband's authority.'

'I know. But to keep her here might be to jeopardise her life. Which is the greater sin?' Eva wiped away the smear of blood with the ribbon. A good job it was red already.

Mutti put down her own sewing and took the strip of fabric from Eva's hands, pressing her thumb against the pinprick still weeping blood on her daughter's finger. 'Tell me the truth, Eva,' she said quietly.

Eva wiped her other hand across her eyes. 'I've spoken to Josef about sending Miriam away, tried to persuade him. He's adamant she's safe with us. But I know what Germans can do.'

Mutti stared into the middle distance, as if replaying a scene in her head. 'You paid a terrible price for risking your safety.'

Eva nodded, mute with misery. The faint sound of a lullaby threaded through her mind.

'It's wrong to disobey your husband.'

Eva nodded again. 'I know.'

'But two wrongs don't make a right.'

Eva stared at Mutti.

'Have you planned to send Miriam away?'

'She's on a list,' Eva whispered. 'An Englishman is making arrangements. I've given him money and a photo of Miriam. I'm waiting to hear when a family have sent for her.'

Mutti picked up her sewing again. 'Then I suppose we'd better hurry up with these clothes,' she said.

9

It had been a long time since Pamela had last visited Liverpool Street station. They'd caught the train from St Pancras for the ski holiday. Not that she'd had much opportunity to look round, with Hugh calling loudly for porters and Will needing the lavatory just before the train was about to leave.

But today she'd arrived early. She'd purchased a platform ticket from a surly man at the kiosk and wandered in, intending to buy a cup of tea from the café whilst she waited for Margery and the others to arrive. But the sight of the vast, splendid concourse made her forget her plans. A train waited at the central platform, impatiently belching steam. Pamela tipped her head back to follow the white clouds as they drifted upwards, slowly dissipating until they mingled with the shafts of sunlight slanting in through the iron fretwork lining the roof. She caught a glimpse of the large station clock. Twenty to five. Still plenty of time.

Another train had pulled in. The staccato slamming of doors added to the cacophony: the guards' whistles, the clanging of porters' trolleys, the undulating murmur of voices. Stations had their own particular smell, too: a mixture of steam, soot and humanity. A bubble of anticipation formed in Pamela's stomach.

She tried to imagine the scene as the children would see it.

Thank goodness it was a sunny day, and still warm. It must be horrible to arrive in cold rain, at the end of a long, harrowing journey. She'd heard the Nazis were making things as difficult as possible for the children. They weren't allowed to say goodbye to their parents in public; they had to travel via Holland so they didn't 'contaminate' German ports. Their luggage was often ransacked by guards searching for valuables. It would be frightening and humiliating for them. She wondered what state they'd arrive in. Margery had said that some were as young as four. Poor little mites.

She cleared her throat and took out her compact. The hot air of the station had made her face glow a little; she dabbed at it with her powder puff. She'd thought carefully about how she should dress. She didn't want to appear snobbish or wealthy. That might intimidate the children. In the end, she'd found a red suit at the back of her wardrobe. She hadn't worn it for a couple of years, so the skirt was a little longer than the current fashion, but at least it still fitted her. She'd teamed it with a modest straw hat, which didn't obscure her face too much. It was important the children saw how pleased she was to welcome them.

She glanced in her mirror again and practised her friend-liest smile. Then she hastily replaced the compact in her handbag before Margery saw her. It wouldn't do to appear vain. Especially not today, when she was representing the Friends in this important role.

A sudden surge of people headed up the platform. It was hard to see human forms under the canopy of hats. Many of the men wore boaters; there were boys in caps and women in conical trilbies with undulating brims. Some wore straw hats like herself. Pamela wondered what the children would wear. Would some of them have benefited from the clothes parcels they'd been sending out for years now? She suppressed a smile at the thought of a little boy wearing the blue jumper with a train motif she'd knitted the summer she was recuperating from her accident. And how lovely to think that Will's cast-offs might have provided for some of these children already. Yet it was a small gesture, considering how much they'd lost.

The station clock said five to five now. Pamela pushed her handbag under her arm to avoid losing it in the crush, and joined the throng making its way to the gates. She enjoyed feeling anonymous, part of the station's bustle rather than an outsider looking on. She'd arranged to meet Margery by the café. No time for a cup of tea now. But it didn't matter. Why should she indulge her own desire for refreshment when those poor children had probably travelled for hours without food or water? She hoped their hosts had prepared filling meals for them. Although no amount of food could make up for the loss of their parents. She twisted her wedding ring round her finger. Please God this chaos in Europe would be quickly resolved. Please God Chamberlain would stave off war. It mustn't happen again.

Will's eager young face flashed into her mind. Keep my son safe, she silently begged. Then pushed away the thought that she'd offered to welcome these Jewish children in some absurd pact to ensure her son's safety. She was here to represent the Friends Committee for Refugees and Aliens. She had a job to do. Margery Weston was depending on her.

It was five o'clock by the time she arrived at the café. Margery strode forward to give her a powdery kiss and introduced her two colleagues: an earnest-looking man called Patrick Smith, enveloped in a black ulster raincoat in spite of the weather, and a young woman with brown curly hair – Sarah someone – who smiled at Pamela shyly.

Margery brandished a sheaf of papers. 'The train arrives at five fifteen.' She glanced down at the top sheet. 'Platform ten, I believe. We will collect the children there and shepherd them over to the staff gymnasium, where they will be met by their foster parents.'

Pamela and Sarah nodded, but Patrick Smith frowned as though the information was already too much to take in.

Margery ignored him. She looked at her watch and stepped forward in her stout brogues. 'Right. Let's go.'

No matter how many times Pamela had imagined this scene, it was still a shock to see the children. Some of them were indeed very young. She watched a small girl peering with huge dark eyes over a teddy bear she clutched to her chest. Beside her stood an older boy bundled up in a thick coat and large scarf. She imagined their anxious mother pressing the toy into her daughter's hands, then turning to fasten her son's scarf before bravely waving them both goodbye, a tight smile forced onto her white face. Older children stood behind carrying battered cases and looking around nervously. All of them had brown labels tied round their necks and carried gas masks. Pamela drew in a sharp breath. In Britain, occupation was only a remote possibility; in northern Europe, it was a terrible reality.

The four of them accompanied fifty or so unnaturally silent children over to the gymnasium, then herded them behind the thick rope strung across the middle. On the other side of the rope stood the foster parents. For a moment, Pamela wished she were one of them, craning her neck to look at the children, wondering which little hand would clasp hers as she escorted them home. But instead she stood meekly behind Margery, who was booming out the names on her list.

As each child's name was called, sometimes twice if they didn't understand Margery's pronunciation, they would walk forward, to be greeted at the rope by their foster family, and the group would move off together. Pamela went to stand by the rope so she could help with the process. Sometimes two children were called together. But the little girl with the teddy bear was marched off by a formidable woman in a tweed suit, whilst her brother went with a young mother carrying a baby in her arms. Pamela drove her nails into her palms to stop herself calling out that she would take both children, anything to keep the siblings from being separated. But she knew Hugh would be appalled if he returned to find refugees in the house when she hadn't asked his permission. That conversation would have to wait.

By the time she got back to Hampstead, she was exhausted. She half expected Hugh to be home, but he hadn't yet returned from Westminster, and it was Kitty's half-day, so there was a cold supper in the kitchen.

Pamela wandered disconsolately from room to room. The walk from the Tube had been pleasant, the evening air still warm. But the house was stuffy. It smelled sterile somehow. She imagined walking up the front path, a child in each hand, showing the boy to Will's old room (she hadn't worked out what would happen in the holidays) and the little girl to the spare bedroom, propping her teddy up against the wooden headboard. Sitting the child on the bed, brushing her hair . . .

This was ridiculous. She must keep busy. She went over to her writing desk and drew out some sheets of paper and her fountain pen. By the time Hugh came home, she was six pages into a letter to Will. Whether Will would be interested in the narration of her visit to fetch the refugees in such intricate detail was another matter. But at least writing made her feel better.

After a rather cheerless cold chicken salad on trays in the drawing room, giving Hugh a shortened version of her afternoon, Pamela went into the kitchen to make coffee. As she assembled cups and saucers, and waited for the kettle to boil, she made up her mind to broach the subject of having a child to stay. She couldn't look on any longer as other people did their bit. Perhaps she should remind him about Quaker responsibilities. They had so much room at home and so much to give. Surely he couldn't have an excuse not to?

She placed his cup on the small table beside him. 'I found it very hard this afternoon,' she said. 'Seeing those poor Jewish children go off with families and knowing I wasn't bringing one of them back here.'

Hugh took a gulp of coffee, realised it was too hot, and put his cup down.

Pamela picked up her own cup and sipped at it carefully. She tried to keep her voice mild. If she could imply that this was a perfectly reasonable request, Hugh might be more willing to agree. 'Darling . . . may I foster one of the children?

114

There is plenty of room here; we could give a little boy or girl an excellent home.'

Hugh frowned. 'Pammie, you have enough to do looking after me – and Will when he's here. Besides, I know your leg still hurts sometimes. You can't possibly run around after a child.'

Pamela's spirits plummeted. Hugh was right. Her leg *did* still hurt occasionally. But that was nothing; she was prepared to put up with it to do her bit. She remembered the pressure of Agata's body as she'd leant against her on the hospital bed, smelled her sweet, milky fragrance, saw her bright eyes, heard her laughter when they played with the doll.

'Please, Hugh. I must do more to help these children. People all over England are making huge sacrifices. I've been brought up to help, not sit around all day. Kitty does all the housework. And you're spending such long hours at the office, darling.'

'Do more charity work then.'

Pamela took another sip of coffee. 'I spend hours at Bloomsbury House with the Friends committee. But I need to do more. I have to be active. We're *Quakers*, Hugh. We *help* people.'

Hugh picked at a loose thread on the armchair. 'What do you think I'm trying to do at the FO, Pammie? I'm using every bone in my body to keep this country out of a war.'

'I know, darling, and you're doing an admirable job. But that's *you*. *I* need to do something too.'

Hugh stood up and collected her coffee cup, dropping a kiss on her head as he did so. 'Not a child, Pamela. It'd be too much for you, with everything else going on. Too much for *us*.' His gesture had been kind, but his voice was firm. Unequivocal. He took the cup and saucer into the kitchen.

Pamela sighed, but inwardly she still felt some hope. Maybe there was something she *could* get Hugh to agree to. She leant back in the chair and crossed her legs in an attempt to appear relaxed. 'There's a British man working to bring children across from Czechoslovakia,' she said as Hugh returned and sat down.

'Oh yes, I've heard of him. Winton. Good chap. Comes from round here.'

'Indeed. I think he's a stockbroker.' That would impress Hugh. 'But he took time off work to go out to Prague and rescue those children.'

'Very commendable.'

'He's back in England now, but he's looking for volunteers to go over to Prague and escort more children back.'

Hugh shot forward in his chair. 'You're not suggesting I go?'

'No, not you. Me.'

'Absolutely not. Czechoslovakia is an occupied country. Far too dangerous.'

Looking keen would only incite Hugh further. 'Darling, I have to do something more than just sorting out clothes for refugees.'

'Out of the question.'

Pamela cleared her throat. 'Margery Weston has been out to Germany several times. Her husband is happy to let her go.'

Hugh snorted. 'If I were Margery's husband, *I'd* be only too happy to see the back of her for a couple of weeks.'

Pamela smiled thinly. 'How did you manage when I was in hospital?'

'All right, I suppose. Kitty stepped up.'

'Exactly. And I'll go when Will is away, so I won't be neglecting him.' She smoothed down her skirt.

'Over my dead body.'

She leant forward. 'Hugh, I'd be under the protection of Nicholas Winton the whole time. You said yourself he's a decent chap. And I'd be going as a Quaker. You know the Germans trust us.'

Hugh examined his nails. 'That's true.' They'd been called 'Hun-lovers' in the Great War, but the Germans had let them in to feed the children.

'Precisely. They know we go in peace. Besides, I still know a bit of Czech. I could be useful to speak to the children.' She'd been popping down to Mrs Brevda's quite regularly since she'd recovered from her accident, on the pretext of getting garments made or altered but really to practise her Czech. Mrs Brevda seemed quite happy to let Pamela sit next to her whilst she sewed and chat to her in her native language. Pamela wasn't sure why she'd felt the need to work on her Czech. She wanted to keep her brain busy and she'd thought it might come in useful one day. Perhaps this was the occasion she'd been subconsciously preparing for.

'Hmm. I could get Halifax to send someone out with you, I suppose.'

Pamela hardly dared speak. 'And it won't take long. Three days at the most. You'd hardly miss me.'

Hugh stood up. 'I hope you won't regret this, Pamela.'

Pamela stood too and put her hands on his shoulders. 'I won't.'

'But no foster children!' Hugh strode out of the room.

Two weeks later, Pamela was on the train for Prague, squashed into a carriage next to portly Margery Weston, who seemed to consume a new packet of sandwiches every half-hour. Eileen Jackson sat the other side of Margery, and Beth Seddon was opposite with two more women who'd joined them at St Pancras. Both had fallen asleep before Pamela had a chance to ask their names. In the corner sat a slight man almost obliterated by a copy of the *Times*, only his homburg and a pair of skinny lower legs visible. Pamela wondered if he was Halifax's man. If it was, he clearly wasn't going to talk. And he didn't look brawny enough to be much of a bodyguard.

There was a crackle of greaseproof paper, and the pungent smell of boiled eggs filled the air as Margery offered Pamela yet another sandwich.

Pamela shook her head and tried to summon a smile. How could the woman eat so much? She herself hadn't even touched the ham roll Kitty had pressed into her hand that morning. 'You'll look after Mr Denison, won't you, Kitty?' she had said as she'd pushed her lunch into her bag and fastened it. And Kitty had nodded confidently. 'Don't you worry, ma'am. He won't even notice you've gone.'

Pamela swallowed. She hoped he *would* miss her. But at least Will would be at school, and Hugh seemed to be spending more and more time at the Foreign Office these days, as the threat of war intensified. She'd kissed him goodbye breezily. 'I'll be back before you know it. And it's so good to feel as though I'm finally doing something.' Hugh had sniffed. 'Aren't all those hours you spend on your charity work enough?' The trickle of refugees from Europe had now become a flood. Earlier in the year the committee had moved from Drayton House and into Bloomsbury House. The work had increased hugely. But Pamela still felt she could do more to help the children. Last time she'd only got as far as Liverpool Street station. Now she was going all the way to Czechoslovakia.

She leant her head against the padded rest. Agata's little face came to her mind again, then Tomas's too. She had no reason to suppose they were Jewish, but they were still living in an occupied country. She wondered how Jan was managing.

Her thoughts travelled to the refugees she'd welcomed earlier that year. As far as she could tell, they were settling in well, learning the language, going to school. Children were adaptable, but they must miss their parents terribly. And they them. How awful. She'd never be able to cope if she didn't see Will every few weeks. But at least he was safe. These poor Czech children had already faced who knew what dangers.

10

Josef was surprised to see five places laid for supper. 'Do we have a visitor for Shabbat?' he asked Eva.

'No,' she replied, reaching out to light the candles. 'I thought Miriam could join us this evening. Stay up late for a treat, now she's turned five. It's time she learned more about our customs.' She waved her hands above the candles to gather the light to her face.

Josef nodded. 'I'll be able to say the daughters' blessing over her.'

Eva smiled, a little thinly, Josef thought. 'I was hoping you would.'

Josef went in search of the wine for the Kiddush cup whilst Eva placed the challah on the table then called up for her parents.

They came down with Miriam. Eva's mother had tied a scarf round the child's head. Josef smiled at his daughter's round face encased in the dark material. Her bright eyes were wide with curiosity. One day she'd be as beautiful as her mother, he was sure of it. It was sad they'd had no more children, but Miriam was such a blessing to them. They really should be grateful. Each night he thanked Adonai that they still had her with them. Thank goodness they hadn't had to send her away like some of their friends' children. His work at the Institute was still going well; the Nazis were clearly pleased with him, although lately there had been talk of a new project, which made him a little anxious. The antisera were nearing the last stage of development, but maybe he could spin things out a bit longer. Make the new project wait, whatever it was.

With the whole family assembled round the table, Josef began the Shalom Aleichem, and the others joined in. Eva must have taught Miriam the words: the child's clear voice rose above the rest, strong and confident. Josef smiled at her and stood up to place his hands on her head. 'Well done, Miriam. You sang that beautifully. Now I'm going to say the daughters' blessing over you. "May you be like Sarah, Rebecca, Rachel and Leah . . ."' As he spoke the familiar words, something made him glance across at Eva. Her mouth was trembling. She dashed a napkin to her eyes. Josef finished the blessing and went round to his wife to put his arm round her. 'All right, *Liebling*?'

Eva cleared her throat. 'Of course. It was so lovely to hear you bless Miriam.' She put the napkin to her face again. 'You almost made me cry!'

Josef kissed her head, feeling its warmth through her headscarf. 'She's a precious girl.'

Eva nodded. But her lips stayed closed.

Josef reached for the Kiddush cup.

Once in the night he thought he heard Eva stifle a sob, but when he leant over to talk to her, he heard only the slow breaths of someone deeply asleep. Perhaps he'd imagined it. But he didn't imagine her tired eyes the next morning, or her shaking hands as she broke her bread roll into pieces and put one into her mouth, chewing it listlessly as if it were cardboard.

'Eva, are you sickening for something? Perhaps you caught a cold in your thin dress yesterday?'

Eva smiled wanly. 'I'm fine, dear. Really.' She turned to Miriam. 'Finish your breakfast, darling. You need to keep up your strength.'

Did Josef imagine it, or did Eva's mother and Eva exchange glances at that? Really, he was becoming oversensitive. Must be all this talk at work. It had unsettled him. He took a quick sip of water – they'd long since run out of coffee – and stood up. 'I'll just get ready for the synagogue.' He went upstairs to get his prayer shawl. But when he came down, Eva was still at the table. 'Aren't you going to get changed, *Liebling*?'

Eva shook her head. 'You were right, Josef. I really don't feel well. You go on without me. I'll keep Miriam back. Mutti finds it hard to look after her on her own.'

Josef nodded. 'I knew it. I can always tell when you're sickening for something.' He kissed her cheek. 'Take care of yourself, my dear. I'll go and fetch your parents.'

Eva nodded. 'Kiss your daughter too.'

'Of course.' Josef went across to Miriam and gave her a hug. 'Look after your mother, little one.'

He cast a glance at Eva's face as he left the room. It was as white as his lab coat.

As soon as Josef and her parents left, Eva dashed upstairs. She hauled an old carpet bag down from the top of her wardrobe and filled it with the clothes that she and Mutti had so carefully been sewing for weeks. Mutti had already said goodbye to Miriam before leaving for the synagogue, although she was careful to make her farewell casual enough not to alert Abba or Josef's suspicions. Eva felt a pang as she looked at her mother's handiwork. Her parents would be bereft without their precious granddaughter, and she couldn't even imagine Josef's reaction. But she kept telling herself she was doing the right thing. She added a pile of jumpers and underwear, then fastened the bag.

Once they were on their own, Eva broke the news to Miriam that she was going away for a while. She tried to present her forthcoming journey as an adventure, implying that she'd be back home quite soon. And she prayed that that would be true.

'May I take Lilli?' asked Miriam, who had followed her into the bedroom.

'Of course, darling. Lilli will look after you.' Eva squatted down in front of her daughter and put her arms round her. 'Whenever you feel sad or lonely, give her a big hug – and I'll be hugging you too, in my heart.' She swallowed, her mouth suddenly too dry to speak.

Miriam's expression was solemn. 'I will, Mummy.'

'Come on then, *Liebling*.' Eva took her daughter's hand and led her down the stairs. She opened the front door, checked the street was empty – all their neighbours would be at the synagogue – and hurried Miriam down the road.

Already the sun was hot, the pavement sticky under their feet. The handles of the carpet bag dug into Eva's hand, and soon her palm was slippery with sweat. Miriam began to whine at the fast pace, and Eva slowed a fraction.

'How far, Mummy?'

'Not long now, then you'll be able to have a nice long rest on the train.'

'Mummy . . .' Miriam stopped suddenly and Eva tried to resist the urge to pull her on.

'What's the matter, *Liebling*?'

'Will the train take us over a river?'

'Why, yes, it will cross the Elbe at some point.'

'And will the train fall in?' Miriam wrapped her arms around her chest.

Eva laughed. 'Whatever gave you that idea? The train will cross the river on a bridge. You'll be perfectly safe.'

A small hand found hers.

They passed a few Germans on the way: rolling cigarettes on street corners, standing in menacing groups in their distinctive grey uniforms and shiny black boots watching passers-by, talking furtively to each other. German flags were everywhere. But no one stopped them or demanded to know where they were going. It had been a good idea to miss the service; the Germans assumed that all Jews were at the synagogues. Eva felt guilty at her deception, but at least the decision protected them.

She dared not run for fear of arousing suspicion, but she hurried a protesting Miriam along the cobbled streets, whose houses tilted menacingly towards her. By the time they got to the Wilson station, a large crowd had gathered. There were children of all ages carrying cases and wearing brown labels. They were dressed in winter coats and wore scarves and hats. Far too much clothing for a summer's day. Eva pushed her way through a thick wall of people and led Miriam to a smiling woman in a red suit sitting at a makeshift desk at the side of the concourse.

'Name?' To Eva's surprise, she said the word in Czech. Her accent wasn't bad either, although she was clearly English.

'Miriam Kolischer.' Eva's right eyelid was flickering. She rubbed at it quickly.

The woman bent over the desk. 'Hello, Miriam. What a lovely doll. What is her name?'

'Lilli,' replied Miriam, smiling trustingly at the woman.

How thoughtful of these British people to supply a Czech speaker. Not many foreigners bothered to learn their language. Eva knew a little Italian from her music studies, and she spoke German fluently, of course, as well as Czech and Hebrew, but her English was minimal.

The woman consulted a long list, locating Miriam's name near the end. 'Miriam, dear.' She leant forward again. 'You are going to be staying with the Williams family, in Wales. They've chosen you specially. I'm sure you will be very happy with them.' She looked across at Eva and nodded at her kindly. The staccato beat of Eva's heart smoothed a little.

She wasn't really sure where Wales was, but she seemed to remember from when she'd looked at a map of the British Isles that it was very far from London. Poor Miriam. Another long train journey.

The British woman wrote something on a brown label and passed it across to Eva to place round Miriam's neck. Like a parcel, Eva thought. 'Platform One,' said the woman. Then she smiled again and invited the next family up to the desk.

Eva led Miriam across to the growing group of parents and children standing near the gates to Platform One. Most of the children had both their mother and father with them. And often one or two siblings. There weren't many mothers on their own with just one child. Eva wondered again if she should have told Josef. But he'd have been bound to stop her. Perhaps if Mutti had opposed her as well, she might have thought twice, but her mother had been supportive. Her stomach clenched. It was nine years since the attack in the cemetery, but she wondered if Mutti still felt the helplessness of a mother who hadn't been able to protect her child. Was this why she was encouraging her to send Miriam to safety? Poor Mutti. She'd suffered too.

She glanced at the children again. Some were crying, their arms wrapped round their mothers. Others were looking around them anxiously. Miriam's plump little face wore a puzzled expression, and she held tight to Eva's hand.

Eva rubbed at her right eyelid again. It was flickering as though it had a thread attached, being pulled by an invisible hand. She swallowed. Britain was safe. Their government was holding Hitler off. She'd been so excited when the letter had come, mercifully when Josef was at work, to advise her that a British family had offered to take Miriam. It was the right thing to do. The letter confirmed it. Besides, it was only for a few months, until all this business was over.

The crowd by the barrier was much larger now, and Eva held Miriam protectively close to avoid her getting squashed. Her little body felt strong and warm against hers. Beside her, a woman in a green dress was stooping down to do up the buttons on her daughter's coat. Poor child. It was stuffy in the station, the hot steam making it even more stifling, but the mother was determined to keep her daughter warm. Maybe she thought she was keeping her safe too. The boy next to her was sitting on his suitcase, which bulged slightly under the weight, talking to a tall man with long payots and a huge black beard. The man bent down to stroke his son's hair. Eva's breath caught in her throat. So many Jews missing synagogue. Whatever would the rabbis say?

Some of the German soldiers at the station were staring at the families with impassive faces and hard eyes. Eva's blood started to pound again. Others, though, looked uncomfortable at the sight of so much distress, and turned away. Eva swallowed. She'd regarded all Germans as enemies for so long, it was hard to remember that they were people too.

Eventually someone opened the gates and the crowd surged towards the waiting train. Eva had been looking around for someone she knew but could see no one familiar.

Suddenly Miriam pointed. 'There's Sammie!' she cried.

Eva followed the direction of her finger and saw a young lad in an overlarge jumper, clutching his mother's hand and looking around him with worried eyes. He seemed about Miriam's age.

'Does he go to your school?' Eva hadn't seen him before.

'Yes. He's in 1a.'

It was a shame it was a boy. And not a child from Miriam's own class. But at least it was someone. Eva led Miriam over towards Sammie and his mother.

'Excuse me.' The woman looked up. 'My daughter says she knows your son from school.'

The woman nodded. She had brown curly hair and an open face.

'Perhaps they could sit together on the train.'

'Of course. You'd like that, Sammie, wouldn't you?'

The boy shrugged, but there was a flicker of relief in his eyes. His mother opened the door and motioned the two children in.

Sammie's mother and Eva climbed into the carriage too. Miriam sat on a polished wooden bench near the window, her feet barely reaching the floor, with Sammie opposite her. Some children were even perched on the overhead luggage nets. Eva placed Miriam's suitcase on the seat beside her daughter, undid it and drew out Lilli. Miriam seized the doll and hugged it to her chest. Eva delved into her pocket for some bread and an apple. It had taken a lot of bartering to secure the fruit, but she had been determined that Miriam should have something good to eat on the journey. She snapped the case shut and heaved it into the luggage rack. Then she sat down beside her daughter and put an arm round her. 'Now, Miriam. Do you have everything you need?'

The child nodded, her eyes full of uncertainty.

'Make your bread last. You may not be given anything else for a while.' Eva tried to keep her voice calm. 'And remember what I told you. Whenever you miss us, hug Lilli and it will be as if you are hugging us too.' The tears gathered. 'It won't be for long, dear.' They threatened to overspill. 'You'll be back before you know it.' She dashed a hand across her eyes. 'And think how you'll have grown!'

Miriam didn't speak, but buried her head in her mother's shoulder.

A whistle screeched.

'We need to go!' Sammie's mother put a hand on Eva's arm.

Eva nodded and stood up. She couldn't speak anyway. She followed the other woman out of the carriage, shut the door and looked in through the window. Miriam was clutching Lilli, and Sammie was inspecting his sandwiches.

Suddenly Miriam started to cry, deep, shuddering sobs. 'I don't want to go!' she shouted. 'Please don't make me, Mummy. I want to stay with you.'

Eva's heart lurched. Without thinking, she wrenched open the door, leapt into the carriage, seized her daughter not stopping to collect her case, and jumped down onto the platform holding Miriam tight. She would take her back home. Josef need know nothing. And perhaps he'd been right all along. Maybe Miriam would be safe. Maybe they could all carry on as normal.

She pressed Miriam to her, exulting in her little girl's solidity and almost faint with relief. But as she turned to make her way back down the platform, she caught sight of a group of German soldiers smoking and laughing. Suddenly, blood pounded affrettando in her ears, and her stomach swooped before she could even register what she'd heard. She hadn't felt this terrified since the night in the cemetery. She was distraught at leaving Miriam, consumed with apprehension and anticipated guilt at Josef finding out. But this total horror was new.

She forced herself to look again. Amid the group of soldiers was a young man with white hair. Could it be Otto, her tormentor from the graveyard? Bile rose in her throat and her heart thundered. As her knees buckled beneath her and Sammie's mother reached out strong arms to steady her, she made another decision. She thrust Miriam back into the carriage and forced her onto the bench, ignoring her daughter's screams. When the guard approached to slam the door, she jumped off without even having time to say goodbye.

As the train pulled away, it was relief as much as terror that coursed through her. But the sound of Miriam's howls of distress would haunt her for the rest of her life.

It was only when she walked past the soldiers as she made her way out of the station that she risked a proper look at the white-haired German. It hadn't been Otto at all. She'd made a mistake.

11

The guard's whistle blew. Pamela put her head out of the window to check that all the children were safely on board. Further down the platform, a wailing child was being forced into a carriage by a clearly agitated mother. How awful. As the train pulled out, Pamela hurried down the corridor to check on the little girl. As she did so, she caught the mother's eye. There was no time to call out that everything would be all right, even if she could find the words, but in that split second of contact she concentrated all her efforts on silently assuring the woman that she'd protect her child. She saw the woman turn to her companion and they put their arms round each other. She couldn't bear to think how hard it must be for them to hand over their children. She twisted her wedding ring round her finger as she thought of Will, and silently thanked God he was safe.

She found the little girl, her face buried in her doll, sitting by the window, her small legs dangling. Opposite her was a boy of a similar age, imperturbably munching on a hunk of black bread. For a second Pamela thought of Margery Weston, who no doubt had purchased new provisions and was tucking into them heartily. How strange that some people could carry on eating even in the most extreme of circumstances. She herself certainly couldn't manage a morsel.

She sat down carefully next to the child. Her long hair, probably carefully brushed by her mother, was frizzy where it had rubbed against the seat. Pamela longed to smooth it but didn't want to scare her. The girl had brown frightened eyes in a white face and looked about five or six. 'Seef por ardku?' Pamela asked. *Are you all right?* Mrs Brevda had taught her well. She was quite fluent now.

The little girl nodded woefully.

'Yak-say-manyouyesh?' *What's your name?*

'Miriam,' the girl whispered.

Pamela gently stroked the doll's hair. 'Jakka hezka panenka.' *What a pretty doll!* Thank goodness she'd had all that practice with Agata. She reached out to shake the doll's hand, just as she had with Agata's doll in the hospital. The child gave a half-smile. Pamela gestured to her to hand the doll over, and soon they were playing hide-and-seek with it. Even the little boy joined in. By the time the train pulled to a halt an hour later, the children had started to laugh a little.

Pamela walked up the train to find out why they had stopped. They were at a station. *Terezin*, the sign said. She located Margery, who was gesticulating at an official with a hand that still clutched an apple. Tiny bits of the fruit's flesh flew through the air. 'Ah, Pamela. Perhaps you can help.'

'I'll try.' Pamela stepped forward and exchanged a few sentences with the man. 'Apparently some important papers are missing. We can't cross into Germany without them.'

Margery blew out her cheeks. 'Oh no. How frustrating. I was assured everything was in order.'

Pamela bit her lip. They had such a long way to go, and already there was a holdup when they'd barely started.

Margery had no choice but to dispatch Patrick Smith back to Prague to collect the necessary papers. Pamela looked out of the window to see the black ulster coat scuttling self-importantly up the platform, ready to catch the return train. Perhaps Smith was more competent than he'd appeared.

It had been nice to be back in Prague, however briefly. Despite the pain of her accident, and the horror of Ada's death, Pamela still had some good memories of Czechoslovakia: the warmth and kindness of the people . . . the beauty of the landscape . . . even the food had been interesting, though very different to Hampstead fare. Most of all, it was tremendous to feel she was doing something. She had her part to play: registering the children, issuing brown labels, trying to console distraught mothers. It had been a very long time since she'd felt she was genuinely helping. I feel like a Quaker again, she realised. At long last the guilt of compromise, hypocrisy even, was beginning to recede. Hugh was doing his bit at the Foreign Office; she was rescuing refugees. Finally they were working as a team.

Their train waited at Terezin for four hours, while others moved through the station past it. Four hours of checking on the children, joining in with 'Hoppe, hoppe Reiter', which they seemed to want to sing countless times, making sure they didn't eat all their food, placing blankets over those who had fallen asleep, comforting those who were distressed. And all the time listening to Margery's infuriated rants and feeling her own blood pressure rise alarmingly. By the time Patrick Smith finally returned with the vital papers, and the train jerked into action, Pamela was exhausted and frustrated. They had so much time to make up.

The motion of the train lulled more children to sleep, and eventually Pamela felt she could relax. For the first few hours the windows were filled with mountains and forests, just as when they'd travelled through Germany for their ski trip. She'd forgotten how beautiful the country was. How could such splendour and tranquillity have spawned such a warlike people? Adolf Hitler was a powerful man, there was no doubt about that. Thank God Chamberlain was holding him off for now, but Pamela had seen the worry and fear etched on the faces of the people at the Wilson station. Occupation was a terrible thing. She hoped it would never come to that in Britain.

When they stopped at Cologne, German officers boarded the train. Pamela heard the thud of their boots as they made their way up the corridors. She looked out of the window. Nazi flags hung from each lamp post; there were black swastikas in white circles and posters of Hitler everywhere. The air crackled with tension.

Suddenly their compartment door burst open and a German officer appeared, lurching slightly in the entrance. Pamela's mouth turned paper-dry, and she held her breath. The officer strode up to Miriam and motioned to her doll. 'What have we here?'

Miriam held out the doll with a shaking hand. The man grabbed it and dangled it out of the window, his fingers forcing the little cloth limbs to jerk up and down. 'Help me,' he cried in a high-pitched voice, then laughed at his own pantomime. Miriam was frozen with terror.

The little boy shifted in his seat. Pamela put her palm on his shoulder to restrain him, then strode over to the window.

'Stop it,' she said, as vehemently as she dared. 'You're upsetting the children.'

She had no idea if the officer understood her words, but he'd caught her tone. He shrugged, drew the doll back in and tossed it onto Miriam's lap. Pamela hoped he'd leave them alone after that, but instead he hauled the children's cases down from the luggage rack. As he dropped them on the floor, one of them burst open, revealing a neat stack of clothes.

The German pulled the garments out and flung them behind him, creating an untidy pile of skirts and dresses, several made from the same material. Something caught in Pamela's throat. Miriam's mother must have sewn them for her. She was obviously expecting them to be apart for some time. The officer grabbed another lot of belongings from the suitcase and dropped them on the floor. There was a smashing sound.

'I can assure you everything here is in order,' Pamela said.

The German ignored her.

Anger tightened in a band across her chest. 'Enough!' she shouted. She marched up to the German, snapped the suitcase shut, and hauled it across the floor away from him. 'What kind of man are you that you victimise defenceless children? You should be ashamed of yourself,' she hissed, putting as much venom in her voice as she could. Even if he didn't speak English, there was no doubt about her anger. Let him attack her if he wanted – the man in the homburg would surely come to her aid soon – but these children were terrified. They had barely anything of their own. How dare he ransack their cases?

The German scowled. Pamela stood her ground. Where on earth was the homburg man? 'Keep away from these children. Their things are not yours to take.' She made a shooing gesture with her hand. 'Get out this minute!'

The German's eyes bulged. He aimed a kick at the suitcase, then left the compartment.

Pamela's legs were suddenly hollow. When she knelt down quickly in front of Miriam, it was as much to stop herself falling over as to reassure the child.

'Come on, dear,' she said in Czech. It was almost impossible to speak, her mouth was so dry. 'Let's repack your suitcase.' She started to refold the girl's dresses and place them carefully back in the case. A photo in a broken frame had slid under the seat. She picked it up to see a smiling Jewish couple, the little girl seated between them. 'Don't worry,' she told her. 'We'll get this mended for you when we get to England.' The child gulped and hugged her doll tightly.

Pamela heaved the cases back into the overhead rack.

'Will you be all right now?'

Miriam and the boy both nodded.

She strode into the next-door compartment to find the man Lord Halifax had supposedly sent to keep an eye on her still sitting behind his newspaper, his homburg intact. The pages shook slightly in his hands.

She stood in front of him, hands on hips, until he lowered his paper. His face was pale and his forehead gleamed with sweat.

'I thought you were here to help,' she said.

The man swallowed. 'Er, sorry. Got engrossed.' He wiped his palms down his trousers. 'Are you all right?'

136

'I am now. It would take more than one thieving German to scare me. But I was led to believe that you were here to protect us.'

'Um. Yes. But you seemed to have it under control. I'm more of a diplomat, you see, if anything escalates.'

Pamela raised her eyes heavenwards and exited the compartment.

Eventually the scenery became flatter, and they passed a blur of windmills. The train chugged to a halt. Pamela looked out of the window and saw smiling girls in Dutch national costume holding out trays of food and drink.

Margery appeared in the doorway. 'Let's get the children out. Stretch their legs. Looks like the locals have put on a bit of a spread.'

The children drank the cups of hot chocolate they were offered, but some of them just stared at the bread. 'It's wet!' said a small boy with a cloth cap, making a face as he sank his teeth into one of the white rolls.

Pamela laughed. 'It's not wet,' she told him. 'Just soft. Have you never seen white bread before?'

The boy shook his head.

'All the bread in England is soft and white. You'll soon get used to it,' Pamela told him. That wasn't the only thing he'd have to get used to. Not having his mother tuck him into bed, or saying prayers with his parents, being away from his home, his village, his friends. And who knew how long for? She just hoped all the guarantors would be good people. For a second she imagined pushing a little girl on a swing at the park, reading her stories by the fire, holding her hand as she took her to school. Hugh had been adamant. No foster child. But at least she was doing something.

They finally got off the train at the Hook of Holland and led the children onto the ship. Some of them looked frightened when they saw how big it was.

'I bet most of these children haven't been on anything bigger than a paddle steamer in Bratislava,' chuckled Margery.

Pamela helped a small boy readjust his rucksack. 'So many new experiences in one day,' she replied. It was getting dark now, the sea an inky black, grey plumes of smoke from the ship the only lighter colour in the sky. The quayside smelled of herrings and salt water. 'Come on.' She put her arm round a little girl sucking her thumb. 'You've got special beds on the ship. I'll show you.'

As they crossed the invisible Channel, which rocked and tilted beneath them, the sound of singing drifted out from the cabins: 'Kde domov můj, kde domov můj.' *Where my home is, where my homeland is.* It was the Czech national anthem.

The train finally ground into Liverpool Street station at nine that night. Pamela stood up stiffly to help the children collect their luggage and to lift the little ones onto the platform. She had to go back twice, once to retrieve a lost teddy and the second time for an abandoned jumper, but eventually they were all out and trudging down the platform. She caught up with Miriam, who was dragging her suitcase along the ground, oblivious to the way it twisted and jolted.

'Not long now,' she told the little girl. 'Let me take your case while you go up the stairs.' The child was almost sleepwalking, her eyes half closed, her dark curls a limp tangle around her face. Pamela walked behind her, in case she fell, as Miriam stumbled up the steps.

In spite of her own exhaustion, Pamela felt a surge of triumph. They'd escorted over two hundred children to safety; maybe even saved their lives. It was awful that families had been split up, that young children were being brought up by strangers whilst their parents pined – and who knew for how long – but at least they were safe. Thank God for England and Chamberlain. And for that wonderful Nicholas Winton who'd set these rescues in motion.

She followed a ragged line of children into the large hall. By now, the routine was familiar. The host families craning their necks, the Czech children timid and apprehensive. One by one they were paired off. Eventually only six children were left: five young boys and Miriam. Pamela remembered her being pushed onto the train by her mother at Wilson station. Poor child. She went over to her. 'Don't worry, I'm sure someone will come for you soon,' she said in Czech.

A policeman was striding across the concourse towards them. 'Still some left?'

Pamela nodded. 'I don't know what's happened.'

'Bound to be hiccups with a crowd this size,' said the policeman. 'Tell you what. Give it another half-hour. If no one has claimed them by then, I'll see what I can do.'

'All right. Thank you.' Pamela turned to the others. 'I can wait,' she said. 'No point us all staying.'

'Well, if you're sure,' said Margery. She rubbed her stomach. 'I don't mind telling you I'm looking forward to some British food again. My cook was under strict instructions to prepare a large chicken casserole to welcome me home!'

Pamela smiled thinly. 'I'll let you know how I get on.'

'Do, dear.' Margery and the others were already striding towards the exit. 'Thanks for staying!'

Pamela turned back to Miriam and the boys. 'Now, can you teach me "Hoppe, hoppe Reiter" again?'

In the end, no one turned up for the children. Pamela was relieved when the policeman reappeared. 'There's a taxi driver just finishing his shift. Says he'll take the boys home with him if you like. He and his wife would be happy to help look after them.' He must have seen Pamela's anxious expression, as he added, 'Don't worry, those lads will be safe with him. I've known him for years, he's a good chap.'

'That's very kind,' replied Pamela. 'I'll take Miriam with me. Just until we can sort out what's happened.'

'Of course, ma'am.' The policeman tipped his hat at her and motioned to the boys. 'Come with me, you lot. I believe there might be some fish and chips in the offing.' The boys wouldn't have understood him, but they obediently picked up their rucksacks and cases and followed him out of the station.

Pamela held out her hand to Miriam. 'Come on, dear,' she said. 'We're going to Hampstead.'

*

As soon as Josef opened the front door, and ushered Eva's parents in, he knew something was wrong. The air in the hall was stagnant. Where was the savoury smell of cholent that normally greeted him? His stomach had rumbled during the last part of the service and his mouth had watered at the thought of the slow-cooked onion and potato, the richness of the beans and barley, the spiciness of the paprika. Eva was no longer able to buy beef, yet she still managed to concoct a good dish without it. But today there was nothing. No sound either. Perhaps Eva was sleeping – she certainly hadn't looked well – but where was Miriam?

He climbed the stairs. Eva wasn't in bed. She was sitting at the dining-room table, her eyes bloodshot, her face translucent in the midday sun. Anxiety inched up Josef's spine. 'What is wrong, Eva?' He was dimly aware of his mother-in-law tutting behind him as she rattled the blech on the stove and placed the pot of cholent on it. 'Eva?'

At last she raised her face to his. Her fingers clutched a photograph of Miriam, one Josef had never seen. It looked as if it had been taken in a studio – Miriam's smile seemed a little forced, as though she'd held the pose for a long time. How strange that Eva hadn't shown it to him before.

'Where's Miriam?' he asked.

Eva took a long, shuddering breath. 'Gone.'

Something clanged on the stove.

'Gone? Where?' Josef sat down next to her. He prised her fingers away from the photo and wrapped his hands round them.

Eva finally looked him in the eye. 'She's on a train for England.'

'No!' The word was out of his mouth before he'd consciously framed it. 'What have you done?'

Eva rubbed at an eyelid. 'She was on a list. A place came up. I took her to Wilson station this morning.'

'Why was she on a list? Who put her there?' Josef released Eva's hands and thumped the table. 'I told you to keep her here.'

'I know. I disobeyed you. I'm truly sorry for that. But I'm not sorry I sent our child to safety. It's the best thing for her. I'm certain of it.'

'Whatever possessed you, Eva?' Eva's father's voice was calmer, but no less firm. 'Disobeying your husband like that?'

Eva turned a blotchy face to him. 'I'm sorry. But you know that Germans are not to be trusted. I had to keep my child safe at all costs.'

Josef stood up. '*Our* child, Eva.' There was no sound from Eva's mother. Had she known? It didn't matter now. What did matter was that his wife had expressly ignored his instructions, had put his beloved daughter on a train with strangers and sent her to a remote land in the misguided notion that she was keeping her safe. She was safe *here*, with her family. Protected by his job, protected by their love. He picked up the photo from the table with trembling fingers. She was so young, so vulnerable. He looked at her brave little smile, her bright trusting eyes, and pressed his lips to her face, whilst fat, silent tears ran down his cheeks.

Part Two

1939–1944

12

Even though she'd known the announcement was coming, it was still a shock. Pamela curved her arm round Miriam, who had her thumb in her mouth, and glanced at Will, who was turning up the volume on the wireless as Chamberlain's sombre voice spooled out, announcing the 'state of war' between Britain and Germany.

'You can imagine what a bitter blow it is to me that all my long struggle to win peace has failed,' the prime minister informed them. 'Yet I cannot believe that there is anything more or anything different that I could have done and that would have been more successful.'

Pamela imagined Hugh's grim face as he sat by the wireless in his office. He'd looked so defeated lately. There were drooping folds of skin under his eyes and his face had a permanent pallor despite the warm late-summer days. He'd done all he could to bring about peace. The government had looked the other way when the Sudetenland had been invaded; failed to come to Czechoslovakia's aid when Hitler's troops marched into Prague; stalled to keep the Russians on board. But the action on Poland had been a step too far. That morning, Chamberlain announced, the British ambassador in Berlin had handed the German government a final note stating that, unless they heard from them by eleven o'clock they were prepared at once to withdraw their troops from Poland, the two countries would be at war. Hitler's silence spoke volumes. Chamberlain had had no choice.

The Michaelmas term at Marlborough hadn't yet started, which was why Will was sitting with them in the parlour, his face bleached by the strong morning sunlight flooding in through the window. He'd spent the summer playing tennis and cricket at friends' houses and looked young and healthy in contrast to poor, tired Hugh. This would be his last full year at Marlborough. He'd be taking his Higher School Certificate next summer. Hugh was keen for him to stay on an extra term to take the Oxford exam, but Will wasn't so sure. Pamela watched her son's serious expression as he listened to Chamberlain's announcement. Will knew all too well that this was a failure of his father's work for the government, but did Pamela imagine the flash of excitement in his eyes too?

She shivered slightly and turned to Miriam. Thank God the child was still with them: the Williamses had written a few days after her arrival to tell them they couldn't take her. Mrs Williams had found herself unexpectedly pregnant and was feeling too ill to look after another child, her own brood having grown up. They'd asked Winton not to return the money they'd sent; it was the least they could do. And despite Hugh frequently muttering that they should find Miriam a proper foster family, or send her to Hinton Hall, the Czech school that had been set up in Whitchurch, near the Welsh border, so far Pamela had managed to avoid him taking further action. Truth be told, he was spending so much time in Whitehall that he left for work before Miriam was awake and didn't return until after her bedtime. Apart from the few hours he snatched with them at weekends, he barely registered her existence. And often Pamela would arrange for Miriam to stay with her parents on Sundays. Miriam adored them. She often spoke to Pamela about 'Oma' and 'Opa', her maternal grandparents. Perhaps she found being with older people reassuring.

Pamela had told herself not to get too attached to the girl. It would be so easy to treat her as the daughter she'd never had. When she'd first got married, she'd wanted several children, just like Mum. Her own childhood had been poor and chaotic, yet happy too. She'd wanted to replicate that. But Hugh had been resolute. 'One child, Pammie. Then we can afford to give him or her a good education. Your parents didn't have a bean. And look where that left you, still playing catch-up.'

Pamela had firmed her lips at that, but Hugh had been right. She'd been terrified for years in case she accidentally dropped an 'h' or referred to 'the lav' and not 'the lavatory'. Hugh had been a cosseted only child, well provided for financially, educated academically and socially. He never had to sit at a dinner party wondering which fork to use. He wanted the same for his own offspring. And when Pamela had given him a son, he'd been overjoyed – no need to try for another child. A boy was all he wanted. Pamela had learned to suppress the vision of a little girl with golden ringlets, or a tumble of dark hair. She hugged Miriam a little tighter, inhaling the faint scent of Pears soap. Perhaps she could pretend the child was hers. Just for a while.

When the announcement finished, Will reached out to turn off the wireless. 'Poor Papa,' was all he said.

'Yes.' Pamela got to her feet, disturbing Miriam. She

rested her hand on the little girl's dark hair. 'He tried so hard. They all did.'

Will shrugged. 'So I suppose we're at war.'

'I suppose so.' Pamela started as a wailing sound burst through the window. 'What on earth?' She grabbed Miriam's hand and motioned to Will to stand still. 'Surely that can't be the Germans already?'

Will looked anxious for a few seconds, then, when nothing else happened, his face relaxed. 'They'll be testing the air-raid siren, I'll bet. Nothing to worry about, Mother.'

Pamela put her hand to her chest. The galloping beat was still there. Was this what it was going to be like now? The constant fear and panic? The eking-out of food, the lurch of dread before turning on the news, the false optimism, the terrible sense of loss? And the last war had been fought on foreign soil. What if the Germans invaded this time? Britain could be an occupied country. She swallowed. How ironic if she'd rescued Miriam from danger only to submit her to new peril. Would she and Will grow up German? She blinked away the vision of her son in a Nazi uniform, forced to fight. Or Miriam never seeing her parents again. Hugh and his pacifist colleagues had failed to ward off war. But she'd fight for her children's safety with every breath in her body.

The shrill sound of a telephone had her heart drumming again. Kitty's footsteps pattered down the hall. 'Mr Denison for you, ma'am,' she announced.

Pamela's heartbeat slowed a little. 'Oh, thank you, Kitty.' She turned to Will. 'It's Papa. Keep an eye on Miriam, will you?'

'Of course.' Will drew the little girl onto his lap. 'Listen carefully, Miriam. I'm going to tell you a story.' Although her English was still limited, Miriam seemed to love the sound of Will's voice, and to enjoy snuggling up to him. It was clear she missed her parents terribly, still cried for 'Mutti' each night, but Pamela could see that the little girl was gradually relaxing in their company, particularly Will's.

Miriam put her thumb in her mouth – Pamela hadn't the heart to break her of the habit – and leant against Will. He reached out absent-mindedly to smooth her curls and Pamela felt something catch in her throat.

She was feeling calmer by the time she picked up the telephone. 'Hugh?'

'You've heard the news, I take it.'

'Of course. Will turned the wireless on just after eleven.'

'Sad day.' Hugh's voice was husky.

'Indeed. Let's hope it's all over quickly.'

'They said that in the last war, remember.'

Pamela did remember. Over by Christmas, they'd said in 1914. How was anyone to know it would drag on for four terrible years? This war could be the same. Or even longer. 'When will you be back, Hugh?'

'No idea. There's an emergency cabinet meeting. Could go on all night.'

'I see. I have to go over to Liverpool Street later. There's a new trainload of children arriving. Biggest yet. I'll ask Will to babysit Miriam.'

'Righto.' Pamela could hear someone speaking to Hugh in the background. 'Got to go. See you when I see you.'

'All right, darling. Much love.'

Hugh blew a kiss down the telephone, then the line went dead.

Pamela checked that Will was still looking after Miriam, then rang for Kitty. 'Would you bring us some strong tea, Kitty? And maybe some of that gingerbread Miriam loves.'

'Yes, ma'am.' Kitty departed for the kitchen.

Will had set up a snakes and ladders board on the floor and was sprawled beside it, with Miriam sitting cross-legged on the rug. As usual, Lilli was propped up beside her. Pamela had managed to find some similar material to the cloth of Miriam's skirts, and Kitty had run up a little set of clothes for the doll.

'Count the squares in English,' said Will.

'One, two, three . . .' Miriam intoned with barely a trace of accent.

'Good.'

Miriam's face was flushed from the room's heat and her dark hair gleamed in the light. She'd put on a bit of weight over the last few weeks and already looked sturdier. The daughter I never had, Pamela thought again, watching the little girl smiling up at Will as he shook the dice.

Kitty arrived with a tray and placed the cups and saucers on the table. Her hands shook as she poured the tea. *I could have made that tea*, Pamela told herself. Had she become too grand lately? She always tried to be courteous to Kitty, not bark orders at her without so much as a thank you as some of her friends did with their servants, but she'd been preoccupied with Miriam recently, as well as the regular influx of Czech children. And there was always more running around to do when Will was home. Still, perhaps she put upon Kitty too much.

'Come and sit down, dear,' she said. 'Why don't you take tea with us? I'll go and get another cup.'

'Oh no, ma'am. I've the luncheon to finish.'

'That can wait, Kitty. Come on.'

'Yes, come on,' said Will, springing up and knocking the dice flying. 'There's far too much gingerbread just for us. And Miriam won't want any.' He winked at Kitty.

'I do, please,' Miriam protested, jumping up too.

Will laughed and passed her a plate. 'Eat up then. Or I'll have yours.'

Miriam put a whole piece of gingerbread into her mouth and looked at Will with bulging eyes.

But as Pamela disappeared to fetch Kitty's cup, she thought she heard the poor girl sniffing.

She returned quickly from the kitchen and poured Kitty's tea. 'Have some sugar, dear. It's good for shock.'

Kitty picked up the bowl and took a heaped teaspoon, which she stirred thoughtfully into her tea.

Pamela leant forward. 'Is it the war, Kitty?' How stupid of her. She'd been so concerned about Will and Miriam that she'd forgotten Kitty's father had been killed at Ypres.

A tear dropped into the girl's tea.

Pamela passed her a handkerchief and waited whilst Kitty dabbed her face and composed herself. She'd resisted having a maid when she and Hugh first got married. Mum had fed and clothed them all without help, so why shouldn't she? And she'd resented Hugh, truth be told, for forcing her to put on airs and graces just because he was in the Foreign

Office. In the end it was Mum who'd made her see things differently. 'You'll be paying the girl a good wage, won't you? She can take the money back to her poor widowed mother. It'll be such a help to the family.' Perhaps it *was* a way of helping. And it freed Pamela up to devote her time to Will once he came along, and, later on, the Friends committee. She'd always tried never to pull rank on Kitty, though. It wouldn't have felt right.

She put an arm on the girl's shoulder. 'Why don't you pop home, Kitty? Check your mother's all right. I can manage here.'

Kitty's eyes were red-rimmed, but she gave a weak smile. 'Thank you, ma'am. If you're sure you can manage, I'll do that.'

'Good.' Pamela beamed as Kitty scuttled off. 'Will, I think Miriam's had enough now.' Miriam had crumbs round her mouth and a very smug look on her face. 'Can you carry on with your game while I get luncheon?'

Will nodded and bent down to pick up the dice. 'Come on, Miriam. I want to teach you to play cricket this afternoon!'

Pamela found herself looking forward to welcoming the new contingent of children, despite the circumstances that brought them here. She hadn't been back to Prague since she'd taken on Miriam; it wouldn't be fair to the child to leave her – she'd already been abandoned by her own parents, even if it was for good reason, and it might unsettle her if Pamela disappeared for a couple of days. There were other volunteers who could take her place on the train, and she was more than doing her bit taking on a Czech child. Sometimes she wished she could be Kitty, looking after Will and Miriam at home, but her desire to help those poor children prevailed. She'd continued to welcome each new group arriving at Liverpool Street. They were up to number nine now. This one had been weeks in the planning: two hundred and fifty children, the biggest yet. How heartening to be able to rescue so many – even though an England at war was hardly the safe prospect the parents had been promised. But at least they hadn't been occupied. Yet.

She retrieved her usual red suit from the wardrobe. It had become her uniform by now. She pushed her feet into her brown brogues and fluffed up her hair. No lipstick. She didn't want to look too alien to the children. Perhaps just a dusting of powder so her face didn't glow too much in the steamy air of the station.

It was impressive what Nicholas Winton had achieved. He'd put adverts in the newspapers asking for volunteers to take on the Czech children, and the British people had responded to the call, finding space in their homes and kindness in their hearts for these poor refugees. Letters and cheques from possible guarantors had flooded in. Fifty pounds was three months' salary for a lot of people. And not all the foster parents looked rich. For some of them it must have been a huge sacrifice, but they'd done it gladly, with generosity of spirit. Despite their famous reserve, her fellow countrymen were kind people. For a second she thought of Ada's little family. They'd been kind too. She couldn't save Agata and Tomas, she hadn't kept in touch with them, but she'd been on the receiving end of Czech generosity. It was nice to feel that in some way she was reciprocating.

As Pamela caught the train to Liverpool Street, an image darted into her mind of Will and Miriam playing snakes and ladders on the parlour floor. It was good for Will to have a sister, even a temporary one, and she was glad that she herself was now personally involved in the refugee work. She could look the other foster parents in the face, knowing she was one of them.

It was humid in the station. The lingering warmth of the early September day combined with the usual fug from the steam and the crowds of people. In front of Pamela a couple of plump pigeons pecked at the ground, searching for crumbs. They'd have precious little to eat if rationing was brought in like in the last war. She pressed her stomach with remembered hunger. During the school holidays she had four mouths to feed, five including Kitty, assuming she didn't decamp to a munitions factory as many girls had done last time. She'd been tempted once herself when she saw how much her friends had earned. But her parents would have forbidden her to make instruments of war, even if she'd wanted to, and when she'd seen those same friends' skin turn yellow from the TNT, she'd known she'd made the right decision.

Mum had worked miracles to feed them all during the Great War. Got up at five to bake her own bread, gone without sugar herself for months so she could still make the apple crumble they all loved. Pamela wondered what sacrifices *she* could make. Hugh would be all right. There would still be plenty of food at the Foreign Office, but maybe she ought to ask Mum for some of her old wartime recipes. What a shame they didn't live in the countryside, where they would have room to grow their own produce.

One of the pigeons flapped its wings and took flight in a blur of grey and white. Maybe it sensed it might soon have to travel further afield for food.

By the time Pamela reached the gymnasium, a crowd of

foster parents had already gathered. Margery was presiding at the front of them with a large sheaf of typed paper, licking her pencil and ticking off names.

'Ah, Pamela. Good to see you. No sign of the train yet.'

Pamela glanced at her watch. Two minutes to five. The trains from Prague could be up to several hours late after such a long journey. 'Do you think today's declaration could make a difference?'

Margery blinked rapidly. 'I hope not, dear, although the thought did cross my mind. This might be the last contingent for a while.'

Pamela nodded. 'Thank God we've got a large number out already.'

Margery glanced down at her list. 'Six hundred and sixty-nine.'

Pamela did the sum in her head. 'So it will be just under a thousand once today's lot come through.'

'Marvellous. A thousand dear little souls saved.'

Pamela was suddenly too choked up to respond.

By six there was still no sign of the train. Pamela went to ask at the station office, but there hadn't been any communication from Prague. She wondered if the children had even boarded the boat in Holland.

'I'll make an announcement,' said Margery. 'Suggest people go off for a bite to eat whilst we keep vigil here.'

'Good idea,' replied Pamela. 'That should keep the Bishopsgate café owners happy.'

Margery waved her plump arms to attract the attention of the crowd.

Eventually only a couple of women were left. Pamela wandered over to them. They looked like sisters, both with wispy white hair and pink shiny faces. Neither of them was an inch above five foot tall. 'Do you want to go and get a meal?' she asked them. 'I doubt the train will be in for a while, and if it does arrive, we'll keep the children safe here until they can be collected.'

The two women exchanged glances. 'We aren't hungry,' said the slightly taller of the two.

'Need to keep your strength up. It could be a long night,' boomed Margery, striding over and catching the last bit of the conversation.

Again the glance. 'I'm going to have a cup of tea,' suggested Pamela. 'I think the café is still open and we can check on the trains coming in if we sit by the window. Won't you join me?' She stretched out an arm to point the way.

'Well, perhaps just a cup of tea,' murmured one of the sisters.

But when they reached the till, it was clear they meant literally one cup, to be shared between them.

Margery raised an eyebrow as one of the women dug in her purse for coins. 'How strange.'

Pamela watched as one sister piled up halfpennies and farthings on the counter and the other sister rummaged through her pockets. Eventually they found enough money and followed Pamela and Margery to the table with their precious tea, which they proceeded to take turns to sip from.

Pamela leant forward. 'Silly me!' she said. 'I meant to buy a cup of coffee. Can't have been concentrating.' She pushed her teacup across the table towards the sisters. 'Can't take it back now, but I haven't touched it. Would one of you help me out?'

Another exchange of glances, and then one of the women accepted.

Pamela went back to the counter, purchased her coffee, and asked for some biscuits to be brought over.

'Good idea,' said Margery, when a waitress deposited a plate of digestives in front of them. 'I expect there'll be rationing before long. Might as well stock up whilst we can.' She seized a couple.

Pamela firmed her lips and slid the plate nearer to the sisters.

By eight o'clock the train had still not arrived. They'd eked out their refreshments for as long as they could, but the rattling of keys and the sound of cashing-up suggested the café owner was trying to close. They traipsed back to the empty gymnasium and stood talking in the chilling air.

The sisters were called Win and Dolly. They'd travelled up from Devon that morning.

'When we saw the notice in the newspaper, our hearts went out to those poor children,' said Dolly. 'We don't have much money, but we cashed in some National Savings Certificates to pay the guarantee and our train fare.' No wonder they had nothing left for food.

'We picked a little girl from the pictures Mr Winton sent us,' added Win, rummaging in her bag to show them the photo. 'Rebecca, she's called.'

Dolly's eyes misted over. 'We can't give her much. But she will be loved.'

Win took her sister's hand. 'Very much loved,' she confirmed.

Pamela smiled at the sisters and spoke in a voice that was suddenly hoarse. 'That's an admirable gesture,' she said.

'I'm sure the little girl, whenever she arrives, will be very happy with you.' She turned to Margery. 'But I really have to get off now. I've left Will with Miriam, but it isn't fair to expect him to babysit for too long. And Hugh won't be back for hours. Today of all days.'

'Of course,' said Margery. 'You go, dear. Win and Dolly can come back with me.' She brushed aside the sisters' protests. 'Nonsense. I insist. Cook will have a lovely roast dinner ready. And we've plenty of room.' She turned to Pamela. 'I'll let you know if I hear anything, but I wouldn't imagine the children will arrive until the morning now.'

The telephone remained silent all evening. Pamela finally went to bed around midnight, and Hugh stumbled in in the early hours. 'How was it?' she asked through a fog of sleep.

'Grim,' Hugh replied. 'You?'

'The train from Prague didn't arrive.' Her senses were sharper now and she propped herself up against the pillow, watching as Hugh struggled to take off his socks. Poor man, he was so tired he could barely function. 'I hate to bother you, darling, but could you make enquiries as to what has happened?'

Hugh grunted. 'It'll be the declaration. Communications have been all over the place all day. But I'll see what I can do. Two hundred and fifty children can't just have vanished.'

'Of course not,' replied Pamela, pummelling her pillow straight again. 'I'm sure everything will be fine.'

But why did she feel a lurch of dread as she turned over and tried to get to sleep?

13

Josef was hunched over the table, his back towards Eva, his fountain pen scratching across the paper.

'Your loving Abba and Mutti,' Eva intoned to the back of his head, where even his kippah perched reproachfully.

Josef paused to translate the words in his head, then committed them to paper in his black scrawl. He read the letter through silently, then slid it across the table for Eva to sign. He still hadn't turned round. His head remained bowed.

Once again Eva wished she knew English and could write to Miriam herself. What use was operatic Italian when you needed to tell your precious daughter how much you loved her? Miriam could only read and write a few words of Czech when she left for England, and although Mrs Denison had a smattering of Czech that she assured them she would use to help Miriam keep up her native language, it was English that she was taught at school. So it was Josef, with his scientist's familiarity with the language, who could write to her. Eva could only dictate the words she longed to put onto paper. Yet it was doubtful Miriam would be able to read the letter herself, not having been at school that long. Probably Mrs Denison would read it to her.

She took the letter from Josef and went to fetch an

envelope. At least she knew the address off by heart and could write that on her own: *32 Templewood Avenue, Hampstead, London.* She added a few kisses underneath her signature, then folded the letter and slid it into the envelope. Even paper was becoming scarce these days. They were down to their last ten sheets. Josef had to write with tiny pen strokes, and daren't make a mistake for fear of taking up too much space. She left the letter in the hall to post later.

Josef was still bent over the table, lost in thought, so Eva traipsed into the kitchen, where Mutti was chopping vegetables. Weak sunlight picked out the white threads in her hair. As usual, Abba was out wandering the streets. Each day when he returned, he looked older than the last.

Her mother held up a green-tinged potato. 'These are in a pretty poor state. I'm cutting out more than I put in.'

Eva grabbed a rubbery carrot and hacked off the fern-like leaves that sprouted from its head. 'The tops will give a bit more volume. And I won't peel it. Josef always says there are more nutrients in the skin than the flesh anyway.'

'Good idea. I wonder what Miriam is eating. I've heard they only have white bread in England.'

Eva tried to visualise Miriam sitting at a grand English dinner table. 'The family sounds quite wealthy. I expect she's spooning jam from a silver bowl.'

Mutti's tired face briefly lit up at the thought, then sagged again as she resumed cutting.

Eva put an arm round her mother's thin shoulders. 'Josef has written another letter.'

'Did he give her our love?'

'Of course.'

'I just hope it gets through. Now that Britain's joined the war, it's going to be much harder to send letters.'

Mutti nodded. 'We'll have to pray it reaches her. And that she is safe there.'

Eva rested her head against her mother's, trying to blot out the whistle of bombs and the screaming of children, the sounds that haunted her ears these days. 'I did do the right thing, didn't I, Mutti? I thought I was sending her to safety, but now I feel like I've thrown her into the lions' den.'

Mutti stroked her hair. 'You weren't to know Germany would take on Britain. At least it's an island. Much harder to occupy. I'm sure it's safer than most countries in Europe these days.'

'I still don't know if Josef will ever forgive me.' Eva sighed. 'I'm not sure I forgive myself.'

Mutti dislodged her gently, went over to the stove and tipped the vegetables into the pan. 'Abba and I pray for our little granddaughter every night,' she said. 'I know Adonai will keep her safe.'

'I hope you're right.' Eva reached into the cupboard to take out the soup bowls, and saw Miriam's little pink plate perched beside the adult versions. She'd meant to hide it away, but Mutti had stopped her. 'It'll be like we're pretending she never existed,' she'd said. 'We must leave all her things ready for when she comes back.'

So they'd kept her bedroom just as it was, left the little row of stuffed toys lined up on the windowsill, placed the rocking chair Abba had made in the corner of the room, arranged the tea set at the bottom of the bed. And either

Mutti or Eva popped in each day to make sure nothing was allowed to gather dust.

Without Miriam, life was just routine. There was no excitement, no purpose. Buoyed up by the joy and challenge of raising a child, Eva hadn't realised how humdrum her existence was below the surface: the cooking, cleaning, washing, ironing that defined her days. And wartime restrictions had made those tasks infinitely harder. But without Miriam, the tasks were chores, with no games, no stories, no play, no fun to imbue them with laughter.

Music had given her purpose once. Although that was a routine, and a strict one at that, there was the joy of discovering new melodies, new patterns; the quiet satisfaction of mastering a difficult piece, the triumph at sharing it with an appreciative audience. I had no idea this was how my life would be, she thought. Is there nothing left to give it meaning?

She'd found a battered old English textbook in a dusty bookshop in the Staré Město and had tried to teach herself the language. But the book was so old and the ideas expressed so irrelevant to her world that her progress was slow. What was the point in learning how to say 'Pardon me, but your postilion has been struck by lightning' when you wanted to ask your daughter whether she'd made friends at school, or how the Denisons were treating her, or whether she missed her poor Abba and Mutti? It was so frustrating.

Having to communicate through Josef felt like a punishment. He never ceased to remind her that she shouldn't have acted on her own initiative; she should have consulted him first before sending Miriam away – even though she insisted she had and it was his stubbornness and naïvety that had made her act as she did. There was frost between them for weeks; she doubted if it would ever thaw.

There was some bittersweet news, though. She'd bumped into Frau Golder in the street the other week, the mother who'd given her Mr Winton's contact details, and she had told Eva that the last train of children that should have been bound for England had never left the station. It was terrible for the poor parents, but Eva couldn't help but be relieved she'd sent Miriam out earlier. Despite Josef's still simmering disapproval, she was sure her daughter was safer in England, despite them now being at war, than she would have been in Prague.

Once the soup was cooking, and Mutti had gone back to her room for a lie-down, Eva went into the hall to fetch her basket and coat. Even a few precious minutes away from the hurt and condemnation in the house, a chance to be on her own, to breathe again, would do her good. 'I think I'll pop down to the post office now,' she called to Josef.

But he detained her. 'Leave that, *Liebling*. I can take it down later. I'd like to talk to you first.'

Eva took off her coat. Surely not another lecture? Hadn't he said enough? For once, though, it was not Miriam Josef wanted to talk about, but his work.

'Now that the antisera research is complete, I've received a new commission,' he told her, massaging his forehead.

'Oh?' Eva drew up a chair to join him at the table, still thinking about Miriam. She hoped this wouldn't take long. Lunch would be ready in an hour; she didn't want to wait until the afternoon post.

Josef rubbed the space between his eyes. 'I was happy to do the antisera work. I knew it would save lives, give people hope. Even though I was sponsored by the Nazis, I had a clear conscience. And I know this kept our family safe.' A sideways look of reproach.

Eva drew in a slow breath. She wouldn't allow herself to be provoked. 'So what's changed?'

Josef took off his watch in an almost unconscious gesture and fiddled with it. He didn't look at Eva. 'Even before the war started, the Nazis were manufacturing Pervitin.'

'Pervitin?'

'It's a methamphetamine-based drug. It helps users to stay awake. Gives them feelings of euphoria. Invincibility. The troops were given it when Hitler invaded Poland.' He put his watch back on again. 'It's probably what made them so powerful.'

Eva's attention sharpened. 'So the Germans conquered Poland *whilst on drugs*?'

Josef nodded.

'Bastards.'

He didn't even reprimand her. 'It was such a success that the Nazis want to produce it in vast quantities. They need thirty-five million tablets.'

'So where do you come in?'

'At the moment it's expensive and time-consuming to create. Dr Svoboda and I have been commissioned to research faster, cheaper methods of Pervitin production.'

'No, Josef, you can't! The Germans are not to be trusted. They are brutal and inhumane as it is . . .' She fought down the bile that rose in her throat. 'If you give them drugs they will become demonic!'

Josef looked at her through exhausted eyes. 'I know,

164

Liebling. But doesn't it say in the Torah that we are to help our enemies?'

'We're supposed to give them bread and water, yes. It'll heap live coals upon their heads. But not help them overpower us. There's nothing in the Torah that says that.'

Josef's head slumped. 'I know. I've been clutching at straws. Trying to find a way to square this with my conscience. But I'll have to say no and face the consequences.'

Eva shuddered. Those consequences could be terrible. Maybe she had done the right thing sending Miriam away after all. 'Isn't there anything else you could do?'

The watch was off again. Josef wound the strap round his fingers. 'There's talk of some work with hydrogen cyanide. The Nazis want to develop it as a humane killer for vermin. A pesticide, I think. So we can be more efficient at crop production.' He looked a little evasive.

'Well, surely that's something positive,' Eva said.

'Yes. It's highly toxic, of course. But we should be able to find a way to work with it safely.'

'Well, isn't that your answer?'

Again Josef wouldn't look her in the eye. 'Yes, I'll see if I can persuade them to put me on that.'

Eva gently took the watch from his hands. 'I understand what it's like to have a torn conscience,' she said. 'Believe me, I struggled with myself for weeks trying to decide whether to send Miriam away or not.'

Josef stiffened. 'That's why you should have discussed it with me.'

'But you were so adamant. So determined that your work protected us all.' Eva covered Josef's fingers with her own.

165

'Now it seems we are all vulnerable. I did what I thought was best, Josef.'

For once he didn't turn away, or stand up, or argue with her. He just said, very sadly, 'I know.'

And somehow that hurt more than anything.

14

'Miriam! Letter.' Pamela opened Miriam's bedroom door, releasing that indefinable little-girl scent, so different from the boyish earthiness of Will's room, and peered in. The cream candlewick bedspread was carefully smoothed, the little pink brush and comb she'd bought her lined up on the dressing table, her linen nightdress tidily folded on the wicker bedside chair. But no Miriam. Pamela paused to look at the small pile of books piled by the bed. *Peter Rabbit*, *The Story of Barbar*, *The Enchanted Wood*. She was reading them to Miriam each night, although recently the little girl had started to read the first couple of paragraphs herself, her little forefinger with its chewed fingernail stabbing at the words, pronouncing them carefully in barely accented English.

Hugh's mutterings about sending her to Hinton Hall still hadn't come to anything. Officially they'd been at war for nearly a year now. Tea had just started to be rationed, much to Kitty's disgust, but other than that, little had changed in Hampstead. Thank God the Germans had left them alone so far. There was no reason to send Miriam away.

Others had been less lucky. There was still no news of what had happened to the last train from Prague. Win and Dolly had departed tearfully back to Devon without the child they'd longed to love, and the refugee committee had

167

reluctantly disbanded, with access to Europe now effectively shut off. Hugh had tried to track the children down, but with no success. 'No one knows what's happened to them. It was just their bad luck they were due to leave the day war was announced between us and Germany.' Pamela had been horrified. No matter that over six hundred children had been rescued; it was the loss of the two hundred and fifty that would always haunt her. Thank God Miriam had arrived safely. She tried to concentrate on Miriam and blot out the terrible speculations about the others.

'Ah, that's where you are.' She flung open the kitchen door to find Miriam sitting on a small stool, a slightly battered Lilli beside her as usual, helping Kitty make gingerbread at the kitchen table. Her face was flushed, and a few blobs of ginger-bread mixture hung in the tendrils of hair that had escaped her long plaits. 'Kitty, isn't that our sugar ration?'

'Yes, ma'am. I've been saving it up. Neither of us takes sugar in our tea, and without Master Will and Mr Denison around to have their usual three spoonfuls each – not that there's much tea to offer these days – I've managed to put some by.'

Pamela laughed. 'Fair enough. And Miriam does love her gingerbread.' She stepped forward to tease the sticky globules from the child's hair.

Miriam was squashing the dough in her chubby hand, flat-tening it out on the flour-covered table and carving little shapes in it with a blunt knife. Kitty was greasing a large tray with smears of precious butter.

Pamela drew up a chair. 'Do you want to open your letter, Miriam?'

Miriam shook her head and carried on with her carving.

'Come on, missy,' said Kitty. 'This lot needs to go in the oven.' She prised Miriam's handiwork from the table, ignoring her wail of protest, and placed the shapes on the tray. Only a small gluey ball remained. As Kitty turned to slide the tray into the oven, Miriam popped it into her mouth. Her little face grew even more flushed.

'Wash your hands, Miriam,' said Pamela, lifting her off the stool and carrying her towards the sink. She clutched Miriam round the waist with one hand, supporting her weight on her raised knee, and turned on the tap with the other, then pushed Miriam's fingers under the running water. Gosh, the child was heavy. She'd grown so much in the last few months. She set her back down on the floor with a grunt of relief and went to fetch the towel.

Miriam sat down again and Pamela joined her, handing her the towel so she could dry her hands. Kitty was scrubbing at the residual stickiness on the table and piling bowls and knives into the sink. The first wafts of ginger sweetness drifted out from the oven.

Pamela handed Miriam the letter and Miriam opened it silently. She drew out a single sheet of thin paper, covered in immaculate copperplate, and handed it to Pamela. 'You read it, please.'

Miriam was coming on well with printed words in books, but her father's dense handwriting confounded her. Even Pamela found it hard to decipher sometimes. 'My darling child,' she began. It would be a relief when Miriam could read her own letters. It was very hard to hold back the tears when her parents' distress was so evident between the lines. 'I hope you are being a good girl and not getting in the way of Mr and Mrs Denison.' Pamela looked at Miriam over the paper. 'Of course you're not getting in the way, are you, dear?'

Miriam shook her head. The plaits made a pendulum motion.

'We are very busy here. Oma and Opa are still with us and send their love. Mutti keeps us all well fed, although there is little food in the shops now. I am working hard at the Institute.' Pamela knew that Miriam's father was a scientist. She wondered what kind of research he was involved with. But it was Eva her heart heaved for. Miriam's father obviously didn't want to worry his daughter, but Prague had been occupied for seventeen months now. Food stocks must be severely depleted. It would be very hard for the woman to feed the four of them. Miriam had never mentioned a Czech version of Kitty; Eva must have to do everything herself. Pamela reached out to push the wisps of escaped hair back behind Miriam's ears. All she could do was take very good care of the poor woman's daughter. And pray to God that she could return her safe when the time came. She'd miss her dreadfully, of course, but she had her own child; it wasn't fair to keep another's.

The rest of the letter was desultory. Little snippets of news about the neighbours, visits to the synagogue, a book he was reading, the neighbourhood cat. Pamela imagined the poor man casting about for acceptable titbits to pass on to his daughter, when probably what he really wanted to write was: 'Life is dreadful, we miss you horribly.' She read out the daughters' blessing that he ended every letter with. She knew it by heart now.

When they'd first taken Miriam on, she and Hugh discussed what they should do about the child's Jewishness. Margery had told her that some rabbis had been to Nicholas Winton one day to complain that the child refugees were being sent to Christian families. Winton's response had been terse: 'If you prefer a dead Jew in Prague to a live one being brought up in a Christian home, that's your problem not mine.' He'd never heard from them again.

Pamela had been careful not to serve her pork to eat, not that there was much in the shops anyway, and she and Hugh had taken her to a Quaker meeting one Sunday soon after she'd arrived, but the child had fidgeted throughout the service and the following week they'd left her with Kitty. It had occurred to her to ask the Segals down the road if they would take her to their synagogue, but she didn't want to trouble them. The Kolischers' letters hadn't contained any request to provide for the child's faith. A few months in a whole lifetime wouldn't hurt, and she could recommence her Jewish education once she was back in Prague. That would have to do.

That night, Pamela couldn't sleep. When Hugh rolled in at two o'clock, she was still awake. Churchill had taken over from Chamberlain that May and was demanding meetings at all hours of the day and night. 'The man never rests,' Hugh growled. 'So we can't either.' He was snoring within minutes.

Pamela must have drifted off around three, but was woken by a particularly ear-splitting snore. The room was full of loud popping sounds. She sat bolt upright, ready to prod Hugh, then realised there were lights too. Sudden flares that lit up the room, then instantly vanished.

The siren started wailing and her stomach swooped. 'It's a raid,' she yelled. Hugh was struggling to surface from deep layers of sleep. 'We're being bombed.' Pamela's heart thrummed in her chest.

Hugh shot up, but Pamela was already on her feet, delving into the wardrobe for the box of emergency supplies she'd assembled the previous autumn: biscuits, a torch, a flask of water, a pack of playing cards. She reached for her dressing gown from the hook on the door and threw Hugh's across to him.

'I'll get Miriam up. Kitty's at her mother's.' Thank God Will was at school.

Hugh nodded, his hair a brush in the dim light, his face folded in on itself with exhaustion.

Pamela tiptoed into Miriam's room. She felt a pang of guilt as she saw the little girl's dark hair across the pillow, heard the gentle rise and fall of her breath. Her thumb was jammed in her mouth as usual. Pamela stroked her face. 'Miriam, dear.'

No response.

The alarm was more insistent now, the sound pulsing through the darkness. Then came the boom of a huge explosion. Pamela scooped Miriam into her arms, ran onto the landing and lugged her down the two flights of stairs as fast as she could.

Hugh was already in the basement, dragging two old armchairs they'd consigned there years ago across the floor.

'Here, give her to me,' he said, and Pamela passed the child across. Hugh grabbed her and slumped into one of the chairs with Miriam on his lap. She curled up, still half asleep, sucking furiously at her thumb. Pamela sped back to get the box of supplies, ignoring Hugh's protests that it would be safer to stay where she was. She retrieved the box from the bedroom floor and made her descent again, pausing briefly at the kitchen door before deciding not to bother making tea. She'd delayed taking shelter long enough.

When she returned for a second time, Hugh had his head tipped back, staring at the ceiling, and Miriam was fast asleep. Pamela grabbed a blanket from her box and made a little nest with it on the floor. She took a cushion from the other chair and placed it on the blanket. Then she scooped Miriam from Hugh's lap and laid her gently on the makeshift bed. Miriam stirred, wriggled a bit, then went back to sleep. Pamela breathed out slowly.

Down in the basement, the sounds were muted, the noise of the bombing stifled by the thick Edwardian walls. Nearby, the boiler rumbled and a water pipe groaned. The air was thick and stagnant; the room dank, cave-like.

'Do you know how long it will go on for?' Pamela whispered.

Hugh shrugged. 'No idea. We've got off lightly so far. Probably our turn now.' The whiteness of his face belied the casual tone of his words. Pamela felt the hot rush of adrenalin. She thanked God again that Will was at school.

As she shut her eyes, a vision flashed in of her teenage self watching a Zeppelin hanging in the air, making a terrible throbbing sound. A boy with a bugle had cycled through the streets warning them of its approach. As Pamela gazed through her window, the Zeppelin had caught fire, triggering a huge cheer from those still outside. The great whoosh of flame lit up the night sky until it was as radiant as day. Then the great white ball slowly crumpled and sank down to earth. She had hated fires ever since.

She was determined to shut out the other memories. The eager faces of Tommy's friends as they'd marched off to war. The haunted eyes of their mothers when they'd failed to return. All the dead. All the grief. Please God, not again.

She shifted in the other armchair. Without the cushion to soften it, the back was digging into her. Thank goodness Miriam was asleep. It was amazing how the child could switch off from what was going on around her. Perhaps she'd learnt that in Prague. Pamela wondered what horrors she'd seen there. What would her parents say when they realised their only child was sheltering from a bomb attack with the very people who'd offered to protect her?

She made a decision. 'Hugh.'

'Mmm?' Hugh had his eyes closed.

'I think you're right. We can't allow Miriam to stay here. The Germans could keep this up for weeks. It's not safe. It would be irresponsible when she's been entrusted to our care.'

Hugh was looking at her intently now.

'Let's send her to Hinton Hall as you suggested. She'll be out of danger there. And surrounded by other Czechs, people who know her language and culture. The Germans won't bother with the countryside. It's the towns they want to destroy.' Will was safe in Marlborough for the same reason. They'd have to tell him not to come home for his next exeat.

Hugh nodded. 'You'll need to arrange transport for her.'

'I'll see to it in the morning.' Outside, a high-pitched whistling sound was followed by several loud bangs. Pamela winced and shifted again in the chair. It was going to be a long and terrible night.

15

Eva wandered disconsolately around the market square. Three years ago she'd come here with Miriam when the air was alive with the blare of the oompah band, the cry of traders, the odour of pickles and onions. Now it was a ghost of its former self. Ramshackle stalls, bereft of produce to weigh them down, swayed in the wind, their wooden struts weathered and discoloured. A few defiant traders, blowing on their fingers to keep warm, presided over half-empty barrels of bruised apples or earth-encrusted turnips. A gust of wind sent an empty paper bag cartwheeling along the ground.

Eva went up to a stallholder standing in front of a crate of rubbery-looking parsnips. She plunged her hand into the pile to see if there were fresher ones underneath, ignoring the man's scowl, and drew out a couple that looked almost edible.

'Thirty heller,' the man demanded. He avoided her eyes.

'That's outrageous,' said Eva. 'Here . . .' She dropped a couple of coins into his grubby palm. 'I'll give you twenty, no more.'

The stallholder glowered but nodded. Eva put the parsnips into her basket. If she could get some onions, she could make vegetable stew that evening. No hope of any meat, but she still had a little salt that would give it some flavour.

But she hadn't come here just to buy vegetables. She was really looking for a present for Miriam. Her daughter would be seven soon. How Eva longed to buy her a doll's house, with little pink shutters and tiny wooden beds. What fun Miriam would have examining all the rooms, dressing the small figures, sitting them at the table to eat miniature food made from clay, pestering Mutti to help her make doll's clothes. Eva could almost imagine her daughter's voice as she acted out conversations between the characters. Last year Abba had managed to get some wood and had carved Miriam a beautiful hobby horse. Mutti had made the head and reins from leftover scraps of material and Josef had come up with a pair of little wheels to fasten to the end. But the horse had spent all year propped up behind the door of Miriam's old bedroom, waiting for a rider who never arrived. Even if there were a doll's house to join it, what were the chances of Miriam ever coming back to play with her toys? Or still being young enough to enjoy them if she did?

Eva trudged over to a stall near the centre of the square. There was a long queue of people in front of it. Perhaps there'd been a new delivery. But as she drew closer, she realised it wasn't food that was displayed on the large table but an assortment of household objects: broken crockery, a few tawdry necklaces and a couple of small paintings with mildewed corners.

She couldn't imagine what people would want with any of those things, but decided to queue anyway. Perhaps she'd get Miriam one of the necklaces. It might make her feel more grown up. And perhaps Eva could find a way of posting such a small item to England.

When she joined the end of the line, the person in front of her, a middle-aged woman with salt-and-pepper hair and deep brown eyes, turned round and smiled.

'What have you got your eye on?'

Eva smiled back. 'It's my daughter's birthday soon. I thought I might get her one of the necklaces.'

The woman craned her neck to see the items on the stall. 'That green one is pretty.'

'Yes, it is. Let's hope someone doesn't buy it first.'

'I'm sure you'll find something.'

Eva shrugged. 'It seems strange that this is the most popular stall when there's nothing to eat.'

The woman laughed. 'Yes. You can't make meals from china and metal. But perhaps when there are pretty things around, life becomes a bit more bearable.'

'Perhaps.' But Eva didn't need things. It was only music that made life bearable. And there hadn't been much of that since she'd sold the piano.

The woman shuffled forward as a man left the front of the queue clutching a battered old book.

'I wonder where all these goods came from,' Eva mused.

'Oh, haven't you heard? They are mostly from empty houses. Jews who've been sent off on the transports. No matter how carefully they secure their property, people get in, take anything they fancy, then sell it on.'

Eva froze in horror. 'How can people be so heartless?'

The woman shrugged. 'Those Jews'll never be back for their belongings. Might as well be of use to others.'

Nausea surged up Eva's body. She nodded at the woman. 'You buy the necklace,' she said. 'It's a bit tarnished for me.'

178

Then she strode away quickly before she could hear the reply.

*

Will scrawled his name in the battered exercise book on the hall table, pushed against the heavy front door and walked briskly down the college drive and into the Pewsey road. Luckily the high street wasn't far away; he didn't need to catch a bus into town. He had a pass for the afternoon and a couple of coins in his pocket, the result of some careful economies with his allowance, and he was determined to buy a present for Miriam for her birthday. He knew it wasn't for a while but if the bigger plan he had in mind paid off he may not see her again for months.

He'd been teaching her to play snap on his exeats with some old playing cards, and she'd picked it up quickly. One time, he'd shuffled the cards after a game and laid a few on the table. 'See that black shape there, Miriam? It's called a spade.'

'Spide,' she said.

'No, not spide, sp-a-de.' He drew out the long 'a' in the middle.

'Spade,' said Miriam. And grinned.

'Well done.' Will took out a club, a heart and a couple of diamonds, repeating the words carefully and receiving a near-perfect imitation in response.

Mother said Miriam had a musical ear; she certainly listened carefully, and her English was coming on really well.

He turned into the high street and looked at the spread of

shops in front of him. Perhaps he'd get Miriam a game. Something more sophisticated than snap. She'd enjoy playing a board game with him, and it would be a good way of increasing her vocabulary. He found the toy shop halfway down the street and opened the door, triggering a jaunty ring from the bell and an even jauntier 'Good afternoon, sir' from the shopkeeper, who was standing behind the counter doodling on a pad. 'What can I do for you?'

'I'm looking for a game.' Will glanced round the shop, noting the empty shelves, the faded covers of the books, the dusty-looking puzzle boxes. 'These toys are new, I take it?'

The shopkeeper laughed, a little hollowly, Will thought. 'As new as we can get them. There's a shortage of toys these days, like everything else. And people are too busy trying to fill their children's stomachs with food to worry about buying them games.'

'Of course.' Will cleared his throat. 'Nevertheless, I take it you do have some games for sale.'

'Indeed I do.' The shopkeeper emerged from behind the counter and led him over to a shelf where a few boxes were lined up. 'There's Monopoly, Ludo, snakes and ladders . . .'

Will frowned. Monopoly was too difficult, and they had snakes and ladders at home already. But Ludo might be fun. 'I'll take this one, please,' he said, carefully removing the box, which was vivid with primary colours. *Suitable for ages 6 and above*, it said. Perfect.

'Right you are, sir. That'll be a shilling.'

Will handed over one of his coins. The man wrapped the box in newspaper and passed it over. Will nodded his thanks and exited the shop. Now he could spend the rest of his time seeing if he could track down some black jacks and sherbet dabs to restock his tuck box. He'd loved those sweets since he was a boy. But the decision he'd made recently would turn him into a man.

If he was successful, he would never be going back to school.

*

Miriam dipped a spoon into the pot of sticky sweetness, turning it to catch the drops, then held it over her bread until the thick liquid streamed down and spread to a golden puddle. She folded the bread up, and crammed it into her mouth. The bread was as tasteless as ever, but then the honey reached her tongue and she closed her eyes at the blissful surge of sugar.

'Come on, Miriam.' Vera nudged her with a sharp elbow. Vera had escaped Czechoslovakia in a suitcase. Her parents had carried her across the border to safety. Perhaps all those hours of having to hold her limbs still had made her more free with them now. Miriam passed the pot on reluctantly, and Vera plunged her spoon in.

The barrel of honey had come all the way from Buckingham Palace. 'Aren't you lucky?' said Pan Čapek, the headmaster. 'This was a present from the Argentine government, but the royal children insisted it was sent straight on to you.' Miriam imagined the English princesses in their golden crowns and long sparkly dresses packing up the honey to send to Hinton Hall. How kind they were.

Miriam loved being with other Czech children at the school,

181

and it was wonderful to speak her own language again. At night, in the dormitory, they'd whisper their stories. One of the other girls told her about little Rene, who'd crossed the Pyrenees on foot with his mother. A border patrol had spotted and killed their companions, but Rene's mother told him to lie still and pretend to be a rock. By creeping and hiding they'd eventually managed to get away to safety.

Most of the children had accounts of escape and rescue. Miriam's own experience had been quite ordinary in comparison to some. But after a while they stopped talking about the past. The teachers were kind, the beds were soft, the lessons were fun, and apart from the odd letter from their parents, reminding them how lucky they were to have escaped, they just enjoyed being together.

She tried to put all worries about Mutti and Abba to the back of her mind. She still missed them terribly, but the only way to cope was to avoid thinking about them too much. Although concern about the recent lack of letters was beginning to gnaw through her well-constructed defences. Perhaps they'd sent a letter to Hampstead by mistake and Mrs Denison had forgotten to send it on. She hoped something would arrive soon.

Their first lesson of the day was singing, Miriam's favourite. There was a rumour that a very important man was coming to see them, and they were practising Czech songs to welcome him.

'Poor President Beneš, having to flee his country like that,' said Paní Černý, their music teacher, pushing back the wisp of hair that always escaped her bun. 'We must make sure we sing all the songs beautifully, to cheer him up.'

Miriam didn't need telling. Mutti had taught her that she should always sing her best, regardless of whether anyone was listening. She joined the other children standing in rows at the back of the room, making sure she was as far away as possible from fat Ester Hirsch, who droned like an old tractor.

Paní Černý sat down at the piano and adjusted a manuscript that was propped up on the metal rest. '"Okolo Třeboně",' she called out, playing a G major chord. 'Go.'

Miriam straightened her back as Mutti had instructed her, and took a deep breath right from her stomach, until her chest felt huge with air. Mutti had taught her this song; she knew it well. The first notes slipped out of her as sweet and smooth as the honey she'd eaten for breakfast. Olga and Hana, either side of her, were singing beautifully, and she felt Hans Becker's breath on the back of her neck as his voice rang out behind her. The familiar folk melody surged like waves on the sea, and Miriam felt wrapped in a warm swell of voices. Apart from a distant rumbling from Ester further down the row, they performed the song well.

'Keep singing.' Paní Černý abandoned the piano and walked down the rows of children, inclining her head to hear each of them sing a cappella. When she got to Ester, she firmed her lips but said nothing. Miriam tried to make her own voice soar as the teacher approached. Paní Černý stopped in front of her, the wisp of hair lifting in the breeze of their voices, then smiled and walked on.

At the end of the lesson, the teacher kept Miriam behind. 'Would you like to sing a solo in front of President Beneš?' she said.

'Yes, please!'

The teacher laughed. 'Good girl. Come back after lessons and you can practise.'

Miriam hugged herself as she left the room. A solo in front of their president. How wonderful. But deep in her tummy she felt hollow. How she wished she could see her family in the audience as she sang, to catch Mutti's eye, to glimpse Abba's proud smile, to watch Oma and Opa mouthing the words and beaming at her. Her first solo and no one from home to hear it. She must draw a picture of herself singing at the concert. If her family couldn't be here for real she would make sure they could see what everything looked like.

She practised every evening for the next few weeks, going over the song again and again until every note was perfect. She sang as she explored the meadows and fields around the school, or paddled in the pond, filling the air with the sweetest sounds she could make. She sang in the weekly bath they were allowed, enjoying the sound her voice made echoing round the steam-filled room. She went through the words in her head as she drifted off to sleep. Even if Mutti couldn't be there to hear her, she would still make her proud.

When Miriam stepped forward to sing her solo, her legs felt spindly. She was amazed she'd managed to get to the front of the stage without falling over, but as soon as Paní Černý started to play, she forgot her nerves. The music was so joyous she wanted her voice to follow it for ever, up and down, light and bright and full of happiness. And when she heard the applause, she realised that other people were happy too.

After the concert, Miriam was invited to sit next to Mr Beneš whilst he had tea in the staffroom. Apparently he'd asked for her specially. He had long strands of hair combed across the back of his head and little thin bits in front, like a baby's. His moustache was the same shape as Herr Hitler's in a picture she'd seen of him, except it was grey not black. His eyebrows were thick and dark, but underneath he had friendly brown eyes.

'Where did you learn to sing like that, my dear?'

'My mother taught me.'

Mr Beneš took a sip of his tea. 'Is she a singer too?'

'No, she played the piano. Before I was born.'

'You must miss her and your father very much.' A drop of brown tea clung to Mr Beneš' moustache. He brushed it off with the back of his hand.

'I do. But we write often. Except . . .' Miriam wiped her palms across her skirt, 'I haven't had a letter for a long time.' Perhaps Abba was too busy working, or Mutti too tired from trying to find food for them all. Last time he'd written, Abba had told her that Šťastný, the neighbourhood cat, was about to have kittens. They must have been born by now.

Mr Beneš was looking out of the window. When he turned back to her, his face was sad. 'It is a very difficult time for the Czech people. I wish I could do more to help.'

'Can you go and see my parents to ask why they haven't written to me about the kittens?'

Mr Beneš sighed. 'I wish I could, but I'm afraid the Germans will not let me back into Prague. I have to live in London until the war is over.' He paused and took another sip of tea. 'But if you like, I will try to make enquiries.' He opened his jacket and patted the inside pocket before drawing out a pencil and a small notebook, which he passed across to Miriam. 'Write your parents' names and address here and I'll see what I can do.'

Miriam took the pad and balanced it on her knee. *Josef and Eva Kolischer*, she wrote carefully, *18a Maiselova, Praha 1, Československo*, then passed it back.

Mr Beneš tucked the pen and pad back inside his pocket and smiled at her. 'I'll do my best, little songbird.'

Two weeks later, a letter and birthday card arrived from her parents. They were well, and so were the kittens.

*

Pamela propped the hastily scrawled instructions against the flour canister and read the list of ingredients. 'Cauliflower, parsnips, carrots . . .' Thank goodness Kitty had been to the greengrocer's that morning and brought back a plentiful supply of vegetables. And thank goodness they hadn't yet been rationed. Many women were growing their own food now, digging up lawns and flower beds to plant root crops, but Pamela doubted much would flourish in their little town-house garden. As long as the shops still had enough produce, it was easier to buy what she needed. She'd planted a few herbs in window boxes, much to Hugh's amusement, but that was her only attempt at self-sufficiency. She reached for the bunch of parsley she'd just picked and buried her nose in it, savouring the fresh, grassy smell. At least there was something home-grown to put in the pie.

She consulted her sheet again and started to break up the head of cauliflower, enjoying the satisfying crack at each severance. The florets looked like miniature white trees as they lay on the tea towel. A felling of arboreal ghosts. She went to throw the woodier stalks in the rubbish bin, then stopped herself. Waste not, want not. She grabbed a knife and chopped them up.

Kitty had the afternoon off and Pamela had decided to cook as a surprise for Hugh. They'd been to the Savoy last week with the American ambassador, and the chef had served the pie there. It had been delicious: chopped cauliflower, parsnips and carrots in a strangely meaty sauce. When she'd asked the waiter for the ingredients, Monsieur Latry had appeared personally and delivered the hastily written-out recipe to Pamela with a bow. 'How did you make that sauce taste so lovely?' she'd asked. 'Brandy, red wine?' The chef had given a Gallic shrug and pointed at one of the ingredients on the list. 'Marmite,' she'd read out loud. Hugh had laughed.

She stripped a carrot of its skin in one spiral and laid it down ready to chop later. It was nice to do something methodical for a change. She'd spent too many hours lately trying to think what to write to Will and Miriam, constructing letters that made the dull routine of her life sound carefree and exciting, or popping down to her parents to check that the incessant air raids hadn't gnawed at their already raw nerves any further. They'd had it bad in the East End, having to decamp to the air-raid shelter in the Whitechapel Road night after night, and some of their friends had even had their houses destroyed. Pamela had tried to persuade them to live with her and Hugh, at least for a while – they had plenty of room and didn't have to share their basement with anyone else – but her father was adamant he wasn't going to leave his home, and Pamela knew better than to oppose his stubbornness.

At night, as she lay in the darkness listening for whistles and sirens, she composed endless messages to her family, her mind on a permanent loop. Words were so tiring. How soothing to concentrate all one's efforts into peeling, chopping and mixing. But it was selfish of her to stay at home. Her Quaker values forbade her from getting involved in the armed services or any direct war work. She had to find other useful refugee work she could do.

She reached into one of the cupboards, pushing aside a tin of powdered custard, a can of marrowfat peas and a packet of salt, until her fingers closed on the distinctive black jar. It had been Will's favourite as a young child. Kitty used to spread it on toasted bread that dripped with butter and cut it into soldiers. By the end of the meal, Will's mouth would be circled with brown and his breath yeasty. He hated having his mouth wiped with a flannel; no matter how hard she tried to distract him, he'd see it coming and duck his head at the last moment. She always packed a jar of Marmite in his school trunk. Last term he'd gone off with one of Hugh's razors too, keen to initiate himself in the ritual of shaving. How strange that men who spent their boyhoods avoiding having their faces wiped would spend their adulthood sawing and scraping at their skin to eliminate every stray bristle.

Will had eventually agreed to stay on at Marlborough for an extra term to study for Oxford. He brought piles of books home each exeat, but Pamela had caught him more than once fiddling with model planes when he should have been revising.

She fervently hoped the war would be over before he started his degree.

She pulled down a saucepan from the rack above the stove and half filled it with water before tipping in the vegetables and adding a couple of teaspoons of Marmite. She'd make the pastry while the stock boiled. There was some mashed potato in the larder left over from last night's supper, so all she had to do was mix the flour and dripping.

She began rubbing in the fat with her fingertips as she had as a child. 'Cool hands make good pastry,' her mother used to say, wiping her own red hands on a towel and motioning to Pamela to take over. There was an art to making pastry, lifting the flour above the bowl and letting it fall to make it light and airy, pressing out the lumps between thumb and forefinger as you did so, until the mixture stopped looking glutinous and began to resemble fine breadcrumbs.

The stock began to bubble on the stove, its steam sealing the windows and imbuing the air with an earthy smell. It was cosy in the kitchen. Pamela scraped the blunt side of a knife down each finger to remove the last vestiges of sticky flour, then reached out to switch on the wireless. The Andrews sisters' voices joined the choir of culinary sounds. She ran her hands under the tap and went to fetch the bowl of mashed potato from the larder.

At first she didn't notice the telephone ringing, there were so many other noises, but something intuitive caused her to push open the kitchen door, listen for a second, then dash into the hall to pick up the receiver.

'Hampstead 4529,' she replied, a little breathlessly, wiping her hands down her apron as if the caller was inspecting her for tidiness.

'Mrs Denison?'

'Yes.'

'Francis Heywood here.'

'Oh.' Will's headmaster. Why ever was he calling her? She collected herself. 'Is anything the matter?'

'I just wondered if William was with you?'

Something jumped deep in Pamela's stomach. 'No. Isn't he at school?'

She could almost hear the frown coming down the line. 'We haven't seen him since luncheon. He missed rugby practice this afternoon and wasn't in his prep session afterwards. His belongings are still in his dormitory but William himself appears to be missing.'

'Oh dear. I'm so sorry.' Pamela swallowed down a surge of nausea. 'I'll contact my husband and see if he knows anything.'

'Yes, please do. I hope to speak to you again shortly.' There was a click followed by a dull buzzing sound. She replaced the receiver.

But a rather brusque Hugh, clearly annoyed at being summoned from a meeting, didn't know anything either. 'Probably some boyish jape,' he said. 'Let me know when you hear from him.'

'Of course,' replied Pamela, trying to keep her voice steady. 'I'll contact you straight away.'

Mr Heywood's secretary said much the same thing. Pamela returned to her baking with a heavy heart.

*

190

They ate the pie in silence. Pamela feared that even the sound of Hugh rolling the doughy pastry around his mouth, with a slightly martyred expression, would be too loud for them to hear the telephone or the doorbell. Her mother had been right. After Mr Heywood's call, anxiety had flooded her body with heat and her sweaty hands had ruined the pastry, and even though she'd carried on making the pie in a daze, her thoughts were elsewhere. The resultant creation was bland and flabby, nothing like the crisp, buttery crust of Monsieur Latry's famous dish. Not that it mattered any more. All that mattered was finding Will.

As soon as she had got off the phone from the headmaster, she'd telephoned all Will's friends' mothers to see if they knew anything. They'd called the school back a couple more times, but no one could give them any information. In the end, they crept into bed and lay rigid in the darkness, neither wanting to admit their wakefulness to the other.

Hugh left early for Whitehall. When Pamela glanced at his face as he put on his shirt in the half-light, it was pale with exhaustion, a film of pink across one eye.

'I'll let you know the minute I hear anything,' she said.

Hugh just nodded, slipped on his jacket and left.

Pamela stumbled out of bed and trudged over to the window. She'd been too distracted last night to hang up her clothes so had just dropped them on the chaise longue that lay in the recess. She picked them up now and stepped into her girdle. She had a couple of old corsets in her drawer but hardly wore them. The garment factories had stopped making new corsets – the steel was needed for the war – and anyway girdles were much more comfortable. Mind you, there was a rumour that rubber would soon be rationed; she might have to make the girdle last a long time. She drew on some stockings, did up her brassière, then dropped her slip over her head. Finally she pulled on her green blouse and skirt and did them up quickly. No need for make-up today; she didn't intend to go anywhere. Even if she had a car, they didn't have the petrol for her to drive round looking for Will as she longed to do. She felt so helpless staying at home.

Kitty had let herself in earlier that morning and was already in the kitchen making breakfast.

'Morning, Kitty.'

'Good morning, Mrs Denison.'

Pamela looked at the still full plate of toast on the kitchen table. 'Did Mr Denison not want his breakfast?'

Kitty firmed her lips. 'Wouldn't have a bite. Just a gulp of tea and then he rushed off.'

'Oh dear.' Pamela's legs felt as though they might buckle. She sat down and told Kitty about Will.

'He'll be back when he's hungry,' said Kitty, pouring Pamela a cup of tea and adding a heaped teaspoon of sugar from their dwindling stock. 'Would you like me to fetch that into the dining room for you?'

Pamela rubbed her eyes. Her legs still felt too fragile to support her. 'Do you know, I think I'll take breakfast here.'

Kitty slid the plate of toast towards her. 'Right you are.'

The hours dragged on. Hours of trying to write to Miriam. Attempting to force down bloater paste sandwiches with a dry throat, racking her brains for any more of Will's other friends' parents to call, walking past the telephone again and again, willing it to ring. Her feelings swung between anxiety and anger. Had he run away to get out of his Oxford exam? Or to visit a girl somewhere? Was he lost and frightened? How on earth could he do this to them?

By five she was dozing in the sitting room, exhausted by a day and night of anxiety. But she shot out of her chair when the front door clicked. Too early for Hugh, and anyone else would knock. Could it be . . .? She ran out into the hall, and there was a triumphant-looking Will, already taller and broader than a few weeks ago, rubbing his fingers through his hair, his face flushed, his eyes shining.

'Kitty! He's back.' Pamela threw the words over her shoulder, then rushed to embrace her son, grasping the solid warmth of him and inhaling the reassuring smell of hair oil and cologne.

Kitty bustled out of the kitchen with a plate of sandwiches in her hand. 'Good evening, Master Will. You've given your parents quite a shock.'

Will released Pamela gently and nodded. He motioned to her to precede him into the sitting room, and Kitty deposited the plate in front of him.

'I'm sorry, Mother,' he said, reaching for a sandwich.

Pamela tried to look furious, but the relief was too strong. 'The school telephoned me yesterday afternoon. We've been out of our minds with worry.'

'I know. I'm sorry. I couldn't tell you beforehand; I knew you'd try and stop me.'

Something icy crept up Pamela's spine. 'Stop you doing what?'

Will sighed and put down his sandwich. 'I've been to Boscombe Down. I walked there last night from school. Slept in a barn overnight, then joined up first thing this morning.'

Two words bored into Pamela's brain. 'Joined . . . up?'

Will nodded. 'I'm sorry, Mother. But I'm in the Royal Air Force. I passed the medical yesterday.' He swallowed. 'I'm now a pilot under training.'

Blood pounded in Pamela's ears. 'No! Will, you can't be. You know how we feel about war. What about school? What about Oxford?'

'They're for kids.' Will kicked at the edge of the rug in front of him. 'I couldn't stay on at school when boys my age are fighting for their country. The guilt and frustration was eating me up. I had to do something.'

'No, you didn't! We're *Quakers*, Will. If you really wanted to do something, you could have driven an ambulance.'

Will's face was red. 'Or carried stretchers like Uncle Tommy and ended up being shot anyway. What's the difference? At least this way I'm not a coward.'

Pamela was on her feet. 'My brother was *not* a coward! Have you any idea what courage it took to be a conchie when you got spat at every day, when your parents' garden was ransacked each night? When your own mother opened her front door to find human excrement on the doorstep?'

Will rubbed the space between his eyes. 'I'm sorry. You're right. Uncle Tommy was brave. You all were.' He stood up too and put his arm round her. 'But I have to take a different path.'

Pamela lowered herself back down into her chair, covered

194

her face and spoke through her hands. She was horrified that Will wanted to fight when all his life he'd been taught the values of peacemaking. 'Wait until your father hears about this,' she said wearily.

16

In the brightly lit laboratory, Josef, wearing a stained and hole-ridden lab coat, was setting up equipment. He lined up a test tube, a syringe and a pipette on the polished dark wood of the lab bench. The test tube rolled slightly out of line so he straightened it, briefly admiring the precision of the arrangement. Then he selected a couple of round-bottomed flasks from the shelf behind him and placed them parallel to the other items. Finally he greased two rubber stoppers. It was important they fitted tightly: he didn't want any gas escaping. The laboratory was filled with the usual sounds: the drone of the fume cupboard, the gurgling noise from the water pumps, the whirr of automatic stirrers. They shut out the outside world, sealing him in the safe, familiar space.

Josef loved science. He loved its precision, its demand for absolute concentration, the way it rewarded often mind-numbing patience and hard work with electrifying discoveries. Like now. After months of repetitive, time-consuming effort, he was almost there.

Since Miriam had left, he was spending more and more hours at work. In the laboratory he had control: they were his experiments, his research. He still found it hard to be with Eva, although they were both trying hard to get over the hurt and mistrust.

Every day more people from the Jewish quarter disappeared. Sometimes, if Josef couldn't sleep, he would look out of the window at dawn to see another family standing disconsolately on the pavement, a small pile of luggage beside them, waiting to be picked up by a truck. Lists of names were published each day. And each day he scanned them frantically to see if his and Eva's were there. For a while he'd been relieved that Miriam was in England; at least she was spared this daily fear. But recently the newspapers had been full of the raids the Germans were launching on London. He just hoped the bombing wouldn't extend to the countryside. They hadn't had a letter for a while, although the last one had been full of descriptions of her singing in front of President Beneš. In spite of his anxiety, Josef felt a frisson of pride that others were recognising his daughter's talent.

He inserted the delivery tube into a stopper, which he twisted into the neck of one of the round-bottomed flasks. Then he carefully unscrewed the bottle of ammonium hydroxide solution and poured in a small amount, before attaching the other end of the tube to a second container. He lit the Bunsen burner and turned down the flame. It wouldn't do to generate too much heat or he'd end up with water vapour along with the ammonia.

So engrossed was he in his task that he failed to hear the door open. He only realised he had company when he found Dr Svoboda beside him, watching the bubbles form in the liquid as the gas escaped from the water.

He turned to acknowledge his colleague. 'Good morning, Doctor.'

'Morning, Kolischer. How's it going?'

'Just creating some ammonia first to see if I can refine the process.'

'Good.' Dr Svoboda laid a sheaf of papers on the table and peered into the flask. 'And do you think we'll be able to manufacture the hydrogen cyanide in the quantities we require?'

Josef hesitated. 'Just how much do we need?'

Svoboda's gaze travelled past Josef's right ear. 'About ten thousand tonnes.'

'Ten thousand tonnes? Just for a pesticide?'

Again the failure to meet Josef's eyes. 'The Nazis want to try it out in prisons.'

'Why?' Josef tried, and failed, to draw his colleague's gaze back to him.

Dr Svoboda reached out and smoothed the top sheet of paper. 'The prisons are overcrowded, the cells riddled with vermin. They plan to evacuate the prisoners, then use the gas to cleanse the rooms. After a few hours, when the gas has dispersed, the prisoners will be allowed back into a vermin-free environment. The perfect solution.'

Josef was calculating rapidly in his head. 'Something still doesn't add up. This is much too much gas. Even for overcrowded prisons.'

Dr Svoboda was looking at his fingernails now. 'Well, there is talk of using it as a humane killer for cattle.'

'Why don't they just shoot them? Much safer. No danger of poisons in the food chain.'

Dr Svoboda shrugged. 'It's not for us to question, Kolischer. Our job is to carry out instructions. Keep up with your research, please.'

It was only when his colleague left the room that Josef realised the sheaf of papers was still on the table.

*

As the plane hurtled along the runway, its engines screaming, Will swallowed at the crescendo of pressure in his ears. Just when the noise became almost unbearable, the Albatross eased into the air and climbed steeply. The landing gear folded itself in with a distant thump and the engine steadied to a throb. Will leant back on his seat and unclenched his fists. Ridiculous to be getting so anxious when he was off to start pilot training himself, but he hadn't realised how noisy big planes were. The Albatross was a huge passenger aircraft; things would be very different in a single-seater.

He leant his head back against the rest, suddenly tired. It wasn't just the busyness of the last few days: the packing, the paperwork, the arrangements for the flight to Canada. It was the emotional exhaustion of the confrontation with his parents. Papa had been furious. Adamant that Will should stay on for his Oxford exams, even if it meant deferring entry, appalled that he had joined up without consulting him. Mother had been all silent, injured reproach: how could he, a Quaker boy, go against his entire upbringing, the beliefs they all held dear (that *you* hold dear, Mother, please don't claim to speak for me, he'd wanted to say but he couldn't bear to see the hurt on her face).

Strangely, it was Miriam who made him waver most. They'd gone up to Shropshire to see her, the metronomic swoosh of the windscreen wipers the only sound for miles as they drove through the rain-soaked countryside, so that Will could say goodbye and give her her birthday present. She'd said nothing; just wrapped her arms round his waist and buried her face in his shirt. When he released her, the shirt was streaked with tears. How could he put her through another separation? But how could he live with himself if he didn't do his bit? The RAF had lost so many good pilots, so many brave lads giving their lives for their country whilst he'd done nothing more than sit at a desk and study. So when the representative had visited Marlborough that day, pleading to the sixth-formers to apply for training, he'd wanted to volunteer straight away. It was only the thought of his parents' reaction that held him back. But after a few hours practising drop kicks by himself at the far end of the field, he'd made his decision. In spite of the arguments, in spite of the tight knot of fear in his stomach, he was sure it was the right one.

The engine was much quieter now. All around him chaps were talking, laughing or passing round chocolate. Will was lucky to have a window seat. He didn't feel ready to join in with the camaraderie just yet, and it gave him an excuse to keep looking out of the porthole. Already the jumble of fields and roads looked tiny, the treetops like dots of green fur, the occasional vehicle a Matchbox car. Soon they would be crossing the wide expanse of the Atlantic, miles and miles of sea until they reached Canada. He'd never been beyond Europe before. Never been in an aeroplane come to that – they'd travelled to Czechoslovakia by train. The knot of fear started to loosen, replaced by a bubble of excitement. He was sorry for Mother and Papa, sorry he had hurt and angered them, but he was eighteen, for goodness' sake, old enough to think for himself, to break free from the shackles of privilege and protection and make his own contribution. In some ways, his life was just beginning.

He eased his legs out under the seat in front of him, and pulled from his pocket the manual they'd all been issued with: *Elementary Flying Training*, it said on the blue cover. Underneath was a predatory-looking owl, its wings outstretched. The book was no thicker than his thumbnail.

There was such a need to train new pilots that Britain could no longer cope. Besides, the best instructors were needed for aerial combat themselves, not putting nervous new recruits through their paces. Lads were being sent all over the Commonwealth to get their training. It was just as well Will was en route to Canada. He had to put some space between himself and his parents. Otherwise he might have a nervous breakdown before he even started.

He opened the training manual at the first page. By the time the plane reached Montreal, he knew almost every word off by heart.

17

Eva came home from a visit to the synagogue one autumn day with a paper bag under her arm.

She placed it on Mutti's lap as her mother sat darning by the window, the fading afternoon light remorselessly illuminating her white hair and deep wrinkles. Mutti's left hand was inside one of Abba's black socks, the material stretched over her palm, whilst the fingers of her right hand deftly sewed up a hole. Yet as soon as the hole was closed, new fissures appeared in the thin fabric. It was an impossible task. The heel was more darn than wool. She took a pair of scissors to cut off a thread, then rolled the sock into a ball and placed it on the windowsill to join a growing pile.

'What have you bought me, my dear?' She rustled the paper bag. 'Hamantaschen?'

Eva frowned. 'I'm afraid not. Just more sewing.'

Mutti opened the bag and drew out a yellow star. It was about the size of her palm and edged with black. Two triangles on top of each other. *Jude*, it said.

'So this terrible indignity has come at last.'

Eva shrugged, feigning nonchalance. 'We were warned.' If they let themselves be upset by the new ruling, it would be another victory for the Germans. She put her hands on her hips with remembered anger. 'I can't believe they had the cheek to charge us for them, though.'

Mutti rummaged in her sewing box for some yellow thread. 'Fetch me the coats,' she said. 'The stars are badges of honour. We'll wear them with pride.'

Eva nodded, blinking at the sudden rush of tears. 'With pride,' she echoed.

Later that evening, after they'd tried, as usual, to make their watery stew last for as long as possible, Eva and Mutti cleared the kitchen table whilst Abba and Josef settled down to listen to the World Service. Then Mutti resumed her sewing, squinting under a dim standard lamp, while Eva took out her writing implements from the drawer. She unscrewed the lid of her fountain pen slowly and angled a sheet of her precious notepaper on the table.

She'd loved receiving Miriam's letters. She and Josef had been thrilled when Miriam wrote to them about singing in front of President Beneš; Eva was so proud her daughter's talent was being nurtured in England – another confirmation that she'd been right to send her away. But this would be the hardest letter she'd ever had to write. She'd spent too long shielding Miriam from the realities of life in Prague. Too long dictating to Josef long letters about Šťastný's latest litter of kittens or Oma's chilblains or Opa's rheumatism. Searching for tiny scraps of their meagre lives that wouldn't alarm their child. She'd let on about the food shortages, trying to imply it was fun to invent new recipes. But now it was time for absolute honesty. Miriam might never hear from them again; she needed to be told the truth.

Despite the harsh contents of the letter, it felt good to be writing to Miriam for herself at last. Miriam was being taught to read and write in Czech in her new school, though she read better in English thanks to the diligence of the Denison family. But most of her teachers were Czech, and there would be older children at the school who could read her the letter if necessary. Maybe one of them would hold her hand when the painful words sank in.

Eva rested the top of the fountain pen against her front teeth for a few further seconds whilst she thought of the best way to start, then she began to write.

My darling Miriam,

I'm afraid I have some difficult news for you. You must be very brave and try to understand what I am writing as it is very important. Keep this letter safe, perhaps in your little suitcase or under your pillow so that you can read it again and again. You may need to show it to some grown-ups if you don't hear from me for a while.

As you know, your dear Abba has been doing some important work at the Institute of Science here in Prague. He has helped invent a medicine that will save hundreds and thousands of lives. The Nazis have been very pleased with his work and it has kept us safe.

Some of our neighbours have not been so lucky.

She paused as she relived the sound of German soldiers pounding on Paní Kratz's door in the early hours, pictured again their kind neighbour's pinched white face as she came to Eva's door to ask her to keep her jewellery and paintings safe until she returned, heard anew the rumbling of the truck as it drove the old woman away. Each day there were new summonses for the transport. No one knew where people were being taken. There was a rumour that it was Poland. Each day more families left the Josefov under armed guard, the Jewish quarter becoming emptier and more desolate. Eva had always told herself they were protected from their unfortunate fellow Jews' fate, but Josef's decision had stripped them all of this security. They now lived in constant fear that they would be next.

She took a deep breath and resumed writing.

A few days ago your father was asked to find a way to make a chemical in vast quantities. He can't be sure, but he fears it may be used to kill people, including our people. He had a very difficult decision to make. We all prayed very hard, and we believe Abba did the right thing in refusing to create this chemical. He is not prepared to have any part in something that may be used for evil purposes. But the Nazis are bound to be angry with him and that puts us all in danger.

It is possible we may have to leave our home and go and stay somewhere else, with some other Jewish people, for the rest of the war. I fear we will not be allowed to write to you from there, so please don't worry if you don't hear from us for a long while. We love you very much, Miriam, and will be hoping and praying that we will all be together again soon, back in our own home as a family. Until that time, you must be very brave. Remember what I told you – whenever you feel sad or worried, give Lilli a big hug, and I'll be hugging you too, in my heart.

All our love, precious girl,

Abba and Mutti

She quickly averted her head so her tears did not fall on the paper. Miriam would be very upset when she read the letter, but she had written to them about the kind teachers and friendly children at Hinton Hall; it was clear she was happy there, and well looked after. Most importantly, she was safe. There were good people there who would comfort her and keep her busy. And there must be many other children in similar positions or worse.

Eva curled her hand into a fist. What a monster Adolf Hitler was, to separate children from parents, destroy the closest bond, make orphans or prisoners of vulnerable people. She and Josef had endlessly discussed how they might escape Czechoslovakia. But it was too late, the borders had long since closed; they were in danger of being killed if it was discovered they were trying to flee. And her parents were too old to cope with the perils involved. They had no choice but to stay and wait until their names came up for transportation.

She felt the staccato thump of blood in her ears. It was only a matter of time until they left the Josefov. And despite the optimism of her words, deep down she feared she might never see Miriam again.

*

Will pulled the stick back and opened up the throttle gently. He swung the nose of the Tiger Moth left and right as she taxied down the runway. The biplane gathered speed and he held the throttle fully open and applied the rudder to keep it straight. When the Tiger had climbed to seven hundred feet, he levelled it off, then leant back slightly and wiped a slick of sweat from his forehead. This was his sixth flight, and already taking off was starting to feel more instinctive.

Maslen put his thumbs up and Will permitted himself a grin. So far so good. But as he turned his head to look down at a miniature flock of sheep below, the Tiger tilted and swayed. He immediately steadied it. The Tiger had a reputation for separating good pilots from great ones. He hoped he'd make one of the latter, but there was so much to remember. Like not rocking the fuselage, for example. Yet pilot training beat cramming history facts for Oxford hands down.

Captain Maslen, Will's instructor, was the epitome of calm. He was rarely seen without a pipe in his mouth. He would puff away until the last moment, then hand the pipe to one of the ground crew before climbing into the plane. Later, he would arrive back on the runway with an outstretched hand, ready to resume smoking. His uniform was so infused with the scent of tobacco that even the cockpit was filled with its rich, sweet smell.

Maslen never raised his voice. All instructions were delivered in mellow tones, the only sign of anxiety a slight increase in firmness and volume. Once, when Will had mangled a take-off, he glanced down and saw the instructor's knuckles whitening, but that was all.

'Want to try a roll?' asked Maslen casually.

Will swallowed. 'Yes, please!'

The instructor reached out to grab the controls. 'Watch the wingtip.'

Will dutifully turned his head. The world shifted sideways.

He laughed in excitement as the horizon swung around them, the bright autumn trees and fields turning to sky. Then they were properly upside down and he looked down in horror at his harness. The leather strained against him. What if it hadn't been fastened properly, or snapped mid roll? But before he even had time to finish the thought, they were straight and level again. He was still laughing as the world regained its proper order.

18

In Prague, the last months of 1940 and the whole of 1941 crawled along painfully and already it was halfway through 1942. More and more decrees had been passed. Jews were now forbidden to travel more than thirty kilometres from their place of residence. Eva again felt thankful that she'd got Miriam out as soon as she had. Then Jews were barred from owning businesses, visiting restaurants, cinemas, theatres, sweet shops and barbers. They were only allowed to shop at three in the afternoon.

When the summons came, it was almost a relief, they'd anticipated it for so long. One early summer morning, Eva woke to several sharp knocks on the door, and a corresponding lurch of dread. Josef was still asleep, so she tugged on her dressing gown, stumbled down the stairs and opened the front door a crack. At first she was worried someone might see her in her night clothes, but the looming presence of a man in a dark overcoat, bearing the familiar yellow star, drove out the embarrassment. She smelt the animal reek of her own sweat. The man held out a sheet of typed paper. 'Sign here, please.'

Eva took his pen and scrawled her name with shaking fingers.

'Don't worry.' The man stepped a little closer. He had

kind eyes in a lined face. 'You won't be going far. It's only Terezin.'

Eva nodded, her throat too dry to speak. At least Terezin was still in Czechoslovakia. But it was a fortress nonetheless. Had been since the eighteenth century, when political dissidents were tortured there.

She trudged back up the stairs, her heart pounding, to wake Josef. Her parents' names were on the list too. She hoped they'd be spared in deference to their age. But it seemed the Germans made no allowances for seniority; no one was exempt from their cruelty.

As she paused on the landing, trying to compose herself, she heard gentle snores coming from her parents' room. They'd be lying side by side as always, like a pair of kippers in a tin, drawing warmth and comfort from each other's bodies, even in sleep.

She took a deep breath and tiptoed into her own bedroom. Josef was still motionless, hunched under the blankets, his breaths an even rhythm. At the foot of the bed was a bulging carpet bag. Eva had packed it weeks ago with essential items: sleeping bags, warm underwear, sturdy shoes, a first aid kit (Josef had insisted on that), torches, candles, notebooks. They would wear as many clothes as they could and squeeze the others into the bag. They were only allowed to take fifty kilograms each. Fifty kilograms from a lifetime's possessions. She had a sudden memory of trying to buy Miriam's birthday present, and coming across the market stall selling Jewish belongings from ransacked houses. It was horrific to realise that the possessions they themselves left behind could well suffer a similar fate.

She crept back into bed. Josef lay, comma-like, on his side. She curled her body around his for a precious few seconds, absorbing his warmth and trying to imprint the smell of his skin, his hair upon her memory. Then she stroked his back to wake him to the news he'd been dreading.

By five in the morning they were all on the tram – at the back, of course; only Aryans were allowed to sit at the front – and on their way to the exposition hall. As they entered the building, Eva was hit by the stench of chlorine. She heard a babble of voices and saw anxious people sitting in packed groups. Babies and small children cried incessantly. One elderly lady tore her false teeth out of her mouth and threw them at a group of soldiers prowling past, then shrieked at them from her gummy mouth.

At the back of the hall a row of stretchers supported bundles of rags that scarcely moved. Eva noticed a man perched on his suitcase with a violin thrust under his chin, playing the same passages from Beethoven's concerto in D major again and again.

How was she ever to find space in a room so crammed with busy humanity? The floor was marked with squares, each about two metres wide. Eva, Josef and her parents followed them round the room until they found one that matched the transport numbers they'd been given. Nearby was a mound of filthy mattresses. They took two and sat down. Mutti tried to make tables out of their suitcases.

'How long will we be here for?' asked Josef.

Eva shrugged. No one seemed to be moving.

Mutti was watching two little girls traipsing round the room arm in arm. One had plaits tied with white ribbons, the other a pudding-basin haircut. They were a little older than Miriam.

'Thank Adonai Miriam is in England,' said Mutti, echoing Eva's thoughts.

Josef reached out and took Eva's hand. 'Assuming she's safe there.'

Eva forced a smile. 'She's in the countryside, dear, you know that. She's safe and happy.'

Josef was looking round the room at the people being coerced into rows. In front of them a red-faced mother was jiggling a crying baby, watched by a grim-faced officer. Josef buried his head briefly in Eva's shoulder. 'This is my fault,' he muttered. 'If only my stupid conscience hadn't got the better of me.'

Eva brushed his cheek with her fingers. 'What choice did you have? They would have got us in the end.'

'But if I'd realised sooner, not been so pig-headed about my job, maybe we'd have been able to escape.'

'But how were you to know what the Nazis were planning to do?' Eva hadn't realised she'd raised her voice.

Abba, who was silently mouthing the words of the Talmud, looked up, and recited aloud: '"Whoever destroys a single life is as guilty as though he had destroyed the entire world and whoever rescues a single life earns as much merit as though he had rescued the entire world."' He looked steadily at Josef.

'Thank you,' Josef replied.

Mutti handed them each a metal mess tin. 'They're calling us for lunch,' she said, clutching at Abba as she struggled to pull herself up.

'Lunch?' said Eva. 'It's only half past ten.'

212

'But have you seen the queue?' asked Mutti.

Eva followed her mother's gaze. A long, ragged line of people snaked round the building. Everyone was holding mess tins. Some people talked in low voices, others stared vacantly into space. A smell of boiled potatoes and gravy filled the air.

It wasn't until half past two that they got their portions and wandered out into the courtyard to eat, trying to make the powdery mounds of potatoes and watery liquid last as long as possible, before rinsing their tins under the spigot and going inside to try to rest on the foul, lumpy mattresses, stomachs clenched in fear as to what would happen next.

'*Achtung. Achtung!*' Eva watched through sleep-deprived eyes as yet another queue formed. Children this time. The Germans seemed to think they could wake them up at any hour of night or day. Now it was a milk allocation. At least the kids were being given something healthy. They had no chance of growing big and strong on the rations they'd been supplied with over the past few hours. If they were allowed to grow at all, that was. Eva leant up on one elbow and watched a toddler clutching her mother's hand as she stumbled a few paces to close up the gap in the queue. The child's hair was plastered to her head, her eyes dull. Eva pictured Miriam when she'd last seen her at the station. She'd been terrified and tearful, sure, but at least she was healthy. And by all accounts she'd flourished at Hinton Hall. She wondered if she'd got her letter yet, and how she'd reacted. She closed her eyes. Best not to think about that. Better to create a safe place inside herself. In the warm glow behind her eyelids, she imagined Miriam singing her heart out in front of President Beneš, her voice soaring, her eyes shining. Her mouth curved with pleasure at the picture.

When Miriam was a toddler, she loved to creep under Eva's piano stool whilst she played. Sometimes, when Eva reached out a foot to press the sostenuto pedal, she would feel Miriam's little hand stroking her shoe and hear the tiny gusts of breath she made when deep in concentration. At other times, the child would pull herself up and stand holding onto Eva's legs, her face buried in her lap. And then she would play as gently as possible so as not to disturb her.

As Eva drifted off to sleep, it was the memory of Miriam's beautiful voice that soothed her.

But that night, Eva dreamt about Otto. His confusion, nervous brutality and strange laugh; the weight of his body as he pinned her to the ground, his beery breath, his grasping, clammy hands. She heard again the jeering boys . . . felt the loss of her clothes . . . her Star of David chain. She awoke with a start, a slick of sweat on her forehead, her mind full of dread. Was Otto here? Was that what had prompted the nightmare?

She sat up and surveyed the room. All around her people were waking up, rubbing their eyes, folding clothes, searching for mess tins. A few German soldiers stood in one corner, watching them, but none of them had white hair. Her pulse slowed; she felt it steady its rhythm. She took several deep breaths, her hand on her chest.

'Are you all right, Eva?' Mutti's concerned face.

'Yes, just a bad dream.'

'The usual?'

214

Eva nodded. They rarely spoke about the incident in the cemetery. But sometimes she saw the stain of wine seeping across the white lace cloth as Abba dropped the Kiddush cup; heard Mutti's scream of horror at her torn clothes and bruised body. And the memory would flood her mouth with the sharp taste of bile. She'd have to remind herself again and again of the lullaby she'd composed at the sanatorium, until she felt calmer.

At six a.m., they were given instructions to wait in the courtyard. They gathered their scant belongings – they'd handed in their valuables on arrival with little hope of seeing them again – and waited to board the train. The already quiet crowd fell silent as the tannoy crackled and a strangely emotionless voice rang out:

'Good morning. We trust you have slept well.'

Abba grimaced.

'We are pleased to tell you we will soon be taking you to a new land, a land where you can avoid persecution and start a new life.'

'A land flowing with milk and honey, perhaps?' muttered Abba. Mutti shushed him.

'You will be taken care of. Things will go well for you,' the voice continued. 'You will be helping to establish a new town where Jewish people can live freely. All will be well.'

Josef turned a hopeful face to Eva. 'Perhaps it is the truth?' he whispered.

She turned her head away.

Eva sat by the window, looking out as the train ploughed through the Czech countryside. The land was flat, patchworked with fields of varying shades of green, their boundaries marked by lines of poplar trees. From time to time a meandering river glinted in the sun. Sometimes she saw clusters of houses, with bright splashes of geraniums in window boxes. Outside a whitewashed bungalow an elderly woman was watering her flowers in the warm sunshine. Eva longed to change places with her, to spend her day weeding and tending her plants, watching them grow and thrive, seeing out the war in peace and anonymity. How could she ever have resented the tedium of her days in Prague? Her present self envied the predictability of her past. Better to be stultified by boredom than gnawed by fear.

She reached for Josef's hand but continued to gaze out. There were blue-grey hills in the distance; nearby, elderflowers foamed in the hedgerows. And at the edge of the wheat fields red poppies twined themselves around the crops' pale stalks.

Josef squeezed her hand in his. 'I wonder what the journey to England was like for Miriam.' None of them had ever been abroad.

'Much like this, I suppose.'

'She must have grown quite a bit by now,' added Mutti, who was sitting opposite them with Abba. 'I expect she's wearing one of the larger skirts we made her.'

Eva pictured Mutti's bright red and orange shawl that they'd cut and stitched that distant spring. Miriam had been in England for three years now. She had probably grown out of all the skirts, although Eva didn't like to tell Mutti that. She tried, and failed, to imagine her daughter in English clothes. Did they even have a national costume? Shropshire was near to Wales, wasn't it? She'd once seen a picture of a little Welsh girl in a book. Perhaps Miriam was wearing one of those strange black hats and a starched white apron. Would her hair be long or short? She hoped she was brushing it carefully. Maybe she still used the ribbon Eva had made her to tie it back. Did she still hug Lilli and think of them, or had she lost the doll by now? If Miriam had sent a reply to her last letter, they'd never received it. And Eva suspected she would never be allowed to write from Terezin. No matter what the voice on the tannoy had said, she had no doubt it was a prison they were going to.

She fingered the yellow star on her coat. Mutti had been right. At first she'd felt ashamed to wear it, and the curious, mocking or sympathetic glances she received reinforced this. But after a while she'd learned to smile when she saw other Jews in the street, as if the star was indeed the badge of honour Mutti had declared it. Eventually she felt as if she had been wearing it for ever.

There was a loud click as the carriage door was opened, puncturing Eva's thoughts and setting her heart thrumming.

Several SS men entered. '*Achtung!*'

Everyone stood to attention. A cherry rolled across the floor, but no one dared retrieve it. Eva saw the panic in her mother's eyes. Abba straightened his shoulders in an attempt to look brave, but he only succeeded in looking even more like a frightened old man. She didn't dare turn her gaze to Josef.

Next to the SS officers was an *Ordner*, a Jewish boy, pressed into helping the Germans. His eyes darted nervously around the room as he muttered under his breath. 'Twenty-eight women, six children and twenty-six men,' he reported in a high, hoarse voice.

217

One SS man looked him up and down, glanced around the compartment and left without a word. The boy followed him.

They all shakily lowered themselves to their seats again, and gradually people started to talk once more.

Eva noticed a woman in the corner of the carriage in a dark blue headscarf. She was gripping her basket, her knuckles whitening through the skin. At the sound of a blow from the next compartment, she leapt up as though to run in, then slumped against the wall. 'My son,' she murmured.

A few minutes later, the boy appeared, his face swollen and red. He squeezed his mother's shoulder. 'I got the count wrong,' he said. 'Don't worry, I won't die from a slap.'

The train rumbled on.

They were at Terezin by midday. The sun was high in a piercing blue sky as they assembled their belongings and stumbled off the train. Heat radiated from the metal tracks and a dribble of sweat ran down Eva's back. She wore a long-sleeved blouse and a thick jumper under her winter coat. Ridiculous clothes for a summer's day, but she knew she'd be glad of them when the weather turned cold. All around her people were similarly dressed, wearing as many of their garments as they could to save carrying them. Josef was already mopping his forehead with his handkerchief.

They traipsed along a bumpy road, past children who stared at them from in front of their houses before their parents shooed them inside. Eventually they came to a large building, eighteenth century in style, which looked to have once been painted yellow but now had chunks of plaster missing, revealing red brickwork underneath. It appeared deserted.

'How come there are no people?' Mutti whispered. 'So many transports have gone here. Where are their passengers?'

Eva looked up at the windows of the building. Some were broken, the holes filled with paper or rags. And despite the glare of the sun, she could make out ghostly faces pressed up against them. A few people waved, but no one emerged.

'That's Sudetenland, the men's dormitories,' one of the carters explained. 'They're not allowed out.'

Eva registered the two terrible facts: that people were imprisoned on a beautiful summer's day. And that men and women were separated.

Sure enough, as they approached the accommodation building, a voice rasped out: 'Men to the left, women straight on.'

Blood throbbed in Eva's ears. So it was true. How could they tear husbands from wives, mothers from sons, brothers from sisters? What inhumane mind had determined that? But there was nothing to be done. Better deal with this with dignity than rant and rail to no purpose. She quickly wound her arms round Josef's neck and pressed her cheek to his. 'Goodbye, my darling.' Josef hugged her in return, his face white with shock. But over his shoulder, Eva saw Mutti sobbing as she clung to Abba, saw her father's bleak expression, her mother's despair. Her parents had rarely been separated in four decades. They had endured so much together, but their marriage had sustained and empowered them. How were they ever going to cope apart?

19

At the airbase, Will was trying to write a letter home. It was hard to know what to say to his parents. Papa was still furious with him, and Mother worried so. He picked up his pen.

Greenham Common
13th June 1942

Dear Papa and Mother,

    I do hope you are both well. Have you heard from Miriam lately? Please give her my love when you next write.

    There's no need to worry about me. Everything is fine. I have to say I absolutely love flying. I adore being up in the clouds. The sense of space and freedom is enormous. I feel closer to God up there than ever I did at the Quaker meetings.

Mother would be pleased at the reference to God. And it was true. Will had never understood how she could commune with the Almighty in a stuffy room full of people punctuating the silence with their sniffs and coughs. He'd tried hard but felt his own prayers raining down on him as they failed to penetrate the ceiling.

But it was different when he was airborne. Up in the sky, nursing the Hurricane through thick cumulus clouds and into the blue expanse, soaring and wheeling in the sunlit silence, higher even than larks and eagles, he knew God's presence. How strange that in the midst of war he could feel such peace.

His writing was becoming a bit faint. He unscrewed the barrel of the pen and filled it up from the little pot of Winsor & Newton in front of him. He scribbled on the blotting paper to check the ink was coming through, then resumed his letter.

I should be due some leave soon so I'll try to pop home. Will Miriam stay in Shropshire for the holidays? It would be splendid to see her again.

After his initial training in Ontario, he'd been shipped back to England on the *Queen Mary* with a cargo of American troops. He'd lain awake at night listening out for U-boats – it would be ironic for an RAF pilot to end up being torpedoed – but they'd made it safely across the Atlantic. After a fleeting, and somewhat frosty, visit home, he'd made his way to Greenham Common for his advanced training.

He'd been in flying raids over Germany for months now, but the strict need for discretion, combined with a concern not to alarm Mother, had caused him to be vague about his activities. Best to keep to the day-to-day news.

Some Czech pilots arrived the other day to join the squadron. I got chatting to the chaps one night in the mess, and one in particular, called Tomas Belinsky. After his mother died when he was young, he emigrated to Poland with his father and two sisters to live with their aunt. Just as well, as he'd never have been allowed out of Czechoslovakia once the Germans got in. He joined the PAF, which re-formed in France, and has been over here for two years. He's a great chap and we've become good friends. I hope you have a chance to meet him sometime.

All love for now,

Will

*

Up at Hinton Hall, Miriam was also composing a letter. She was perched on her bed, an uprighted pillow at her back, writing in careful italics on the paper she'd begged from Matron that morning. The Denisons had sent her a fountain pen last Christmas. It was important she keep the letter neat, so that her parents could see how good her writing was. She didn't want to make any blots.

Dearest Mutti and Abba,

I know you said you might not be able to write for a while, but I am worried about you both. Abba must hate not being able to work at the Institute. He was very brave to stand up to the Nazis. I pray for your safety every night. How I wish President Beneš were here to help me get in touch. I keep thinking about you and wondering how you are managing. Have you moved to a new address? If so, could you send on the details? I do hope this reaches you. It was lovely to receive a letter in your own hand, Mutti. Even though I have written this in

English, my Czech reading is coming on well. I could understand almost all of your words.

How are the kittens? They must be cats by now. I wish I could see them. And how I wish even more that I could see you. I miss you all so much. On Saturdays we are allowed to go into Whitchurch. I cycled there last week with my friend Olga. We went to see *Dumbo*, which was fun. Afterwards we were allowed to spend our pocket money in Woolworths. Some of the children bought presents for their mothers. I so wanted to buy you something, Mutti, but I knew there would be no point in sending it. In the end I bought a penny whistle and some sweets. I thought I could learn to play the whistle as a surprise for you. But it doesn't make a very nice sound and I know you would much rather hear me play the piano.

She paused as a memory of Mutti trying to get her to play their old piano in the apartment sidled into her mind. She remembered her mother making her sit up so straight her back hurt. Mutti's thin fingers bored into her shoulders as she squirmed on the stool. She could hear children having fun outside. It wasn't fair that she had to stay in and practise when others were enjoying themselves. But strangely, she'd never felt that with singing.

She gripped the pen tightly and repositioned it on the paper.

I'm pleased to hear you were proud of me for singing in front of President Beneš. He was a nice man and seemed to enjoy my solo. I have continued practising with Paní Černý. She has taught me Smetana's 'Píseň česká'. Do you know it? It is beautiful and makes me think of home. I wish you could hear me sing it. Sometimes, when we perform one of our concerts, I look out into the audience – mainly teachers and other pupils (the ones who can't sing!) – and imagine you there, listening to me, your head on one side. I know you would be proud deep down, but I expect you would criticise me too. You always pointed out my faults when I played the piano. But I know now you did it to make me better. And I will be better, dearest Mutti. I will always try my hardest for you all.

Please try to keep in touch, even though you say it is difficult. I worry about you all so much, particularly now Abba has got into trouble, but I am sure he did the right thing.

I expect Abba is reading this letter to you and maybe to Oma and Opa as well. If so, I send you all a big kiss and a warm hug!

All my dearest love,

Miriam xxx

*

Hampstead
22nd June 1942

Dearest Will,

Thank you for your last letter. It is good of you to find time to write when life is so hectic. I listened to

Winston Churchill on the wireless last night. He spoke of how we shall fight Hitler in the air until, 'with God's help, we have rid the earth of his shadow and liberated its people from his yoke'. That made me think of what you and all our gallant boys are doing for us up in the skies. I must confess it made me well up to think of your courage and determination. I know Father and I were unhappy about you being engaged in active combat. And we still are. But my feelings are mixed and there is a good swelling of maternal pride along with the fear and worry. And it is wonderful you feel so close to God up in the sky. Stay safe, my darling boy.

Your new friend Tomas sounds interesting. It makes me think of a young Czech boy I met while in the Prague hospital. He was also called Tomas, and was rarely without a toy plane in his hand. Of course, invite him back here if you get the opportunity. I would love to meet him.

Life in Hampstead rumbles on as usual. As you know, Father finds Mr Churchill difficult, but listening to him last night, I was awed by his firmness and faith. Perhaps, after all, he is the right man for the job.

Kitty has very little to do without you and Miriam around, so I have set her to giving your rooms a thorough clean. And of course she spends hours queuing for food, poor dear. Cheese and eggs are now rationed, so no more lovely fluffy omelettes. Instead we have horrible powdered egg, so much more difficult to cook with. I do hope you are getting enough to eat. I would much rather go without myself than know you are hungry.

I've been helping the Collinses at the end of the road. They have a girl about your age, Janice: you may remember her. Anyway, their house received a direct hit in the last bombing raid. They were all out at the time, thank goodness, but they stayed with us for a few days until they found temporary accommodation. I spoke to some of the neighbours and we've been able to pass on some clothes and a few household items to them. Don't worry about our house, though – it's sturdy enough to withstand anything.

Father continues to be busy. I see so little of him these days: just early in the morning and late at night. And after the Friends meeting on Sunday, he just wants to sleep. So I am keeping busy knitting, and sewing new clothes for Miriam. She is growing so fast and there are hardly any children's garments in the shops these days. I've managed to get some new wool from Mrs Arnold's and will knit you a jumper. It will be a blessing to know I am helping to keep you warm when you are on combat. Mrs Arnold's son is out in France. She worries about him so. And do you remember Josephine Palliser's girls? They're both in the WAAF. Perhaps you'll come across them too!

Miriam writes often and I think she is happy in Shropshire, but she hasn't heard from her parents in a while. Their last letter was very worrying. Apparently poor Mr Kolischer was asked to make some chemicals for the Nazis – he's a scientist, remember – but he refused and now they fear they'll be deported. Poor things. I wonder what has happened to them. It must be hard for

Miriam to have her family so far away, and possibly in danger. Thank goodness she has us – I'm sure she thinks of you as a brother now.

Well, I must go, as Kitty has asked what she should cook for supper. Father seems to have become quite fond of Lord Woolton pie, so perhaps I will ask her to prepare that. He has given me strict instructions not to make it myself.

Look after yourself, my darling boy, and write when you can.

Greatest love,

Mother xxx

20

Still no letter from Abba and Mutti. Miriam hardly dared look at the hall table when she came downstairs to breakfast. Day after day she'd glanced at the polished wood surface, desperately hoping for an envelope with Abba's neat copperplate handwriting on it, or even Mutti's scrawl, seeing as she had written the last letter. But there was nothing. A few of the other girls continued to get letters, and most tried to hide their joy at hearing from their parents when so many of their friends received nothing, but the pile of correspondence on the table was getting smaller each week.

Miriam was becoming more and more worried. If her parents were all right, she'd surely have heard by now. It had been very brave of Abba to stand up to the Nazis, but it would have put them all in danger too. Sometimes Miriam couldn't breathe she felt so anxious.

She glanced at the grandfather clock in the hall. Its huge wrought-iron hands only said half past seven. As usual, she'd woken up early, her stomach churning. There was half an hour before she had to go into the dining hall to queue up for the usual gluey porridge and slices of flaccid bread. She opened the front door and stepped outside. No one would miss her for a while.

After the coolness of the school hallway, with its dark wood and stone floor, the air outside felt warm and inviting. Miriam walked down the driveway and struck out towards the meadow. She always preferred outside to in. Tramping across the long wet grass, she closed her mind against her worries and pretended she was back home in the Czech countryside, walking through the fields with Mutti after taking the train out of Prague for the day. She could feel her mother's cool hand in hers, see her lively eyes as she told her stories of the operas and symphonies she'd learned as a child. Sometimes she'd ask Miriam to sing to her, and Miriam would hum the villanelle or 'Okolo Třeboně', the song she'd later sung for President Beneš. What a good job she'd known it already, and had practised it under Mutti's critical eye. Her mother must have been so proud when she'd read about her solo.

A skylark twittered overhead and Miriam tipped her head back to listen, closing her eyes against the already bright glare of the sun. Mutti had once played her a piano arrangement of Vaughan Williams' *The Lark Ascending*, and she felt the spiralling notes rise in her throat and drift on the summer air.

She walked towards the pond, watching the surface ripple and smooth in the breeze. At once Abba's warning tone filled her ears. 'Swimming is dangerous, Miriam. You can pick up all kinds of germs. And it's easy to catch cold, even on a warm day.' But the temptation was too strong.

Mr Čapek had taught them all to swim last summer, although they weren't allowed to go in on their own. She looked around to check no one was watching, then tugged off her school blouse and skirt, rolled her socks into a ball, stuffed them into her shoes and waded in, still wearing her vest and pants. The water was deliciously icy on her legs. She pushed off from the bottom, ignoring the initial clench of cold on her shoulders and back as she launched herself under the surface, and swam across the pond with rapid strokes until her body tingled with exertion. As always, exercise drove all thoughts from her head. All she could feel was the slap of water on skin as her swimming slowed to a steady rhythm. Surely, on this summer morning so full of warmth and hope, she'd return to find a letter from her parents, and all would be well with the world. She had a sudden vision of yellow paper on gleaming wood and took it to be a good omen.

But after hastily scrambling into her clothes and striding back across the field, lifting up strands of her hair with her fingers so the sun would dry it more quickly, she returned to find the dining room already full, and a bowl of rapidly congealing porridge, kindly salvaged by one of her friends, awaiting her at her usual place.

She'd no doubt be reprimanded for going absent without leave. But worse still, as she'd rushed through the hall, her wet underwear clinging to her skin, she'd registered that there was still no letter from either of her parents on the table.

*

The only way to cope was to retreat into yourself. Eva remembered her piano-playing days, when she'd imagined herself as a breve, surrounded by space and silence. She'd had a bedroom all to herself at her childhood home. A place where she could read and dream without having to answer questions or make desultory conversation. It had been her refuge, her sanctuary; it nourished and calmed her. She tried to recapture that feeling

230

now. Concentrating on her inner world of hope and memory, blotting out the horrors of the dormitory – the stench of urine and unwashed bodies, the reek of rank food and dirty mattresses; the scuttling of rats, the constant itching from fleas – withdrawing into a world that was clean and whole.

She'd done that after the attack in the cemetery all those years ago, wearing a mask of stoicism. Didn't the prophet Isaiah say, 'I set my face like a flint, and I know that I shall not be ashamed.'

But it was hard to ignore Mutti's harsh breathing beside her. Eva pressed her hand to her mother's forehead: it was only four inches away from her own, so tightly were they packed on the mattresses. Her palm came away filmed with sweat. Mutti was murmuring in her sleep and her body radiated heat, even in the stuffy room. Eva turned carefully onto her back and stared at the ceiling. If Mutti were no better in the morning, she'd go to the Council of Elders and see if she could persuade someone with medical knowledge to look at her.

She turned over and tried to find that tranquil place in her mind. But sleep evaded her.

Mutti didn't stir when the dormitory leader gave the morning call, or when Eva tried to rouse her too. She eased her mother's body gently over to avoid her getting bedsores, and a spurt of diarrhoea shot across the bed. Shocked and worried, she blotted it as best she could. She'd have to smuggle the sheet to the laundry later. They were only allowed to wash their clothes every three weeks, and then only three kilograms' worth. But she couldn't leave the sheet like that. It would smell horrible, and besides, it could spread disease.

She crept along the mattress to retrieve her clothes from the hook on the makeshift rack at the end of the bed, climbed down the ladder and slapped a bit of water from the washstand bowl onto her face. No point in trying anything more; there was already a long queue building up behind her. The other women were setting off to see if there would be any breakfast. Then Eva would be expected to report for work. But if she skipped breakfast, she might just manage to catch Aaron Rathstein.

As she left the women's barracks and crossed the courtyard, she thought she glimpsed a familiar face in the distance: the receding hair, round spectacles and benign expression of Gabriel Schmidt, a former piano tutor. Mr Schmidt had taught at the conservatoire in Prague, and sometimes given private lessons. Was he really at Terezín too? Perhaps she should make contact? But she dared not linger now. She hurried down the Park Road, keeping her face down, slipped into Magdeburg barracks, made her way to the Council of Elders building and knocked on Mr Rathstein's door.

'Come in.'

A weary figure sat behind a desk. In front of him were several pieces of paper with what looked like names on. As Eva watched, Aaron Rathstein scratched two out, gazed into space for a few seconds, then added a few more.

'Good morning, Elder.'

He laid down his pen and pushed the papers aside. 'Good morning, young lady. What can I do for you?'

'It's my mother. She's sick. I couldn't wake her this morning.'

Mr Rathstein took off his glasses and rubbed his eyes. 'Sick?

Sick! Everyone is sick. What am I to do? Do you know how many people died yesterday?'

Eva shook her head.

'Over a hundred! More and more each day. It's probably typhus. Most of them are.' He replaced his glasses and gnawed at a bit of loose skin beside his thumbnail.

'Then what do you suggest I do?'

Aaron Rathstein stood up, went over to a cupboard behind him and pulled out a drawer. 'Here . . . aspirin.' He dropped two white tablets into her hand. 'Give them to her if she wakes up. Try to find some clean water. It's all I can offer.' He motioned her out of the room.

Eva slid the tablets into her pocket. The clock on Mr Rathstein's wall had said ten to seven. She needed to be at work by seven. She'd try to pop back at lunchtime – another missed meal – and hope her mother slept all morning.

She trailed off to the laundry, the workplace she'd been assigned when they first arrived at Terezin. Before she'd become ill, Mutti had been directed to the sewing room. At least she'd gained some pleasure from doing something she was good at; Eva had no such aptitude or affection for washing clothes. As she pushed open the heavy wooden door, the usual aroma of cheap detergent and soiled bedding greeted her. The whirr of big machines, the hiss of irons, the creak of mangles was almost deafening. Already her armpits were prickling from the heat. She heaved up one of the bundles from the doorway, deposited the pile of dirty washing on the floor and started to sort the items.

She was dropping garments into one of the huge boiling coppers when a woman sidled up to her. She recognised

Elsa from Dresden block, although she wasn't in the same dormitory.

'Have you heard the rumour?' Elsa asked. Her dark frizzy hair curled even more tightly in the hot, damp air of the laundry.

'No, what rumour?'

The woman half turned her head, then placed her mouth near Eva's ear. 'More transports.'

'More transports. Surely not! We've *been* transported – from Prague. Isn't this enough?'

'Apparently not. There's a woman in my dormitory, Ruth, who has been summoned with her husband and two children. They have to pack tonight.'

Eva retrieved two more garments and dropped them in the copper, triggering a swift release of steam. She wiped her forehead with the back of her hand. 'Where are they going?'

'To the east, apparently. Another camp.'

'Why?'

'According to her, it's a work camp.'

'A *work* camp!' Eva almost laughed. 'And isn't it a work camp here?'

The woman shrugged and sidled off.

Eva continued to add clothes to the copper, but as she did so, her mind raced. What if Terezin were just an interim centre? What if there was worse to come? How on earth would her mother manage another train journey in her condition? She had to get word to Josef.

At lunchtime, she went without rations again, ignoring the hunger that gouged her stomach, and raced back to Mutti. Her mother was still hot, and her skin had a yellow hue, but at least she was conscious now. 'Eva. I have such a headache,' she whispered.

Eva fetched a tin mug from the washstand and thrust it under the tap, then reached into her pocket for the aspirin and held them out to Mutti. But Mutti struggled to swallow them, retching and retching as Eva patted her on the back and tried to get her to take more liquid. Eventually, after two more trips to get water, the tablets went down. Mutti lay back on the mattress, exhausted.

Eva delved in her rucksack for pen and paper and scribbled a note to Josef to inform him of her mother's illness and ask him if he'd heard anything about the transports. She folded the paper up small, then hurried back to the laundry and managed to hand it to one of the porters when he came to deliver a new batch of dirty washing.

'Can you take this to the Sudetenland barracks?' she whispered.

The porter nodded, prised open the heel of his boot, slid the letter in, hammered the heel back with his palm, and departed.

The next day, the same porter handed her a return note from Josef. *Have spoken to Abba. Your mother might have typhus. She must be quarantined. Speak to one of the guards. They're terrified of the disease. They'll get her moved.*

Eva wondered how poor Abba had reacted, knowing how ill his beloved wife was. She must do all she could to save Mutti.

But how would she get permission? Jews were forbidden access to the SS-Service Club and there were surprisingly few

235

guards on the streets. Maybe the sorting house in Usti barracks, where confiscated property was checked. She set off along Station Road, past the park, already carpeted with autumn leaves, and across Eger Street to the depot.

Sure enough, two German guards were presiding over a pile of belongings: penknives, watches, books, even a cake. As Eva approached the building and the figures came into focus, her stomach suddenly contracted and her legs threatened to give way. Surely not? Surely it couldn't be, after all this time? But yes, one of the heads bent low over the table of objects was white-blond, and even if his hair didn't identify him, his voice and way of holding himself did: Otto. How could she have found herself in the same camp as him? It seemed as if the world was truly conspiring to torture her. She drew in a sharp breath and willed her body to stop shaking. She couldn't control the knot in her gut, or the pounding of blood in her ears, but she could and would make her voice sound firm.

'Excuse me.' She tried to adopt an unconcerned expression.

The guards looked up. Was it Eva's imagination, or was there a flicker of recognition in Otto's eyes? Was there any vestige of her sixteen-year-old self in her nearly thirty-year-old body? Her hair colour was the same; she was still slim – probably thinner after years of food restrictions – but this Eva was tired and grim. If there was recognition, it quickly passed. His eyes were blank again.

'Yes?'

'My mother is sick. We think it might be typhus.'

A look of revulsion crossed Otto's face. Josef had been right about the German horror of illness. He reached for a piece of paper and scribbled something on it. 'Take this to the matron at the Long Street hospital. She will know what to do.'

Eva grabbed the paper and departed before her knees could give way.

21

They scrambled at first light. The sky was a gunmetal grey, the air sharp with autumn cold. A nimbus of breath escaped from Will's mouth as he dashed towards the Hurricane, strapping on his helmet and doing up his Mae West as he ran. The ground crew, who had already started the engine, helped him into the cockpit.

Will checked the controls, taxied out and took off. Tomas had been just ahead of him and was already climbing steeply. Will followed his trajectory. They made it across the channel without incident, and had just reached the northern French coast, when he heard a voice on the radio transmitter scream, 'Fifty thousand plus bandits approaching from south-east. Twenty-six thousand feet.' Damn. That was about ten thousand feet more than the Hurricane was comfortable with, but needs must. He opened up the throttle.

A rapid glance down and sideways revealed puffs of black smoke. He flew towards them: the signs of ack-ack fire were harmless by now, but they might show him the position of the enemy bombers. Nothing yet. The AA couldn't have been accurate.

He climbed higher. The clouds were magnificent up here. Majestic anvils towering above a vast snowy landscape. He was a tiny speck flying over drifts and swirls and heaps of whiteness under a brilliant blue sky.

Up above him the Jerries were making smoke circles, silver trails that coiled like snakes. Will climbed higher and glimpsed a slanting black line to his right. Bombers. He turned towards them and set the gun button to 'fire'. Visibility was poor, so he opened the hood and was hit by a blast of freezing air that would have taken his breath away had he not been wearing his oxygen mask. The rapidly closing bombers were now surrounded by black dots: Me 109s. They were in for it this time. He couldn't see Tomas.

As they attacked, Will noticed the cannon fire from the top rear gun of a Dornier – little squirts of white smoke flicking into the slipstream. The cockpit was filled with the reek of cordite.

Suddenly three explosions ripped down his right-hand side. Cannon shells. He whipped into a right-hand turn over another Hurricane. There were two more explosions and something hit him hard in the right leg, but he didn't feel any pain. Waves of hot air washed into the cockpit. His stomach lurched; the Hurricane had gone into a spin. He jammed his right foot on the rudder bar and pushed with all his might. Nothing. Tried again. Still nothing. His hand was poised to push the stick forward, but he was still rotating frighteningly fast. And losing height rapidly.

He'd have to bail out. He yanked back the roof, fumbled his straps undone, leant out and pushed with his feet on the dashboard. Nothing happened. He jerked back into the cockpit, undid his oxygen bayonet connection and tried again. This time he came out straight away, but fell forward, missing the propeller by inches. The sky swung alarmingly above him, then steadied. He yanked the release ring. The parachute streamed out beneath his feet and there was a sharp jerk. He was suspended in eerie quietness at about two thousand feet. The Hurricane blazed past him and spun down directly underneath before bursting into flames.

Will parachuted down into enemy-occupied territory.

*

Pamela sat at her dressing table brushing her hair. It had been a while since she'd last had a perm, and it was looking a bit lank. She leant forward and fluffed up the sides with her fingers. Better. She rummaged around in her drawer to see if she could find that pink lipstick Hugh liked. Kitty was at her mother's today, and Pamela had volunteered to do the shopping. She ought to look at least a bit presentable if she was to stand in queues for hours. She'd read a magazine article that said it was a woman's responsibility to maintain personal standards – it was her bit for the war effort – though she could think of better things she could be doing to help people.

As she leant forward again to apply her lipstick, she caught a flash of navy and silver out of the window, and heard the click of the gate and the crunch of gravel on the path. She stood up to look out properly. A telegram boy was at the front door, an envelope in his hand. She raced down the stairs, her stomach churning, seized the telegram from the apologetic-looking boy and managed to whisper, 'No reply,' before her legs gave way and she collapsed onto the bottom stair.

Should she open it now, or wait until Hugh got home? A

vision of another telegram, propped on a mantelpiece, flashed into her mind. It had glared at them all day, haunting the room with its terrible power, until her father had come home to open it, and announced Tommy's death in a broken voice. Not again. Please God, not again. She took a deep breath to steady herself and slid her thumb under the flap.

Regret to inform you that your son, William Denison, has been reported missing in action as of 3rd July 1942. A letter following this telegram giving all available details follows.

She snatched at the words, trying to grasp their sense, then laid the telegram down on knees that shook uncontrollably. Oh Will. What had happened? Please be alive, my darling, please. Missing in action could mean anything. He could be a prisoner of war . . . injured . . . lost at sea . . . She closed her eyes and sent up a silent prayer for her son's life, then stumbled down the hall to telephone his father.

'I knew we should have stopped him,' said Hugh in a voice that was hoarse with shock and grief. It was two in the morning, but there'd been no point going to bed. Fear and anxiety had driven out all attempts at sleep.

Pamela put her elbow on the arm of the chair and rested her forehead on her fist.

'But what could we have done? It was already a fait accompli when he got back from Boscombe Down.'

'I could have contacted someone high up in the RAF and got them to block Will's application.'

241

'And face accusations of nepotism? Even Winston couldn't prevent his nephew from being captured in Norway.'

'Giles Romilly was a journalist, not a fighter pilot. He was just in the wrong place at the wrong time.'

'So was Will.'

'You've changed your tune. I thought you were furious with him for not upholding Quaker values.'

'I *was*. I *am*. But I'm a mother too. Will's heart wasn't in his Oxbridge exam. He'd never have got in. Too busy reading up about planes and ignoring his school textbooks. And anyway, if we'd stopped him joining up, insisted he'd done something safer for the war effort, he might still have risked his life. Like Tommy.'

Hugh stood up and put an arm round her. 'I'm sorry. It must have been such a shock for you getting another telegram like that.'

Pamela nodded, mute with grief.

'And we don't know what's happened to Will. I'll make enquiries in the morning. See what I can do.'

'The letter should arrive soon. That will tell us more.'

'Indeed. Come on.' Hugh held out his hand. 'Let's at least pretend to get some sleep.'

Pamela followed her husband wearily up the stairs.

The next day, she was sitting bleakly at the breakfast table, nursing a cup of stone-cold tea, when there was a knock on the door. She sprang up, heart hammering, and rushed into the hall in time to see Kitty open the door to a young man in RAF uniform. For a second, she thought it was Will. But the cry of joy caught in her throat. This man was a good head shorter than Will, and altogether lighter in frame.

He smiled faintly and started forward, his hand outstretched. 'Tomas.'

But Pamela ignored his attempted handshake and reached out to hug him, her fingers pressing into the comforting thick wool of his jacket. She caught the familiar whiff of hair oil and cologne.

'Mrs Denison. I came as soon as I could.'

Pamela motioned to him to follow her into the sitting room. 'Tea, please, Kitty – and as much bread and butter as you can rustle up.'

'Yes, ma'am.' Kitty scuttled off to the kitchen.

Tomas sat down. He took off his hat and laid it on the floor before running his hands through his hair.

Pamela sat too, trying to ignore the frantic beat of her heart. She knew that good manners required her to comment on how nice it was to meet Tomas after all Will had said about him, to ask after his health, his family . . . but all she wanted to do was find out about her son.

Tomas knew that too. 'I saw Will go down,' he said.

Pamela felt as though her heart was inching its way up her body, weighing down her tongue. She stared at him, willing him to continue.

'The Hurricane hit the ground and exploded.'

She clapped her hand over her mouth to stifle the surge of nausea. Her body was one long scream.

'But I'm pretty sure Will bailed out. I saw a black figure floating through the air before the Hurricane fell.'

He stood up awkwardly and stumbled towards her. He

knelt at her feet and grasped her hands. 'He's got a good chance, Mrs Denison. I know it.'

Pamela felt the strength in Tomas's warm fingers. Hope rose in her like a breath. Her cheeks were wet, but she kept her hands in his.

'Thank you, Tomas,' she whispered.

Eventually the letter arrived. It was from Will's CO. He began with some very complimentary remarks about Will: his courage, his openness of character, his charming manner, even his faith. He confirmed Tomas's theory that Will had bailed out, and went on to say that in the circumstances there was no reason to suppose he was dead. If he'd become a prisoner of war, they would hear from the Red Cross within a month. If he'd escaped, they wouldn't get any news until he'd made his way safely back. Both options gave reason for hope.

But it was the waiting that drove Pamela mad. The Collinses were probably getting fed up with her, she spent so much time popping over to make sure they were all right. But she had to help someone. At least Hugh could forget his anxieties for a few frantic hours at the FO. Some days she wished she could go with him.

In the end, she begged Hugh to let her go to Hinton Hall to see Miriam. 'I need to tell her about Will face to face. She's so fond of him.'

Hugh agreed. 'I'll try to arrange for someone to drive you there. I hate to use my position in this way, but I think the occasion merits it.' He glanced at her with a worried frown.

Pamela knew her hair was lank, her nails bitten to the quick. But she couldn't seem to do anything other than think of Will. She longed to see Miriam, to hug her warm little body, to fill her arms with a living, breathing child. Nothing would assuage the horror of her son's disappearance, but seeing Miriam would help. She was sure of it.

Two days later, she found herself sitting in the back of Hugh's official Bentley being driven by a government chauffeur all the way up to Shropshire. To her surprise, the driver was a woman, in WAAF uniform, with intelligent brown eyes and pinned-back dark hair. Her name was Kate. For a second Pamela wondered if she'd ever met Will; she was so young and pretty, and he'd have liked her, she was sure. But after wrinkling her forehead, Kate said she didn't recognise the name. Of course, it was a long shot. There were thousands of men and women in the air force. Pamela pushed down the thought that Will had died without ever having had a girlfriend. He'd played tennis with the sisters of his Marlborough friends, but never brought anyone home. They hadn't expected him to. He was still a schoolboy. She looked out of the window at the blur of green and brown fields, the distant hills, the occasional sparkle of water. Could she ever enjoy the beauty of the countryside again without him?

Eventually the car rumbled up the drive to Hinton Hall. Kate rushed round to open the door for Pamela, who unbent her stiff body and stood up.

'I'll wait here until you're ready, ma'am,' said Kate, smiling.

'Oh, won't you come in? I may be a while. And I'm sure you can grab a cup of tea and something to eat here.'

Kate shook her head and produced a flask and some sandwiches from the glove compartment. 'Don't worry. I'll be fine.'

Pamela nodded and walked up the drive.

She thought she would take Miriam for a walk round the grounds, break the news about Will by a bed of delphiniums whilst skylarks flew overhead, but the headmaster, Mr Čapek, insisted she use his office, a small, cramped room with a muddle of cricket bats and lacrosse sticks piled up in the corner. Before sending for Miriam, he confirmed that the Kolischers hadn't been in touch for a while, and that Miriam was clearly worried by the recent lack of letters.

As she watched Miriam's shoulders slump, and her eyes fill up, Pamela felt a body blow of guilt. How could she inflict another loss on this poor child, who hadn't heard from her parents in months, just for her own comfort? How selfish of her to want to hug Miriam without a thought for the girl's own grief.

She tried to keep her voice calm and happy. 'You mustn't worry, dear. Mr Denison and I are positive Will will return. He'll be back soon, you'll see. And perhaps the bombing will have lessened by then and you can come back too. We'll all be together again!'

'And my parents?' Miriam whispered.

Pamela sighed. 'Communications are all over the place in Europe.' Was she beginning to sound like Hugh? She put her arm round Miriam. 'It must be very frightening for you, but do try to be brave. Never give up hope.' She wondered if her words were as much for herself as for Miriam.

Miriam nodded, but didn't seem convinced.

'Let's go for that walk now.'

Pamela had let go of Miriam in order to follow her down the narrow corridor, but took her hand as they stepped out into the warm summer air. A gardener in a cloth cap and short-sleeved shirt was pulling up carrots from a vegetable plot, releasing an earthy odour. He tipped his cap at them as they walked by.

'How is your singing going, Miriam?'

Miriam's face brightened. 'Well, thank you.'

'Can you sing me something?' Pamela's eyes were smarting in the sunlight, but it was good to be out in the fresh air.

Miriam started to hum a tune quietly. It sounded happy and folksy.

'And with the words?'

Her voice soared.

By the time they were on the road again, Pamela's heart had eased. Mr Čapek seemed a good man – he looked strong and sporty, quite unlike the thin, scholarly headmaster at Marlborough – and it was obvious Miriam had many friends at the school. Had Miriam been distraught at Pamela's news, she might have been tempted to bring her back to London, but really it was better to risk her being upset in Shropshire than endangering her security in Hampstead. Poor child: someone else missing from her life. She must be so scared about the lack of communication from her parents.

Pamela couldn't bear to spend the whole of the return journey looking out of the window. The sky was already darkening, purple clouds bruising the horizon. Soon there would be nothing to see.

'So tell me about how you came to be in the WAAF,' she said to Kate, more out of politeness than genuine interest.

Kate's mouth twitched. 'I have three brothers in the RAF,' she said. 'I wasn't prepared to stay at home sewing whilst they had all the fun.'

'Fun?' Pamela turned to stare at her.

'I'm sorry. That was thoughtless of me. You must be so worried about your son.'

Pamela gripped the handles of the brown handbag that lay on her lap. 'It's all right. I think Will probably did have fun.' She swallowed. 'He always seemed so alive when he came back on leave.'

Kate nodded. 'That's it. I've worked in radar control, tested aerial guns, even manoeuvred barrage balloons. Sure, we're not on the front line, but the work we do is vital.' She stopped talking to overtake an elderly man on a bicycle. 'I'm exhausted most of the time, but life has never been so exhilarating.'

Pamela smiled. That was how Will had felt. She opened her handbag, drew out a packet of mint humbugs and offered one to Kate.

'Worried I'll fall asleep at the wheel?'

'No, I meant to give these to Miriam. She loves them. But I forgot.' Pamela laid her head back on the rest, her eyes prickling.

'Her loss, my gain, ma'am,' said Kate. But her smile was sympathetic.

'You're welcome to them.' Pamela leant forward again. 'Here, I'll put them by the handbrake so you can help yourself.'

'Thanks.' Kate delved inside the packet. 'Have you been able to do any war work yourself, Mrs Denison?'

Pamela told her about the refugee committee. 'But we've had to stop for now. Most channels into Europe have been blocked.'

Kate chewed thoughtfully. 'I've heard the Red Cross are looking for volunteers. You might like to get involved there.'

'I might.' Pamela reached absent-mindedly for a mint and put it into her mouth. Kate was right. She'd been so aimless since the refugee work had dried up. Her Quaker values prevented her from actively supporting war work, and Hugh was keen for her to stay at home. But now, with Will gone, she needed something more to focus on, to break the tension of waiting for news. A part of her felt too exhausted to do anything, but she knew that was anxiety; there was no physical reason. And in a strange sort of way, if she helped people through the Red Cross, she'd feel as though she was helping Will too. She smiled at Kate. 'Thanks. I'll look into it,' she said, then laid her head back again as the car purred on through the gloom.

22

Eva stood with Abba and Josef at the hastily dug grave in the Bohušovice basin, blinking back the blur of tears as she watched her mother's body being lowered into the ground. This was to be one of the last burials. Already the building of the vast new crematorium was nearing completion. Another insult to Jews, who abhorred the burning of bodies. Eva was glad her mother would have a proper grave, even if her death had come far too soon, exhaustion and typhus claiming her before her time. She buried her head briefly in Josef's shoulder, then glanced behind her. Long shadows reached across the grass from the towering city walls behind them. A chill wind whipped at Eva's headscarf and reddened Abba's wet cheeks. She reached for his hand and held it.

'No more suffering, my dear,' he whispered.

Eva glanced at her father's face. But it wasn't to her that his words were addressed. His gaze was fixed on the grave.

'I'll see you in Gan Eden.' In front of him, in a shaft of watery sunlight, two white butterflies were performing an elaborate dance in perfect symmetry with each other. No matter how far apart they were, their movements were perfectly synchronised.

Eva squeezed Abba's hand. She thought of her mother's compassion after she had been attacked, the hours Mutti had spent sewing Miriam's clothes, her support over Eva's decision to send Miriam to England, the times she had pretended not to be hungry so Miriam could eat more, her selflessness, even in her last illness. Yes, Mutti would be in Gan Eden now.

As they traipsed back to their barracks, Eva glanced over at the small fortress. She'd been sent there once to collect some laundry, and had meandered across, savouring the rare chance for some fresh air. She'd lingered on the bridge, gazing down at the dry moat, and noticed a tangle of forget-me-nots with their sky-blue petals nestling among the weeds. How she wished she had some now to place on Mutti's grave. Perhaps she could pick a few the next time she was sent up to the fortress.

She wondered if she should risk trying to contact Miriam. The punishment for attempting to send letters was severe. Back in January, nine prisoners had been hanged for trying to write home; besides, even if she got away with a letter, it was very unlikely that any communication would get through. And why upset the child with the news of her beloved Oma's death? She'd find out soon enough.

Eva left Josef to escort a suddenly frail Abba back to the Sudetenland barracks whilst she returned to her dormitory in the Dresden block. Her bereavement had given her a day's reprieve from laundry duties, but the drudgery would start again tomorrow.

*

251

Pamela opened the wooden box and placed a tin of rice pudding in one corner and one of herrings in another. She wedged packets of tea and biscuits in the middle and laid the more fragile items, the bars of chocolate and cigarette packets, on top. Then she closed the lid firmly, slapped on a label and tied the box with string.

It felt good to have a focus again, now that the Collinses were finally back on their feet and no longer needed her help. Even Hugh had finally recognised she needed to do more. This time she was packing food, not clothes, and it was going to prisoners of war, not refugees. As usual, she wondered if one of her parcels would reach Will. She pictured him tugging at the string and wrenching open the lid before seizing on the chocolate. Would he devour it all at once, or savour it piece by piece? He'd never taken up smoking, but he'd probably be able to trade the cigarettes for more chocolate. And for a while, the creamy sweetness might give him a brief respite from the horrors of captivity and rekindle memories of his safe and happy childhood. She'd often popped penny bars of Dairy Milk into his tuck box for school.

'Any more, Mrs D?' Archie Higgins was trundling his trolley down the aisle, collecting boxes as he went.

Pamela started. Had she really only packed one box? 'Sorry, Archie. Can you come back in ten minutes and I'll have a couple more for you.'

'Right you are.' Archie touched his cap.

He was a nice lad, about Will's age. If Will hadn't been so headstrong, he too might be helping pack boxes in a Red Cross depot rather than mired in misery in a prison cell. Pamela firmed her lips. She mustn't think about Will; it was much better to keep busy. She reached for a tin of cocoa and started assembling the next container.

*

A few weeks later, Eva met Gabriel Schmidt face to face. She and Elsa had been delivering some laundry to the SS-Service Club in one of the huge black hearse carts that everything was transported in at Terezin, when they came across a group of men with hoes and rakes, en route for the gardens. Schmidt's face broke into a smile and he beckoned her into the shadow to the side of a barrack building.

'Eva Novak!' he exclaimed.

'Gabri. I thought I saw you a while ago, but I wasn't sure.' She smiled at the musician's familiar benign face. They had got to know each other well at the conservatoire. Gabri was much older, an excellent composer and pianist, although he'd still had to give piano lessons to supplement his income. They'd once played a duet together under Professor Novotny's watchful eye. Gabri was a kind and generous man, and it was another sadness from Eva's past that she no longer came across him. How strange to meet again in this awful place.

'Eva. Come on!' Elsa rattled the handles of the cart, annoyed at the delay.

Gabri glanced up. Already the garden gang was twenty metres away. 'Meet me at Dresden courtyard at eight tonight. I have something to show you.'

Eva smiled and returned to Elsa, who scowled and jerked the cart away.

*

253

By eight, it was completely dark. In the summer months, boys had played football on the courtyard, but now winter was approaching and all outdoor games had ceased. Eva looked up as Gabriel approached, his breath a white cloud in the cold air. Dry leaves crunched under his feet.

'Eva!' He kissed her warmly on both cheeks, and Eva instinctively looked around, whether for Josef or Germans she didn't know. 'What happened to you? One minute you were one of the bright stars at the conservatoire, and the next no one knew where you'd gone.'

Eva scratched at a flea bite on her arm. It was one of hundreds. 'I decided to give up my career,' she said. 'I got married . . . had a family.'

Gabriel nodded at her, but his gaze was intense. 'So, music's loss then.'

Eva shrugged. 'And you? Do you still compose?'

'A little. Even in here.' He looked round the courtyard, but nothing stirred. There was a distant clatter from one of the dorms, and, further out, the sound of someone shouting, but nothing close by. 'But I have a new project now.' His eyes gleamed in the darkness. 'Come with me.' He led her through the town park, across the main road, and into a room in the boys' home. 'Here's the gymnasium.'

Eva's stomach clenched as she looked round the cavernous room, with its peeling paint and stale-sweat odour. Ever since that first terrifying glimpse of Otto, her senses had been on high alert. Now she imagined him skulking behind the wall bars or lurking in the shadows. Or, worse still, bursting in with a group of armed guards to punish them. She put her hand against her chest to calm it.

'Come this way.' Gabriel beckoned her across the echoing room, produced a small torch from his pocket and illuminated a large shape in the corner. 'Look!'

The beam lit up a battered baby grand piano, shrouded in dust. It had no legs.

In spite of her terror, Eva was intrigued. 'However did it get here?'

'Someone discovered it a few months ago in Sokolovna, just outside the town limits. It was moved here in secret a few nights back.' He led her over, squatted down and placed his hands on the yellow keys before playing an A flat major scale. The sound wasn't bad. Perhaps someone had tuned it. She knelt down beside him and fingered the first few notes of the villanelle. Why that piece she had no idea, but it brought a shadowy Professor Novotny to her side, listening critically, a faint smile on his lips. For a second she imagined herself back in the rehearsal room at the conservatoire, preparing her piece for the Rudolfinum concert. Such an innocent child she'd been then. She'd had no idea she'd spend the rest of her life jumping at shadows, trying to suppress the horrors that threatened to engulf her.

'What a beautiful melody,' said Gabriel.

Eva stopped. 'I haven't played that for a long time.' Not since she'd sold the piano at the apartment to pay for Miriam's passage to England. She'd have had to dispose of it later anyway. Jews were no longer allowed to own musical instruments. She straightened up, reeling slightly at the touch of dizziness. 'But surely this is forbidden?' She looked round the room again to reassure herself it was empty.

Gabriel stood too, a little more slowly. 'The Germans are surprisingly relaxed about music here,' he said. 'Some of the prisoners have formed a chamber choir.'

'Really? And the Germans know?'

'They've made it clear they will turn a blind eye. Maybe they think it's harmless.' There was a liveliness in Gabriel's expression that Eva had rarely seen in Terezin. How had she not known about this? She'd been too busy worrying about Mutti and Abba – and Josef, come to that – and getting through the back-breaking work at the laundry, to find out about any cultural activities. 'But I have bigger plans.' Gabriel turned to the piano again. 'If I can get someone to clean and mend it, would you be prepared to play for us?'

Eva wrapped her arms across her chest. 'I'm completely out of practice.' She hadn't played at concert level for twelve years. Her hands were puffy and reddened from the laundry, her back hurt so much she could barely sit up, she was exhausted and still aching with grief. Piano playing was from another time, another life. Yet her fingers tingled and she stretched a palm across her leg and pressed out a chord.

'Many of us are. It'll come back to you. There'll be easier pieces at first. We are just finding our way in.'

'Why do you want to do this? Does it help to keep your mind off things here?'

Gabriel laughed. 'A little, yes. Perhaps it gives us a sense of purpose.'

'And is that worth the risk?'

He traced a circle on the ground with his foot. When he looked up, his eyes were fierce. 'Those bloody Nazis think they can break us. They shame us, work us till we drop, remove every shred of our humanity. But they can't take our creativity. Or our souls.'

'So music gives us hope?'

'Hope . . . identity . . . defiance. A legacy.'

Eva glanced at Gabriel's white face. There were dark folds under his eyes; his cheeks were almost hollow, his hair sparser than she remembered. But his eyes revealed a spirit that would not be suppressed.

'You won't believe how many musicians and singers are here: Gideon Klein, Pavel Haas, Ada Hecht. I know we can work together to produce something immensely powerful.'

'I had no idea Gideon was here. And Pavel too. I knew them distantly. But to have an opera singer is amazing.'

Gabriel stepped forward, took her arm and shone his torch towards the exit. 'And to have a pianist of your calibre is amazing too. I believe we can produce the best performances of our lives. Will you join us?'

Eva glanced back at the piano. She'd thought that chapter was closed. But then she'd thought she had a future as a wife and mother. Now Miriam was in England – she hadn't seen her in over three years – and she and Josef could no longer live together as man and wife. Gabriel was right. Who knew what the future would bring? There were more and more rumours about transports to the east. Harsher conditions. Perhaps death. Was life just about surviving the monotony, or creating something extraordinary? The fire that had been ashes for so long started to be rekindled. She grinned at Gabriel. 'Count me in,' she said.

*

The following night, after the usual watery beetroot soup and hard roll that served as supper, Eva went alone to the gymnasium. She was tired of playing cards with the other women in her dormitory or writing desultory letters to Josef in the hope that someone with a pass could smuggle them across to him. It was virtually impossible to speak to her husband, yet seemingly the Germans allowed male and female musicians to mix freely. Gabriel had offered her the chance to renew her passion, to be part of something momentous. How could she have refused?

She rummaged in her rucksack to find a torch, and discovered that if she propped it on top of the piano, she could angle it to illuminate the keys. At first she was fearful of being heard at this late hour. But then she remembered Gabriel's assurances that the Germans condoned music practice, and started to relax.

She knelt down and tried a few major scales, forcing her stiff fingers across the keyboard. Then several minor ones, followed by some arpeggios, a few chords and a chromatic scale on each hand. Before she knew it, an hour had passed and her fingers were throbbing. In the middle of her practice, she'd half expected Mutti to come in and reprimand her for working too hard, so vividly had she been returned to her girlhood, but of course the door had remained closed, and, apart from the mouse in the corner, she had no company all evening.

Before she staggered to her feet, she played the whole of the villanelle. Gabri had been right: it had come back to her. Perhaps she could be of use to the choir after all. For a whole hour she hadn't once been aware of bed bugs, or grinding hunger, or the still painful separation from Miriam. And just as Gabri had promised, she'd remained uninterrupted the entire time.

*

Pamela wiped a film of condensation from the window and glanced out. After weeks of dull winter days, a white sun lit up pavements glittering with frost, and sugary drifts piled up on roofs. She retrieved one of Hugh's old scarves from the hook in the hall, wound it round her neck and buttoned her winter coat over the top. Then she tugged on an old cloche hat and dug deep in her pockets for her winter gloves. She hesitated about whether to retrieve her gumboots from the basement, but decided that brogues over her lisle stockings would be sufficient.

It was pleasant to leave the cheerless house behind and stride down Templewood Avenue towards the Heath. Even with the cold wind reddening her nose and making her eyes water, the weather was invigorating. She felt more alive than she had for weeks, in spite of the sight of bomb-damaged houses with their boarded-up windows and patched roofs. Technically they were still in danger, but their old house hadn't shed so much as a brick. In some ways, she'd have felt less guilty if it had. Her own parents were much more vulnerable in the East End, even though they'd refused to give in to Pamela's increasingly frantic requests to stay with her and Hugh. There'd still been no news from Will, and who knew what had happened to Miriam's parents. It didn't seem fair that she'd been kept safe when others were suffering so much.

Already she could see the criss-cross of canes in the distance: a few months earlier, runner beans had wound their way round them, but the plants had long since withered, leaving behind bamboo skeletons. As she came closer, she saw newly dug beds dotted with frilly-leaved cabbages, their tight-packed hearts beaded with dew. There'd been allotments up on the Heath for a few years now, and she felt the usual pang of guilt that she still hadn't produced any food of her own apart from the pot of yellowing parsley that moped on her windowsill.

She said good morning to a man pounding at the earth with a pickaxe, whilst a small girl, possibly his granddaughter, inched towards a tame robin perched on a spade, holding out a few crumbs of bread on her white palm.

The man tipped his hat at her. 'Lovely day.'

Pamela smiled. 'If a bit chilly.' She watched him wipe his brow with his handkerchief. 'Although I dare say it's warm if you're working.'

'It is that,' he agreed. 'Pleased to do my bit for the war, though.'

Pamela nodded. 'We've had it quite bad round here.' Only last week, on the corner of West End Lane and Dennington Park Road, a wedding party had been hit by a high-explosive bomb. Ten people were killed, including two babies. The only family member to survive was the father of the young soldier who was getting married later that day. It had been all over the front page of the *Herald*.

She wondered why the little girl hadn't been evacuated. 'Is that your granddaughter?' she asked the man.

'Yes. We lost her mum in the Blitz. Her dad's fighting with the Desert Rats. We couldn't bear to be parted from Joan, so we kept her with us.'

'That must be hard for you. My son is missing in action. I'd give anything to have him back home.'

The man's face creased in sympathy. 'I'm so sorry.'

Pamela turned to go, then changed her mind.

'Is it difficult to secure an allotment?'

The man leant on his pickaxe. 'Normally, yes, but I've been saying for a while that this is too much for me. I could give you a small patch of mine if you like.'

Pamela had a sudden memory of planting carrot seeds with her father, the thin brown specks nestling in her palm. She'd checked the ground each day until the first feathery leaves pushed through the soil. Then she'd picked them too early. Her father's laughter at her fistful of tiny yellow roots came back to her through the years.

'I'd like that, thank you.'

'We'll be finished here soon, but if you come back tomorrow at the same time, we'll sort something out.'

'Thanks, I will do.'

The man tipped his hat again as she walked on, her body tingling with the prospect of a new activity to fill her days.

Although the edges of the Heath were patchworked with allotments, higher up, the pre-war areas of rough grass and scattered paths were still intact. There was no one else around and Pamela enjoyed the solitude of her walk. It was good to stride out in the winter sunshine, to feel her leg muscles flex and tighten, to swing her arms in a brisk rhythm. She'd been cautious for so long after her skiing accident, but now her leg barely troubled her.

As she walked on, she saw the shadowy figure of a boy running through the late-morning mist. They'd given Will a kite for his tenth birthday. She and Hugh had taken him up to the Heath one day to fly it. Will had tugged at Hugh's hand in frustration as they mounted the incline to the point where they were closest to the translucent sky and their ears were cuffed by the buffeting wind. Finally Hugh placed the frantically flapping kite into the boy's hands and told him to hold on for dear life. Then he let out the string, yard by yard, until Will was screaming with the effort of keeping the kite still.

'All right. Let go!' Hugh had shouted.

Will had opened his fingers and the kite leapt out, soaring upwards through the swirling air.

Hugh pulled and released the string and the kite arced through the sky. Pamela laughed at Will's expression of unfettered joy, his movements staccato as he ran with his head tilted back, shouting with delight. She wished she'd brought the little Brownie camera Hugh had given her, to capture this moment. Instead, she'd tried to fix it on the film of memory. But inevitably the cycles and busyness of life had pushed it to the recesses of her mind. Until today.

She pulled her collar up and set off back into the wind, trying to rekindle the memory of a small hand in hers as she retraced her steps home.

23

For once, Eva was glad of the sticky fug of the laundry. Outside, icicles hung from the windowsills and a cold wind whipped down the streets of the ghetto. Despite the fetid odour of the washroom, the constant plumes of steam billowing from the coppers, it was a relief that she didn't have to work in the cold. She wore gloves all the time now, apart from at work, even in bed in the freezing dormitory. It would be disastrous to get chilblains: she could stand the pain, but swollen fingers would not play so well. At least the temporary puffiness from working in the laundry subsided as soon as she went out into the cold; chilblains would be much more long-lasting.

The door banged open, bringing with it a blast of cold air, and Eva looked up to see Gabriel striding towards her, grinning. 'How would you like to play for a performance of *The Bartered Bride*?'

Eva frowned. 'I thought Smetana was banned.'

Gabriel grinned. 'And Mendelssohn, Mahler, Schoenberg, Offenbach . . .'

'So isn't it a terrible risk to play a Czech opera under the noses of the Germans?'

Gabriel mimed a triumphant chord. 'Not when the Nazis are positively encouraging it. They've dubbed it *Freizeitgestaltung*: leisure time. Apparently it's good for us.'

Eva shook her head. 'So husbands and wives are not allowed to live together, we're given meagre rations and worked till we drop – but we can meet openly and play music?'

'That's about the gist of it. Come to the basement of Sudeten tonight. We're to have our first rehearsal.'

That night, in the dim light of a musty basement riddled with damp and thick with stale air, Eva made out the exhausted faces of her fellow prisoners. Most were women; some she recognised from Dresden barracks, or the laundry or the kitchen. Truda Borger was to play Mařenka, Franta Weissenstein Jeník, Bedřich Borges Kecal and Jakob Goldring Vašek. Gabriel was conducting. He motioned Eva to the baby grand piano, now retuned and on new legs, which had been moved there now, and handed her some sheet music.

'You brought this to Terezin when you were only allowed fifty kilograms?'

Gabriel nodded. 'I have lots of music. Much more use than books or extra socks. There's a cello player I know who took his instrument apart, wrapped the pieces of wood in a blanket, together with some glue and clamps, and put it back together when he got here.'

Eva felt her eyes prickle. 'What foresight,' she murmured. 'But Gabri, I haven't practised this.'

Gabriel laughed. 'Nor has anyone else. That's what rehearsals are for.' He tapped a makeshift baton on the table.

'Thank you for coming, everyone,' he said. 'I know we are all exhausted, but I thought a little Smetana might lift our spirits. He represents the heart of our culture. So, ladies and gentlemen: the opening chorus: "Let us rejoice".' He turned to look at Eva, who obediently played the introduction, managing to get it note perfect, and was rewarded by a warm swell of voices singing the triumphant, joyous words of the beginning of Smetana's first act. It was hard to maintain composure at the hope and courage they conveyed.

As she played the last note, Eva gazed across at the chorus. She saw young women whose faces were prematurely lined, girls in faded headscarves and patched jumpers, men with hollows under their eyes, thin, tired, desperate people. But every one of them stood straight and sang their best, with shining eyes and full hearts. Yes, they were Czech Jews, but even here, in the most shaming of circumstances, they delivered the song with pride and triumph: *Let us rejoice*. Yes! Why shouldn't we?

*

Pamela sat by the window, looking out. The street lamp at the end of their front garden drizzled yellow light on the pavement, and misty rain blurred the hedge of the house opposite. It would soon be time to draw the blackout, imprisoning them for another night.

She'd been back to the allotment earlier. The man had marked out a patch about ten feet square. 'All yours.'

'Thank you,' she'd said, reaching down to scoop up a handful of sandy soil. She'd have to get hold of some manure. But carrots would grow there quite happily. Probably parsnips too. And she might even be able to fit in some potatoes. How wonderful to have Miriam and Will home and see their surprise as she handed them bowls of thick vegetable soup made from her own home-grown ingredients. 'How much do I owe you?'

'Nothing,' said the man. 'Just give me some produce from time to time.'

Pamela had laughed. 'It's a deal!'

She glanced at her watch. Nearly six. She'd long since given up anticipating when Hugh would be home. He must be tired of eating heated-up food. She traipsed into the kitchen, bent down to the oven and drew out the pot of lamb stew that Kitty had made earlier. She ladled the contents onto two plates, covered Hugh's with an inverted bowl and set it aside. It would stay warm for a while; later on, she'd boil some water in a saucepan and rest the plate on it to reheat.

She carried her own meal into the dining room. She wasn't hungry – she rarely was – but she still went through the motions, chasing limp vegetables and a tiny piece of meat round the plate with her fork and trying to scoop up watery gravy. She'd meant to do some potatoes to soak up the juices, but somehow she'd lost track of time. There was the end of a loaf in the bread crock. That would have to do.

But as she went to stand up, she heard Hugh's key in the lock, and rushed into the hall to greet him.

'Got away early for once,' he said, wiping his feet energetically on the mat. 'Any news?'

Pamela shook her head. 'You?'

'Bloody Germans. They're supposed to supply us with lists of POWs, but nothing seems to be getting through at the moment. You'd think working at the FO I'd be the first to hear about my own son, but I never get to find out anything.

Apparently, if he's a POW he'll have filled in something called a capture card on arrival. If he's been taken prisoner, that's the first we'll know of it.'

Pamela's stomach lurched with disappointment. 'I suppose we just have to be patient.' She took Hugh's coat and hung it on the hook. 'Supper's ready. I'll bring yours in.'

'Righto.'

She retrieved Hugh's plate from the kitchen and set it on the mat opposite hers. Then she picked up her knife and fork listlessly. Another meal spent trying to pretend all was well, another evening making desultory conversation. Each of them unwilling to discuss their gnawing fears. And the terrible sense of foreboding that increased each day that Will was away.

*

The women gathered round, dressed in newly washed and ironed clothes. The first candle was lit, throwing long shadows around the room, and the dormitory leader approached the menorah and prayed. '*Ma'oz tzur yeshu'ati . . .*' It was strange to hear the words in a woman's voice and not Abba's dear, familiar tones.

They'd been determined to celebrate Chanukah at Terezin that year. In the women's barracks someone had 'borrowed' a white tablecloth, and one of the men, a former carpenter, had given them a menorah he'd carved out of wood. Thanks to the stealth and ingenuity of kitchen workers, there was fresh bread and even a cake. And they'd been making each other presents for weeks out of old scraps. Eva had composed a tune and had spent the last few evenings copying it carefully onto little pieces of manuscript paper Gabri had given her, ready to distribute later. Even if her roommates couldn't read music, she knew they would be touched by the effort. She was pleased with herself. She hadn't written a new tune since she'd created the lullaby at the sanatorium.

Suddenly there was a loud whisper: 'A German's in the building!' It was the watch, who'd run upstairs.

Someone extinguished the candle and the shadows vanished, plunging the room into darkness. Eva grabbed the menorah. 'Run to your rooms,' the dorm leader hissed, and everyone scattered. 'Quietly! Don't let them hear you.'

Eva sped back to her dormitory, thrust the menorah under her mattress and threw herself on her bunk, face down, her heart hammering. The door burst open; she heard the thud of heavy boots and felt her ribcage tighten. A quick sideways glance confirmed what she constantly feared every day in the camp: it was Otto. Her heartbeat increased until it was almost one long note. She watched him stride up to the table, sit down on the bench and fire questions at the dormitory leader. Why was the table so beautifully laid? Where had they got all that bread from?

The dormitory leader stumbled over her replies. Thank goodness Eva had hidden the menorah, although it wouldn't take long for Otto to find it if he was persistent enough. Luckily the woman didn't give anything away.

Eva hid her face again, but she could still hear Otto prowling round the room. The heavy breaths came closer; he was standing by her bed now, watching her. Even with her nose pressed into the blanket, she still caught his stench.

Once again she was back in the graveyard, her clothes being ripped off, her body pummelled and torn. She braced herself for the attack.

He pulled her hair and yanked her head up. 'Wake up, Sleeping Beauty.'

Eva looked into his eyes. Again the flicker of recognition. Stronger this time. She longed to grab the menorah and run out of the room. To run and run until she left Terezin and all its horrors behind. But she'd never get away. This time she had to face her demon. The room held its breath. Eva continued to glower at Otto.

Otto stared back for a second, and something passed between them, then his mouth twisted and he backed off. She dropped her head again and listened to the sound of retreating footsteps, the blood pounding in her ears.

Eventually the watch reported that he'd left the building. The presents were brought out and distributed; they ate supper. But the bread lay heavy in Eva's stomach. Was that man never going to stop tormenting her?

Josef had a pass now. It meant he could come and go on legitimate camp business. He could also see more of Eva. He managed to visit the laundry one morning to speak to her. She was pressing German uniforms in the ironing room. A smell of hot serge filled the air.

'How are you, *Liebling*?'

She reached up to kiss him. His whole face had sagged over the last few months, and his jacket looked like it was made for a much bigger man. The laundress in her yearned to take out its creases, but the wife in her longed for him to return to the fitter, stronger man she'd married – despite his hypochondriac ways.

'I'm well.' She shrugged. 'Tired, of course, but coping.'

Josef sighed. 'It's all this music. Wearing you out on top of everything else.'

'It's the one thing that keeps me going. Everything else is drudgery.'

'Including me?'

Eva reached for the iron. 'Of course not! But we hardly see each other. We're not exactly man and wife any more.'

'No. I feel more married to your father than I do to you!'

Eva laughed. 'I'm sorry, dear. I know you look out for him, and I'm grateful. But we all have to find ways of coping.'

'And music's yours?'

She paused, and a surge of voices filled her chest. 'Yes, music's mine. I didn't think I would ever take such pleasure in it again, but the standard is so high here. We're lucky to have some of the finest musicians here at Terezin.'

'Lucky?' Josef's voice sounded bitter. 'How can anything be lucky in a place like this?'

'Maybe "lucky" is the wrong word, but in a funny way, I do feel alive again.'

'And didn't you feel alive with me?'

'Of course!' Eva realised how her words must have sounded. 'I loved . . . love being your wife, looking after Miriam, spending time with my parents . . . but things are different now.'

'Terribly different. And it's all my fault.'

'Josef. We've been over this. We all make decisions. It was me who decided to send Miriam away, remember. I had to live with that.'

Josef patted her shoulder awkwardly. 'It was the right decision.'

Eva nodded. After *The Bartered Bride*, there was talk of a children's opera. She would have loved to hear Miriam sing, to swell with maternal pride at her daughter's solo, to share with her the joy that music brought. But that was a selfish thought. Besides, Miriam was getting opportunities to sing in England. And it was much safer for her there. Eva had learnt to suppress a pang every time she saw a mother with a child Miriam's age. She'd be nearly nine now. But she also felt huge relief that Miriam wasn't facing the daily privations of Terezin. 'Yes, it was the right decision,' she echoed.

'But I worry about you,' said Josef. 'You'll make yourself ill with all these rehearsals.'

Eva shook her head. 'They invigorate me. I go to bed with music in my ears, melodies in my heart. I wake up looking forward to the next practice. It gets me through the day.'

'I know. Just be careful you don't overdo things.'

A thought occurred to her. 'It isn't just music, you know. Aaron Rathstein is appealing to everyone with specialist knowledge to give lectures. You could talk about science.'

Josef laughed hollowly. 'What, tell everyone how to make hydrogen cyanide?'

'No. Not that, of course. But you could talk about your work on the antisera. People would find it interesting. And I want everyone to know what a good person you are.'

'Maybe I will. That's a good idea. Thank you. Maybe I'll prepare some notes this evening.' Josef left the laundry, forgetting to kiss her goodbye.

Eva picked up the iron again. She knew his omission

stemmed from absent-mindedness rather than lack of affection. Her suggestion about a science lecture had struck a chord, and she was pleased he had something else to think about.

They both had their passions, she and Josef, but unlike other couples at Terezin, who yearned for each other and felt their separation terribly, those passions lay elsewhere. For Eva, it was music that quickened her pulse and made her heart leap in her chest, and she'd rekindled that ardour in the most unlikely of places.

*

Up on the allotment, Pamela held the garden fork upright, intending to plunge it into the frosty ground, but as she pressed down, the prongs shot along the icy surface, barely leaving a mark. She dragged the fork back to a vertical position, placed a wellington boot on either side, pushing herself up until she was suspended above the earth, then drove down with all her weight. This time the prongs dug in half an inch or so, but when she climbed off, the fork had stuck fast. 'Damn!' She looked round, but the mist-enveloped allotment was silent, the corpses of long-abandoned vegetables shrouded in white, the trees skeletal in the shadowy air.

She heaved the fork out of the ground and tossed it down, panting with effort. Then she knelt on the freezing soil, pulled off her gloves and clawed at the earth with her bare hands until she'd gouged out enough for a little cairn of stones and lumps of clay.

It was useless trying to garden in this weather; she'd

known it as soon as she'd wiped the condensation off the window that morning and glimpsed the thick fog outside. But she couldn't bear to spend another day in the morgue-like house, listening to Kitty pad around as if frightened of making a sound. She had to feel the grip of the wind on her face, the frozen soil on her fingers, the ice under her bitten nails.

Ashes to ashes, dust to dust. It had been winter when Tommy had died. They'd buried him where he'd dropped, close to the front in a French field. His comrades must have pounded at the earth with spades and pickaxes, hewing a shallow grave out of the hard mud, constantly alert for the sound of gunfire, then lowered his body and covered it with earth. After the war, her parents had been informed that he'd been transferred to a military cemetery. They'd never visited it. 'He's in our hearts,' her mother had whispered, wiping her face. 'We'll treasure him there.'

Pamela drove out the thought of Will joining Tommy in France, uncle and nephew in the same foreign soil, and sat back on her heels. Sweat prickled her armpits and her cheeks burned. At least she was warm now. She'd hoped to dig the ground ready for some early planting, but there was nothing more to be done today. And she was due at the Red Cross later. She picked up her gloves, thrust her dirt-encrusted hands into them, then set off home through the still-white streets.

She had put her key in the door and was about to wipe her boots when she saw a battered white card on the mat. Her chest tightened. Could this be the capture card at last? She picked it up with shaking fingers. It had Will's familiar spidery handwriting, and a German postmark. It was from somewhere called Hammelburg. The words *Fill up this card immediately* were typewritten across the top. Then, *I am a prisoner of war in Germany*. Next followed scant details in Will's own hand: his name, rank and squadron. Under 'Sound', he had written *Yes*. The word 'wounded' had been crossed out. Underneath, in more typed letters, it read, *Do not reply to Hammelburg, await further information*.

Pamela leant against the wall, trying to hold the card still. Thank God. Will was safe. A prisoner, but safe, and apparently unharmed. She'd wait until her heart stopped racing, then she'd telephone Hugh.

*

The Bartered Bride was a spectacular success. Not only was the performance of a high standard, but the opera revived a little of the prisoners' lost national pride. It was painful to be reminded of their past, sure, but it stirred something in their hearts that made them stand a little taller, frown a little less, smile a little more. Music was a powerful medicine.

Josef had been in the audience the first night, along with Abba, and both hugged Eva warmly afterwards.

'Well done, my darling,' said Josef.

'You played just like you did as a young girl,' said Abba with a proud smile.

Eva made a face. 'I doubt that. But it was marvellous to be performing again.'

Josef nodded as though he finally understood.

Sometimes Eva felt as though she'd been a little harsh with Josef. He'd been under no illusion that theirs was a love match when he married her, but she'd tried hard to look after him, to make him happy. She was no competition for his first wife, who seemed to have been the perfect hausfrau before an untimely bout of pneumonia. Yet Josef was a devoted father to Miriam, and the years when she was tiny, and they all lived together in Prague, were happy. Josef had spent hours creating puppets for his little girl, making her laugh with their antics, and the love he showed his daughter had increased Eva's affection for him. But with Miriam gone, and Josef's long months of silent reproach hanging between them, there seemed little left to hold them together.

She'd been content to share a mattress with Mutti before her mother had become ill; the physical separation from Josef had made the mental separation possible. Now there were two women sleeping in Mutti's place. New prisoners were arriving at Terezin every day; the place was bursting at the seams. Sometimes, in bed, they all had to turn over at the same time in order to coordinate their movements and so take up as little space as possible. It reminded Eva of sardines in a tin. Not that they'd eaten sardines for a very long time.

She was glad that Josef had followed her suggestion and put himself forward for science lectures. His enthusiasm for the project had assuaged some of her guilt at the hours she spent in rehearsal. Josef was a thorough, if occasionally pedantic lecturer, but there were many scientists in Terezin who flocked to hear him. His popularity gave him confidence. In their separate ways they had both found light in the darkest of places.

24

One evening, after another performance of *The Bartered Bride*, Gabriel asked Eva to stay behind. 'There's someone I'd like you to meet.' He looked out where the audience had been sitting and beckoned to a young girl who lingered in the back row. 'Hana. Please come forward.'

The girl walked up the aisle towards Eva. At the sight of her, something fluttered in Eva's chest. Hana had blonde hair and a shy smile. She looked older than Miriam – twelve or thirteen, perhaps – but something about her reminded Eva of her own daughter.

'Hello.' Eva reached out a hand to her.

The girl's eyes shone. 'I loved the performance, Mrs Kolischer,' she murmured. 'It was like a beautiful dream I want to have again and again.'

Eva smiled at Hana's enthusiasm.

'I think I'll be singing "Faithful loving" even in my sleep.'

Eva laughed. 'Do you sing yourself?'

'A little. But I prefer to play the piano.'

'I was like that too. I used to play for hours.'

'I heard you were one of the conservatoire's star pupils.'

'Did you go to the conservatoire yourself?'

Hana looked down at the ground. 'I had private lessons with Mr Schmidt. Until music was banned.'

'And now here you are in Terezin, where music is not banned.'

'I know. In spite of all the bad things here, it is wonderful to go to concerts again.'

Eva stood up and relinquished her seat at the piano. 'Will you play for me, Hana?' she said softly.

Hana looked reluctant, but sat down without demurring. She placed her hands on the keyboard, gazed into the middle distance for a second, then started to play. She sat up straight to start with, then, as the piece progressed, dipped one shoulder and leant into the keys as if trying to merge with the instrument, pulling and coaxing as much poignancy from the keys as she could.

As the sound of a delicate lullaby threaded through the room, Eva gasped and Gabriel put out a hand to steady her as the blood plummeted from her head.

Hana stopped playing.

'Eva, are you all right?' asked Gabriel 'When did you last eat?'

'No, it's not hunger,' whispered Eva. The room was still swaying and her heart was galloping. She put a hand to her chest.

Gabriel rushed to get a chair and Eva sat down gratefully. 'How do you know that tune?' she asked Hana.

Hana blinked at her. 'I-I found it,' she said.

'Found it where?'

Gabriel moved protectively towards Hana. 'Eva. You're frightening the girl.'

Eva ignored him. 'I must know where you found that music,' she repeated. 'It's vital that you tell me.'

Hana hung her head. 'At my parents' house. In a cupboard.'

'You can't have!' Eva was almost shouting now.

'I did.' Tears formed at the corners of Hana's eyes and her face flushed pink.

Gabriel laid a hand on Eva's arm. 'Eva. If Hana says she found the music in a cupboard, we should believe her. I've never known her tell a lie. You're tired, my dear, perhaps we should have this conversation another time.'

Eva dashed a hand across her eyes. Perhaps Gabri was right. Her heart was still hammering and she still felt light-headed, but it was the conclusions she had drawn, the only conclusions she could draw, that were distressing her more than anything. She needed time to think. And perhaps to speak to Hana alone.

'I'm sorry,' she whispered, and stumbled out of the room. She didn't need to look back to know that Hana and Gabriel were staring at her, rigid with shock.

Eva spent a sleepless night, staring at the ceiling, oblivious to the sighs and rustles around her, as her mind wrestled with the implications of her encounter with Hana. The dormitory was even more crowded now, new consignments of people arriving at Terezin almost weekly, but for once Eva wasn't aware of the cramped conditions, the freezing cold, the constant itch from burrowing bed bugs. All she could think of was Hana.

As soon as her shift at the laundry finished, she hurried back to the practice room in the Dresden basement. A second grand piano, replacing the original one, had been brought across from Prague and installed in the gymnasium, as well as a number of instruments. It was extraordinary the licence the Germans were permitting them for their leisure – whilst all other aspects of their lives were so restricted. She had only just entered the corridor when the sound of the piano reached her. It must be Hana: she had a way of pausing a split second before she played a phrase. Gabriel did it too; he must have passed it on to his pupil. Thankfully she wasn't playing yesterday's lullaby. In fact it was the first triumphant chorus from *The Bartered Bride*. Note perfect. She must have memorised it.

Eva stood in the doorway watching Hana play. Sunlight poured through the window, lighting up the dust on the top of the piano and illuminating each strand of the girl's unusually fair hair. She played with complete concentration, her eyes intense with focus, a half-smile on her lips. Eva wondered again how the child had got hold of that melody.

Hana broke off as Eva approached the piano. She darted a frightened look at her, as if fearful of a repeat of yesterday's questions. It was important that Eva was gentler this time.

She squatted down beside the piano stool. 'You play beautifully, Hana.'

Hana managed a faint smile. 'Thank you.'

'How did you know that piece so well? You don't have any music.'

'Mr Schmidt taught me it. I know it by heart now.'

'It's a difficult piece for someone your age to master.'

The girl sat up straighter. 'I'm twelve. I've been playing for eight years.'

'A long time. And I can't imagine you ever shirk your practice.'

'Never. In fact my mother often tells me . . . *told* me to stop.'

'Told?'

Hana's face was rigid. 'My parents left Terezin a month ago. They were in one of the transports.'

'You poor child. But how come you didn't go with them?'

Hana's hands shook and she placed her fingers on the keyboard to steady them. 'I was on the list, along with my mother. But my father begged the commandant to release me.' Her voice became hoarse. 'He offered to go instead . . .'

Eva reached out to cover Hana's fingers with her own. 'A brave man.'

Hana barely moved. 'The bravest.'

'And have you heard from your parents since?' More and more people were being transported from Terezin to the east, but no one really knew what awaited them, despite the rumours.

'My mother said she would try to get a message through when she got to the next camp, even though it was a terrible risk,' said Hana. 'We agreed on a signal. No matter what she wrote, if her handwriting sloped up, it would mean conditions were better where they'd gone. If it sloped down, things were worse.'

'And what happened?' asked Eva.

Hana took a battered postcard from her pocket and showed it to Eva. *We are well and happy*, it read. *This is a nice place and we are living a good life.*

The writing clearly sloped down.

Hana was too distressed for Eva to ask her the question that had tormented her all night, but she spoke to Gabriel before the next performance.

'Are you all right, Eva?' he asked as she arranged her music on the grand piano.

Eva nodded. 'I had a shock.'

'What kind of shock?'

Eva paused. How could she tell Gabri the truth? Besides, she had to compose herself for the performance. It wouldn't be fair on her fellow musicians and singers to allow herself to become upset. 'I wrote that lullaby Hana played,' she said. 'Many years ago. I didn't think anyone else knew of its existence.'

'Perhaps you left a copy at the conservatoire by mistake.'

Eva lifted her already perfectly arranged score in front of her face and shuffled its pages. 'Of course. That must be it,' she replied, and replaced the score on the rest, trying to keep her fingers steady.

Gabriel bowed. 'Good luck this evening,' he said.

Eva looked out into the audience. 'Thank you.'

But the question was burning her up. Gabriel asked her to teach Hana the music for *The Bartered Bride*, so she would have an understudy if she ever got sick – or worse. Eva spent hours with the girl, going over the pieces again and again, adjusting a chord here and a phrase there. She was as tough on Hana as she'd been on herself all those years ago. But Hana never complained, despite the fact that she must have been exhausted.

They were finishing their practice one day and Hana had lingered to chat. Their breath came out in clouds in the freezing basement air. Hana pulled the sleeves of her jumper over her hands.

'Do you remember that song you were playing when I first met you?' asked Eva.

Hana's expression was guarded. 'Yes.'

'Tell me again how you discovered it.'

'In my mother's cupboard. She was out one day when I was sent home early from school with a temperature, and I was looking for something else when I came across it.'

'What were you searching for?'

She failed to meet Eva's eye. 'My birth certificate.'

'Why?'

'I never looked like my parents. They weren't musical like me, although they always encouraged my love of it. They were quite old when they had me. I went through a phase when I wondered whether I was adopted.'

'And did you find the certificate?' Eva tried to keep her voice mild.

'No. I've never found it. But I did come across the manuscript for the lullaby. I committed it to memory so my parents wouldn't know I'd been looking through their private cupboard and discovered it. I often play it to myself, although I still can't work out why they had it when they themselves weren't musical.'

Eva leant forward a fraction, towards the girl. 'Hana, the reason I was so strange that day was because *I* wrote that piece. No one else has ever seen it.'

'So why was it in my mother's cupboard?'

'I don't know. I wrote it for a baby. A baby I had in secret and had to give away.' Her words hung in the suddenly thick air. 'The only thing I could create for my child was a lullaby. A lullaby I hoped might comfort her when I no longer could.'

She held her breath as Hana turned away and gazed silently

282

out of the window. A clock at the back of the room pulsed in time with her heart.

When Hana finally turned back and met Eva's eyes, it was with complete understanding. 'It did comfort her,' she whispered, her white cheeks glistening with tears.

That night Eva dreamt of the attack again. The stench of beery breath was in her nostrils, the slime of spit on her cheeks. Her body recoiled from hands that grabbed and grasped and pulled; the memory of brutish thrusts. Her ears rang with taunts. Could something so terrible have produced something so beautiful? There'd been no possibility of justice.

When she'd finally arrived home that night, tearful, shocked and torn, her parents had coaxed the truth out of her, then exchanged horrified glances. Later, she lay in the bath and her mother tenderly sponged away the blood then wrapped her in a towel. She didn't move as Mutti dabbed gentian violet on her bruises, but curled up like a child when she was eventually put to bed.

At first she failed to register the lack of menstrual cramps: the pain in her head drove out everything else. But when, after three months, her period failed to arrive, and she slowly realised that the almost constant nausea was not just from shock, she confided her terrible suspicion to Mutti. Dr Parizek confirmed the pregnancy. The child would be born in six months.

Later, as Eva lay in bed, she heard her anxious parents whispering. She could imagine the content of their conversation: how would Mutti deal with the gossip at the kosher butcher's? How could Abba face the talk at the Kotva? What about Eva's music? The performance at the Rudolfinum? How could she bring up a baby when she was still a child herself?

By the morning, Mutti had a suggestion. 'There's a sanatorium in the Carpathian mountains. Doctors send people with TB there. But there's a wing for unmarried mothers. We will make enquiries . . .'

Eva had nodded, still numb with shock. Two weeks later, she was on a train. And a year later, she was married to Josef.

They let her hold the baby for five minutes. Her precious daughter had hardly any hair, just faint white down on her soft little head. Her blue eyes were trying to focus. What was she saying to her mother? *I know you love me.*

And now they were together again. Although clearly Hana was still grief-stricken for her adoptive parents, she seemed to be gradually coming to terms with the fact that Eva was her biological mother. But Eva couldn't bear to tell her she was the child of a rape. Hana had had to cope with so much – this would devastate her. But then perhaps the fact that her life was so grim, that she had hardened herself to deal with its horrors, meant that she would be able to deal with this now. Who knew whether she'd ever see her adoptive parents again? But here, in Terezin, against all the odds and in the most unlikely of places, both her biological parents had been brought together once more.

Eva was developing a good relationship with Hana. She reminded her so much of herself at that age; she even played the piano with some of the same mannerisms. Hana treated her affectionately. But how could she tell her about Otto?

She listened to the scratch of bed bugs as they skittered over the walls. They were everywhere these days. She daren't look up at the ceiling in case one dropped on her face. It was hard to know where the bed bugs began and the fleas ended. They all wanted to violate her, to suck her flesh, to infiltrate her with their poison, leaving their legacy of angry red bumps.

By the morning, she was resolved. She would have to speak to Otto next time she saw him. But she hadn't yet worked out how or when that chance would come.

The infestations had been getting worse. Each group of new arrivals to the ghetto brought new vermin. Now there were lice to add to the fleas and beg bugs. The rooms were crawling with them. It was impossible to concentrate on anything other than the itching, burning and stinging sensations. At night the air resounded with scratching sounds as people tried desperately to relieve their discomfort. The next day, their arms and legs would be raw and running with blood.

One morning, the gendarme came into Eva's dormitory and made an announcement: 'Everyone out. You're to take all your belongings with you and live in Hamburg barracks for a few days. The whole of Dresden will be fumigated.'

Eva reached to the end of the bed for her bag and hastily stuffed in all her clothes, her tin mug and plate, her cutlery, the photo of Miriam and a torch. Not much to show for all these months at Terezin. 'I expect we're being upgraded,' she said. 'Five-star accommodation instead of four.'

Nobody laughed.

Within half an hour, the dormitory was empty. As they

walked down the corridor, en route to the Hamburg barracks, they passed men in boiler suits and masks holding huge cylinders of gas with hoses attached. Eva shivered.

She and the thirty other women rearranged their belongings in a room that was as dismal as the last: bunks stacked three tiers high, filthy mattresses, a single cracked washbasin, very little space and no privacy.

'It'll be Zyklon B,' Josef told her later when they managed to meet up outside the kitchens. 'The gas the Nazis wanted me to help produce. Maybe they've changed their minds and it was just to kill vermin after all.'

'Do you really think so?' asked Eva, raising an eyebrow.

Josef kicked at a loose stone on the path in front of him. His eyes were dull and sunken in their sockets. How strange that the man who had been such a hypochondriac in Prague rarely mentioned his health in Terezin. Hardship produced all kinds of courage. 'Ten thousand tonnes is still a huge amount, even for all these infestations,' he said.

'I suppose it depends what kind of vermin you want to exterminate,' muttered Eva.

Josef nodded, his face a white mask.

Eva thought of Hana's postcard from her adoptive parents. What were they doing to those prisoners in Poland that was so terrible? Whatever it was, she had to protect the girl at all costs. Once again she marvelled at the strange and almost unbelievable circumstances that had delivered Hana to her care. She'd got one daughter to safety – and even a bomb-torn Britain was safer than Terezin; now she had to save the other too.

*

286

It was a couple of weeks later, at a packed performance of the Smetana opera, that she noticed a shadowy figure at the back of the audience: Otto. He stood with some of the other German guards, watching the production.

As luck would have it, he was still chatting with a group of uniformed men at the end. She quickly slipped off her piano stool and made her way towards him, on feet that felt as though they were wrapped in cotton wool, preventing her from making contact with the ground. 'May I have a word with you, sir?'

Otto reddened as his companions jeered and made some raucous comments. So he hadn't become so hardened that he couldn't still feel embarrassed? Surely that was a good omen?

Her heart was pounding in a frantic rhythm as he led her quickly out of the building. But it was still busy: people were streaming out of the door, talking noisily about the performance. Eva felt a flash of pride as someone mentioned her playing in glowing terms.

'Somewhere more private?' she asked Otto, wanting to gulp the words back. Was she luring the lion into the den and trapping herself in there with him?

He nodded, beckoned her towards another door and ushered her in.

They were in a small storeroom. It was piled high with old chairs and desks, a battered paraffin heater, a box of old papers. It smelled of mould. It gave them privacy even though being this close to Otto on her own was terrifying.

She swallowed. 'Do you recognise me, sir?'

Otto came closer and shone a torch at her face. She smelled again his beery breath, noticed the full lips, the still blond hair, although a shade darker now. There were still traces of the confused, aggressive boy who'd raped her and become the father of her child, despite the hardened soldier he now appeared.

She put a hand out to the wall to keep herself upright. 'Let me help you remember,' she said. 'The Jewish cemetery. Prague, 1930.'

Otto flushed again. 'What of it?'

'You were there with a gang of Hitler Youth. I'd taken a short cut home from the conservatoire. Your whole gang attacked me. But it was you who raped me. I got pregnant. The child, a girl, was adopted. But she's here in Terezin. Hana. She's twelve years old.'

Eva watched the expressions of guilt, shame, disbelief and denial sluice across Otto's face.

He finally settled on defiance and glared at her with hard eyes. 'You can't prove anything. You're making this up.'

'I could be. And no, I can't prove it. But I would swear to you on my life that Hana is your child.'

There was a shout from outside and Otto looked alarmed.

Eva needed to stop him from leaving. Otherwise this was all a waste of time and put her in even greater danger. She pleaded with him with her eyes. 'Hana is your daughter. Come and watch our choir practice one day. You'll hear her play the piano. Her features are unmistakably yours and she has your blonde hair. She's an excellent pianist, with great talent.'

Was it Eva's imagination, or did a split second of pride register on Otto's face before he closed it off?

'Ridiculous. Get back to your barracks.' He thrust open the door of the storeroom and almost pushed her out.

'Of course.' Eva slipped past him.

'And not a word of this to anyone,' he shouted after her.

Eva hurried back to Dresden. They'd returned to their old dormitory after a few days, and for a blissful week there'd been no vermin to plague them. She wondered if she'd done the right thing in speaking to Otto. She'd taken a huge risk – he could get her deported, send her to solitary confinement. Worse . . . But the glimpse of satisfaction on his face when she'd mentioned Hana's piano skills, his urgent request at the end for her not to tell anyone – surely they were hopeful signs? She'd done all she could for now. She'd just have to hope that he'd protect Hana when the time came.

Josef still didn't know her terrible secret. When they were courting, she confessed she wasn't a virgin; he'd have found out anyway on their wedding night. He knew she'd been raped and had a breakdown. But on Mutti's insistence, she'd kept quiet about the baby. Her parents had set their hearts on Josef marrying her. They didn't want to jeopardise her chances any further. And it hadn't affected Josef's attitude to her as it might have done with many men. He had taken her on, and been a good husband in his own way.

When Eva had fallen pregnant, Mutti advised her to have a home birth. Luckily, Miriam had come so fast there hadn't been time to summon a midwife, so Mutti, to her deep joy, had delivered her own grandchild. And there'd been no one present to discover the existence of the earlier pregnancy. The secret remained.

A few weeks after the first successful performance of *The Bartered Bride*, Gabriel asked Eva if she would consider getting involved in a production of *Brundibár*. She'd heard about the children's opera whilst she was still in Prague. Hans Krása and Adolf Hoffmeister had written it for a competition run by the Ministry of Education and Culture.

'But isn't it dangerous to perform a story about an evil man with a moustache in Terezin?' she asked.

Gabri laughed. 'Apparently the SS don't think so. They've even commanded Krása to rework it. I've asked some artists to create audition posters and I'll put them up around the ghetto. Our first meeting will be on Thursday.'

That evening, over fifty children crowded into the gymnasium to find out more about the opera. Gabri asked them all to sit down, then explained the story.

'*Brundibár* is about two children,' he said. 'Their names are Aninka and Pepíček. I will be looking for a young girl to play Aninka and a boy to play Pepíček. You will need to be able to sing and act. Anyway, in the story, the children's mother is ill. Although the doctor says she has to drink milk to make her better, the family can't afford to buy any. But Aninka and Pepíček are determined to make her well. One day they notice an organ grinder playing tunes. People are putting money into his hat. The children realise they could sing for money too and use their earnings to buy milk. So they stand near him and start to sing. People come close to listen to their beautiful voices. But the evil organ grinder tries to drown out their singing. Luckily, a sparrow, a cat, and the children of the town come to Aninka and Pepíček's aid. They all sing louder than the organ grinder and win the battle. The children make enough money to buy their mother the milk she needs and she gets better.'

Eva watched the children's faces as Gabri related the story. Some of the little ones sucked their thumbs. A girl with pigtails was plaiting the hair of the girl in front of her. Some looked at the ground, some gazed at Gabriel open-mouthed. But they all listened attentively and clapped when he'd finished. Eva could tell from his wide smile that he was delighted by their response.

'Can you play the victory song, please, Eva? We'll get them to sing it in groups of five and keep back those who show promise.'

'But what about those you turn down? Won't they be upset?'

'Well, there are only three solos. We'll put those who can't sing at the back of the chorus. And persuade any growlers they'd rather paint scenery instead!'

Eva laughed. 'All right. Line the first group up for me.'

Gabriel divided the children up and sent the first lot across to Eva. She sang them the victory song then asked them to join in. One lad of around thirteen had promise, the rest she advised to join the chorus. Gabriel pencilled the boy in to play Brundibár, the organ grinder.

They found Pepíček three groups later: Hans, a little lad with a huge voice who looked as though he could act too. But none of the girls was suitable for Aninka. They were either too tall, too shy, or clearly couldn't sing. By the time the last group was sent up, Eva had almost given up hope.

She picked out three growlers straight away. Why did they always sing louder than the others? She sent them to Gabriel to persuade them of the joys of scenery painting, then kept the other two, both girls, back.

'Can you sing the song again, please?' She struck the first note.

They both sang well, but the elder of the two, a pretty girl with a sweet face, had a particularly good voice, and a clear grasp of tempo. 'What's your name, dear?'

The girl coloured slightly. 'Erika.'

Eva tried to suppress the thought of how well Miriam could perform the role, or even Hana despite her protests against singing. Yet this girl had talent. She beckoned Gabriel across. 'I think we might have found our Aninka,' she said.

Five new women had been assigned to the dormitory. Five more bodies packed into a room that was already bursting at the seams, five fewer spaces on the beds. Sometimes Eva felt she couldn't even fill her lungs with air; she had to take shallow breaths or there wouldn't be enough oxygen to go round. It wasn't long before the fleas started to bite again, probably brought in by the newcomers.

She lay in the freezing darkness, trying to scratch as silently as she could. She hadn't seen Otto again since that night. All she could do now was wait. They had started to rehearse *Brundibár*, and she was teaching Hana the piano part. They met every spare moment to practise. At first, Hana had asked her about her father, but, perhaps sensing Eva's reluctance to talk about him, she had soon stopped questioning her. She was eager to know about Eva's early life, though, and her lessons at the conservatoire, and Eva was happy to relive her memories, though avoiding all reference to the night in the cemetery.

In turn, Hana told her about her adoptive parents, and Eva was reassured to know her daughter had been happy. Sometimes she wondered if Hana blamed them for not disclosing the truth, but if she did, she didn't mention it. After a while, they talked less and played more. Eva had never felt so in tune with a fellow pianist. They expressed their growing attachment through their playing, and Eva sensed that Hana treasured their time together as much as she did.

Josef complained that even their snatched moments with each other were dwindling, but he understood: he knew how important music was to her. Sometimes Eva wondered how she could have neglected her piano playing for so long after their marriage. But she'd had a home and a husband to look after, and, later, Miriam to care for. Music was a greedy master: it demanded your total commitment and concentration. Years and years of selfless application. As a young girl she'd been happy to give it. She loved to play; music was a channel for her feelings, a means of self-expression. It was in her soul. The rewards were tremendous. But the attack and her subsequent malaise had robbed her of all the joys of her talent. For so long she had associated the piano with misery and pain. Only at Terezin, in the most terrible of circumstances, had she recovered some of her former fervour.

What was music to her now? There wasn't a shred of vanity left in her. She no longer played for people to admire her skill. She played to take their minds off their suffering, to transport them somewhere beautiful and peaceful, to take them to a place, where, if only for an hour or so, all things were possible, however beaten down and exhausted the day's work had left them. Yet it was more than that. To perform *The Bartered Bride* or *Brundibár* was to express their Czech heritage and their solidarity as Jews. When she played, and the choir sang, they

293

were articulating the power of their race to withstand all manner of attack. They were Moses, Joshua, Gideon, Esther, the Maccabees. Small in number, insignificant in stature, but Adonai's chosen people, protected by His love, His power. They would never be extinguished.

As Eva lay awake, she heard the pounding of footsteps down the corridor. The door of the dormitory was thrust open, and the overhead light snapped on. It was a guard from the transport line, rigid in her black uniform, hair pinned back, not an ounce of compassion on her face. Instantly, every occupant was awake, heart rate accelerating, nerves jangling, blood pounding. Fear surged through Eva's body.

'Every woman whose transport number begins with a three is to pack by the morning,' rasped the woman. She was prowling round the bunks, identifying people's numbers from their bags and thrusting pieces of paper into their hands. Moans of horror swept round the room.

Eva lay back on her bed. Her number began with a seven, as did Josef and Abba's. They were safe for now. But as she listened to the terrified whispers, the sounds of frenzied packing, and felt the fear in the room, she knew their turn would come. They'd be herded into the trains and taken off to the east. *The writing sloped down*. Things would be worse. As her heartbeat steadied, she told herself again and again that she had to make Otto believe her. She had to save Hana.

But first she had to tell Hana about her father. When her initial attempts to find out about her conception were rebuffed, she'd obviously assumed that Eva had had relations with a man out of wedlock, which was why the resulting baby had had to be adopted. How on earth was Eva to reveal the terrible truth? Could she say she'd been raped? And that Hana's father was in fact a German soldier, here in this camp! Hana would be horrified. But she had to make her realise she needed Otto's protection, however appalling the circumstances of her conception.

As the darkness closed round Eva again, she rehearsed her speech to Hana. It was vital she get it right.

*

Hugh's face was sterner than usual when he came in that night.

'What's wrong?' asked Pamela as she turned her cheek for his usual perfunctory kiss.

Hugh brandished a newspaper and Pamela caught the words *The New Republic* on the front.

'Isn't that American?'

Hugh nodded. 'Yes, but it's run by people of conscience. There's a chap who's written a piece about the Jews.' He went into the dining room, already laid for supper, pushed the mats and cutlery out of the way and slapped the newspaper down on the table. Then he rifled through the pages until he came to an article entitled 'The Massacre of the Jews'. 'There!'

Pamela picked up her spectacle case from the sideboard and put on her reading glasses.

There are some things so horrible that decent men and women find them impossible to believe, so monstrous that the civilized world recoils incredulous before them. The recent reports of the systematic extermination of the Jews in Nazi Europe are of this order . . .

The words started to swim, and nausea rose in her throat. '*Systematic extermination*?'

Hugh's face was pale. 'Read on.'

There are extermination centers, where Jews are destroyed by poison gas or electricity. There are specially constructed trucks, in which Jews are asphyxiated by carbon monoxide from the exhausts, on their way to burial trenches. There are the mines, in which they are worked to death, or poisoned by fumes of metals. There is burning alive in crematoria or buildings deliberately set on fire . . .

The breath snagged in her throat. 'Miriam's parents?' she whispered.

Hugh's face flushed. 'Possibly. It's so difficult to get news. We've been receiving unofficial reports for weeks, but this is the first time someone has written publicly about the way Jews are being treated.'

'But no one could make this up, surely?'

'It would take a pretty disturbed mind to do that. As I say, it confirms what we've long suspected.' Hugh flicked his fingers at the article. 'Apparently this Varian Fry's a sound chap.'

'How did you get hold of it?'

'Winant brought it over.' John Winant was the American ambassador to England.

'So Miriam won't find out?'

'I sincerely hope not. Poor girl. I doubt American news-papers reach Shropshire, and there'll be a media embargo until we can find out more.'

Pamela pulled out a chair to sit down before her legs gave way. 'How will you do that?'

Hugh took another chair and sat beside her. 'There's talk of getting the Red Cross into one of the camps. The Nazis won't be able to refuse them.'

'The Red Cross? Then maybe I could—'

Hugh put his hand over hers. 'Don't even think of it, Pammie. It'll be the International Red Cross anyway. The Brits may not even be involved.'

Pamela slumped in her chair. 'I see. But at least news will filter back.'

'Indeed.'

'What will we do about Miriam?'

'Nothing. The girl will find out soon enough. We'll wait until we have something more concrete. Let her enjoy her childhood a bit longer.'

Pamela pictured Miriam when she'd last seen her. She'd been subdued at the news of Will's disappearance, and was obviously worried she still hadn't heard from her parents, but otherwise she was suntanned and healthy. Life at Hinton Hall was clearly good for her. 'Well, it's hardly a typical childhood, but you're right, let's wait and see.'

Hugh folded up the newspaper and rearranged the table. Pamela noticed his hands were shaking as he did so. He must be concerned about Miriam. She was too. But she decided to protect Hugh from the thought that was too terrifying to utter: if the Germans could be so cruel to the Jews, how on earth were they treating Will?

25

The winter of 1942 turned into the spring of 1943, and still their summons had not come.

Hana continued to flourish under Eva's music tuition, and the bond of affection between them grew. Eva still felt the painful loss of Miriam, still thought of her each day, trying to imagine what she was doing, but the unexpected thrill of finding the daughter she'd thought lost was a comfort, there was no doubt about it. She told Hana she had a sister, and Hana was fascinated to hear stories of her. The days grew warmer, and mother and daughter spent time sitting outside in the spring sunshine, finding out more about each other. They discovered they both liked carrots but hated turnips. That they both felt full of energy at bedtime but struggled to get up in the morning. When Hana laughed, she wrinkled her nose just like Eva did. It was like being reunited with her younger self.

At the first performance of *Brundibár*, Eva caught sight of Otto in the audience. After the terrible shock of finding out he was a guard at the camp, and her initial dread of bumping into him, he seemed less frightening recently. Confronting him about their daughter had helped: the most important thing was persuading him to protect Hana. He was sitting with a group of SS men, laughing and applauding as a moustachioed boy, revelling in his role as the evil organ grinder, tried to deny the innocent children their freedom. Eva smiled to herself as she played. The symbolism of the play was completely lost on Otto and his cronies. Another little victory for her people.

Gabriel's next project was even more ambitious. 'I thought we should put on Verdi's *Requiem*,' he told Eva. 'I'll bring you the score so you can start practising.'

'Verdi's *Requiem*? Why on earth would you want to perform that?'

Gabri gazed into the middle distance as if the crashing chords of the Dies Irae were already thundering through his head. 'It's a mass for the dead.'

Eva shivered. 'For us, then. It's a mass for us. But we're Jewish. Why would you want to play a Catholic mass?'

Gabri shrugged. 'It's a beautiful opera.'

Eva took a step towards him. 'But that's not all, is it? Come on, Gabri, what's the real reason?'

'Giuseppe Verdi wrote about justice and retribution,' he said. '*Dies irae* means "the day of wrath"; *dies illa solvet saeclum in favilla* means "that day will dissolve the world in ashes". We might be singing a requiem for ourselves.' He smiled grimly. 'But we're making an act of defiance too. It's a requiem for the Germans, a requiem for the Third Reich.' He looked over Eva's shoulder again, as if searching his memory. '*Judex ergo cum sedebit, quidquid latet apparebit: nil inultum remanebit.*'

Eva raised an eyebrow. 'And that means?'

'Therefore when the judge takes His seat, whatever is hidden will be revealed: nothing will remained unavenged,' Gabri recited. His brown eyes blazed. 'We will sing to the Nazis what we cannot say to them.'

Eva's skin started to prickle. 'I see,' she said.

*

One March evening, Miriam and some of the other girls were clustered round Olga's bed in the gloomy dormitory. Unbeknown to the teachers, Olga had got hold of a wireless and managed, after twiddling the dial through a lot of static and crackling, to locate the World Service. The announcer's crisp tones came through. In a dispassionate voice he told them clearly and precisely what was happening to the Jews in concentration camps.

'There is starvation: Jews all over Europe are kept on rations often only one third or one fourth what is allowed to non Jews. Slow death is the inevitable consequence. There is deportation: Jews by the hundreds of thousands have been packed into cattle cars, without food, water or sanitary conveniences of any sort, and shipped the whole breadth of Europe. When the cars arrive at their destination, about a third of the passengers are already dead . . .'

Miriam put a hand to the bed to steady herself as the world tilted sideways.

One of the girls, Monika, started to cry, big fat tears rolling down her face.

'I knew it,' said Miriam, swallowing down the bile that rose in her throat. Is that what Mutti had feared when she'd written to say Miriam might not hear from them for some time? It

300

was appalling to think they might have known what was in store for them. She suspected it had all been to do with Abba's science. She was proud of him for doing the right thing, but terribly worried that his conscience might have cost them their lives.

'Do you think they're still alive?' whispered Frida, a tall, thin girl from Miriam's dormitory.

Miriam pulled the sleeves of her cardigan down over her hands. 'I don't know,' she said. 'Surely I would sense something if they were dead.' She couldn't cry, couldn't feel anything except this curious numbness, as if her whole body was an empty shell. 'Perhaps they escaped the transports. Perhaps they're just living somewhere else but are unable to write to us.'

'What shall we do?' asked Frida.

Miriam looked up at the curtained windows of the dormitory. Outside, the fields and trees would be wrapped in darkness, the March wind ruffling the surface of the pond and bending the grasses; the birds silent in the still-bare trees. For a second she'd wondered about contacting the exiled president to ask if he could help her, but finding a way of getting a letter through from her parents was one thing; rescuing them from a prison camp was another. Although the ex-president was living in relative comfort in Putney, rather than facing the terrible conditions of the camps, he was just as much a captive as they were, and there was nothing he'd be able to do.

She turned to Monika and wrapped her arms round her, feeling the shudder from the girl's chest, the heaving sobs on her shoulder. And finally her own tears came.

*

The first time the choir assembled in the chill, dank air of the basement, Gabri made a speech.

'We sing in memory and with gratitude to Giuseppe Verdi, who composed this wonderful music,' he said. 'But I would like you each to remember someone you have loved and lost. Sing the requiem to them too, in your hearts.'

Eva closed her eyes. She saw Mutti and Abba hugging Miriam when they first arrived in Prague; she saw Miriam's eyes light up at their gifts; she saw them all round the table on that last day, singing the Shalom Aleichem in the candlelight, Miriam's voice rising pure and clear above the rest. But she blinked back the memory. She needed to concentrate on the present.

'Where is our music?' someone asked.

Gabri sighed. 'There is no music. I only have one copy of the score. But I will teach it to you. And you will memorise every word. That way, you can look up when you sing. You can watch me, as your conductor, and you can hold your heads high.'

Eva looked at the choir members. All displayed the familiar white faces and hollow eyes of exhaustion. Yet despite their utter weariness, despite the hunger that gnawed at their very bones, not one stomach rumbled, not one mouth complained. It was as though the prospect of music had made them into souls more than bodies. They were one collective plea for liberation, a united expression of longing for freedom.

Gabri motioned to Eva to play. 'Now, the Dies Irae,' he said. 'The day of wrath, the day of wrath, that day will break up the world into ash.' His strident voice rang out as he sang the first few bars. Then, at his command, the choir sang on their own. At first they faltered over the difficult notes and the challenge of remembering the score. Even by the end of the practice they were scarcely word perfect. Yet despite this, Eva heard sweet, earnest, harmonious voices pouring from battered people. And most of all she heard the sound of hope.

*

Will sat on the thin bench, hunched over the table. He was trying to make the watery stew that slopped around his mess tin last as long as possible. Sometimes, if he was lucky, the cook would scoop up a bit more potato or swede in his long-handled ladle. And then Will's mouth would be filled with something solid and soft and his stomach would feel full, if only for a short while. But today the only solid elements were the globules of fat glistening on the surface of the yellow liquid and a translucent piece of onion floating in its depths. He kept it in his mouth for as long as he could before letting it slither down his throat. He tried not to think about Kitty's apple crumble or even Mother's attempt at Lord Woolton pie. It would be a long time before he'd taste those again. If ever.

The door at the end of the refectory was thrown open and a long line of new prisoners shuffled in. Will watched them with dull eyes as they progressed through the dinner queue and registered their shock at the meagre rations. As usual, he scrutinised the new inmates for anyone familiar, wondering if his flying companions were still on active service, or if any more had been captured. He hoped Tomas was safe. He'd become almost like a brother to him.

The tables filled up, and soon his elbow was jostled by one of the recent arrivals as he struggled to climb over the bench to sit down.

'Sorry.'

'Don't worry,' said Will. 'It takes some manoeuvring.' He held out a hand. 'William Denison. Welcome to the Hammelburg hellhole.'

His companion stared back at him through red-rimmed eyes. His face was lean and pinched, his hair cropped close to his head. He nodded his thanks and introduced himself. Ernest Harper. He'd been with 16 Squadron and had been shot down during reconnaissance duties. Will resigned himself to another tale of capture and imprisonment. After a while, they all blurred into one. And still the war rumbled on. Would he ever be an active part of it again?

*

As Pamela traipsed up Templewood Road, she was aware of the sun on her back. It had much more warmth now; already her blouse was sticking to her skin, and a dribble of sweat ran down the side of her face. She wiped it off with the pad of her thumb. There'd been another air raid last night. She and Hugh had sat in the cellar for hours, wincing at the whistle of bombs and the crash and crack of falling masonry, before the all-clear sounded and they could stumble back to bed. She'd phoned her parents first thing; thankfully they were all right. This morning her eyes were gritty with exhaustion, and a dull headache pounded her forehead. She hoped to God it would clear once she got up to the Heath, and that the soft breeze and huge sky would invigorate her.

As she climbed a grassy bank, she heard a ringing *swee swee swee* sound. A sandpiper flew past her, its clockwork wings flapping, looking for water, no doubt. Ahead of her lay the allotments, a mosaic of greens in the spring sunshine. A few early risers were already digging and hoeing their beds. The low sound of voices drifted back to her, and even a few rumbles of laughter. No matter how disrupted their nights, the gardeners always managed to be back at their allotments the next morning.

She saw Ernie Smith, the man who had leased her some of his land, talking to his neighbour. He doffed his cap at her and Pamela smiled back. 'Any news of your lad?' he asked.

She bit her lip. 'Not since the capture card arrived, no.'

'Don't give up hope. You never know.'

'Indeed,' said Pamela, and hurried past to her end of the allotment. It was hard to know what to say to people these days; they meant well, but it was exhausting trying to sound positive when sometimes all she wanted to do was scream. Today, though, in the balmy air of the Heath, she felt her spirits lift.

She knelt down on the sandy soil, so much warmer now, and started to gouge out dandelions with her penknife, working methodically down the rows and tossing the weeds onto the grassy path to pick up later. Yes, her back ached; yes, there was still no news from Will; yes, this terrible war showed no sign of ending; but crops were growing, the ground was pulsing with life, there were birds in the air and warmth in the sun.

She passed a newspaper stand on her way back. A shaft of sunlight lit up the words on the hoarding: *Heavy RAF raid on Stuttgart*. The sense of hope persisted.

26

Eva sat with Hana on the piano stool. The window was open behind them and the sounds of early spring drifted in: the kick of a football, a distant cheer from the park, the ever-present rumble of a hearse cart, the frenzied buzzing of a fly.

They were working on the Lux Aeterna, the most difficult part of the *Requiem*, and Hana was struggling with the key changes. Eva made her play the section again and again. 'You're nearly there,' she told her. 'Just make sure you take the solo quartet with you. It will sound terrible if everyone isn't totally together.'

Hana's hands flew over the keys. Eva watched her daughter's face, deep in concentration. Her complexion was pale and she had a cluster of freckles around her nose. At the top of her mouth was a tiny mole. Near her hairline, a small scar. Perhaps she'd had chickenpox as a child. Had her mother applied calamine lotion and sodium bicarbonate as Eva had done to Miriam when she'd had the same illness? She wondered which parts of her daughter belonged to Otto and which to her. It was clear that Hana had inherited her mother's musical talent, although her colouring was more like her father's. Not many of the children at Terezin were as blonde as she was.

These days, Eva often glimpsed Otto hovering at the back

of a rehearsal, or watching Hana practise when he thought they couldn't see him. Sometimes she'd look up and see a strangely wistful expression on his face. Was he beginning to accept deep down that Hana was his daughter?

Like the other girls her age, Hana was in the Hauptstrasse barracks. Some of the elders tried to provide a little schooling each day, known as the Programme. But Eva had no doubt that her piano instruction was more important.

Hana's playing came to an end and she looked at Eva expectantly.

'Again,' said Eva.

Once more the ripple of notes. But something was not quite right.

Eva was trying to work out what the problem was when she realised that some of the keys were wet. Tears were running down Hana's cheeks.

'What's wrong, Hana?'

The girl took a long, juddering breath. 'It's too hard.'

Eva turned to her in amazement. 'All this time, I've never heard you utter those words. You've practised and practised and practised, taken all kinds of criticism on the chin, never admitted defeat – no matter how tired you were or how difficult the piece. Why now?'

Hana wiped her face with the back of her hand. 'I'm sorry. I don't know what's the matter with me.'

'Maybe we need to stop for a while.'

Hana nodded.

Eva closed the lid, but they stayed sitting on the piano stool, side by side.

'Why do we have to play this piece? It's so sad.'

'I know. But Mr Schmidt thinks it will show the Germans our spirit. It's an act of defiance.'

'Isn't that dangerous?'

Eva shrugged. 'Probably. But then everything is dangerous here.' She paused. 'You know, Hana, I could get called up at any moment to go on the transport.'

Hana nodded. 'So could I.'

'I'm doing my level best to prevent that.'

'How?'

Eva had managed to evade Hana's questions about her father for weeks. But now she spoke the words she'd rehearsed so carefully that night in the dormitory. 'There's a man here, a German guard, who I think might protect you.'

'Why would he do that?'

She had to tell her daughter the truth, however unpalatable. Time was running out now. She took Hana's hand and covered it with her own. 'Because he's your father.'

Hana's face turned the colour of the ivory piano keys. She took a sharp breath and pulled her hand away.

Eva didn't attempt to make further contact as she told the terrible story of the attack in the cemetery, whilst trying to shut out the memories that came tumbling back.

Hana made a retching sound as though she was about to be sick. 'You're telling me my father is a German and a rapist?'

Eva nodded faintly. 'But your mother is a Czech Jewess who loves you dearly.'

'How do you know he's my father?' The look of horror and suspicion on Hana's face reminded Eva of Otto, but she didn't dare tell her that.

'I know. Believe me, I know.' She didn't mention the laugh.

It sounded ridiculous somehow. But there was no doubt in her mind it was Otto. And by the curious glances he sometimes gave her, Eva suspected he was beginning to acknowledge it.

Hana slumped on her seat.

'Hana. I could be forced to leave Terezin at any moment. I'll do all I can to make sure you stay here. The war can't last for ever. Already there are rumours that the Germans aren't doing so well. It could be over in months. You're young. You can rebuild your life.'

Hana placed trembling fingers on the piano lid.

'If you are left when I go, I want you to play for the Verdi performance. You are quite capable of it. Once we iron out the little problem with the key changes.'

'Do you really think so?' Hana whispered.

Eva marvelled at her daughter. In spite of her horror and exhaustion, a spark of ambition still smouldered. She would need that if she were to survive. If she were to create a future for herself. A future that revolved around music. The future that Eva herself had been denied at sixteen, and quite probably would be denied again very soon.

'I *do* think so. Hana, you play so well. You're skilful by any standards. But for a girl of twelve, you are brilliant. Better even than I was at your age.'

Hana smiled weakly. 'Then I'll practise harder than ever before. I'll make you proud of me.'

'That's what I hoped to hear.' Eva opened the piano lid and rested her fingers on the keys. Then she played Hana's lullaby, the melody she had composed for her baby, with all the love and tenderness she could muster.

*

The summer passed. By November, Abba was fading in front of their eyes. He no longer shared the same dormitory as Josef, but had been sent up to sleep under the rafters with the other frail and elderly. It was freezing cold there in winter and stiflingly hot in summer. The old people at the ghetto were fed smaller rations than anyone else. As a result, they became weaker, and their weakness made them unable to work. It was a vicious circle.

When Josef came to find Eva in the laundry one bitter winter day, his expression was bleaker than usual. 'My dear.' He drew her away from the bubbling copper and led her to the relative quiet of the ironing room.

'It's Abba, isn't it?'

Josef nodded. 'I'm sorry, Eva. The doctor said his heart just gave out.'

Eva thought of kind, solid Abba, presiding over the Kiddush cup smiling proudly at his daughter, or passing Mutti the challah, his face full of love for his wife of nearly forty years. She thought of the bleakness of his days at Terezin without Mutti, the expression of bewilderment on his face. Then something shifted within her. Both her parents were gone now. Despite Josef's presence, and the marvellous discovery of Hana, she felt terribly alone. Yet perhaps that was selfish of her. Abba was at peace now.

She wiped her face with the back of her hand. 'I'm glad,' she said. 'His suffering is finally over.' At least he wouldn't see any worse horrors. It was terrible to end your days at Terezin, but worse to be summoned to the transport and journey into an even more terrifying fate.

'He'll be with your mother in Gan Eden.'

311

Eva nodded. There were no more burials. All the dead bodies were fed into the huge furnaces at the crematorium now, emerging the other side as a heap of ashes. Another insult to Jews. But Abba didn't need his frail earthly body. She tried to picture her parents as young and hopeful, holding hands and laughing. They were together again now, free of pain and worry. They would know peace.

For a second, she thought of Miriam, how upset she'd be at the loss of both her grandparents, but there was no way of telling her. She wouldn't mention it to Hana. Hana had never known Abba, had never gone to the synagogue with him dressed as Queen Esther, had never been fed hamantaschen by Mutti. It was Miriam's loss, not Hana's.

*

For some months now they'd been extending the Prague railway into Terezin. Josef had been one of those assigned to the construction team. 'I'm a scientist, not an engineer,' he'd muttered to Eva when they'd last managed a few minutes together. But life before Terezin mattered little now. Apart from the weekly lectures Josef still gave, which continued to be well attended, he was just part of the workforce like everyone else.

He shouldered his pick and shovel and marched off with the rest of the track-laying team. So many people had been transported from Prague, and still more were being taken off to the east, that Terezin had almost become a transport junction. Laying the tracks meant there was no longer the bleak trudge from the station to the ghetto for people carrying

312

bundles of belongings, the carters alongside taking the heavy stuff and the possessions of people too old or too young to carry much. It was a neat solution, even if the work was relentless and back-breaking for the prisoners assigned to it.

Josef took his hammer and began to pound nails into the sleepers evenly placed along the track. The ground was softening after the winter; all around him were green shoots and buds. Birds sang from the trees. No matter how many deaths the ghetto incurred, nature was responding to the warmth and the sun. A new season was beginning.

Next to him, Ivor, a young man from his dormitory, was breathing heavily as he swung a pickaxe to break up the stony soil ahead of him.

'Your wife is an excellent pianist,' he said to Josef, in between blows.

Josef looked around to check there were no guards watching, then put down his hammer and stood up shakily.

'Yes. She played to concert level as a teenager. I'm pleased she was able to take it up again here.'

Ivor placed his pickaxe on the ground, then rubbed his back. 'An excellent teacher, too. That young girl Hana is coming on so well. I heard her practising the *Requiem* the other day. Beautiful.' He wiped a film of sweat from his forehead with his shirtsleeve. 'She looks a little like your wife too.'

Josef stared at him. 'But Eva is dark and Hana's hair is fair.'

'It's more subtle than that. There's something self-contained about the pair of them. The way they're both so still before they start playing. As if they've locked themselves away.' Ivor had been a poet before he became a Terezin slave. He noticed small details; he was deft with language.

'No talking! Get on with your work.' A guard was walking towards them, his face a mask of fury.

Both men grabbed their tools and dug and hammered for all they were worth. The guard delivered them each a punch to the back as he walked by, and the two men grimaced. But after the pain had ebbed, and Josef could contemplate something other than the throbbing soreness, his face became meditative as he mulled over Ivor's words. Was there more to the growing closeness between Eva and Hana than he'd realised? He felt a stab of irrational jealousy on Miriam's behalf. Of course he was glad she was safe, but was Eva somehow replacing their absent daughter with this child? It should be her own daughter she was teaching so painstakingly at the piano, not someone else's.

He swung his hammer angrily, and Ivor glanced up in surprise as a nail flew through the air.

*

They were working at the Verdi each evening now. Eva would take her place at the piano, Hana beside her, turning the pages and watching her every move, and play each section as Gabriel announced it. Sometimes she had to hold back the tears as the warm voices surged around her, and people who by the end of the day were on their knees with exhaustion, illness or sheer despair found the strength to stand up straight, to pull in their already hollow stomachs, expand their chests and sing with every fibre of their bodies. She marvelled at the resilience of the human spirit, the power

314

from within that allowed a person with no hope to give their all.

Gabriel had said it was the perfect act of defiance, and he was right. As an act of defiance against those who said that Jews were useless, hopeless, redundant to the human race, they sang as sweetly and powerfully as any human being could; as an act of defiance that said that no one could destroy Adonai's people, they sang their hearts out; as an act of defiance that told the Germans, without them even realising it, that the wages of sin were death, they sang the chilling words that convinced them, if only for the moment, that no weapon formed in anger could ever succeed against them. Their bodies were failing, their hope was dwindling, but their souls were alive and transcendent.

Whenever Eva played the tumultuous notes of the Dies Irae and heard the choir sing 'nothing shall remain unavenged', it was Otto's face she was pounding; it was his fate the judge was deciding. And he was found guilty every time.

*

They finished the railway. Josef felt as if it had been constructed from their own sweat and blood as much as iron and wood. Immediately the line was busy: trains came in from Prague bringing hundreds of fearful, weary passengers; trains left Terezin with hundreds more – thinner, less healthy, and even more fearful.

'It's only a matter of time now,' he told Eva. 'We've outlived our usefulness. We'll be going east soon.'

Eva nodded. The summonses had come for all the people whose numbers began with a 5; now they were halfway through the 6s. Josef was 768 and she was 769. It was obvious they would be next.

*

Gabriel was determined that the *Requiem* would be their finest performance yet. Every night, artists worked late on the scenery. They'd managed to find some wooden boards in the ghetto, and someone had smuggled in a set of paints. The result was stunning: dark, sombre backgrounds, huge shadows, thundering clouds. And in the corner, the blinding white of the sun, streaming its light across the darkness.

Eva concentrated all her efforts on training Hana. The girl was finally mastering the Lux Aeterna now, and Eva was proud of her. Sometimes she played for large sections of the rehearsal, Eva sitting beside her to turn a page or whisper a word of advice or encouragement. Under her tuition, Hana was blossoming, gaining skills and expertise far more rapidly than she would have done at the Prague Conservatoire. If she lived, she could become a virtuoso pianist. The musician I wanted to be, thought Eva.

They hadn't discussed Otto again. Eva suspected Hana had buried the shocking news that he was her father deep in the recesses of her mind; it was too awful to contemplate. But at least she had told her now. And she just had to hope Otto would protect his daughter when the time came.

*

When Eva next saw Gabriel, his face was full of shock and anxiety. 'There was a summons during the night. Many of those whose numbers begin with a six have gone,' he told her. 'Half of the chorus have been transported. What on earth am I going to do?' He thrust his hands through his hair.

Eva's own hands started to shake. Hana's number was 694. 'Has Hana gone?' she whispered.

'No. Not Hana. She's safe for now. But Erika, Friedrich, Corrie . . .' Gabriel started to list some of the other musicians.

Erika had been their Aninka. A beautiful child with an exquisite voice. And the others were so young . . . Eva blinked as their dear faces appeared before her. She was reassured that Hana was not on the transport, but devastated for those who were. She took a deep breath. 'All right. Then we train new singers, new musicians. We've invested too much in this to give up.'

Gabriel put his head in his hands. 'How are we going to rehearse new singers from scratch? It took weeks and weeks to get the choir note perfect.'

'I don't know,' said Eva. 'But we can't abandon this. It would be like giving in to the Germans, insulting the memory of those who've gone. We have to dig deeper than ever before and carry on.'

Gabriel slowly peeled his hands away. 'You're right,' he whispered. 'I wanted the production to be an act of defiance. We won't let them stop us.' He took a deep breath. 'I'll ask some of the artists to put up new posters. We will go on.'

*

The next time Eva saw Otto, lolling against the sorting house wall and smoking a Stuyvesant, she forced herself to go up and stand next to him, despite the clammy nausea that his nearness always aroused. He was on his own, and for once the sorting house was empty.

'Your daughter is an excellent musician,' she told him, trying to keep her voice steady.

Otto blew a curl of smoke into her face. 'I've told you. You have no proof she's my daughter. She could be anyone's.'

'Not anyone's, no. Look at my hair. It's dark brown. Always has been. Most of my family have the same hair colour. Hana's is much more like yours.'

Otto laughed, his short hyena bark. 'You could have opened your legs for any Aryan.'

Eva looked at him steadily. 'Or I could have been raped by one. I was a virgin. There was only one man who could have fathered my child.'

Otto shifted his feet. 'You can say what you want. It's your word against mine.'

'I've seen you watching her. You know she's yours. All I want is for you to protect your daughter. I know my days here are numbered. No one has ever come back from the east, have they?'

Otto looked away and shifted as though uncomfortable. 'I'm sure the Third Reich's decisions are the best ones for all concerned.'

A ragged line of men was trailing towards them, carrying garden tools. Eva noticed Otto standing up a little straighter as he watched them. 'Come here,' he shouted. 'I need to count those.' The line obeyed.

Eva pulled her cardigan around her. 'She's yours,' she whispered. 'There could be no other father.'

'Not a word,' he hissed as the men approached. But before she turned to set off down the path, she glimpsed a fleeting expression of panic on his white face.

Once again she was in the cemetery. The boys were there, jeering as usual, but this time they all carried pieces of paper. Eva caught sight of the writing in the moonlight. Each piece of paper had a number on. And each number was the same: 769.

She awoke with a start, her heart pounding affrettando. A torch was being shone into her eyes. And behind the torch was Helga Schmidt, one of the German guards. She shoved a scruffy docket into Eva's hands. 'Your summons. Be quick.'

Eva sat up. Helga shone the torch on the paper. *You are summoned to be transported at 5 a.m. Please assemble at the market-place*, it read. Eva stumbled out of bed and started to pack up her meagre belongings, her heart still hammering. There was the sound of receding footsteps as Helga departed the room and strode back down the corridor.

As Eva approached the marketplace, she noticed Josef almost immediately. He was stooped now, and wore an expression of permanent disbelief, as if he still couldn't fathom what was happening to him. At the sight of her, he stretched out his arms, and Eva stumbled into them. 'At least we're together,' he murmured. Eva kissed his cheek, but as she looked over his shoulder, her whole body froze. Standing with a group of other girls, silent with terror, was Hana.

Eva wriggled out of Josef's arms and rushed over. 'You too?'

Hana nodded. Her face was paper-white and her eyes glassy. 'Mr Schmidt will have to find a new pianist,' she said shakily.

'No!' Eva replied. 'He will not.' She was aware of Josef's cry of surprise behind her, conscious of the scrutiny of the hundred other prisoners who stood there, but it didn't matter. Nothing mattered apart from keeping Hana safe.

She didn't have to look far for Otto. The train had come in and he was one of the soldiers ensuring people got on and were packed tightly enough together. 'Otto!'

He looked up from his task, his eyes narrowing.

'It's Hana! She's due to leave on the train. You have to do something. Please.'

Otto stared at her, his jaw rigid. But he stopped what he was doing.

'I'm begging you. Even if you don't believe me, even if you don't acknowledge she's your child, please understand you are sacrificing a great musical prodigy. Hana is supremely gifted. Don't rob the world of your daughter's talent.'

Otto didn't reply. But he muttered something to one of the other guards and strode off.

By the time it was Josef and Eva's turn to board, Otto still hadn't returned. Eva sat between Josef and a man with a downward moustache and a mouth that followed its shape, her shoulders and thighs crushed by their limbs, straining to look out of the window. Guards were shouting, whistles blowing, people murmuring fearfully. Where was Hana? Where was Otto?

The train started to move, and she pushed herself forward, desperately trying to see. They passed piles of rucksacks . . . carts . . . guards . . . a blur of faces and figures . . . The train increased its speed and the man sat forward, blocking her view. Eva stood up, ignoring the cries of protest and the difficulty in keeping her balance. She pushed her face against the window, trying to scan the rapidly receding groups of people: in less than fifty metres the tracks turned sharp right, and soon she would no longer be able to see anyone. But just before the train took them out of sight, she was sure she glimpsed two figures: Otto, smiling grimly, and Hana standing next to him, a look of shock on her face.

As Eva sagged back against the rough material of the seat, she witnessed the smoke rising from the crematorium, swirling and mixing with the fumes from the train. Hana is safe, Hana is safe, she told herself, again and again, to the rhythm of the train's wheels as it clattered over the track that Josef had helped to build. She laid her head on her husband's shoulder. And Miriam was in England, flourishing under the Denisons' care. She was already showing promise at singing. Maybe she and Hana would find each other and could even perform together at the Rudolfinum one day. Eva smiled to herself. It was an absurd dream, but it helped blot out her terror. She let it play around her mind as the train took her onwards to whatever destination the Nazis had planned for them.

Part Three

1944–1950

27

After breakfast, Hana brushed aside the wall of sour-smelling dresses that hung limply on the end of her bunk, and lay down on the mattress. It no longer sagged under her weight, she was so thin now. She stared up at the grimy ceiling. At least the dormitories were less crowded, with so many people gone. But that made things worse somehow; it was colder and lonelier without the press of bodies; the sighs and groans in the night; the whisperings and murmurings of people in despair.

She hadn't heard from Eva since she'd left. And apart from that one postcard, there'd been silence from her adoptive parents too. Were they even still alive? Hana wiped her cheeks with her thumb and tried to ignore the familiar clench of fear as she wondered, for the thousandth time, what had happened to them all. She blinked back the image of Eva's face as she'd watched her play the piano. She'd worked and worked at her pieces just to catch a fleeting glimpse of Eva's proud smile when she'd played a phrase particularly well, or when the audience clapped enthusiastically at the end. And further back, the memories of the first Mutti she'd known, tying her woollen scarf carefully round her neck so she wouldn't get cold as she walked to school; and her father saying the daughters' blessing over her at Shabbat. She stifled a sob. How was she to find the energy to keep going? Particularly today, when she had to act as though her life depended on it.

Back in June, a delegation from the International Red Cross had visited the ghetto. Hana had been asked to play for a gala performance of the *Requiem*. She'd imagined Eva by her side throughout, and had played with every fibre of her being in her mother's memory. At the end, there'd been a standing ovation.

The Red Cross visit was such a success, a film was now being made at Terezin. It was to be called *The Führer Gives a City to the Jews*.

'Come on, Hana.' The dormitory leader dropped a pile of clothes on her bed. 'You need to get dressed. Filming's starting in ten minutes.'

Hana sat up wearily and took off the grey dress she'd worn for the last two years, which strained under the armpits and was far too short. Then she dragged the white blouse over her head, dimly registering the faint smell of new, crisp cotton. How long was it since she'd worn a garment that wasn't old, and stiff with grime? The blouse was a bit loose, but the material felt soft on her skin, and in spite of her hostility towards the day's events, a little bit of her enjoyed the sensation. She did up the pearl buttons slowly. There was a blue dirndl skirt with embroidery round the hem laid out on the bed. She pulled it over her feet and up her legs, then climbed cautiously down the ladder, clutching at the skirt to stop it falling down. Standing in front of the speckled mirror, she rolled the waistband over a few times until the thickness of the material kept it in place. It made the skirt a little short, but it flared out pleasingly, and at least it wouldn't slip down this way.

There was a low whistle behind her, and Inga pushed her gently out of the way to check on her own outfit: a knee-length serge dress in a rich dark red. 'You look nice.'

Hana shrugged. 'You too.'

Inga took her arm. 'Come on, let's get this charade over with.'

They walked past flower beds blazing with jewel-coloured chrysanthemums, and immaculate lawns luminous in the late summer sunshine. At the end of the road was a crowd of men in new, if ill-fitting, suits; women in smart pre-war clothing that dwarfed their thin bodies, and children with carefully brushed hair and new ribbons.

The director, a tall man with a jowly face and thick receding hair, rushed up to Hana and Inga as they approached. 'Just in time. Come and sit down over here, please.' He pointed towards a table in front of a brightly painted café, and drew out two chairs. Hana and Inga perched on them awkwardly. Someone placed cups of steaming ersatz coffee in front of them.

'You have to look natural. Smile. Laugh.' His furrowed forehead belied the jauntiness of his words.

Hana tried to stretch her mouth into a grin, whilst Inga giggled self-consciously.

The director took a step backwards, frowned again, then rushed forward to place Hana's arm on the table and tilt Inga's face towards her. He nodded to the cameraman, who pressed something on his machine. 'Now,' said the director, running a hand through his hair. 'Start talking. It doesn't matter what you say. Your conversation won't be heard on the film. But try to think of something nice. It's important that you look as though you are having a good time.'

Hana shot a glance at Inga, who shrugged imperceptibly.

Hana's mouth felt stiff with the effort of forcing a smile. Whatever could she think about? She pushed aside the images of Eva and her parents and let her mind focus on the evening ahead. She was playing at a special performance of *Brundibár* that night. She tried to anticipate the joyful notes pouring into the new concert hall, and imagine the applause and congratulations when she'd finished. At last her face relaxed and her pleasure became genuine.

'Cut!' shouted a voice. The director grinned. 'Well done, ladies,' he said. 'That worked well. We did a close-up of you smiling at the end, Hana. Very nice.' He stepped back as one of his aides removed the girls' cups, even though they hadn't finished their coffee. 'You're free now until the football scenes this afternoon.' Hana and Inga stumbled to their feet, smiling grimly.

The director turned to face the group of prisoners who'd been watching the scene. 'All right, everyone, let's have a shot of you queuing at the bank.' The crowd turned towards the hastily erected facade that now stood in front of an old storehouse, and started lining up to resemble a queue. 'Lots of smiling and chatting, please,' he ordered. The prisoners obliged with stiff grins and self-conscious laughter, standing in line to receive worthless camp money. The filming continued.

'At least it's a break from the usual tedium,' muttered Inga as she and Hana wandered back to their barracks. Behind the scenes, nothing had changed: the dormitories were still chilly and squalid, the rations – apart from the luxurious food they were given for the cameras, which was taken away as soon as the filming had finished – were meagre and monotonous, the fleas and bed bugs dined better than they did. And every day trainloads of people with white, haunted faces were loaded onto the transport going east.

As they traipsed down the corridor towards the dormitory, they saw a German officer on his way out: Otto. Inga pressed herself into the wall and looked down at the floor. They'd all learned long ago that it was better not to draw attention to themselves. Hana stood beside her, but as Otto passed, she shot him a look. There was a nod in return. When she approached her bed, she saw a bread roll perched on the grey blanket, beside a sheaf of music. She picked up the roll and pressed it to her nose. It was fragrant and still hot from the bakery.

'Favours?' asked Inga drily.

There'd been quite a few gifts over the months, but normally Hana had discovered them when she'd been on her own. This was the first time there'd been a witness to Otto's generosity.

Hana nodded. 'He seems to have taken a shine to me.' She broke the roll in two and handed half to Inga.

Inga nodded her thanks, then raised an eyebrow. 'And what does he get in return?'

Hana flushed. 'Nothing!' She picked up the music. It was one of Chopin's études. Her fingers itched with the desire to play.

Inga spoke through a mouth still clogged with bread. 'You're expecting me to believe a German officer gives you presents for no reason?'

'All right. He's a fan. He likes my playing.'

Again the raised eyebrow. 'Private audiences, eh?'

'No!' Hana said. 'Come on. We need to get ready to watch the football match.' She picked up a greasy comb and started to drag it through her hair.

Inga gave her a searching look but said no more.

The film was finished in a week. The day after the final edit, the director and the rest of the crew, their usefulness served, were loaded onto a train to the east. The bright shopfronts, the children's playground, the delicious food all vanished. The happy, cheering crowds had done their job in convincing their audience that all was well. The world was ignorant of their suffering. And Terezin was the same as ever, if not worse for having given them a brief reprieve.

Soon after the filming, Gabriel and a number of other key musicians and composers were also on a train bound for the east. Terezin had been robbed, almost in one fell swoop, of its musical talent. Hana never heard from them again.

But less than a year later, things started to change. At first it was just a rumour. 'The Russians are coming,' people whispered at the water pump. 'The Germans are retreating,' they told each other in the kitchen queues. 'The war is nearly over,' they quietly proclaimed as they set off to work each morning. Germans started to disappear. One morning Hana walked past the SS building and saw a number of officers carrying out suitcases and loading them into vans. There were fewer supervisors in the kitchens, fewer uniforms on the street.

Two days later, Otto approached her as she sat at the piano, practising for a concert that evening. 'I may not be here much longer,' he said, looking at her with that curious mixture of pride and incredulity that had begun to characterise his expression now. 'The war has gone badly for us. The Russians are advancing. They've already liberated some of the camps. Go back to Prague when the war is over and I'll find you there.'

Go back to Prague? Much as the thought of freedom elated her, Hana felt a surge of panic. Where would she go? She was fourteen now, but she hadn't had any contact with her adoptive parents for years. Should she return to the house she'd lived in with the Rubensteins? How would she manage on her own? Her heart thrummed in her chest. Otto had done a terrible thing; she could never forget that he'd raped Eva and had failed to save her from being sent east. In those ways he was a monster. But he was still her father – and he had saved *her*. She wanted to ask him to stay, to continue his protection of her. They had spent little time together since he'd rescued her from the transport, yet she knew he kept an eye on her from afar. The extra treats had kept coming, but she made sure she hid them from Inga for fear of more taunts about favouritism. She knew he would no longer have any power if the Russians took control, but perhaps he would keep his word and find her. 'Thank you,' she whispered, confused.

Otto nodded a little awkwardly and strode off.

Then new people started to arrive on transports. This time it wasn't the terrified, yet relatively healthy, Prague Jews, but people from camps in the east. Hana caught sight of a group as they stumbled off the train: men with sallow faces and skeletal bodies, women with shaved heads, wearing rags, children whose haunted faces suggested they'd seen a lifetime of horror. She froze at the sight of them. Things had been bad at Terezin, but no one looked like this.

That night, a new girl was allocated to their dormitory. She curled up on the bed next to Hana's, her face a mask of exhaustion. Hana offered her a glass of water and the girl sipped from purple lips and looked at her through dead eyes. 'Where did you come from?' Hana whispered.

'Auschwitz,' the girl replied.

'Auschwitz? Isn't that in Poland?' asked Hana.

The girl nodded almost imperceptibly, as if even moving her head was too painful.

Hana's mouth was suddenly dry. 'Did you come across a couple called Rubenstein? Or Eva and Josef Kolischer?'

The girl moved her head again. 'There were tens of thousands of us.'

Hana took her hand. 'What did they do to you?'

'Starved us . . . tortured us . . . left us to die. But I was lucky. So many were gassed.'

Something icy inched up Hana's spine.

'*Gassed*?'

'They told them they were taking a shower. But they never came out alive. I saw the bodies afterwards . . .' She closed her eyes.

The room spun around Hana. She tried to shake off an insistent image of Mutti, the skin of her shaved skull stretched tight over a shrunken head, bones like sticks, eyes blank with terror . . .

She gently stroked the girl's back, conscious of the prominence of her spine against the sharp dip of her skin. 'Thank you for telling me,' she said. Then she slipped into her own bed and spent the night trying to ward off spectral figures who clawed at her with nerveless hands, to blot out the sound of inhuman screams, to stifle the rank odour of rotting bodies, the pernicious drift of gas, to extinguish the horror of her parents' and Eva's deaths again and again.

The next morning, there was no sound from the girl's bed. Hana looked across at her. She was lying on her back, her forehead crawling with lice. It was obvious she was dead. And Hana realised she didn't even know her name.

A few days later, Hana woke to a strange silence. Why weren't the guards shouting as usual? Why weren't doors being slammed, trucks rolling? Why weren't people groaning as they faced the tedium of another day? She sat up and looked around. Her fellow roommates were doing the same.

'What's going on?' she asked.

Elsa, the dormitory leader, was already dressed. She opened the door and went into the corridor. Hana listened as her footsteps receded. There was a long silence as everybody waited to find out what had happened. Eventually Elsa returned. 'There's no one around,' she said. 'No Germans, anyway.'

Hana scrambled up and grabbed her clothes. She dressed hurriedly, motioning to Inga to join her. Together the girls explored their block, but apart from other prisoners as baffled as they were, they didn't see a single guard. They walked across the empty street and went into the kitchens, where people were helping themselves to food, seemingly without fear of retribution. Hana looked at a man in front of her, who was tearing up pieces of bread and stuffing them into his mouth. She was tempted to do likewise but didn't think her stomach could stand it. Instead she grabbed two apples, gave one to Inga and nibbled at hers carefully.

'Is it a trick?' asked Inga. 'Do you think the Germans are testing us – that they've gone into hiding to see what we'll do? Perhaps if they find us raiding supplies, they'll reappear and shoot us.'

Hana thrust her apple into her pocket. 'You might be right,' she said. 'But I bumped into one of the guards the other day and he told me he'd be leaving soon. He said the war was going badly, that they needed to escape before the Russians came.'

Inga grinned. 'Then let's make the most of it,' she said.

But the next day, they woke to the sound of gunfire. 'Stay down,' Elsa warned them. 'Hide under the covers.'

Hana stretched her body the length of the bed and pulled her blanket over her head. The blanket smelled foul and the hot darkness was suffocating. It was hard to resist the temptation to go out into the spring sunshine, but better than risking her life.

After several hours, during which Hana was glad of the apple she'd stowed under her pillow, it was evident the shooting had stopped.

'Let's get dressed,' Elsa said. 'I think it might be safe to leave the building, but we'll need to be careful.'

They all followed her advice and soon were emerging stealthily through the door. Hana took a deep breath. The air was still tainted with the smell from the crematorium, but behind that was something floral and uplifting. The smell of hope, she thought. But no sooner had she registered the impression than gunfire started again. They darted back into the building and watched from the shadows of the entrance hall as two men in German uniform ran down the street and lobbed hand grenades through the door of the Long Street building opposite. Inga hid her face against Hana's shoulder as there was a loud explosion followed by screams of pain. They didn't dare investigate. They returned to their dormitory and spent the rest of the day, and long into the night, listening to the rumble of cannon and the sound of gunfire. Once the whole building shook as a shell landed nearby, but no one in Hauptstrasse barracks was hurt.

'I can't believe we've survived all this only to be killed in the Nazis' last stand,' muttered Inga.

'We have to stay hidden,' Elsa said. 'This is a battle between the Germans and the Russians. We'll only get killed if we're caught in the crossfire.'

Hana nodded, and dived under the blanket again. If she played the whole of the *Requiem* to herself in her head, maybe the fighting would have stopped by the time she'd finished. She'd performed the piano part for the choir many times since Eva had left. And each time she and the singers gave their all as an act of defiance. It was a small victory, and the music never failed to rouse their souls.

But she'd only got to the end of the Kyrie when she felt someone shaking her. 'Come on out,' Inga said. 'You must see this.' She was leaning across the end of her bunk, looking through the window. Hana scrambled to join her.

A Russian tank was making its way down the road, a red flag fluttering from its gun mantlet. As the girls watched, people started pouring out of the barracks. Their voices floated up. 'The Russians are here!' 'We're saved!' Hana and Inga rushed to join them. All around them people were shouting and hugging, sharing hunks of bread and jugs of tea, talking feverishly, dragging rucksacks and suitcases onto the street, their hoarse voices singing their national anthems. At long, long last the war was over. They were free.

28

Pamela hadn't been to a Monday meeting for a while, but as she passed the Friends house on the way to the shops one lunchtime, something made her open the plain wooden door that faced onto the street and walk in. As usual, the chairs were arranged in a circle around the table. She recognised a few people – mostly women at this time of day. Old Margaret Jones sat in her customary seat, head bowed, leathery hands clasped in prayer. A few seats away was a young woman Pamela didn't recognise, in a navy suit and a black hat. She was sitting up straight with her eyes closed, a look of anguish on her face.

Pamela slid onto a chair at the end of a row and placed her bag by her side. Then she took a deep breath and attempted to focus on God. She tried to shut out the sound of a clock ticking, to find space and silence in the room's thick air. For a while she just saw the brown glow behind her lids. Then suddenly Will appeared. He was gaunt-looking, with pale skin above a sparse beard. His eyes were gazing straight into hers. And they were smiling. 'I'm coming home, Mother,' he said. 'All is well.'

She sent up a heartfelt prayer and stumbled out of the room.

*

When she let herself back into the house, Hugh was already there, slumped in an armchair, his hand clutching a glass of amber liquid.

'Hugh! What are you doing home? And drinking at lunchtime.'

He placed the glass on the table beside him, held out his arms and drew Pamela onto his lap. 'It's over,' he said wearily. 'Winston will broadcast a statement later.'

'Thank God,' Pamela said. She wrapped her arms round his neck and pressed her damp cheek to his, listening to her own pulse beating in time with her husband's.

Some time later, he gently dislodged her to turn on the wireless. They listened together as Winston's voice boomed out: 'We may allow ourselves a brief period of rejoicing; but let us not forget for a moment the toil and efforts that lie ahead.'

Pamela felt the weight of worry in her husband's hunched shoulders, saw the exhaustion on his lined face. But she didn't tell him about her vision of Will. She didn't want to raise his hopes. Instead she hugged the knowledge to herself. And continued to dream.

*

There had been rumours for a while, so it was no surprise to Miriam when Mr Čapek called them into the hall one morning. It was a late spring day, the woods hazed with bluebells, the lambs leaping in the fields, the air fragrant with wild garlic. They sat on the polished wood floor and listened as Mr Churchill's voice growled out from the wireless. As he spoke of *the evil-doers who are now prostrate before us*, Miriam had a sudden memory of Mutti throwing her to the ground whilst a German plane flew overhead, of papers falling like leaves through the air, of Mutti's frightened face and the palpable alarm in the street. Like a newsreel running through her head, she saw the goose-stepping soldiers marching into Prague, heard the screams of horror, saw the weariness on Abba's face. *We may allow ourselves a brief period of rejoicing*, Mr Churchill continued. But how could they rejoice when most of them didn't know if their parents were alive or dead? Olga's face, next to her, bore the same expression of optimism mingled with anxiety that Miriam imagined hers showed. The English prime minister was right: there was nothing worse the Germans could do now. But what if the worst had already been done?

Mr Čapek was announcing a party back in the hall that evening. There would be cake, lemonade and ice cream. But no amount of delicious food could make up for the continued absence of their parents.

'What will you do now?' asked Olga, as they made their way back to their lessons.

Miriam shrugged. 'Wait to hear from my parents.'

'And if you don't hear?'

'I expect the Denisons will ask me to stay with them, but I still think of Prague as my home.' She wiped her face with her sleeve. 'I can't believe none of my family will be there any more.'

'Me too. Perhaps we could find somewhere to live together. Look for jobs.'

'Olga! We're eleven years old. We won't be allowed.'

Olga smiled her funny little smile. 'Then I suppose we'll have to stay here.'

Miriam opened the door to the classroom. 'If Hinton Hall stays open. It might be closed now the war is over.'

They sat down at their desks. Madame Lebrun was at the front of the class, holding a piece of chalk, just as she had been when they'd been called into the hall.

'If you please, ladies,' she said. 'The war may be over, but there are still French verbs to learn.'

Olga and Miriam took out their exercise books.

*

Pamela wrapped her arms round her chest and adjusted her hat. Even a summer night was cold on the airfield, the wind sweeping across the flat Buckinghamshire plain, the rain splattering her cheeks and drumming on the tin roof of the hangar.

Hugh put his arm round her. 'Not long now.'

Pamela nodded, her heart already thrumming. It was hard to know how she felt; any mother would be elated and excited at seeing her son again after three interminable years. She longed to hold him, to feel his reassuring solidity, to look into his dear boyish face once more. But she was worried too. How had war changed him? And worse still, what had they done to him in prison? Thank God he'd been in Germany and not the Far East. The war was still going on there, and reports were coming out of Japan about how cruelly the POWs had been treated. In comparison, the Germans were humane. But Pamela was under no illusion that Will would have escaped unscathed.

A distant drone suggested the aircraft was approaching. She shielded her eyes against the glare of the airfield lights, finally allowed to be switched on after all this time, and peered into the black sky. 'Can you see anything?' she asked.

Hugh tilted her face slightly so she was looking further west, and pointed. 'I think that's the Dakota.' Two steady orbs of light trailed through the darkness, and she caught the silver ghost of a distant aircraft. Her son was somewhere in that metal tube. For some reason an image of Will skiing, that time they'd gone to Czechoslovakia, came into her mind: flushed, triumphant, ecstatic. Did he still have those ruddy cheeks, those bright eyes? Or was he a shuffling corpse like some of the prisoners she'd seen on Red Cross films? Fear tightened in a band across her chest. She reached out her hand and placed it inside Hugh's, and received a reassuring squeeze of her fingers.

The engine sound increased to a roar and the Dakota approached, angling steeply towards the airfield, before bouncing down on the black lake of the tarmac and screeching to a halt.

Hugh and Pamela waited whilst the staircase was attached. Then the door opened and a line of gaunt grey figures trudged down the steps.

'There he is,' said Pamela. The second man down had Will's thick brown hair, and she caught a familiar look of trepidation. There was another man behind him.

'Are you sure?'

'I'm sure.' She turned a smiling face to Hugh. 'That's our boy.' It took all her willpower not to run across the tarmac and fling her arms around him, to hold him and never let go. She rammed her fists against her sides and waited.

When he reached them, his voice was quiet, his expression subdued. Pamela was shocked how weak his arms felt as he wrapped them round her and stood with his face buried in her shoulder. Eventually she looked up to see the man she'd glimpsed earlier hovering behind him.

'You remember my friend Tomas,' said Will. 'I hadn't realised he'd been taken prisoner too. We met up on the flight.'

'Mrs Denison. How lovely to meet you again.' Tomas stretched out his hand.

Pamela gave him a hug almost as warm as the one she'd given Will. If Tomas hadn't taken the trouble to visit her after he'd seen Will go down, she'd have had even less hope to cling onto.

'It's all right if Tomas stays for a few days, isn't it, Mother? Just until he can get a flight back to Poland.'

'Of course.' Pamela smiled at Tomas. 'Please stay as long as you want. It's the least we can do.'

As she and Hugh led their beloved son and his friend back to the car, a bubble of joy rose in Pamela's heart. At last her life could begin again.

Once they were back home, Tomas insisted on going to bed, despite Pamela's protests, assuring them he would eat in the morning. He was obviously being tactful. She showed him to the spare room, where fortunately the bed was made up, then heated up the chicken soup Kitty had left out for Will and brought it to him on a tray in the drawing room, where he was sitting with Hugh.

'I'm sorry, darling. This doesn't seem much of a hero's welcome.'

Will reached out thin, pale fingers to pick up the spoon. Even the weight of that seemed too heavy for him. 'I'm not a hero, Mother, just a survivor.'

Pamela put her hand on his bony shoulder. 'You'll always be a hero to me. Eat up. You need to build up your strength.'

But Will sighed and put down his spoon. He seemed to have difficulty swallowing. 'The British gave us as much food as we could eat,' he said. 'Some of the fellows stuffed themselves with it and died in agony.'

'Too much for their stomachs, given the state they were in, I suppose,' said Hugh, shaking his head.

Will nodded. 'Luckily I didn't eat too much.' He pressed his hands to his middle. 'But my stomach still feels tender. I'm going to take it easy.'

'Of course,' said Pamela, taking the spoon gently from his fingers and laying it down on the table. She longed to put plates of roast beef and cottage pie in front of him. To look on with maternal delight and incredulity as he devoured bowl after bowl of apple crumble and custard, or rice pudding. She wanted him to smack his lips and ask for seconds. But even if she could procure all this marvellous food, this hesitant, fragile man wouldn't eat it. He was like a wounded wild animal that she'd have to bring back to life. Put out little morsels until he felt strong and trusting enough to relax. She was glad she'd warned Hugh not to ask too many questions, or try to find out what plans Will had for the future. It was only his first day back. Too soon, too raw. They just had to be patient. 'I'm so glad you met up with Tomas and brought him back here,' she told him.

343

Will nodded. 'It was marvellous to find he was on the plane.' He laid his head back and closed his eyes. 'You don't mind him staying?'

'Of course not. I'll look after you both. He'll be a new man by the time he goes home.'

Without opening his eyes, Will gave a weak smile.

They'd decided to leave Miriam at Hinton Hall for the time being. Petrol was still rationed and the summer holidays would be starting soon. They'd bring her home then. The poor girl was still struggling to cope with the presumed loss of her parents and grandparents; meeting up with a dramatically changed Will might be too much. Pamela hoped that by the time she came home, he'd be on the road to recovery.

'I think I'll go up to bed now,' he said.

'All right, darling.' Pamela had insisted that Kitty let her wash the sheets and make up the bed. She'd put a sprig of lavender under his pillow so he would sleep well, and managed to get him some new flannelette pyjamas, although they'd probably be too big. She just wanted to surround him with the comforts of home until they drove out the terrors in his mind. He let her kiss him goodnight, and allowed Hugh to pat him awkwardly on the back, before he trudged upstairs, leaving his parents to mourn the loss of the old Will.

Tomas was still with them a few weeks later. He and Will had walked each day; short distances at first, then, as they both grew stronger from Kitty's cooking, they started to venture onto the Heath. Pamela watched their faces begin to lose their pallor and their eyes grow brighter. Perhaps the Heath was healing them as it had her.

'It will be nice for Tomas to meet Miriam,' Pamela said, before she and Hugh left to collect her. 'Are you sure you two will be all right on your own?'

'I think we can manage, Mother,' Will replied.

'Kitty will look after you, and there's plenty of food in the larder.'

'Off you go,' said Will, ushering her firmly out of the door.

Following Hugh down the hallway, Pamela thought she heard a sigh of relief.

As Hugh drove them back through the English countryside, Miriam announced that she didn't want to return to Hinton Hall.

'I'm eleven now, old enough to go back to Czechoslovakia on my own.'

'But who will you live with?' asked Pamela gently. They hadn't heard for certain that her parents and grandparents were dead, but there'd been no letter from them in years. She wondered if deep down Miriam still nursed a shred of hope. But if she did, she never acknowledged it.

Miriam glanced out of the window at fields of wheat bleached by the hot sun. 'I don't know. There must be somebody.'

'Didn't you say your mother was an only child?'

Miriam nodded.

'So no aunts or uncles? Cousins?'

Still looking out of the window, Miriam shook her head.

'And what about your father's side?'

'My father was much older than my mother. His older brother was killed in the Great War. I don't think there was anyone else.' There was a catch in her voice, and Pamela saw her shoulders trembling. She looked up and caught Hugh's face in the rear mirror. 'Ask . . . her . . . to . . . stay,' he mouthed to her reflection.

'Miriam, dear.' Pamela put a tentative hand on Miriam's knee. 'Why don't you stay here with us for a bit? Until things have settled. Finish your education. You can go to Sarum Hall. Then we'll see how things are. It will be much safer to wait for news of your family in London. I know you fear the worst, but we haven't heard anything for certain. We'd love to have you. You know you're like a daughter to us now.'

Miriam finally turned round and smiled at Pamela sadly. 'Thank you,' she said. 'May I think about it?'

Pamela smiled back. 'Of course.'

Soon after Tomas had returned to Poland, Miriam woke one September Saturday morning to the sound of the wind rattling the letter box and the back gate banging. She looked out of the window. Fast-moving clouds scudded across a bright blue sky. She pulled on the new brown jumper Mrs Denison had bought her and a pair of brown and white checked slacks. More clothes were coming into the shops now. Mrs Denison had taken her shopping last week and she'd chosen the outfit from Debenhams. It was nice to wear her own clothes after that scratchy South Hampstead High uniform.

She bounded down the stairs and into the kitchen. Will was there already, munching on a piece of toast. He motioned to the pile beside him. 'Want some? Kitty's just made it.'

'Please.' Miriam grabbed a piece and smeared it with some of Kitty's home-made jam. Will was looking stronger now. She'd been shocked when she'd first seen him, so thin and pale. Now he was more like the old Will, although he still wore that harrowed expression when he thought people weren't watching him.

'Do you fancy a walk up on the Heath later?' he asked. 'It's such a lovely day.'

Miriam nodded. 'I'd like that.'

'Great. I've a surprise for you. Finish your breakfast and I'll get it.'

Will dashed out of the room, a piece of toast still in his mouth, and returned with a diamond of bright red cloth fixed to a wooden frame, trailing a long piece of string, some of which was wound round a short stick.

'Know what this is?'

'Of course. It's a kite. I used to fly one with my father on Petřín Hill when I was little.'

'Oh, so you're too old to fly one now?'

Miriam shrugged. 'A bit. But I'll go with you if you want.'

Will went into the hall to fetch his coat. He retrieved Miriam's gabardine mac and threw it across the room to her. 'Great. It's the perfect day for it. Come on.'

Will was right. Up on the Heath, the kite soared in the spiralling wind. In spite of herself, Miriam laughed. Will looked so funny dashing backwards and forwards, shouting at the kite as though it were a person. When he handed her the string, she noticed his bright red cheeks, his lively eyes. She was smiling as she took over the flying.

The kite was soon a tiny red dot dancing in a vast and shimmering sky. Miriam felt its power and freedom. Was that how Will felt in a plane? It was marvellous to know he was standing next to her, shouting encouragement, gently guiding her hands, laughing at her mistakes. How could she bear to go back to Prague and leave him behind?

They stayed there for an hour or so until Will announced he was hungry and they should get back for lunch. Miriam tugged at the string and quickly wound it round the stick, pulling the reluctant kite with her. Eventually she tamed it; Will took it from her and grasped it firmly to his chest as they turned to walk back.

'That was fun,' she said. 'Thanks.'

'So you weren't too proud to be a kid again?'

She arched her left eyebrow. It was a trick she'd learned at Hinton Hall, and she was rather pleased with it. 'Nor you.'

Will laughed. 'Things were so much simpler when we were young.'

Miriam nodded. 'Perhaps we need to try to be kids again.'

'We can't wind the clock back, Miriam. But we can still enjoy life. Some of it, anyway.'

'I hope you're right.'

He squeezed her shoulder. 'Please don't go back to Czechoslovakia. Stay with us. It's easy to be natural with you. I miss Tomas so much. Mother and Papa talk to me as if they're treading on eggshells all the time. I need my sister with me.'

Sister! That was the first time he had ever used that word. Miriam smiled. 'Yes, I'll stay,' she said. 'Now that I have a brother to look after.'

*

348

Two weeks later, Will joined Pamela and Hugh in the drawing room. Pamela was knitting a jumper for Miriam, and Hugh had a tumbler of Scotch in his hand.

'Quick snifter before bed, Will?' Hugh jumped up and went to the sideboard. He picked up one of the leaded glasses from the silver tray and motioned to the bottle of whisky.

Will glanced at Pamela's face. 'No, thanks, Papa.'

Hugh shrugged and returned to his seat.

Pamela felt a rush of warmth towards her son. She had no idea whether he'd started drinking during the war. In some ways, she wouldn't blame him if he had. But at least he respected her views in the house.

All those walks with Miriam had reinvigorated him. And it was terrific that he'd persuaded Miriam to stay. He'd looked happier lately too. Thank God their son was coming back to them.

'Have you decided what you'll do now?' said Hugh. Pamela thought they'd agreed not to ask about future plans for a while. But maybe Hugh was so relieved to see flashes of the old Will that he'd judged the time was right.

Will picked at a loose thread on the antimacassar. 'Yes. I've given it a lot of thought over these past few weeks.'

'And?'

Pamela thought Hugh sounded a little aggressive.

'And I've decided to stay in the RAF.'

'What?' Hugh was halfway to his feet, the whisky lurching across his glass.

'But the war's over,' said Pamela. 'Surely you've been demobbed?'

'Of course. But I want to join the regular RAF.'

'You want to *fight*?' Pamela was horrified.

Will smoothed the armchair cover. 'No, Mother. I want to keep the peace.'

'But you could still be engaged in active combat. There'll be other wars, other conflicts,' said Hugh.

Will's tone was weary, as though he'd explained this a hundred times before. 'I'm still a Quaker. I still believe in peace. More than ever since this terrible war. But pacifism isn't the answer. Monsters like Hitler see that as weakness.'

'But Quakers were the only people the Germans have allowed through. We've done nearly all the relief work. Here and in Europe.' Margery Weston had even gone out with a group of volunteers to the Bergen-Belsen camp just after the British had liberated it. Hugh had forbidden Pamela to go with her, but she'd spent weeks packing supplies.

'Of course the Quakers have done a marvellous job, Mother,' Will shot her a warm glance, 'and they always will. We both believe the same thing. We're coming at it from different angles, that's all.'

Hugh cleared his throat. 'So you want to stay in the RAF in order to promote peace?'

'That's it. We need strong forces as a deterrent.'

'And you don't believe there'll be another war?' Pamela could hear the anxiety in her voice. She couldn't go through that again.

'No, I don't.' He smiled at her reassuringly. 'I'm a good pilot. Read my squadron leader's report. I love being up in the sky, the sense of freedom, the responsibility. It's what I was born for.'

Pamela firmed her lips. 'I don't understand you, Will.'

350

'I know, Mother, but I need you to respect my decision. Please.'

Hugh stood up to refill his glass. Pamela noticed his hand was shaking.

29

'I'm sorry, do I know you?'

Hana looked up at the middle-aged woman standing at her parents' old front door. She had permed grey hair and a sharply angled face. There wasn't a measure of compassion on her thin mouth.

'I'm Hana Rubenstein. I used to live here before the war with my parents, Hilda and Kurt Rubenstein.'

'So?' The door closed a fraction. It had weathered over the years, but the cherry-red paint Hana's father had applied with such care was still in evidence.

Hana took a steadying breath, as she did when she had to quell her nerves before a recital. 'So I'm wondering why you are living in a house that belonged to my parents.'

'Jews?'

Hana nodded.

'Well, they're not going to need it now, are they?'

'No, they're not. They died during the war. But I am alive and I intend to live here.'

The door closed a little more. Hana could just glimpse her mother's old pine dresser at the end of the hallway. She wondered if her piano was still in the drawing room. Did this woman sit at the Rubenstein family table eating dinner from their Epiag plates with the pictures of peacocks on, drinking from their blue china cups? She felt her face burn.

'I'm sorry.' The woman didn't sound it. 'I live here now, with my family. You will have to find somewhere else.'

'But it's my house! Our things!' shouted Hana. 'I grew up here. My father paid for it from his wages, my mother loved it.' She had a sudden vivid memory of Mutti stitching the tapestry cushions night after night, crocheting the delicate antimacassars that this woman was now soiling with her grubby fingers.

The woman shrugged and shut the door firmly.

Hana leapt forward and pounded her fist on the hard wood, then kicked it several times, but it remained closed.

Eventually she wandered back up the street, blood pounding fortissimo in her ears, trying to work out what to do next.

It was getting late. Long shadows striped the road. Shopkeepers were shutting their doors and pulling down awnings. A faint sound of music threaded through the cooling air. Instinctively Hana followed it. It was a piano. Chopin. Or possibly Schubert. The yellow building of the conservatoire loomed in front of her, reassuring in its solidity. Had people continued to go there through the war? Taken lessons? Practised? It was hard to imagine life going on as usual.

She hadn't come across Otto since Terezin had been liberated, so she had no idea if he was in Prague or not. And even if he was, she didn't know how she might react to seeing him again. She was still curious about her half-sister, Miriam. Eva had told her so much about her. But it was too soon to seek her out; she couldn't cope with any more changes in her life. She just wanted to find some stability again. And for her, stability always meant music.

She pushed the heavy brown door and walked in.

A woman sat at a desk, typing. She raised her head as Hana entered. 'Do you have a lesson?'

Hana shook her head. How could she tell this woman what she'd come for when she didn't know herself? 'I used to have lessons here, before the war.'

'Who was your teacher, dear?' The woman had kind brown eyes.

'Gabriel Schmidt.'

'You must have been good. He was the best.'

'The best and the bravest.' Hana blinked back the blur of tears.

The woman nodded. 'I heard what happened to him. We've lost so many of our best musicians. The conservatoire feels like a shell now.'

Hana told the woman about the performances at Terezin. *Brundibár* and the *Requiem*.

The woman wiped her cheeks with the back of her hand. 'How like Gabri to use music to fight back. I'm very proud of him.'

Hana nodded. The woman seemed so sympathetic, she found herself telling her about Eva.

'Eva Novak? She was such a promising pianist as a girl.'

'I know. Eva Kolischer now. She got to play again at Terezin. She was marvellous. All I can do is try to live up to her memory.'

'Do you play too?'

'Yes, I took over from her at the performances after she'd left for Auschwitz.'

The woman pressed Hana's hand with her warm fingers. 'You poor child. And where are you living now?'

Hana relayed the failed attempt to regain her old home.

The woman nodded. 'I'm afraid I've heard many stories like yours.' She glanced at the clock, placed a cover over the typewriter and stood up. 'Right, dear. I have a spare room in my apartment; you're coming with me.'

Hana followed her out, making no attempt to stem the flow of tears.

Slowly Prague came back to life. People returned from the forests, where they'd lived on wild berries and stale food salvaged from rubbish dumps, where they'd slept under the stars in summer and in shelters they'd dug out with their bare hands in winter. Others limped out of the prisons and shuffled down long roads across Europe as they returned from the concentration camps. Hana heard of a boy whose wooden clogs had to be removed by a surgeon because the soles of his feet had grown into them; she saw a young woman kiss the ground in front of the statue of St Wenceslas, then faint from exhaustion; she heard of families visiting friends to whom they'd entrusted their belongings for the duration of the war, and being invited to sit on their own chairs and drink from their own glasses whilst their friends denied all knowledge that the possessions had merely been lent.

Some people whispered terrible stories of death and blood and gas, while others claimed that the suffering of living on skimmed milk and doing without butter had been far greater. The pink posters containing long lists of names of people who had been executed for 'crimes against the Reich' were torn down from the walls. Sometimes whole families had been murdered for protecting a Jew or an escaped prisoner.

For months Hana filled her head with music, staying with the kindly receptionist, Irena, at night and attending the conservatoire during the day. No one ever charged her for the lessons. 'You are Eva Novak's daughter,' Irena told her, with awe in her voice. 'She was one of our most promising students. For you there will never be any charge.' And each day Hana became more skilled, more confident and more secure.

*

Pamela alighted from the bus and made her way up Marylebone High Street. She hadn't told Miriam or Hugh about her journey. It was important she found out this information on her own. Then she could choose how to present it. In the absence of any concrete news, they'd avoided speaking to Miriam about her parents. If she mentioned them at all, it was in the past tense, but maybe that was because she hadn't seen them for so long. Their time together in Prague must feel like another life. Yet Pamela wondered if she still nurtured some hope.

As she entered the hall of the Czech Red Cross headquarters, a wave of fuggy heat hit her. It was packed. Everywhere she looked there were anxious expressions, women in head-scarves with pinched faces, old men with sticks, frightened-looking children holding onto their mothers' hands. Pamela remembered how she'd felt when Will had been taken captive, and her heart went out to these poor people. Above the low hum of voices was the frantic sound of the ticker-tape machine, pattering out its deadly news.

There was a hush as a young woman appeared on the balcony, a sheaf of papers shaking in her hands. She read the list in a firm, slow voice. As each name was intoned, there was a corresponding wail of grief from the hall. Pamela could hardly bear to look at the couples who clung to each other, sobbing, the children bawling into their mothers' coats, the white faces of grief and despair.

The young woman was less composed now. Before each announcement she had to take a deep breath to steady herself. Pamela watched as she fixed her gaze upwards, as though she could no longer bear to see the terrible distress her words triggered. What an awful job.

Pamela thought of Kate, who had driven her to Hinton Hall that day she'd told Miriam about Will. Another girl who'd turned into a strong woman. Funny what war did to people. What reserves of courage and determination could be found when undergoing the severest of trials.

'Eva and Josef Kolischer.'

Pamela's attention shifted. That was Miriam's parents. Confirmed dead. Her heart plummeted. Even though they'd feared this deep down, it was still a bombshell. And one she would have to break to Miriam as gently as she could. She waited until the surnames beginning with 'N' were announced, and when she heard the girl read out 'Esther and Samuel Novak', she trudged out of the hall with a heavy heart.

When she was next at the British Red Cross, she begged the desk clerk to find out more, but he could only repeat that the Kolischers were on the list of those killed; whether at Terezin or elsewhere, he couldn't say.

*

Pamela sat by the window until she saw Miriam walking down the street in her navy blazer, a bulging satchel slung over her shoulder. She opened the front door, took Miriam's satchel from her, hung up her blazer, then motioned her into the drawing room.

'Sit down, dear,' she said, 'I've something to tell you.'

But she could see from Miriam's white face that she already suspected the devastating news that Pamela would impart.

30

Four years later, Miriam stood in front of the mirror and pinned a brooch to the lapel of her suit. It was the one item of jewellery she possessed; Mrs Denison had given it to her for her fifteenth birthday. Although the brooch gleamed prettily, she knew the jewels weren't real, just paste emeralds and gold leaf. Nonetheless, it made the brown hand-me-down suit look a little less dowdy.

Although the war had long since ended, clothing was still rationed. And even if it weren't, how would she get the money to buy new things? The Denisons were very generous – too generous really – but no one had expected her to be there that long. Back in 1939, they'd thought the war would be over in a couple of years, or at least that President Beneš would return in triumph to Prague and reclaim the city. Miriam had fantasised for months about arriving at Wilson station, running down the platform towards her parents and grandparents, being swept off her feet by Abba, hugged until there was no breath left in her body by Mutti, then petted and spoiled by them all the way home. Yet none of those things had happened, and the war had dragged on for six whole years. Now the Russians had taken over Prague. Apparently they hated Jews too – if there were even any left to hate.

There had never been another letter from her parents or grandparents. Mrs Denison's news from the Czech Red Cross had only confirmed what she already knew deep down. She was now officially an orphan, with no family left.

Mr and Mrs Denison had insisted she carried on living with them. 'You've always been like a daughter to me, Miriam,' Mrs Denison had said. 'Let's make it official now.' And Miriam, not knowing what else to do, had agreed to stay, but only on the grounds that she would leave school when she'd turned fifteen and find a job. She insisted on paying her way.

Luckily, a vacancy had come up at the Foreign Office. Today was her first day, and she was going in with Mr Denison on the train.

'Miriam, are you ready?' he shouted up.

'Coming.' She walked down the stairs and went to join him in the hall.

'Very nice, dear,' said Mrs Denison, adjusting her brooch. 'I'm sure you'll do very well.'

Secretarial work was hardly the brilliant musical career Miriam had once envisaged, but it would have to do for now.

The crowded train lurched and stop-started its way to Westminster. Miriam sat beside Mr Denison, who was reading the *Times*. Opposite them was a row of men in pinstripes, also reading the *Times*. Even their legs crossed the same way. Apart from their differently arranged heads – one wore glasses, one had thick hair, another was bald – they could have been replicas of the same person. There weren't many women – just a couple of girls in navy and gold school uniform, who alighted at Goodge Street, and a middle-aged woman, swathed in fur, with immaculately stockinged legs, who gazed haughtily over Miriam's shoulder at the advertising posters behind her. There were posters opposite Miriam too, above the woman's head: General Electric Radios, Coca-Cola and Lucky Strike cigarettes. Miriam stared at them and tried to look as haughty as the woman.

Mr Denison's office wasn't far from the Tube station. He marched along the pavement without talking, probably already preoccupied with the day ahead, and Miriam did her best to keep up with him in a pair of Mrs Denison's old court shoes that were a little too big for her and made her feet slip and slide within them. After a bit, they came to a magnificent white stone building with huge windows and statues perched on the roof. A man in a black uniform dotted with shiny buttons opened the door, and Miriam followed Mr Denison inside. He waved his copy of the *Times* in acknowledgement and swept by. Miriam aimed a timid smile at the rather disapproving-looking woman sitting at the reception desk and followed Mr Denison across a mosaic-patterned floor interspersed with marble pillars. Above them was an ornately decorated ceiling from which hung glittering chandeliers. A red-carpeted stairway swept down to the floor. Mr Denison held open the lift door, smiling at Miriam's amazement. She'd never seen anywhere so beautiful before.

'You mustn't be nervous, Miriam,' he said as the lift shuddered its way upwards. 'Everyone will be very kind.'

Miriam tried to stretch a smile, but her lips were suddenly very dry, so she nodded instead. When the lift man pulled back the metal doors and touched his cap to Mr Denison, Mr Denison put a palm against her back to guide her out, then led her down the corridor, knocked on a dark wooden door with *Secretarial Support* written on a gold plaque, and motioned her in.

A middle-aged woman in a suit stood up and greeted him. Her clothes were severe, but she had a smiling face and dark brown curls that made her look friendlier from the neck upwards. 'Good morning, Mr Denison,' she said. 'And you must be Miriam.'

Miriam nodded.

'Good morning, Mrs Ainsley,' said Mr Denison. 'Yes, this is Miriam. Righto, I'll leave you to it. See you at six, Miriam.' He backed out of the door.

Mrs Ainsley took Miriam's coat and hat, showed her to a desk, then began to explain the day's tasks.

By lunchtime, Miriam was bored rigid. She wasn't a typist and couldn't take shorthand – although the Denisons had promised she could be trained in both if she showed an interest – so was relegated to filing, sorting the post and delivering messages. Mrs Ainsley promised she would show her how to answer the telephone that afternoon. Miriam thought she could hardly wait.

At one o'clock, she was informed she could have an hour for lunch. So she retraced her steps of five hours earlier and stumbled out onto the pavement and the white glare of Whitehall. Mr Denison had said he would eat at his club, but Miriam assumed the invitation didn't extend to her. She wandered down the road, onto Westminster Bridge, found a bench and sat there to open up the greaseproof paper package that had been wilting in her handbag since Kitty had handed it to her earlier: corned beef, pickle and thick white bread. Miriam still yearned to taste proper bread – the black loaves they'd had at home – but years of the National Loaf had hardened her, and now she found British bread almost palatable.

She looked across the bridge at the river. The Thames was bright in the sunlight, with a few boats motoring along. It was early spring, and tall sycamore trees lined the banks, their green leaves already unfurling. Other office workers – as she supposed she was now – were sitting on benches, some chatting, some reading. Perhaps she would bring a book tomorrow. That would give her something to do; if she found one with a good enough plot, anticipating the next section of the story might keep her mind occupied during the morning.

She finished her sandwiches and folded the greaseproof paper carefully into a square, then took an apple out of her pocket.

Although the work was dull, the morning hadn't been all bad. Mrs Ainsley was kind and explained things well – not that any of the tasks were difficult. From time to time, people popped into the office: a private secretary, looking harassed and asking for some papers; the tea lady, who handed Miriam a cup of dishcloth-coloured liquid and a Nice biscuit at half past ten; and Hugh, who had seemingly forgotten she was there and asked Mrs Ainsley to book him a flight to Nuremberg in Germany in three days' time. Miriam wondered if Mrs Denison knew about his trip.

She finished the apple, walked over to a nearby rubbish bin

and deposited the core, carefully nibbled to ensure everything edible had been eaten, together with her sandwich packet. Then she glanced at her watch. Still forty minutes left. She wandered over the bridge.

There was an imposing-looking church at the far end, with the faint sound of music drifting from it. Miriam approached. The door was open; next to it stood an easel with a poster advertising lunchtime concerts. Today, apparently, it was Vivaldi's *Four Seasons*. She went in and sat down on one of the hard wooden benches.

Beautiful, stirring music pulsed through her and she felt her heart lift. The orchestra was quite small: only half a dozen violins and violas, a cello, double bass and a harpsichord. Fleetingly, Miriam wondered what Mutti would have made of it. She imagined her mother being in London with her, performing Chopin or Debussy at a lunchtime concert. Miriam couldn't imagine Mutti having access to music at Terezin. She'd died without ever taking up her vocation again. But she'd encouraged Miriam's singing. She'd have been proud of her solo in front of President Beneš.

She looked round at the walls of the church, advertising all sorts of ensembles, and finally found the number for a choir. She took out a small notebook and a pen from her bag, and scribbled down the number. They rehearsed at lunchtimes and early evenings. Perfect. Perhaps she could find something to relieve the tedium of her days after all.

As she made her way back to the office, her footsteps were tuned to Vivaldi's allegro beat.

*

Four months later, Miriam was singing solo at a lunchtime performance of Beethoven's *Missa Solemnis*. Mrs Ainsley was very good at giving her time off – in fact Miriam wondered if she'd only been given the job because of Mr Denison; she'd suspected for a while that Mrs Ainsley was merely finding work for her.

She stepped forward for her part, her voice soaring over the stately chords and majestic cadences. The conductor, a willowy man with a thatch of auburn hair, beamed at her. The chorus felt like a wall of music behind her, their voices providing warm support. It reminded her of when she'd sung for President Beneš with the choir at Hinton Hall, but instead of the sweet voices of schoolchildren, these voices were rich, mature and powerful. As she delivered the final note, she looked out into the audience – quite an impressive array of office workers today – then bowed her head.

'Have you ever had proper singing lessons, Miriam?' asked Mr Fellowes, the conductor, as Miriam packed away her things later.

She shook her head. 'Not really. My mother taught me for a while, although she was really a pianist. Then the music teacher at school helped me.'

'I know an excellent vocal coach. Shirley Mountford. She trains some of the singers at the Royal Opera House. Would you like me to mention your name?'

'Would she be very expensive?' Miriam was earning a small amount now, but she insisted on giving some to the Denisons, and she was trying to save for the future – whatever that might hold.

'If the singer is exceptional, she sometimes gives lessons for free. I can talk to her about you.'

'Yes, please,' said Miriam. It would be wonderful to be properly taught. She smiled at Mr Fellowes, who nodded approvingly, as though he'd bestowed a huge honour on her. Maybe he had.

That afternoon, the talk in the office was all of Nuremberg, where they were holding trials of Nazi war criminals. Mr Denison, who spoke passable German, had flown out a few times; now he asked Miriam if she would like to accompany him, together with Will, who'd been summoned as a witness as a result of his time at Hammelburg.

'You don't have to go if you don't want to,' he said. 'It could be a very difficult trip for you.'

Miriam swallowed. How would she feel being in a room full of people who hated Jews, who'd maybe even been responsible for the murder of her parents? Would she be able to sit calmly whilst her blood pounded and her hands shook? But her parents and grandparents had had no choice about the horrors they'd faced. She'd been sheltered for most of the war; she owed it to them to be brave now.

She fixed Mr Denison with an even gaze. 'I want to go,' she said.

He smiled back. 'Good girl,' he said quietly.

At supper that night, Mr Denison explained a little more about her expected role. 'You'll be taking notes mainly,' he said, cutting off a piece of lamb chop. 'We're on to the minor trials now. We need to collect enough evidence to make a case. Will

will be questioned, of course. I thought it might help if he had company in between court sessions.'

Miriam reached for the pepper. 'I'll do my best,' she said. She had a little shorthand now, enough to get by, thanks to a course at the Pitman College in Oxford Circus that she'd been released for on Thursday afternoons. Shorthand was hard, but easier than music, and Miss Scott, the prim, exacting teacher, had lowered her normal reserve enough to tell Miriam that she was making good progress.

It would be good to spend time with Will again. Since that awful summer when he'd returned from Germany, thin and haunted, he'd been at Brize Norton, where he worked for the central flying school. As far as she knew, he was still in touch with Tomas. 'How can he want to train pilots, after all he's been through?' Mrs Denison had said.

Will had filled out again, his face resuming its ruddiness, and sometimes he even looked happy. Miriam wondered if he had a girlfriend. He'd never brought anyone back home as far as she knew. As a child, she'd fantasised about marrying him, but he was too old for her and they were more like brother and sister anyway. She hoped they'd become close again in Nuremberg. That might help allay some of the terror she was already beginning to feel about attending the trials.

The next day, Mrs Ainsley showed her a long list of German names. 'Mr Denison has asked if you would check these, dear,' she said. 'We'd like you to find out which camp they worked at, what their crimes were.'

'And how would I do that?' asked Miriam.

Mrs Ainsley handed her a sheaf of papers. 'Here is a list

of all the camps in Europe. Just check we have the right names for the right camps.'

Miriam reached out to take the papers and placed the two piles of documents side by side on her desk. It would be a long job. She'd had no idea there had been so many concentration camps in Europe. There were ten in Czechoslovakia alone. So many of her people killed. She'd been told that around six million Jews had failed to survive the war. Her eyes prickled and she felt the familiar lurch of panic at the thought of her parents' and grandparents' deaths. It had been years now, and her life in England was happy enough, but the knowledge that she had no blood relatives left still haunted her.

She picked up her pen, gripping it with suddenly shaky fingers, and steeled herself for the task ahead.

The singing teacher, Miss Mountford, was a beanpole of a woman with a large bosom – as if someone had eviscerated every ounce of fat from elsewhere on her body and deposited it as two pectoral mountains. Perhaps you needed to be well endowed to sing powerfully, thought Miriam, looking down at her own small breasts. She'd been fourteen before Mrs Denison had bought her a brassiere. And even then it felt much too big. Perhaps she should try to eat more.

'Now, Miriam.' Miss Mountford stood at the piano and sounded a note. 'I'm going to play a few scales, and I'd like you to replicate the sound as best you can.' She started with C major, then nodded to Miriam.

Miriam sang only two notes before Miss Mountford interrupted her. 'Shoulders back.' The teacher thrust her own shoulders back, triggering a corresponding wobble from her front. Miriam quickly suppressed a rising arpeggio of laughter.

'And again, please.'

Miriam squared her shoulders and began the scale.

Three notes this time, then, 'More legato, please.'

She delivered the notes more smoothly and even managed to get to the end of the scale.

Miss Mountford firmed her lips. 'You're breathing from your throat. High larynx. Take the breath from further down.' She slapped at her chest, causing a seismic oscillation, and Miriam had to turn a laugh into a cough. 'Go!'

Miriam sang the notes again.

'Better. But your facial muscles are too tense.' Miss Mountford was making exaggerated chewing movements and motioning to Miriam to do the same. 'Now you're more relaxed. And again.'

Miriam continued, trying to keep her jaw supple.

'You're swaying slightly. Stand *still*.'

She did as she was told.

By the time Miss Mountford slapped down the lid of the piano, Miriam realised an hour had gone by and the teacher hadn't praised her once. She obviously thought she was a lost cause, there was so much wrong with her singing. Maybe she'd carried on with the lesson as an act of pity.

'Same time tomorrow?' Miss Mountford asked.

'Oh.' Miriam was amazed. Not only did the woman want to continue her lessons but she even wanted to see her again soon.

Miss Mountford was staring at her.

'Yes, please.'

'You showed great promise today. Keep working hard and you could do well.' She exited the room like a galleon figurehead, leaving Miriam dumbfounded.

31

Two weeks later, Miriam sat between Mr Denison and Will in the back of an armoured car, being driven through the cobbled streets of the Bavarian town on their way to the last of the Nuremberg trials. Most of the major war criminals had been tried and executed by now: von Ribbentrop, Frank, Frick, Kaltenbrunner, Keitel, Seyss-Inquart, Streicher and Rosenberg had been hanged; Goring and Hess had committed suicide the night before their executions.

She looked out of the window at the bombed-out houses and piles of rubble and tried to imagine the sounds of marching feet, cheering crowds, rousing music and a triumphant Führer spitting out his message of hatred to the listening world. She'd not even been born when Hitler came to power; now he was dead himself, shot by his own hand, deep in his underground bunker. But not before he'd claimed the lives of Eva's parents and grandparents. She'd heard the Jews had been told to sing as they entered the gas chambers so they would inhale more gas and die quicker. Had Mutti ended her life with the melody of her beloved villanelle on her lips? She turned her head to hide the glaze of tears from Will.

She must have made a sound, as Mr Denison reached out to hold her hand. 'I'm sorry, my dear. This can't be an easy trip for you.'

Miriam nodded. She'd wondered a few times on the way out if she'd made the right decision, but every time her parents' faces came into her mind, her resolve had hardened. 'I'm here to do a job. And I'll do it to the best of my ability.'

Mr Denison smiled at her. 'I wouldn't have expected anything less.'

Will was very brave in court, standing ramrod straight in the dock and answering the judge's questions loudly and clearly. Miriam winced as she took notes. Will hadn't told her about the terrible food, the solitary confinement, the hard labour, although it was obvious from the mental and physical change in him that he'd had a gruelling time. She knew too that the Germans had treated their prisoners of war a lot better than they'd treated the Jews. She stared hard at the notebook in front of her, to blot out the image of Mutti and Abba, their heads shaved, their bodies stripped as they entered the gas chamber at Auschwitz. All she could do for them now was to be the best daughter she could. Here at Nuremberg, she'd do everything in her power to help Mr Denison make sure the criminals were punished. And afterwards, she'd work at her singing until her voice was so beautiful her parents would hear it from Gan Eden.

*

Hana chewed the inside of her cheek as she lay on her bed frowning up at the yellowing ceiling of Irena's spare room, then winced at the resulting soreness and metallic tang in her mouth.

Irena had been so kind, and the apartment was comfortable if sparse, but it wasn't home. She'd not had a home for ten years now. And there was clearly no chance of going back to the house where she'd lived with the Rubensteins, thanks to that awful woman who owned it now. But apart from the memories, the house was just bricks and mortar really. It was the feeling of being an orphan that haunted her most: all those she'd loved, all those who'd loved her – Mutti, Abba, Eva – were dead. Only her biological father remained alive, but she hadn't seen him since Terezin. Perhaps he'd been in hiding. Until now.

She smoothed the crumpled letter in her hand, then propped the paper against her raised knees to read it, even though she knew the words by heart. It was headed with the impressive lion and unicorn emblem of the British Foreign Office, and was a summons to give witness at the trial of Otto Blumsfeld at Nuremberg.

She let her knees drop and the letter fluttered onto the bed. In normal circumstances she'd never have contemplated going to Nuremberg. How could she testify against her own father? But then she'd noticed the name at the bottom of the letter: Hugh Denison. Doubtless he had no idea who she was – just another Terezin survivor who could testify against a minor war criminal. But Hana knew exactly who *he* was. It was too much of a coincidence. It had to be the man whose family Eva told her Miriam had gone to live with in England. Eva had spoken of Miriam's letters assuring her that the Denisons treated her like a daughter, that Mr Denison was benevolent, if busy, and Mrs Denison was all heart.

Apart from Otto Blumsfeld, Miriam Kolischer, her half-sister, was Hana's only surviving relative. So she'd accepted the summons. It was partly curiosity: she'd never been outside Czechoslovakia in her life, and Prague had felt stifling lately, the houses in some of the old streets off the Staroměstské náměstí tilting so alarmingly it seemed they might topple forward and trap her between them. The roughened cobbles constantly snagged her shoes as though they wanted to rip her to shreds from her feet upwards.

She yearned to see Prague receding at speed from a train window, its spires and towers blurring as she hurtled free of the city's grasp. But it was more than that. Some of the most evil men in the world had passed through Nuremberg. Murderer after murderer had stood in the dock and been sentenced to death or life imprisonment. Some had even died at their own hand. There'd been nothing she could have done to save her family, but maybe she could witness their killers brought to justice.

And then there was Miriam. If she could get to meet this Hugh Denison, maybe she could talk to him about his adopted daughter. Perhaps he'd invite her back to England to meet her. A little bubble of hope rose in Hana's chest at the thought of getting to know her half-sister. Would she look anything like her? Would she be musical? And how would Miriam feel knowing that her mother, *their* mother, had had another child?

It would be a risk going to Nuremberg; she'd accepted the offer of expenses and accommodation, perhaps dishonestly – and she'd have to account for that – but the desire to find out about Miriam had been too strong. Even if she still didn't know whether she could stand up in court and testify against her father.

It was a long train ride to Nuremberg, through half-destroyed villages. She glimpsed ragged children perched on piles of rubble, staring at them forlornly. Women in patched clothes paused in their farm work to rub their backs whilst the train sped by. But at least they were all alive. What would Eva be doing now if she'd survived?

They left the towns behind and the track wound slowly upwards towards the wild beauty of the Böhmerwald mountains, then plunged into the dense forests of Bavaria. Lulled by the endless blur of bottle-green trees and rigid brown trunks, Hana fell asleep for the last part of the journey. But she woke with a jolt when the train finally ground into the station, her stomach clenching and her heart quickening at the thought of what was in store.

After checking in at the small but clean hotel, the details of which had accompanied her letter, Hana spent a restless night before breakfasting early, alone, in the chilly dining room. It was strange to eat by herself; at Terezin you were never alone, and back in Prague, she normally chatted to Irena as they drank coffee in the kitchen before departing for the conservatoire together. Her anxious thoughts reverberated round the room. Why was she here? She still hadn't decided whether she would go to court. The trial wasn't until the next day. She had a little time to come to a decision. But first she had to track down Mr Denison.

She asked the grim-faced receptionist for directions to the British consulate building, where she assumed she'd find him.

Thank goodness her German was still good, although she'd mainly spoken Czech since returning to Prague. But at the consulate, another receptionist, a little less stern this time, informed her he was at the Palace of Justice.

It took another hour, and a number of wrong turns, trudging through the streets in her worn shoes, before she finally arrived at a large old building with a terracotta-coloured roof and myriad windows. She looked up at them, wondering if any German war criminals were staring out, and shivered as she made her way up to the entrance. There was a soldier on guard outside. Fortunately she had thought to bring her letter from Mr Denison, and, after peering at it for several seconds whilst Hana held her breath, he let her in. The action was repeated by the official inside, until she was finally shown down a long corridor with a high gothic ceiling and into a room where a large-framed man was sitting behind a desk. There had been a weary-sounding 'Enter' to the official's knock.

'Mr Denison?'

The man looked up. His face was flushed, whether from exhaustion or annoyance she couldn't tell, but there was kindness in his blue eyes. This was the man who'd welcomed her half-sister into his home, Hana told herself.

He asked her a question in English, to which she couldn't reply, then nodded at the official, who departed at once.

Hana took a deep breath and spoke in her best German, hoping Mr Denison would understand. 'My name is Hana Rubenstein. I was in Terezin during the war. You asked me here to give witness against Otto Blumsfeld.'

There was a movement from the corner of the room, and

Hana realised there was another occupant, a young girl, possibly in her mid teens: slim, with dark hair and a slightly anxious expression. She'd been sitting in a gloomy recess, surrounded by piles of papers, and had been so still that Hana hadn't noticed her.

'Indeed I did,' Mr Denison replied in heavily accented German. 'Is there a problem?'

Hana nodded. 'Otto Blumsfeld was my gaoler. The guards at Terezin made our lives very difficult.'

'A good reason to testify against him.'

Hana took a step forward. 'I'm not sure I can. I was supposed to be on a train to Auschwitz, but he rescued me. He almost certainly saved my life.' She darted a glance across the room. The girl was looking at her keenly.

Mr Denison's words drew her back. 'He might have rescued you, Hana, but he let many other people go to their deaths.'

Hana's heart was hammering. She'd meant to tell Mr Denison her decision, then hope to lead the conversation on to Miriam. She certainly hadn't anticipated saying this much, but there was something in the man's scrutiny, something in the girl's stillness, that made her want to tell the truth. 'It isn't as straightforward as you make out. You see, Otto Blumsfeld was also my father.'

Mr Denison leapt to his feet and came round the desk towards her. 'We'd no idea; why didn't you say?'

The girl was standing too, her expression a mixture of sympathy and horror, although she didn't come near.

Hana looked down at the floor. 'I was in two minds. I wanted to hate him for what he did to my mother; I thought

I could keep my feelings at bay – stay detached.' She drew her hand across her face. 'But now I find myself remembering how he saved me.' A memory darted into her mind of Otto standing awkwardly beside her as the train receded. The train that had carried Eva to her death and should have carried Hana too. She felt a warm hand on her shoulder and realised the girl had approached.

'What did he do to your mother?' Mr Denison asked.

Hana made her fingers into a fist and rammed them silently into her side. 'He was a member of the Hitler Youth as a boy, back in 1930. He attacked my mother because she was Jewish. She became pregnant . . .' She couldn't say any more. Already she felt a heave of nausea.

Mr Denison returned to his desk and sat down heavily. He muttered something to the girl in English, and Hana thought she saw a look pass between them. The room started to swim, and she reached out to steady herself.

'Are you all right?' The girl, this time. Strangely, she spoke in Czech.

'Miriam, take Miss Rubenstein to the bathroom, please. Then perhaps you could go through the papers with her.'

Miriam? Hana's legs felt hollow.

'Please come with me,' said the girl. Her voice was low and clear. But Hana barely registered that. She was too busy taking in the fact that this girl was called Miriam, that she knew Mr Denison, and that she spoke flawless Czech. There was no other explanation. This Miriam had to be her half-sister.

She stumbled down the corridor after her.

*

After Miriam had taken her to the bathroom and waited outside whilst Hana dry-heaved into the wash basin, then swilled out her mouth and tidied herself in the mirror, she showed her into another office, even smaller than the first, and invited her to sit down. Then she drew a chair from under the heavy oak desk that dominated the room, and positioned herself in front of her. Hana gazed at Miriam's face. Was that Eva's expression she saw, or was she imagining it? How could she confront Miriam with her suspicions?

'You speak Czech,' she said, 'and you have a Jewish name.'

Miriam nodded. She was drawing a sheaf of forms from the desk and unscrewing a pen. 'I lived in the Jewish quarter in Prague until the German invasion. My mother managed to smuggle me out to England, where I've lived ever since.'

It all fitted. 'Did you live with the Denisons?' Hana asked.

'Yes! How did you know?' The pen lid clattered onto the desk.

Hana shifted in her seat. 'Mr Denison seemed very protective of you.' She remembered the two of them standing close together in the room. That was how a father and daughter should look.

'He is. But you must know more to make you think that.' Miriam's gaze was intense.

Hana let out a long, low breath. 'I think I met your mother in Terezin.'

'My mother? Yes, she was there.'

'Was she Eva Kolischer? She was a musician, wasn't she?'

'Yes,' Miriam whispered.

Hana reached out to take Miriam's fingers in her own, as much to stop her own hands shaking as to comfort the other girl. 'When we were in Terezin, the guards allowed us to put on musical concerts. They thought it would keep us busy.' She tried to keep her voice steady. It wouldn't help to show she was upset herself, even though she felt the sweat trickling down her back. 'I was . . . am . . . a pianist. Eva – your mother – became my teacher. She taught me to play Verdi's *Requiem*. I acted as her understudy when she performed it in front of the Germans.'

Miriam swallowed. 'And when she left for Auschwitz . . .?'

'I took over. She was a wonderful teacher. A wonderful person.'

'She was.' Miriam blinked several times.

Hana tried to speak as gently as possible. 'Miriam, when I told Mr Denison my mother was attacked, I was speaking about Eva – your mother, *our* mother.' She ignored the sharp intake of breath and fixed her eyes on the navy cloth of Miriam's skirt. She didn't dare look at her face. 'She was raped in the cemetery when she was taking a short cut home . . .'

'How do you know this?' Miriam's voice was hoarse.

'When she came to Terezin, she recognised one of the prison guards – Otto Blumsfeld – as her former attacker. She'd become pregnant on the night of the attack. I was the result. She had me in secret and gave me away for adoption. When she knew she was to be sent to Auschwitz, she asked Otto to take care of me.'

Miriam snatched her fingers from Hana's grasp and shot to her feet. 'I'm sorry. I have to go.' She lurched towards the door and Hana heard the staccato rhythm of her shoes down the corridor.

She sagged in her seat. What had she done? Miriam would never want a relationship with her now. Why on earth had she answered the summons to Nuremberg? She should have refused, stayed on in Prague and tried to put her life back together. But wouldn't Eva have wanted her daughters to get to know each other? And a small part of Hana was pleased that Miriam knew the truth. The girl had spent five years being brought up by Eva, cuddled by her, kissed by her, put to bed at night . . . cherished . . . loved. Hana had grown close to Eva at Terezin, but she could never have Miriam's memories. And she, the firstborn daughter, had been farmed out to strangers kind though they were, whilst Miriam had basked in their mother's affection.

She drew a long, shuddering breath. There was no point in feeling jealous. Eva was no longer alive; Hana couldn't compete with Miriam for their mother's affection. She could only hope Miriam would still want to know her. They'd both lost their mother. They were each other's only blood relatives. She had to find a way of getting close to her.

She was still sitting on her chair, churning over the events of the last half-hour, when she heard a soft knock.

She wiped her cheeks with her thumb. 'Come in.'

It was Mr Denison. He sat down on the chair Miriam had vacated. 'Miriam is terribly upset,' he said. 'I've sent her back to her hotel. My son will look after her.'

Was there a note of accusation in his voice? And there was something in the way he said 'my son', as if the Denisons were closing ranks against her. Miriam had a foster brother to care for her. And she'd been kept safe during the war. All Hana had left was the man who had a dubious claim to be her father. She didn't reply to Mr Denison: even if she could have found the words, she didn't trust her voice.

'My dear, it's clear from what Miriam has told me that you've had a terrible time.' Mr Denison was panting a little, whether from exertion or embarrassment Hana couldn't tell, but at least these words were kinder. 'But she's had an awful shock too.' He paused, waiting for her to speak.

Hana managed a whisper. 'I'm sorry.'

'Tell me everything, from the beginning.'

With Mr Denison's kind eyes fixed on hers, Hana blurted out her story. How she'd been adopted by the Rubensteins, sent to Terezin, her meeting with Eva, the discovery that she was her mother, the music . . . and her last-minute rescue by Otto.

'I see. You have something of a dilemma here.'

Hana nodded. Her voice was stronger now. 'My father did a terrible thing, many terrible things probably. But he also tried to protect me.' A memory slithered in. Otto seeking her out when she was alone practising in the gymnasium, and handing her a hot baked potato in a napkin. She'd eaten it quickly, the floury heat burning her throat, whilst he had looked on, smiling, then taken the napkin from her after she'd wiped her fingers. He'd slipped away whilst she resumed her playing, nourished and warmed from within.

'Yet he didn't rescue your mother. Nor the thousands of others who went to Auschwitz.'

'He couldn't disobey orders.'

'He must have done to save you.'

'I suppose so.' Hana had never found out if Otto had been punished. She'd just been glad to be reprieved. Although

382

at times she was racked with guilt that she was the only one who'd survived.

'Perpetrators of crime have to be brought to justice, Hana.'

'I know. But I am not going to testify against my own father.'

Mr Denison sighed. 'Please think about this very carefully. If you don't testify, Otto Blumsfeld may well walk away scot-free. Do you really think that's right?'

'No. Of course not. But I can't live with myself if I help sentence him to death.'

'He won't get the death penalty. That's reserved for the major war criminals. He'll get a prison sentence. Like all those Jews incarcerated at Terezin.'

Hana shook her head. 'I'm sorry. You'll have to find someone else. I can't do it.' Her stomach was churning, the nausea threatening to return. What was she supposed to do? She had no one to return to.

'Very well.' Mr Denison got to his feet. He patted her hand awkwardly. 'Thank you for coming, anyway. I'm sure Miriam will want to talk to you again. But she needs time.'

Hana managed a wan smile in response.

She returned wearily to her hotel room, almost oblivious to the journey, so consumed was she with thoughts of her meeting with Miriam. She went to bed convinced she'd made the right decision. But all that night, the Dies Irae from Verdi's *Requiem* thundered through her brain. She heard Eva playing the tumultuous notes, and her ears rang with the choir's words: 'Therefore when the judge takes His seat, whatever is hidden will be revealed: nothing shall remain unavenged.' And in the darkness she saw a terrified girl cornered in a gloomy graveyard, and a terrified woman singing in the stifling air of the gas chamber until she could breathe no more.

Nothing shall remain unavenged.

*

Miriam sat in the packed courtroom. The benches were filled with officials and journalists, all wearing suits, some with headphones on their ears. The air was thick with tension. Eventually a tall man with fair hair was led into the dock, flanked by armed soldiers. He looked to be in his mid thirties, with a scattering of freckles on his face and a full mouth that quivered with fear. Hana's father. And Mutti's rapist. She'd been sixteen. Almost the same age Miriam was now. Miriam's stomach clenched; she rammed her nails into her hands.

Mr Denison had been disappointed but resigned. 'Hana would have been our trump card. The other two witnesses have since passed away. We'll have to make do with written statements now.'

'I'm sorry,' Miriam had said. 'I might have been able to persuade her, but I just couldn't cope with what she told me about Mutti.'

'Of course you couldn't,' said Will. 'It must have been a terrible shock.'

And Mr Denison had nodded at her kindly.

But now, in the gloomy room, staring at the man who'd raped her terrified mother and played gaoler to thousands of her people, Miriam wished she'd stayed to talk to Hana. All she'd been able to think about last night was *her* mother seated on a piano stool with this stranger who claimed to be her half-sister; *her* mother waiting patiently whilst Hana

384

played her scales; *her* mother offering Hana advice, making her play again and again until she was note perfect. It was Hana, not Miriam, her legitimate daughter, who'd spent those last precious weeks with Mutti, given her her last kiss, her last hug. Miriam had spent the night trying to banish those painful images from her mind. How on earth was she to cope with this?

She understood her half-sister's loyalty; by her own account Otto had saved her life. But what about Mutti? What about Abba? What about Oma and Opa, who'd died ahead of their time? Not to mention all the other Jewish families. He couldn't be allowed to walk free.

Otto's face was white as the witness testimonies of the dead were read out. Miriam watched the journalists scribbling furiously. Next to her, Will leant forward, frowning in concentration. A nerve flickered in Mr Denison's cheek.

'Do you have anything more to say?' Lord Justice Colonel Sir Geoffrey Lawrence turned an enquiring face to the chief prosecutor, who shook his head.

There was a sudden flurry of activity as an official scurried into the room and whispered into the prosecutor's ear.

The barrister stood up. 'Apologies, my lord, we do have a last-minute witness. May I permit her to give her testimony?'

The judge gave a nod and wrote something on the pad in front of him.

As Miriam looked up, a slight, fair-haired young woman entered the witness box, guided by an official, and gave her oath. Miriam's pulse accelerated.

It was Hana.

32

Six months later, as she stood in yet another interminable queue – for bread this time – Hana wondered if she'd been right to return to Prague after Otto had been sentenced, rather than try to persuade Miriam to take her back to England. But her newly discovered half-sister had clearly been in shock. And besides, there were her music lessons at the conservatoire, not to mention the few piano pupils she'd acquired now and her accommodation with Irena. Too much at stake to risk it all on a whim. And Miriam hadn't exactly been welcoming.

Hana's chest tightened. It had been hard for her too. Miriam had had Eva to herself for five whole years, whilst she'd been farmed out, admittedly to people who'd adored her, but she'd been denied the love of her own mother nevertheless. And Miriam had lived out the war in peace whilst Hana had been subject to the horrors of Terezin. It might have been hard to deal with that whilst living with the very girl who'd had all the advantages, even though they'd both lost their mother now.

Hana was still struggling with her decision to testify against Otto at the trial. Perhaps she'd have to cope with the guilt at betraying her father for the rest of her life. He'd saved her from Auschwitz after all. And she'd seen him look at her with pride, even affection, when she played the piano. Perhaps they could have had a relationship if it wasn't for her actions. She'd never visited him in prison. She couldn't bear to see the reproach in his eyes.

She thought she'd seen him once in Prague, just after the war. She'd been crossing the market square, having bought some fish for supper, when she'd glimpsed a ragged-looking figure in the queue for vegetables. Something about his stance reminded her of him, although he was a far cry from the proud uniformed man in the ghetto. He hadn't seen her, so she kept her head down and walked briskly back to the apartment. Her feelings for him were still so complex, she didn't want to have to deal with them – or him. But testifying against him at the trial had now sealed his fate, and destroyed their relationship for ever.

The air was icy, and a sharp wind tugged at her headscarf. She tied it more firmly, then blew inside her gloves to warm her hands. A woman in front of her was stamping her feet. A toddler with a red nose and streaming eyes grizzled beside her. Since the communists had come in that February day, poor President Beneš trying desperately, but failing, to hold the country together, it seemed to have been perpetually winter. It was hard to believe that five years ago, when the Russians liberated Terezin, the prisoners had welcomed them with open arms. Yet the very same people who'd given them their freedom now held them captive.

She flexed her hands. All this cold was doing nothing for her fingers. When she rested them on the piano keyboard in the conservatoire practice room, they looked pinched and white. It took a lot of playing before they became warm and fluid again. When she first started classes, she'd been assigned to Václav Husa, one of the best piano teachers at the conservatoire. He was teaching her the Chopin études Pan Husa was a patient, if demanding, teacher, and Hana knew she was making good progress.

She was preparing for a concert at the Rudolfinum. Her first. Eva had spoken to her about the concert hall, and Hana knew she was the reason her mother had failed to play there. It was vital she prepared as thoroughly as possible in order to do her mother justice.

Eventually she'd seen a list of those who'd died in Auschwitz. Eva and Josef Kolischer were on it. Hana wiped a wool-clad finger across her face. Eva would never know that her pianist daughter was about to play the piece she'd prepared to play in the Rudolfinum in her memory. But she'd still perform at her very best for her mother's sake.

Two middle-aged men were standing in the line behind her. She could hear snatches of their conversation, but good manners prevented her from turning round to stare. Like most Prague residents, they complained about the lack of food, the never-ending queues, the restrictions on their freedom. Then their talk shifted to a topic that caused Hana to freeze.

'It's those bloody Jews, getting their thieving hands on our supplies,' said one. 'I can't believe so many came back.'

'Probably too many holes in the gas chambers,' his companion replied.

Both men guffawed, and Hana couldn't help darting a look back at them. They were bent over like gnarled old wizards, convulsed with laughter.

Anger tightened in a band across her chest. How dare they? That was her mother they were talking about . . . her adoptive parents . . . her people. All had died the most horrible death

She balled her fists to stop herself turning round again. But there was worse to come.

'I heard they told those miserable Jews to sing songs as they were being gassed.'

'I wonder if they took requests.'

Again the belly-clenching laughs.

White-hot fury radiated from her body. And this time she couldn't stop herself. She turned round. 'What did you say?' She could hear the ice in her own voice.

One of the men looked a little shamefaced, but the other stepped forward until his face was inches from her own, his beery breath filling her nostrils. 'Are you Jewish?'

Hana tried to hold herself still. 'I am.'

He spat on the ground in front of her. 'Then get to the back of the queue.'

The other man spat too.

Hana wanted to pick them up by their lapels and hurl them to the ground. She wanted to hurt them so much they begged for mercy. Let them have a taste of the fear and pain they dished out so nonchalantly.

Instead she looked from one to the other, injecting as much fury into her stare as she could. 'Don't worry. I have no intention of breathing the same air as you a minute longer.' She turned and walked away with as much dignity as she could muster, despite the anger scorching her from inside. She'd have to find another bread queue.

But once out of sight of the men, she put her empty basket on the ground and clutched at the wall for support. Her biological father had been one of those who'd looked the other way whilst her people were sent to the death camps.

He'd betrayed her mother twice: once in the graveyard and once by failing to rescue her from Auschwitz.

Nothing shall remain unavenged.

Yes, she'd made the right decision after all. Anyone who could treat others' suffering with such indifference deserved to be punished.

She bent down slowly to retrieve her basket. On days like this, she didn't know if she could stay in Prague a minute longer.

33

When Hana opened the front door of the conservatoire and approached the front desk, she was immediately aware of a strained atmosphere. Irena was wiping her eyes with a handkerchief instead of greeting her with her usual bright smile. And the cavernous entrance hall, normally filled with a riot of different instrument sounds, was curiously silent.

'What's the matter?' she asked.

Irena blotted her face again, then balled the hanky into her fist. She glanced round the hall and whispered, 'It's Václav, he had a visit from the secret police last night. He's now in custody, awaiting trial.'

Hana gasped. Václav Husa was a superb pianist and an excellent teacher. But he made no secret of his hatred of the communists. She'd often wondered if he'd been too outspoken when he'd openly referred to 'poor President Beneš' over coffee at the Kotva, or talked of getting up a petition to get him reinstated. You never knew who was listening. There were rumours of houses being bugged, informers encouraged to turn in their fellow citizens, people being imprisoned for filing complaints. Prague under the communists was almost worse than under the Nazis.

'Poor Pan Husa.'

Irena nodded. 'Everyone is in shock.' The handkerchief

came out again. 'And of course this affects you, Hana. You won't have a lesson today. Do you mind practising on your own?'

'Of course not.' Hana's mind was clotted with fear for Václav's fate and she felt a rush of panic at losing her teacher. How could they imprison such a talented musician? But then that hadn't stopped the Nazis. She smiled sadly at Irena and trailed off down the corridor.

Two weeks later, Václav was sentenced to six months' imprisonment. He would hate being locked away. There was nothing Hana could do to help him except continue to practise so she could surprise him with her progress when he was finally released.

In the meantime, she had a new teacher. A woman this time: Milada Dedecek. Paní Dedecek was tall and gaunt, with a beak of a nose and small, critical eyes. She worked Hana hard and was meagre in her praise, but Hana knew instinctively that she'd take her to new heights in her playing.

By the summer, she had mastered all of the Chopin études, even the treacherous Opus 10 No. 2 in A minor, the 'Chromatique'. When she first practised the piece, Paní Dedecek had watched her attempts to achieve the second finger stretch on the bottom of the second page a few times, an amused smile on her lips. Eventually Hana gave in to frustration and played a crashing chord before laying her head on the keyboard. 'It's impossible. I'll never do it.'

Paní Dedecek forced her up. 'Enough!' She picked up Hana's arm. 'First you need to relax.'

Hana let her wrist go limp and her hand droop.

'Good. Now place it on the keyboard without tensing it.'

She did as she was told.

'Now play the chromatic line once more, keeping your wrist supple.'

Hana played the line again, note perfect, and laughed with relief.

'There you are, you *can* do it!'

The concert at the Rudolfinum went well. At Hana's next lesson, Paní Dedecek had a proposal. 'How do you fancy a spot of travelling?'

Hana's tummy fluttered with excitement. Apart from her brief trip to Nuremberg, she'd never been out of Czechoslovakia in her life. 'I'd love to.'

'Excellent. There's a concert in London in April. I've been invited to play.' Paní Dedecek gave recitals as well as teaching the piano. 'I'd like to introduce you as my protégé. You could play one of the études.'

'How will we get there?'

'By plane, of course. Then we can stay at a hotel. The concert organisers are paying my expenses.'

Hana's excitement at the prospect of flying for the first time was replaced by a lurch of dread. 'But how much will the flight cost? I have no money.' She'd been given performance pay for her concerts, and there was the small amount she earned from teaching, but she had insisted on passing it all on to Irena for her bed and board. She owed her friend so much.

'Don't worry. I'll see if the expenses will stretch to you. If not, the conservatoire will pay from the contingency fund. Leave it with me.'

Hana could hardly suppress the bubble of joy as she walked back to Irena's apartment. She was going to England. She might be able to see Miriam again and start to get to know her half-sister properly. They had been writing to each other and slowly opening up, increasingly affectionate, though their correspondence was still stilted and unsure. And maybe by April, Václav would be able to come with them.

*

Pamela always asked Kitty to cook a roast dinner when Will came home for the weekend, and this Sunday was no exception. As they sat round the table, their plates piled high with succulent chicken and Kitty's trademark crispy roast potatoes, Pamela gave a fervent amen to Hugh's somewhat brusque grace.

She didn't think she'd ever get over the joy of having Will home. With each visit he seemed stronger, happier. Miriam became more animated in his presence and it was clear Hugh revelled in having another man at home to talk to. Pamela was content to listen as they discussed politics. Clement Attlee had taken over from Churchill after the war. 'Man doesn't say much, but he's like a bloody whirlwind,' said Hugh. He was being kept busy with plans for a European Defence Community, and the ongoing battle to stem the tide of communism. The war might be over, but its repercussions took up much of Hugh's time.

As Miriam leant forward to pick up the gravy boat, something slithered from her lap and fell to the floor.

Pamela bent down and retrieved it. It was a blue envelope. She handed it back to Miriam. 'Is that a letter from Hana?'

Miriam smiled her thanks. 'Yes! I was about to tell you. She's coming to London for a concert.'

Pamela had been so excited when Miriam came back from Nuremberg and told her she had a half-sister. Miriam had clearly been in shock at first, but after a while Pamela had persuaded Miriam to write to Hana, and now they corresponded regularly. It had helped that Hana had testified against Otto Blumsfeld at the trial. Pamela dreaded to think how Miriam would have felt about her otherwise. Now, whenever Miriam received a letter from Hana, Pamela wanted to hear all her news. And she'd reminded her time and again that Hana would always be welcome to stay, even live with them if she wanted.

'There's talk of the Russians closing the borders in Czechoslovakia,' Hugh said.

Miriam's fork stopped halfway to her mouth. 'What about Hana?' she whispered.

Pamela put her hand on Miriam's. 'That's terrible,' she said. 'Hugh, we must do something.'

Hugh poured a stream of gravy over his chicken. 'It won't be easy,' he said. 'Attlee's determined, but he's no match for Stalin.'

'Surely she'll still be able to get across?'

Hugh speared a potato with his fork. 'She'll have to hurry.'

'She can't! The concert's not until April.'

'Then I don't fancy her chances.' His face was grim, and a frown creased his forehead.

Miriam laid down her knife and fork and dabbed her cheek with her napkin.

Will put his arm round her. He wore what Pamela thought of as his plan-hatching expression. 'Don't worry, Miriam. I know you must feel a duty to your mother to protect Hana. There must be a way to get her through.'

Miriam gave him a watery smile.

*

A week later, a letter with a Czechoslovakian postmark arrived at Will's base. He tore it open eagerly, recognising Tomas's distinctive handwriting. The words were innocuous; clearly the censor hadn't seen anything to alarm him. But RAF pilots had their own way of communicating. And to Will's experienced eye, Tomas's letter told him everything he needed to know.

34

It was late March. Already the air was softer and the evenings lighter. It had been another harsh winter, but spring was finally on its way.

As she let herself into Irena's apartment, Hana kicked off her shoes and hung her coat up on the hook, aware of a spark of excitement in her chest. She'd anticipated this moment all day. Irena was out for the evening: dinner with a friend, so Hana had the apartment to herself. Not that Irena ever complained if she played music – in fact she particularly loved Tchaikovsky – but Hana felt less self-conscious on her own. She made herself a cup of coffee, no time for dinner, then fiddled with the wireless until the concert was broadcast at full volume. It was Tchaikovsky's Piano Concerto No. 2, coming from Moscow. Tatyana Nikolayeva was the pianist, and Hana was looking forward to hearing how she played.

She gulped the coffee quickly, then seated herself on Irena's piano stool, waiting for the violins and cellos to deliver their first majestic bars before the piano came in to echo the melody. Then she fingered the notes from memory as Nikolayeva played. The girl was good. She'd just won the International Johann Sebastian Bach Competition and she played with great conviction. Hana sat up straight, imagining herself playing with as much confidence and authority, and was soon lost in the music.

The first movement was just coming to an end when she heard a knock at the door. At first the staccato blows merged with the timpani, but then she realised the sound wasn't coming from the wireless at all. She jumped up, turned the dial anticlockwise until the sound was barely audible, and rushed along the hall to answer the door, faintly aware of the usual boiled-cabbage odour on the communal landing.

A serious-looking young man in a dark suit stood there. At the sight of Hana, he took off his fedora, revealing close-cropped brown hair.

'Hana Rubenstein?' A gentle smile lit up his face.

Hana's heart started pounding. 'Yes,' she whispered, her lips almost too stiff to move.

'My name is Tomas Belinsky. It's all right. I'm a Czech national.'

Hana let out a slow breath. But what if he was just saying that? The secret police were capable of anything. Besides, even Czechs were capable of informing against other Czechs. Especially if they knew they were Jews. She felt a clench of terror.

The man took a step forward and Hana made to shut the door.

'I don't want to come in. I'm just here to give you a message.'

Hana widened her eyes.

'You have to trust me. Does the name William Denison mean anything to you?'

'It might do.' Was this a trick? How had the man got hold of Miriam's brother's name? He looked so kind standing there.

His eyes creased at the corners and his smile was friendly. But her time in Terezin had taught Hana she could trust no one.

'I flew with William in the RAF during the war.'

'I see.'

'You have a passport, I take it?'

'I do.' Milada had helped her arrange one for the concert next month.

'Will and your sister have arranged for you to travel to England.'

Miriam had told Hana about Will. He wasn't really her brother, but she knew they were close. Could they really be behind this? And why did they want her to travel to England? She'd heard rumours about what the communists might do, but nothing was certain.

'The communists are closing the borders. Soon no one will be able to leave Czechoslovakia.' Tomas looked round quickly, then lowered his voice still further. 'This is part of a bigger plan. A huge mission to save Czech pilots and their families. We don't have much time. Pack a small bag – as if you're going on a short trip. You're to catch a train to Brno as soon as possible. There you must purchase a plane ticket to Prague. Your flight is at six thirty-five a.m. on Friday the twenty-fourth of March.'

'But that doesn't make any sense! Why would I want to travel halfway to Slovakia only to come all the way back to Prague again? Besides, I have no money.'

Tomas thrust his hand into his pocket and drew out a bulging envelope. 'You have now.'

Hana opened the envelope. It was full of brown koruna notes. They looked greasy and had obviously been well used.

Should she take them? What if this was a snare and she was arrested for stealing? Her fingers were slippery with sweat.

The man was pleading with her with his eyes. 'You have to trust me, Hana. This is your only option if you want to see your sister again.'

Hana felt her own eyes prick with tears. 'But how do I know I can trust you?'

'You don't know. You just have to take a risk.' He looked over his shoulder, but the landing was still empty. 'Your sister sent you a message. Does "do this for Eva" mean anything?'

Hana tightened her grip on the envelope and tried to smile. 'It does,' she said.

'Good luck.' He nodded at her, then disappeared down the stairs.

When Irena came home later that evening, flushed from wine and conversation, Hana was waiting for her.

'Hana! You're still up. And you haven't even switched on the lamps.'

Irena bustled round the small apartment room, drawing curtains and turning on lights. The concert had long since finished; the wireless was emitting the low rumble of a late-night 'news' programme. Communist propaganda, no doubt. She turned it off. 'How was the Tchaikovsky?'

'I don't know. I only heard part of it.'

Irena stopped fiddling with things and came and sat by Hana. 'Whatever's the matter? You're looking very pale.'

Hana told Irena about her visitor. She drew out the envelope she'd stowed behind the clock on the mantelpiece and showed her the contents.

'Goodness.' Irena's eyes opened wide.

'What do I do, Irena?'

'Let me think.' Irena hurried into the kitchen and started opening cupboards. There was a hiss as she lit the stove and the sound of liquid being poured into a saucepan. After a few minutes, she returned with two cups of hot milk, one of which she handed to Hana. 'Do you want some vodka in yours?'

Hana shook her head.

Irena sat down and sipped her drink thoughtfully. 'I think you should go.'

'You do?'

'Tomas told you it was a risk, and there's no doubt it is. But he mentioned your mother's name, didn't he? And your half-sister and her adoptive brother.'

'But he could have got those names from anywhere.'

'He could. But why go to all that trouble? Apparently when Václav was arrested, he was just frogmarched outside and bundled into a van. No subterfuge.'

Hana swallowed. Václav still hadn't returned. 'Maybe it's different for women.'

'Maybe. But you haven't done anything for the last four years except keep your head down and play music. You aren't a threat to anyone!'

'No, but Milada wants me to travel to London next month for a concert. Perhaps that's got the authorities rattled.'

Irena put her cup down slowly. 'If what I hear is true, you won't make that concert, or any other concert abroad for that matter. Your visitor was right. The Russians are going to close the borders. This could be your only chance of escape.'

The fog of indecision in Hana's mind suddenly cleared. Irena was right. She should trust Tomas. She should believe that Miriam and Will had organised this. She would do it for Eva, just as he'd said. She stood up. 'You mustn't breathe a word of this.'

'Of course not.' Irena hugged her. 'But I'll miss you so much.'

For the second time that evening, Hana felt the prickle of tears. 'How can I ever thank you? You rescued me when I had no hope.'

'Nonsense,' said Irena. 'How could I not look after you? Your mother would never have forgiven me. She was such a talented girl . . .' She gazed into the middle distance for a second, then collected herself. 'Now go and pack.'

Hana did as she was told.

*

Miriam was just filing the last of a vast pile of papers when the telephone rang. She reached across her desk and picked up the receiver. 'Whitehall 4897.'

'Miriam, it's me. Can you speak?'

'Will!' Miriam looked round the room, but she already knew it was empty; the other secretaries were still on their lunch hour. 'Yes, I'm on my own here. How lovely to hear from you.'

'Thanks, but it's not a social call, I'm afraid.'

'No?' Miriam reached out to doodle on the blotting paper in front of her, whilst still holding the receiver with the other hand.

'I've heard back from Tomas. He's been to see Hana and she's agreed to the plan.' Will had told her that ex-RAF airmen were no longer wanted as Czech pilots, presumably because they'd had too much contact with the West during the war. Apparently they'd had their passports confiscated and were under observation by the secret police. Tomas had told Will he thought it was only a matter of time until they were arrested and interrogated – maybe even imprisoned. 'Hana will be landing in Erding, near Munich, just after eight on Friday morning. I've got permission from the RAF to take a biplane across to bring her back.'

'That's marvellous, Will. And will you bring her straight to Hampstead?'

'That's the idea. But not me, you!'

'Oh!'

'She's your half-sister. I need you to come out to Germany with me. We're in this together.'

Miriam drew a big exclamation mark on the blotting pad. 'Count me in!' she said.

Miriam was careful to pick the right moment. She waited until Hugh had left for work, excusing herself from travelling with him on the pretext that she had a headache and would take the morning off. Hugh grunted. 'Shall I inform Mrs Ainsley?'

'Yes, please,' said Miriam. She hoped her anxiety about her forthcoming conversation was making her pale enough to convince Hugh the headache was genuine. 'I'll come in later if I feel better.'

Hugh nodded, dropped a kiss on Pamela's head, then strode

off down the hall. Once Miriam heard the front door bang, and had reassured herself Kitty was busy washing up in the kitchen, she took a sip of rapidly cooling tea and deliberately caught Pamela's eye.

'I may have to go away for a day or two,' she said.

'Oh?' Pamela took a bite of toast absent-mindedly. 'Does Hugh know?'

'No. Will does, though.'

'Will?' Pamela stopped chewing.

'He's been in touch with Tomas. You remember Mr Denison told us the other day about the communists closing the borders in Czechoslovakia? Well, it turns out there's very little time left.'

Pamela swallowed. 'Poor Tomas.'

Miriam looked at her steadily. 'And poor Hana.'

'Of course. How awful. She'll be trapped. Wasn't she supposed to be coming to London soon for a concert?'

'Indeed she was. The thing is . . .' Miriam twisted the corner of her napkin into a rope, 'Will and I – and Tomas – are going to help her escape.'

'Oh no.' Pamela was on her feet. 'What are you doing? I must tell Hugh.'

Miriam's stomach swooped as she stood up too. She walked round to Pamela's side of the table and put her arm round her. 'Please don't tell Mr Denison,' she said. 'If he finds out what is happening, he'll be obliged to report it. It might jeopardise Tomas's plans.' She searched around for something else to convince her. 'It'll endanger Will.'

Pamela sank slowly back down. 'Not again, please,' she whispered.

Miriam's heartbeat slowed a little. 'It'll be fine,' she said. 'The plan has been very carefully thought out. But we need your help.'

A little more colour had returned to Pamela's blanched face. 'Yes?'

'You'll need to cover for me while I'm away. Can you tell Mr Denison I'm visiting my old friend Olga from Hinton Hall for a couple of days?'

'I can't lie,' said Pamela. 'You know that. But if he asks I'll say I don't know where you've gone. That will be the truth.'

Miriam nodded. 'And there's something else.' She twisted her napkin again. 'I'll be bringing my visitor back here . . .'

*

Hana sat up stiffly and pushed her hair out of her eyes. The airport bench wasn't the most comfortable of beds, but after Terezin, she could sleep anywhere. With the money Tomas had given her she could probably have afforded a hotel for the night, but she didn't want to squander it. Who knew how long she'd have to make it last.

She'd walked the eight kilometres from Brno station to the airport last night, sticking to minor roads, terrified that someone would stop her to search her belongings, or to question what a young girl was doing out on her own on a damp March evening. But she only saw an old man riding a bicycle, who smiled at her as he pedalled his way up a hill.

She glanced up at the big airport clock: 5.30 a.m. Time to go to the washroom to freshen up as much as she could. Irena had telephoned ahead from the conservatoire to book her ticket, and she'd collected it from the airport office last night. So far so good.

By the time she emerged from the washroom, a crowd had gathered by the gate, awaiting the plane to Prague. She tucked herself in behind a rotund woman in a headscarf, who yawned every few minutes, then muttered under her breath.

The woman was surrounded by luggage: two bulging carpet bags embellished with florid roses, a tatty brown holdall and, somewhat bizarrely, a man's briefcase. Hana wondered if she'd received the message not to bring too many belongings. It was strange how some people interpreted the restriction. After three years at Terezin with only fifty kilograms' worth of possessions, and after limiting herself to only a few essential purchases since, she herself had long since learned to live on very little. Perhaps everything would change if she got to London.

The crowd started to move forward and Hana took her passport and papers from her bag, trying to keep her hand steady. When she got to the desk, the official stared at her for several seconds, then bent to scrutinise her documents. He took his time, checking every line carefully before handing the items back. Hana gave him a thin smile, which he didn't return, then made her way onto the tarmac, trying to look as though she did this journey every day.

Outside, a weak sun was trying to break through an opalescent sky. The wind was brisk, cuffing Hana's ears and ruffling the headscarves worn by some of the older women. Most people were only carrying small bags, but there were a few, like the woman Hana had seen earlier, who struggled with a large array of luggage. A waiting steward came forward to take one of the woman's carpet bags, but he was frowning as he did so. She caught a glimpse of Tomas, sitting in the cockpit in a smart uniform, but he didn't acknowledge her. It was reassuring to see him in an official capacity, though.

She was shown to a seat near the front of the aircraft. A thin man was already positioned near the window, looking through the porthole. He didn't turn round as she sat down. To Hana's annoyance, the rotund woman was standing opposite her in the aisle, attempting to stuff some of her luggage into the overhead compartment. Once again the disapproving steward came to her aid, before the woman slumped down beside Hana. Hana bit her lip.

Finally the plane taxied down the runway and Hana allowed herself to breathe more naturally. It picked up speed until the engines were screaming. Her ears roared. There was a rustle as the woman next to her drew a packet of mint humbugs from her pocket and offered her one. Hana shook her head.

'Do have one, my dear, it will ease the pressure on your ears when you swallow.'

Hana took her advice. By the time the plane took off, the dull pain in her eardrums had subsided.

She tried to relax as the engine note settled, but when, a few minutes later, the plane suddenly lurched to the left, she felt a wave of sickness. She bent forward to retrieve the brown paper bag tucked into the back of the seat in front of her. The plane was full, but it was impossible to tell who was intending to defect, like her, and who was a potential informer or even in the secret police. Hana swallowed, a series of rapid gulps, both to suppress the desire to vomit and to calm her taut nerves. Still bent over, she wiped the sweat from her forehead, then eased herself back, trying to disturb her body as little as possible. The sick feeling abated.

To distract herself, she watched the stewardess wander, apparently nonchalantly, down the aisle and enter the cockpit. Above the drone of the engine, she heard the click of a lock being turned. Saliva pooled again in her mouth.

Next to her, the fat woman was already asleep, her head tipped back, soft snores emanating from her slack mouth. The man next to her had barely moved, but Hana registered a tightening of his jaw.

Then the cockpit door opened again and the stewardess emerged. She walked calmly back down the aisle, checking on her passengers. Hana wondered if she'd fully understood the dangers of the flight. But if she had, the implacable expression on her face did not alter.

Hana leant back in her seat and closed her eyes, trying to imitate the stewardess's composure. But inside her head all she could imagine was the secret police waiting to pounce, and all she could do was to beg Adonai again and again to let them arrive safely. It would be a long and tense flight.

*

Miriam stood with Will under the trees at the edge of the US airbase at Erding. The biplane in which they'd travelled to Germany was parked on the tarmac in front of them. Will wore his RAF uniform and Miriam was dressed in warm trousers and a jumper. Despite this, they still shivered from time to time, as much from fear and anticipation as from the cold.

408

'What's Hana like?' asked Will.

Miriam stared up at the early-morning sky; the sun was buried behind a bank of clouds and a small sliver of moon still showed. Will had said the weather was perfect for Tomas's flight. He'd have to navigate Russian airspace and the plane would be less visible through an overcast sky. The American air-base Commander had been alerted about the mission, and had agreed to let the Czech pilots through, but it was still very risky. She tried to summon Hana as she'd seen her at Nuremberg. 'She's fairer than me. Maybe quieter, too. It's hard to say.'

Will gave her a sad smile. He'd taken to smoking a pipe recently, and his breath carried a trace of the rich, sweet scent of tobacco. His cheeks were ruddy and some of his dark hair fell over his forehead. She'd loved sitting beside him in the plane, watching him command the controls with such confidence.

Are you in love with him? Hana had written once.

Of course not, Miriam had replied. *He's my brother.* Although truth be told, it was hard to find someone who matched up.

Will's instructions had been clear. 'Once Tomas touches down, watch the plane like a hawk until you see Hana alight. Then sprint across the airfield, grab her and bring her across to me. I'll have the engine running and we can set off straight away. The authorities know about this, but we still can't afford to delay.'

Miriam strained her ears and thought she heard the faint throb of an approaching plane. She gazed upwards. Nothing yet. 'Did you hear something?' she asked Will.

Will stood stock still, listening. 'Yes, that sounds like the Dakota.'

Miriam looked up again. There was a moving shape in the far distance. As it crossed a cloud, it was briefly silhouetted. Simultaneously the throbbing increased. 'This must be them.'

They watched the aircraft approach and heard the changed engine note as it prepared to land. The wheels bounced along the tarmac and eventually the plane came to a halt.

'Are you watching?' asked Will.

'Of course.'

Miriam couldn't make out the figures in the cockpit, but soon the stairs came down and a series of passengers descended. Some looked shocked as they realised this wasn't the Prague destination they expected but an unfamiliar airport in West Germany. Others strode confidently towards the arrivals area, elated relief registering on their faces. Will had given more details on the way over. Three planes, supposedly travelling to Prague from rural airports, were going to be hijacked by ex-RAF pilots and flown to Erding. The site had been chosen as it was a similar distance from the rural airports as Prague and therefore would be less likely to arouse suspicion in non-defecting passengers.

The mission was fraught with danger. There could be secret police on board. Something could go wrong with the takeover. The pilots of the planes might fight back. A panicking passenger could ruin everything. Miriam's stomach was churning more and more with each of Will's revelations. 'But it's been carefully thought through,' he assured her. 'There are eighty-five passengers in total, twenty-six wanting to escape to the West. Family members of the pilots are not allowed to travel with them. That's why they need three planes. And why it has to be a triple hijack.' He wiped away a slick of sweat on his forehead with his jacket sleeve. 'It'll be a terrific coup if they can pull it off.'

'Or a terrible tragedy if they don't,' added Miriam.

Will stared silently ahead.

'Will?' Miriam plucked at his sleeve, her whole body tense with foreboding. 'I think that's the last of the passengers, and I still can't see Hana.'

*

Pamela wandered into the bedroom for the umpteenth time that day. For years it had served as a spare room: sometimes Will brought a friend home, and her parents had slept there once or twice, although these days they preferred their own beds. It had been Tomas's refuge when he'd stayed with them for a few weeks after he and Will had been released. She liked to think it had been a sanctuary.

She smoothed down the pale pink candlewick bedcover and adjusted the little brush and comb set on the dressing table. As an afterthought, she'd popped into Dickman's for a bottle of Yardley's English Lavender. Hana had spent all those years in the ghetto, then there were probably very few luxuries in the shops once the communists came in. There was a bar of lavender soap too, nestling in the underwear drawer, and she'd taken the liberty of buying a few smalls so that Hana could have something new. Miriam had insisted on hanging a couple of dresses of her own in the wardrobe, brushing away Pamela's offer to buy some. 'We don't know what size she is. I would imagine she's still very thin. Anyway,

411

it will be fun to take her out and let her choose some clothes herself.'

Pamela had nodded. They'd need to feed her up too. She'd ask Kitty to make one of her suet puddings.

When Will and Miriam had asked her if Hana could stay with them, at least for a while until she found her feet, her answer was an unreserved yes. She'd always imagined having a houseful of children, despite Hugh only wanting one. They loved Will dearly, and he was the most marvellous son – if a little headstrong at times – but she'd ached to give him a brother or sister, and she knew he'd often yearned for one too. So when they'd taken on Miriam, and she and Will had become so close, Pamela felt she'd finally produced the sister he lacked. And now there'd be Hana too. She and Miriam had the same mother; they were blood relatives. And both talented musicians. Much as she wanted to love and protect another girl, though, she hoped Hana's arrival wouldn't threaten Will and Miriam's closeness.

And then there was Hugh. He hadn't wanted them to keep Miriam at first, although now he doted on his adopted daughter. It was lovely to see them go off to work each morning, chatting and laughing together. But how would he react to having another girl in the house? One he hadn't given permission to stay? He didn't even know about the whole escape plan. If he did, he'd be horrified.

Pamela closed her eyes and offered up a silent prayer. Please let everything go well, she begged. She glanced round the bedroom once more, then went downstairs to check on dinner.

*

As the Dakota touched down at Erding, Hana looked out of the window to see large numbers of fighter aircraft outside, marked with blue flashes and white stars. Another Dakota lay ahead of them. Presumably one from one of the other destinations had got in first. The woman next to her jerked awake. 'Have we arrived in Prague?' she asked.

Hana couldn't risk telling her the truth. 'I would imagine so,' she replied.

The woman leant over Hana and ducked her head to see through the window. 'Doesn't look like Prague-Ruzyně.'

Hana shifted in her seat, uncomfortable at the closeness of the woman's bulk. 'When did you last fly there?' Damn, she should have said 'here', but the woman hadn't seemed to notice.

'Last year.'

Hana shrugged. 'A lot can change.'

The woman gave her a puzzled frown, then sat upright again.

As they taxied down the runway, the stewardess was telling people to stay in their seats. She walked briskly down the aisle to the rear of the aircraft. When she'd passed their row, the man next to Hana stood up suddenly and pushed his way into the aisle. 'Treason!' he shouted.

There was a collective gasp. Hana's neighbour ducked down and Hana became aware of a man to her left swallowing hard. She glanced at his white knuckles as he gripped the armrest.

The man advanced on the cockpit and rattled the still-locked door. 'Let me in,' he demanded. 'Treason!'

Hana's stomach lurched and blood roared in her ears. Surely he couldn't sabotage the escape, not when they'd come so far?

413

Suddenly she heard the sound of running. Four men in khaki uniform, wearing helmets and carrying guns, rushed down the aisle. 'US Military Police,' the front one shouted. He grabbed the man's arm, pinning it behind his back, whilst his fellow officer thrust him to the ground.

The remaining two policemen ushered the other passengers to safety. 'Get out quickly. No one is going to get hurt. You are in Munich.'

The man writhed on the floor, still shouting. 'Don't give up, comrades, it would be treason. As long as we are on board, we are in the territory of Czechoslovakia. You mustn't leave it.' One of the officers clamped his mouth shut.

Hana climbed down from the aircraft on shaky legs, barely able to carry her own bag. Suddenly it was removed from her grasp by a slight figure, grinning broadly. Miriam put an arm round her. 'It's me, Hana. You're safe! It's over. You've made it through.'

Hana tried to smile back, her heart too full to speak.

Miriam took her hand and led her across the lush grass to the side of the runway. 'Come and meet Will,' she said.

And Hana followed her half-sister towards the biplane, where Will was waiting to take her home.

Epilogue

1968

'Ready?' whispered Miriam.

Hana nodded. Oscar had told them it was a full house, although she knew that already. By the swell of sound coming from behind the curtains, it was clear there were hundreds of people waiting for the performance to start. She heard the usual rustle of programmes and sweet papers, the babble of excited voices, the billow of anticipation. She loved that moment before the curtain went up. People had come from all over Czechoslovakia to hear this concert, emboldened by the Prague Spring. They were not going to be disappointed.

She grasped Miriam's hand briefly and squeezed it. This was for Eva. 'The performance of our lives,' she whispered. 'For Mutti.'

Miriam smiled, and blinked several times. It wouldn't do to cry now, not when she'd held everything in for so long. She took a deep breath and nodded her assent as Oscar signalled he was going to raise the curtain.

As the velvet drapes lifted, and the audience at last glimpsed Hana seated at the huge grand piano, and Miriam to one side, there was a huge round of applause. Both women bowed their heads. Then Hana raised her hands and played the first few notes of the villanelle as Miriam watched her, waiting to sing her part.

Their mother never had her chance to perform the villanelle at the Rudolfinum, but now her daughters did it for her. And if Hana's playing was even more brilliant than usual, and Miriam's voice more beautiful than ever, maybe it was because Eva's spirit was with them, lost in wonder and joy at the sound of her daughters, giving them her blessing, in peace at last.

Author's Note

It's often said that truth is stranger than fiction, and in my research for *The Child on Platform One* I came across several improbable events: the rescue of hundreds of Czech children from under the noses of the Nazis by a London stockbroker; a concentration camp where Jews were allowed to put on music concerts; a three-way hijack enabling ex-RAF Czech pilots to escape communist Prague. Yet all these episodes really occurred. I set myself the task of coming up with a collection of characters and a narrative that threaded them together.

I first became interested in the Nicholas Winton story when I stumbled across the YouTube clip of Esther Rantzen congratulating this modest hero fifty years after the last Kindertransport had left, surrounded, unbeknown to him, by a sea of adults whom he had rescued as Czech child refugees. It makes for poignant viewing (https://urlzs.com/2SFW). That led me to research German-occupied Prague, and it was then that I read of the extraordinary events at Terezin (known to the Germans as Theresienstadt), where Jews had been allowed to paint, sing, play instruments, give lectures and act. Most notably they put on a performance of Verdi's *Requiem*, ironically and subversively declaring God's judgement on the Germans listening. As I mention in my acknowledgements, there is a DVD of the story of this event, but you can get a taste of it here: https://urlzs.com/Ut4Q.

I knew from Vera Gissing's autobiography, *Pearls of Childhood*, that the children at Hinton Hall heard about the treatment of the Jews when listening to a radio announcement in March 1943. Try as I might, I couldn't find a transcript of this, so I have taken the liberty of attributing to the World Service the words of Varian Fry, taken from his article 'The Massacre of the Jews', published in *The New Republic* on 22 December 1942. The full article makes shocking reading (https://urlzs.com/GANk). Even more shocking is the fact that the Allies knew about the death camps at this stage but seemingly did nothing about them.

Vera Gissing's book provided me with much of the information about the lives of those young Czech refugees. To find out about the experience of being interred in Terezin as a young girl, I found *Helga's Diary* by Helga Weiss very useful.

I would also recommend the DVD *Nicky's Family* for more information on the Nicholas Winton story.

It has been a humbling experience to write of those who demonstrated creative brilliance in the darkest of circumstances. To be gifted in music, drama, art or design is to be blessed; to share those gifts from under the gallows is remarkable.

Acknowledgements

I am indebted to so many people who helped me write this book: the cheerleaders and morale boosters, the critics and editors, and those experts whose brains I remorselessly picked so I could pretend I knew something about science, music and medicine. Any unintentional mistakes are my own.

A big thanks in particular to the following:

My wonderful agent Anne Williams.

The amazing Sherise Hobbs and the terrific editorial team at Headline.

The ever wise and generous Stephanie Norgate and Jane Rusbridge.

My husband Paul (for keeping me sane!).

Laura and Richard, for being so supportive of their mother.

Kate Lee and Jacqui Pack for their loyalty and enthusiasm.

Helen and Dominic Bevan, Nick Smith, Jenny Alexander and Ceilidh Botfield for their musical knowledge, particularly Dominic, who talked me so helpfully through the experience of singing Verdi's *Requiem*.

The Defiant Requiem Foundation, for kindly sending me their DVD.

Carolyn MacDonell, for passing on her mother's memories of travelling to England from Germany in 1937 as an eleven-year-old refugee.

... ot Czech history and for
... ...less questions.

... ... and informative Terezin guide.

... ...hompson for kindly supplying medical informa-
...on.

Sue Greenhalgh, Libby Morgan, Dave and Jude Thompson, Tessa and Drew Forsyth, Alex Burn, Anne Hudson, Julia Arthurs and the staff of Godalming College, particularly the wonderful English department, for all-round support and encouragement.

Read on for an extract of
Gill Thompson's heartrending novel

The
Oceans
Between
Us

Prologue

Even after all these years he still dreads plane journeys. The take off is the worst: the rush of tyres on concrete, the scream of engines, a crescendo of pressure in his ears.

There's a light touch on his hand. He looks down. Her fingers on his white knuckles.

'All right?' she says.

He nods, then looks out of the window. The plane is climbing steeply, the runway already a biscuit-coloured blur. The landing gear folds itself in with a distant thump and the engine steadies to a low throb.

He wipes his forehead with the back of his sleeve and leans his head against the rest.

She squeezes his hand. 'Well done. You'll be fine now.'

Yes, he will be fine. He always is. But this time there is another anxiety. Not the journey but the destination.

He pats his jacket pocket and feels the firmness of the expensive cardboard against the warm wool. No need to take the invitation out again. He knows the words off by heart.

And suddenly he's a young boy once more, excited to be going on a long journey to a land full of hope and opportunity. How was his eager twelve-year-old self to know what was really waiting for him?

He glances at his companion. They are deep into a long

marriage; her face as familiar to him now as his own, her hair shorter than when they'd first met. His breath still catches at the sight of her. He reaches out to stroke her cheek. 'I'm glad you're here with me.'

'Wouldn't have missed it. It's been a long time coming.'

He's suddenly too choked to speak. He swallows and runs a finger round his shirt collar. 'Forty years' he says. His voice sounds hoarse.

'Half a lifetime. But you got there in the end. Just as you said you would.'

The seat belt signs have gone off. She reaches under the seat, pulls a leather bag onto her lap, and reaches into it for her bottle of water. She passes it across to him.

He takes a long sip. She always knows the right thing to do.

'I just wish I'd got there sooner. It's too late for some people.'

'Those who can will come. And remember who you're doing this for.'

He nods, then turns to the window again. The horizon is striped with brilliant colours: turquoise, orange, green – all radiating from a fiery, sinking sun. They'll soon be hurtling through a dark sky in their metal tube, for miles and miles until they reach Canberra. And the ceremony they will attend.

This day is the one he's fought for. He closes his eyes and the faces of the past appear before him.

No one had listened to them then.

They would listen now.